D1083793

Gripped by Drought

by

Arthur Upfield

LONGWOOD PUBLIC LIBRARY

Novel © Bonaparte Holdings Pty Ltd, Australia.

First published 1932 by Hutchinson & Co Ltd, London, United Kingdom.

This edition published 2011 by Lulu.com, 3101 Hillsborough Street, Raleigh NC 27607-5436, United States of America.

Rights owner Kees de Hoog, Australia.

Cover photograph © Justin Mott

ISBN: 978-1-4466-2734-1

Also available on-line from the Arthur Upfield Bookshop (www.lulu.com/kdehoog)

When Bony Was There: A Chronology of the Life and Career of Detective Inspector Napoleon Bonaparte by Kees de Hoog

Eccentric Minds: A Homage to the Bony Novels of Arthur Upfield by Graham Jackson

Up and Down the Real Australia: Autobiographical Articles and the Murchison Murders by Arthur Upfield

Up and Down Australia: Short Stories by Arthur Upfield

Up and Down Australia Again: More Short Stories by Arthur Upfield

Author's Preface

There is no greater Australian drama than a three-year drought, and such a drought, associated with drought in the human heart, is the theme of this plain tale for plain people.

The course of this fictitious drought is based on the course of a real drought. I have followed the weather records over an actual three-year drought period, and no city critic can say that such a drought is impossible. Similarly, I have followed actual wool prices over the same period. And, finally, the succession of mental phases which the "new-chum" in the bush proper must live through, or else desert to a city, is real and based on personal experience.

I should like to add that my original title for this work was the one all-sufficient word *Drought*. It was found, however, that already a novel under this title was in circulation, so that regretfully the present more sensational title was substituted.

Kalamunda, W.A

TO MY FRIEND
E. V. WHYTE
to whom I am indebted
for the pastoral statistics
and other data which have
made this story possible.

CONTENTS

THE FIRST YEAR

THE SECOND YEAR

THE THIRD YEAR

GRIPPED BY DROUGHT

PART I

THE FIRST YEAR

CHAPTER I

DIAMOND DAYS

1

THAT morning of early June, when Feng Ching-wei rode a spirited dapple-grey mare beside the River Darling in western New South Wales, found his mind busied with a problem that Time was beginning to describe as a Sin of Omission.

Following considered judgment he had, six months before, refused to take twenty-one shillings a head for nine thousand wether sheep, because the price offered had been half a crown below his own valuation. The morrow would witness the arrival of the prince whose steward he was; and, in rendering account of his stewardship, he might give just reason for dissatisfaction, not for failing to increase the talents lent him – namely, sheep – but for not having decreased them. The number of sheep on the great Atlas sheep-run that morning really should have been less by nine thousand.

A superb day that tenth of June – a calm, sparkling, intoxicating day, to be found only in the hinterland of Australia during the midwinter months; a diamond day, for the azure sky was reflected by the pools of water lying in the clay-pans, the golden sunlight was reflected by the myriad leaves of the giant gum trees bordering the river in a stately avenue a thousand miles long, and the very atmosphere was a brilliant crystal that magnified and brought near the western line of red, whale-backed sand-dunes.

The horse was walking on her toes, her neck arched, her nostrils patches of vivid crimson, her foam-flecked mouth working ever at the restraining bit. Horse and man were passing over a bar of red sand which, crossing the grey river flats from the distant pine lands, stabbed at the river's flank. Tiny shoots of grass gave to certain of its slopes in alignment with the eye a faint tinge of emerald. Three days previously it had rained.

No more than the horse had the rider lived in China. Born thirty-one years before on the gold diggings of Tibooburra in the north-west of the State, of his parents Feng Ching-wei remembered nothing. He had been adopted by Old Man Mayne, the creator of Atlas from the wilderness, who had begun to despair of ever having a son of his own. However, when Feng was four, Frank Mayne was born, and the two boys, reared in the same nursery, later attended the same schools and were articled to the same squatter. When Old Man Mayne died in the first year of the Peace, both boys returned to Atlas, where Feng was content to remain firm friend and shrewd financial adviser to the young master who had become sole owner of nearly seventy thousand sheep and a Government leasehold of over three-quarters of a million acres.

The fight Old Man Mayne had fought to leave his son an inheritance was one of grim, almost savage, tenacity, governed by the motto, "What I have I hold." After the three-year drought at the beginning of the century, he had consolidated the financial foundations of Atlas. The nineteen-thirteen-fourteen drought had failed to weaken those foundations, although the flocks were atrociously depleted. When Frank Mayne succeeded to his inheritance he faced the booming postwar years, and a succession of gratifyingly large annual wool cheques had sent him on a three-year world tour, leaving Feng Ching-wei sole arbiter of the destinies of Atlas. And on the morrow Frank Mayne was returning to Atlas, bringing with him an English wife and an eleven-month old baby boy.

Whilst Feng rode homeward, following the track winding among the wide-spaced box trees growing on the river flats, he recalled the moments when he had sat in the Atlas office with Frank Mayne's letter before him. The words, the quickly written, impulsive words, lay beneath his hands, which trembled. *"Ere you get this, old man, I shall be married."* Married! Frank in England and married! And twenty miles south of Atlas – Ann Shelley!

They three – Ann Shelley, Frank Mayne, and Feng Ching-wei – were of the same class and generation. They had grown up together, even schooldays failing to come between them. Whilst there never had been a declaration of love between Ann and Frank, before he went away young Mayne had hinted that after he had had his fling he would propose marriage to Ann. With the

9

arrogance of youth he had said it, and Feng then had no doubt that Frank would propose and that Ann would accept him. But Frank married suddenly in England, and he never suspected the hurt he thereby rendered Ann Shelley, the hurt that rebounded from her to his lifelong friend, Feng Ching-wei.

2

WITH the fates of Ann Shelley and Frank Mayne burdening his mind, Feng Ching-wei did not at once see the sun-reflecting car, which emerged from a belt of mallee, speeding towards him at an outrageous pace. It was some seconds after the mare first became excited that the increasing hum of the engine penetrated his curtain of day-dreaming. Then, looking up and recognising the low-hung body of the Tin Tin car, he reined off the track and dismounted. The car slowed to a stop, a gloved hand was waved to him, and the blue silk scarf floating out over the rear of the single-seater beckoned him. With quickened heart-beats he led the horse close to the machine, behind the steering-wheel of which sat the mistress of Tin Tin Station – Miss Ann Shelley.

"Feng! I have been hoping to meet you," she exclaimed gaily, her grey eyes alight, her face flushed by the quick rush through the air.

"Meeting you makes a lovely day perfect," Feng murmured.

"It makes me feel very young – meeting you," was her parry. "You know, Feng, even though we 'growed up' together, and you are four years older than I, you make me always feel – well, juvenile. Your face is without a line; your black eyes regarding me so benevolently are inscrutable. I have never been able to read your thoughts. No wonder you play poker so well! Will you be glad or sorry to step down from the Seat of Atlas to-morrow?"

"I shall not regret abdicating, Ann," he said with slow, perfect articulation. "I have done my best to govern Atlas, yet would I rather occupy the position of Grand Vizier; because in that sphere responsibility is less, and I can fill my mind with matters other than sheep and money, fodders and rain."

"Your pictures?"

"Exactly – my pictures. Whilst I paint I am a god. At all other times I am a – worm. For three years I have seldom been a god."

He was smiling at her with his old trick of quizzical

penetration. His semi-veiled eyes gleamed with the warmth of friendship. He was master absolute of himself.

"You will want now to have me sit a few more times to finish my portrait. I – well, things at Atlas will be different, won't they?"

Search though she did she failed to observe any change in his expression.

"That is undoubted, Ann. Even so, Mrs. Mayne surely will be as pleased as I shall for you to visit Atlas often. I was hoping that when Frank was again firmly established on the Seat of Atlas you would give me a few more sittings. You see, the portrait that has been occupying both our time and our interest was not satisfactory, almost finished though it was. And you know what I do to a canvas with which I am not satisfied."

"You did not destroy it?"

He inclined his head. She accepted the inclination as his reluctant assent. She did not see his eyes.

"Feng, you are wicked!" she chided him, genuine regret in her musical voice. "It promised to be your best picture. And now – I'm afraid I shall not be able to come to Atlas very often."

Looking up, the swords of their gaze met. What he saw in her eyes hurt him. He said: "I believe I understand. The mountain shall go to Mahammod."

"You are one of the understanding kind, old boy. It's three years since he went away, but Time has been a poor doctor. The rain came just in time, didn't it? Did I not say that the dry spell would not last?"

"You did," he assented, again smiling. "You predicted rain to me on the telephone, having observed a bunch of steers racing about with tails elevated. If the frosts hold off, we should show a good picking of grass by shearing time. Another good rain next month, and a further fall in August, will assure us summer feed. How many do you expect to shear this year?"

"Somewhere about thirty thousand, I suppose. My lambs have done well, in spite of the dry spell. Well, I must go, Feng. Everything ready at Atlas?"

"Everything, thanks to your assistance. I should have been hopelessly at sea had you not come to my rescue with the decorations and the furniture."

"I did it to help you," she said softly, adding, with a touch of colour in her cheeks, "and Frank. But you'll say never a word about it, will you? It – it was my real present to him."

Unconsciously falling into the imagery of his race, he said: "If the greatest-souled man climbed to the top of a mountain peak a hundred miles high, he would see standing on a peak he could never hope to reach, a woman."

"She would be very cold, Feng," Ann said with smiling lips, but with misty eyes. "*Au revoir!*"

The engine hummed. Feng Ching-wei stepped back, hat in hand. He was smiling calmly when the girl let out the clutch pedal.

"Au revoir, Ann!"

She waved to him and was gone.

3

CONTINUING his meditations, Feng walked on homeward, the mare docilely following. Australian born, reared in the omnipresent bush among Australia's bluest-blooded squatocracy, educated in Australia's best schools, there was nothing in his gait or his physical appearance to betray his ancestry. Weighed in European scales he was by no means ill-looking, descended, as he was, from stock much above the coolie class. As a man he was a credit to Old Man Mayne's judgment of human pedigree, which was as sound as it notably had been in the case of cattle, horses, and sheep. His gabardine-slack encased legs were straight, his body lean and supple, his hands as well formed as those of any polished aristocrat.

The track presently led him to the river bank at one of its sharp bends. That morning the stream was low, trickling from deep hole to deep hole – the inevitable hole washed out at every sharp elbow. The water was brown. But yesterday it had been as clear as crystal. The rain had sent down a freshet.

The woman fishing with a hand-line failed to hear the approach of man and horse. She was seated ungracefully at the rocky edge of a large, deep hole; and, observing her, Feng halted, so unusual was it to meet with a female sundowner. For that she was a sundowner, a tramp, was evident. On the branch of a fallen tree partly buried in the bank was laid a rolled "swag", composed of blankets and personal effects, and near-by a billy-can blackened by half a thousand camp fires.

"Good day!" called Feng.

The woman stood up, and turned round to look at him on the bank far above her.

"Good day, mister!" she replied in a faint Irish brogue containing a hint of hostility. "How far to Atlas homestead?"

"From here it would be three miles. Surely you are not travelling alone?"

"An' wot's agin it? Are you objectin'?"

"Not at all," Feng told her politely.

Slightly amused, he watched her climb the bank. Her bare arms were mahoganied by sun and wind, and in circumference were enormous. Feng felt dwarfed when she stood before him, not by reason of her height, which was no more than his own, but rather by her breadth. Her weather-beaten face, with its button of a nose and now grim mouth, was not unpleasing, but the glint in the wide-spaced, small blue eyes forewarned him.

With her hands on her hips she said: "Me name is Mary O'Doyle. County Clare, me. Any argument?"

Feng masked surprise and slight perturbation with a guileless smile, saying: "I am a man of peace, madam. If to address you is an offence, you must excuse me, for I did not know it. You will admit that a woman carrying a swag is unusual."

"For a year I've carried it. Ever since me second husband died beneath the wheels of a table-top wagon," she said in truculent explanation. "It just shows you, mister, wot drink will do to a man. The blackguard! He left me without a farthing, me as was a gentleman's datter."

"For a year! Have you been on tramp for a year?"

"Sure! Would ye be havin' me live on me husband's relations? An' 'im dying in drink. Faugh! 'Enery Jones was a weakling in drink. Six pints would knock 'im rotten. 'Ad I 'ave known, I would niver 'ave married 'im. I would 'ave stuck to me honoured maiden name av O'Doyle. To go an' fall off 'n a wagon, 'cos 'e was drunk!"

"Where are you making for now?"

"Wot's that to do with you? Ain't this a free country?"

"Decidedly. Yet I was considering. I thought, perhaps, I might be of assistance to you."

For twenty seconds Mary O'Doyle was occupied in examining Feng Ching-wei from his feet upwards to his head. Then: "You're a Government 'Ouse man. I know you! You're the manager of Atlas Station."

Once more the slow, upward-moving scrutiny, insulting in its minuteness. But when her gaze crossed his the belligerent expression vanished, and the hard curves of her body appeared to soften.

In quite a different tone of voice she said: "Could you give us a job, mister? I'm broke, an' me shoe-leather is thin, an' – and I'd like to sleep in a bed o' nights atween sheets."

"What can you do?" inquired Feng doubtfully.

"I kin mend an' sew an' scrub an' cook."

"Then why are you on tramp? A woman with your abilities need never sleep out of a bed."

Once again fell the mantle of truculence. "That's right, mister! Go yer gab! How old am I? How many times 'ave I bin in the jug? 'Ave I bin rescued from the streets? Go on – let's 'ave it – all the catechism!"

Looking into the woman's blazing eyes, Feng thought he understood her attitude that moment to represent her sole armour against the world with which she was in perpetual conflict. Masculine in physical strength, even so she appealed to his sense of chivalry, and unexpectedly, even to himself, he made up his mind.

"Come along to Atlas," he said with a disarming smile. "I will inform the housekeeper of your coming."

"Is it a job ye'll be givin' me?" Mary O'Doyle demanded with lingering suspicion.

"I'll find you one."

"Thanks, mister! I'm coming," Mary said firmly, and dashed down the bank to retrieve her hand-line, her swag, and the billy-can.

A diamond in the rough. Indeed, it was a day of diamonds.

4

"ATLAS!"

The thrill expressed in Frank Mayne's voice when he saw the red-roofed, white-painted buildings of the homestead march out of the river gums to meet them, caused his wife to glance at him sharply. Mayne himself was driving the station car, and beside him sat Ethel with the boy sleeping on her lap. She wondered at the ecstatic look on his face even whilst she pondered on the strange absence of any thrill in her own heart at coming to her new home. Here, over all the buildings she was to be queen, to face a future all unknown. To her husband it was a known equation, to use his own words, and he strained to reach it as a hound on the leash. A minute later they drew up before a group of people standing at the open gateway in a white-painted paling fence that appeared to keep in a neat line the thick mass of the bamboo hedge within.

"Hallo, Feng!"

"Hallo, Frank!"

Feng Ching-wei grasped the hand held out to him, and beamed into the hazel eyes of the man he had always regarded as his brother. He was dressed immaculately and with distinction – greater distinction than Mayne in his Bond Street cut clothes. His dress, his manner, and his cultured voice reached Ethel Mayne's fastidious standard.

Mayne said, when his wife was assisted from the car: "Meet Feng Ching-wei, my dearest friend! Feng – my wife!"

Mayne took the child from her arms to permit her to shake hands with Feng. With inherent grace Feng bowed. He saw a tall, slender woman whose hair and eyes were dark, whose complexion was creamy white – a really beautiful woman.

"Permit me, Mrs. Mayne, to extend an official but none the less sincere welcome to Atlas," he said. "You arrive as the mistress of a district larger than some European States. I assure you, you will find us all your devoted subjects."

"Thank you Feng! As my husband's lifelong friend, I shall, if you will allow me, call you Feng," she said, in the clear, well-modulated voice of one used to cultured society. There was, however, unnecessary emphasis on the words "thank" and "allow", due no doubt to high-school elocutionary training.

"You honour me, Mrs. Mayne. Now to introduce you to – well, the executive officers of your State. This is Mrs. Morton, the housekeeper."

A tall, grey-haired woman, rigid in carriage, dressed in severe black, stepped forward. Her hand left her side to offer welcome, but, no response being made, was quickly withdrawn. Ethel Mayne bowed her head stiffly. Her expression was subtly changed. It was cold. Mrs. Morton flushed, bowed in return, and retired several paces.

"I shall be glad to have you show me to our apartments, Mrs. Morton, and later take me round the house."

"Very well, madam," assented Mrs. Morton, with equal coldness. Ethel frowned. Feng, sensing strain, introduced the accountant, who had been appointed when he had undertaken the management of Atlas. The accountant was tall, white-haired, beyond sixty years of age.

"This is Mr. Barlow, Mrs. Mayne," Feng said suavely. "Mr. Barlow's finger is always on the financial pulse of Atlas."

Barlow had observed Mrs. Mayne's aloofness towards Mrs. Morton, and merely inclined his head. Ethel nodded coolly. Her husband grew hot with annoyance, and checked an impulse to explain that Barlow was their social equal, and was counted as a friend from the years he had served Old Man Mayne. Feng noted the flash that sprang into Mayne's eyes, and calmly went on with the introductions.

"This is Mr. Noyes and this is Mr. Andrews, both of whom are serving their articles with us. Mr. Noyes comes from near Cobar, where his people are squatters. Mr. Andrews' people are stock and station agents and financiers of Sydney."

Feng was enjoying himself. In introducing these jackeroos he purposely published their connexions. A woman more subtle than Ethel would have discerned the cynic behind the bland mask.

"I am very glad to meet you," she said, smiling graciously at each. "I hope to come to know you both much better after we are settled."

They bowed and fidgeted, as young men of nineteen are apt to do, before withdrawing with ill-concealed relief. Despite Feng's recommendations, both Andrews and Noyes were less uncomfortable on the back of a buck-jumping fool of a horse than in their peoples' drawing-rooms. They did not hear Feng when he again spoke:

"And now, Mrs. Mayne, last but by no means least in either physical weight or loyalty – Aunty Joe! Aunty Joe was Old Mrs. Mayne's nurse-girl, who shepherded both Frank and myself from countless childish dangers, and can be guaranteed to shepherd your baby boy from every danger too."

A vision in pink stood before them. A shining, ebony-black face, crowned by snow-white hair, beamed first on the master of Atlas, who grinned at her, and then on the new "missus", who examined her as though she were a brontosaurus. Time had matured Aunty Joe, yet still was she straight of back and strong, despite her fifteen stones.

"Mine tinkit I orl funny here," she cried, her hands pressed hard against her vast bosom. "Oh, Boss! Gibbit me!"

Aunty Joe ambled towards the wide-eyed child in Frank's arms. The boy, observing her approach, cried: "Oo-o Oo-o!" Wonderful blue eyes were wide; the smile angelic.

But it was Ethel who took him from Mayne's arms, almost snatching him to her. Without a word she hurried to the house veranda, followed by the rigid Mrs. Morton.

Mayne was astonished. Feng's eyes were veiled by lids that almost hid them. Aunty Joe's broad face had changed in expression from sunshine to rain. Her wide mouth trembled.

"Aunty Joe, listen to me," Mayne said softly, passing an arm around her shoulders. "Missus come from far country where no lubra live. She does not understand, but bime-bi she let you have Little Frankie. 'Member how you jumped into the river that day I fell in at Sheep Bend?"

Aunty Joe blinked her eyes. Her hands flew up to his, which rested on her left shoulder. And then quickly she turned and faced him, and he saw how hurt she was.

"Ole Aunty Joe unnerstan', boss. Bime-bi orl thing goodo. Bime-bi missus gibbit me likkle fellow. Oh my!"

Without warning of her departure she rolled away towards the kitchen. Mayne squared himself and sighed almost audibly. When his eyes met Feng's gaze the scene was still reflected in them, although he was smiling.

"Feng, old man, I'm darned glad to be home," he said. "I want to rush about all over the place, and see all the old faces and things. But look! The sun's gone. Is the medicine chest stocked?"

Feng's eyebrows rose interrogatively at Barlow.

"There are, I know, ointments and lotions in the chest, Mr. Mayne," Barlow stated in his thin voice, his light-grey eyes twinkling.

"Then let's sample the lotions. Come on, Feng! You, too, Inky Fingers! Let's drink to Atlas and prosperity."

With the energy of youth, with the sparkling impulsiveness of his boyhood, Frank Mayne slipped one arm through that of Feng, and the other through that of the old accountant. Whilst they walked towards the office he pressed their arms to his sides, and spoke of the season, the prospects, of anything but his wife.

CHAPTER II

ATLAS

1

ABOUT eleven o'clock the next day Mayne and Feng Ching-wei emerged from the wicket-gate in the south side of the white paling fence that enclosed the big house with wide verandas on three sides, the river skirting the east side. It was a sparkling morning, windless and cold. High in the great gum tree growing on the river bank near the wicket-gate, a score of Major Mitchell cockatoos – pure white with rose-tinted underwings and multi-coloured crests – greeted them with harsh, defiant cries.

The house they had left was a rambling bungalow structure built of stone quarried twenty miles away, cooled by twenty-foot verandas, and double ceilings beneath the galvanised iron roof. Beside the eight bedrooms, there were a breakfast-room, dining- and drawing-rooms, a spacious study, and a billiard-room. The kitchen and servants' quarters were in a separate building, connected with the house by a covered way.

The main gate in the paling fence was on the west side. Directly opposite this, beyond the road that led to the township of Menindee up north and to Wentworth, beyond Tin Tin Station, down south, was the long weather-board and iron building devoted to a spacious office, a store like a well-stocked grocer's shop, another store stocked as a combined ironmonger's and saddler's shop, and the quarters of the bookkeeper and the jackeroos, which included their combined dining- and sitting-room.

When Mayne and Feng left the wicket-gate they proceeded south along the river bank, the former walking quickly, evidently anxious to reach a goal, obliging Feng to lengthen his stride.

"The speed limit is only two and a half miles an hour," he good-humouredly remonstrated.

"Hang it, man! I'll race you for a pound," Mayne challenged.

"I am over thirty," Feng rejoined in his suave manner. "You are the Master of Atlas. For us to run would be out of character, as the novelists say. Go slowly! Notice the condition of your kingdom. Every wall and roof was repaired and painted last April. The interior of my cottage was done as well."

South of the office and store building was a square-built bungalow containing seven or eight rooms, and entirely surrounded by unusually wide verandas protected by canvas blinds now rolled up to the roof. Like every other building there, its walls were painted white and its roof red.

"It all looks darned good!" Mayne said, joy in his voice.

A hundred yards farther south they reached a substantial bridge of hewn red-gum timber spanning a creek in which water lay even at that time, forming an outlet from the river proper. Beyond the creek, lining its south bank, was a cluster of small buildings forming the station hands' quarters, dining-room and kitchen. Farther up the creek stood the giant corrugated iron shearing shed, flanked by the shearers' quarters, the blacksmith's and carpenter's shops on one side, the maze of sheep-yards and runways on the other. Beyond the buildings stretched the grey river flats bearing the wide-spaced box trees, between which sometimes it was possible to see the red sand-hills a mile or more distant.

When over the creek bridge and passing the men's quarters they caught sight of the men's cook in his kitchen. From the blacksmith's shop came the ringing blows of hammer on iron. Back of them, beyond Government House – so named because it housed the station's governing authority – a steam-engine methodically chugged at its labour of pumping water from the river to the big reservoir tanks set high on piles, so that gravitation might force the water to taps in the garden, the kitchens, and other offices.

Proceeding downstream for a quarter of a mile, they skirted three large huts, or rather small houses, occupied by married people. About them played several small children.

Mayne frowned. "No school, Feng?"

"The teacher decided that no longer could she resist the call of the city."

"Is another one coming?"

"I am hoping to hear so by the next mail."

Mayne hurried on, satisfied that nothing had been neglected. The average number of children of school age belonging to his employees was only six, which was below the number for which the Educational Department would supply a teacher. Atlas paid the teacher's salary.

High above the slowly moving grey-brown stream the two men walked for twenty minutes, when they came to rapidly rising ground that took them almost one hundred feet above the then level of the river. Here the river turned eastward, countless bygone floods having scooped out a great hole in its bed and formed precipitous cliffs where it was turned by the iron-hard limestone forming the high ground. On the summit grew two immense gum trees born centuries before ever Dampier saw Australia.

2

OLD MAN MAYNE'S wife had had one failing to set off her many virtues. Predeceasing her husband by five years, the old man invariably extolled her virtues, but never mentioned the one failing, which was a rarely silent tongue.

He created an arbour where he might withdraw to smoke his pipe in peace, and ponder the sheepman's ever recurrent problems, whilst gazing far and wide over his vast domain.

Forty feet up, on the lower branches of one of the two trees on the high ground of the river bend, he had caused to be made a stout platform, on which had been placed a sawn square of timber to serve as a seat. The great branches above the platform gave excellent shade from the summer sun. From it the sitter could view thousands of acres of the run. It had become known as the "Seat of Atlas".

It was the objective of Mayne and Feng Ching-wei this sparkling June morning. Sitting together on the great wood block, Feng was more interested in the open face of his companion than in the scenery which at once absorbed Frank Mayne.

At their elevation the slight undulations of the land were unmarked. Save to east and north, where the river trees cut off the view, the far-flung horizon was almost as level as at sea. Here the sky was as brilliant – nay, its brilliance was heightened by the land covered with dark-green scrub in the foreground merging into black toward the background. Pure crystal light above, mysterious darkness below, met with a sword-edge on the horizon.

To the north the deep-cutting river, marked by the avenue of tall gums, ran almost straight for three miles before it deviated north-east. Ten miles up-river lay the northern boundary of Atlas. Fifteen miles south ran the southern boundary, beyond which a low ridge marked the position of the Tin Tin homestead. As far as the eye could reach westward, and farther, far beyond the horizon, seventy miles away, lay the western limits of Atlas. Mile after mile, thousands of acres added to thousands of acres, paddocks with forty-mile boundary fences – mulga forests, pine ridges, salt-bush plains – all under the government of him who sat with Feng Ching-wei.

Originally, Atlas had comprised eleven hundred thousand acres, but the State Government had resumed block after block of land under closer settlement schemes, giving this applicant twenty thousand acres and that man thirty thousand; taking from Atlas, in bites here and there, three hundred thousand acres, so that now in shape Atlas was similar to a Cubist's drawing of a German sausage. Along the river frontage the width was about twenty-five miles in a straight line; at the western end its width was forty-five miles; somewhere about the middle the width was only five miles.

Atlas! Mayne's inheritance: a state, a country of nearly eight hundred thousand acres; a sheep-run seventy miles in length. And the population of Atlas never higher than forty. Nowhere, save to the immediate south, could a house be seen, or even any indication of the white man's lordship excepting at one point on the horizon where, south of a clump of big pine trees, the sun flashed on the vanes of a revolving windmill.

3

FOR quite a long time neither man on the Seat of Atlas spoke a word. He who was born at the edge of the restless sea and has returned after years of absence; the blind man who, by miracle, again can see; the dungeon captive of long years restored to freedom and the light of day – these and such as these know just how Frank Mayne felt this morning whilst seated on the romantically named Seat of Atlas. During many months the bush had called – softly, sweetly, alluringly. He had heard the call in the streets of London and New York, in the depths of the Black Forest, on the canals of Venice, amid Alpine snow and ice, and on the sun-heated steps of the Great Pyramid. His ears had hearkened vainly for the sough of the wind through pines; his nostrils had twitched to catch the scent of gum leaves burning in a camp fire. Amid the roar of traffic he sometimes fancied he heard the musical tinkle of a horse-bell; in slush and rain he had pictured such days as this; whilst the glitter of ice and the touch of the raw east wind had brought to memory their antithesis, the scorching summer sun of Central Australia, where one lived with the minimum of clogging clothes and could really breathe. At a thousand unexpected moments, in a thousand tones of elfin music, the great, the vast, the humanly indescribable, the alluring, the masterful, the all-conquering bush had called, called, insistently called.

And at last he had answered the call. Love had kept him away in strange lands. Now he knew that love of woman and by woman would not much longer have held him from obeying the call; knew that he had almost reached the breaking-point; that had his wife not finally consented to return with him to the bush he would have returned alone. Such as he are as the slaves of an autocrat.

After a while he explained something of this to Feng, surprising himself as well as his friend with his eloquence. It was the moment when he realised how firmly he was gripped by Atlas, by the Australian bush which is known no more intimately by bushmen than is London by Londoners. Feng Ching-wei was

22

wholly sympathetic. Whilst lacking the inherent land-love that possessed Mayne, he yet understood much. It is said that no man leaves the Darling River who does not strive to return that he may die beside it. Mayne had returned, and knew he wanted never again to leave it, and felt joy in the knowledge that he was its slave.

Frank Mayne sat staring over the bush-darkened land lying beneath the sky as the sea-bed beneath fathoms of translucent water. Watching him, his friend saw that he was changed, much changed. To be sure, he had not altered greatly in physical aspect, although his face was without its old-time tan; but it seemed as though during his travels he had caught fire from some mysterious spiritual fount, a negative personality having been electrified into a positive one. He wondered if the change had been brought about by travel or – love. The artist in him cried out now to paint the face of his loved friend: in the old days he had painted it merely for friendship's sake.

"Well, what do you think of Ethel?" Mayne asked abruptly. Wide, fearless hazel eyes gazed deep into the slanting black eyes.

"I think," Feng began, "I think Mrs. Mayne is a very beautiful woman. The tall slimness of her figure arouses my admiration whilst I have never seen a more perfectly oval face. The dark brown, almost black eyes and the black hair bring up in startling relief the pale, beautifully chiselled features. How old is she?"

"She is twenty-five," Mayne replied a little impatiently, as though a catalogue of his wife's good looks was not what he required.

After a pause he said: "Do you think I have done right?"

"Surely you love your wife, Frank?"

"With all my heart and soul, and every nerve and fibre," was the earnest reply. "And yet –" Mayne again turned to stare out over Atlas.

Feng laid a long-fingered white hand on his friend's arm. "We used to say: 'Trouble divided is trouble vanquished'," he murmured softly.

When Mayne next spoke his words were deliberately candid. "I am wondering whether it was right or wrong of me to marry Ethel. There was no mistake about my loving her, nor do I think there was any about her loving me. Her father is a dean of the

Church of England. Ethel comes from genuine English gentlefolk, and her ideas of things conventional, of things hallowed by a thousand years of tradition, are as fixed as these river gums. You have no idea; can have no idea, of the caste system of England, its rigid iron boundaries which really are no less rigid in the provinces now than they were before the War. To some extent money counts, but money does not count in all things.

"I am greatly afraid, Feng, that she will find our easy bush conventions most irritating. The majority of people in Great Britain, even the educated classes, cherish many illusions regarding us. Retired squatters and blatherskiting politicians appear to have given people over there the idea that a sheepman is a millionaire, and the working man almost as well off. Time is going to destroy that illusion, which my wife holds in common with thousands of Britishers, and I am beginning to be fearful that disillusionment will affect her love for me. If it does, our social laxity will become trebly irritating to her, and, doubtless, her reaction to us will make us all, as well as herself, very unhappy."

"If you find that she does not take kindly to us, Frank, then you must take her back to England and there make your home."

"That is what I can't do." Mayne suddenly stood up and swept his hand in an arc. "I've told you how it has got me. All that is mine, and I can't give it up. I don't want to give it up. I shall never be able to give it up."

"Don't you think you are making a sand-hill out of an ants' nest?" Feng said slowly. "You think that because Mrs. Mayne disapproved of the reception given you at the Menindee Hotel, because she did not make a fuss of Mrs. Morton and old Barlow, and almost ran away from Aunty Joe, she will never come to accept our standards. Really, you must give her a chance, Frank. You must credit her with common sense. It is said, and I believe with truth, that a new-chum finds the first six months in the bush pass easily as a period of novelty, but during the second six months the bush becomes loathsome and the torment of homesickness intolerable. After this second phase has worn away, the mystic allure of the bush begins to exert its power, so that even should he return to his homeland he will feel always that sweet allure."

"You may be right, Feng. You generally are, you know."

24

"I think I am right now. Be advised. Don't keep Mrs. Mayne here too long without a change. Even if you do not want to leave Atlas, take her for a trip to Melbourne and New Zealand this coming summer. Remember, too, we are a tolerant people towards the new-chum. Mrs. Mayne will settle down eventually. Her ideas may be cast-iron, but her common sense will find the flaws in the metal."

4

"I have endeavoured to carry out your policy in all respects," Feng said, when by tacit consent the subject of Ethel Mayne was dropped. "In breeding I have striven to continue the production of a robust merino, annually buying the best Bungaree rams and culling the ewes with severity. My aim has been your aim – to breed hardy sheep, long in the leg, with a big frame, and growing wool of a medium strength. Wool first and the meat market second."

"Good! That was Old Man Mayne's policy after nineteen-ten."

"At the beginning of this year," Feng went on, "Atlas was clear of all debt, the bank account being twenty-one thousand pounds to the good. Last shearing we shore fifty-nine thousand sheep, cutting seventeen hundred bales of wool, which topped at twenty pence halfpenny per pound. We should shear more this year than last year, and I have been regretting not having accepted twenty-one shillings a head from Adelaide buyers for nine thousand wethers."

"A guinea a head!" echoed Mayne.

"Yes. At that time, early last January, I thought, as apparently you now do, that a guinea was not a reasonable offer, and I declined. I should have closed. I did not, thinking that this year's weather conditions would have equalled last year's. I thought it wise to hang on for a better price, which March rain would undoubtedly have made."

"It didn't rain in March?"

"No. I offered to let the wethers go at one pound, but the highest offer then was only fifteen shillings. The market has been slowly falling all this year. I decided to hold the wethers and then sell off the shears at the coming shearing, besides culling the flocks most heavily if the season did not improve. No rain fell in

25

April or May, and the young lambs suffered severely from lack of green feed. Every day now I regret more not having sold those surplus wether sheep in January for a guinea a head."

"Regret? Stuff!" Mayne exclaimed. "No man could know that the year would be dry, Feng. I would not have sold at a guinea, because the price then was about twenty-three shillings."

"But having those wethers now makes Atlas slightly overstocked," Feng pointed out.

To which Mayne rejoined in a brisk business tone, quite unlike his everyday speech: "We'll sell off the shears, as you said, and cull heavily. Anyway, the rain has come and the market is bound to harden. Old Man Mayne always overstocked Atlas, according to our more modern ideas. We'll not make the very few mistakes he made, but profit by them. Come! It must be time for lunch. We'll put in the afternoon among the books, and you can formally hand Atlas back to me. I'm taking over from to-morrow morning, and to-morrow morning your well-earned holiday starts."

5

AT half-past seven the next morning Frank Mayne met the hands working on the east end of the run outside the office, where they were waiting to receive the day's orders. By then he knew the location and the condition of each of his flocks, the work of each man in the immediate past and in the present, and he found himself as much master of affairs as if he never had been absent. So he began briskly and confidently to organise the work of the day.

There was one man among the group not directly working for Atlas, and when the others had been detailed to the various kinds of work this man approached Mayne. Of medium height, nattily dressed in riding-boots, gabardine trousers, and serge jacket. It was obvious that he was highly strung, for when he spoke ingrained nervousness was revealed.

"Can – can I have a word with you, Mr. Mayne?" he asked with unmistakable English accent.

"Certainly. What is your name?"

"I'm Tom Mace."

"Oh! Mr. Ching-wei was telling me about you. I understand you have been making an excellent living at rabbiting."

26

"Y – yes, but not so excellent when a good deal of lost time is taken into account." Mace began to stutter and became silent.

"Well, go on, Tom. You can talk to me as you would to Mr. Ching-wei," Mayne said encouragingly.

With an effort Mace controlled his tongue. "I've – I've a proposition to make, Mr. Mayne," Mace began quickly. "I got about two hundred pounds clear out of the rabbits this last summer, and I am wanting to buy a truck. You see, I've been using a horse and dray at the dam-trapping, which is all right in a way, but wastes a lot of time when I've to take a load of skins to the railway at Ivanhoe. If I had a truck I could cart my skins in a day, instead of almost a week, when I am earning nothing. But I don't want to get a truck on time payments. The payments when they come due would worry me. I – er –"

"Well?"

Mace saw sympathy and kindliness in Mayne's eyes. "You see, it's like this, Mr. Mayne. A new truck would cost two hundred and twenty pounds. I'd have to keep back twenty-five pounds for floating expenses, and I am wanting to know if you would put up fifty pounds if I mortgaged the truck to you."

"Humph! How many rabbits did you take off Atlas last summer?"

"Close on eighty thousand and two hundred and thirty-seven eagles as well."

"Eighty thousand! You did fine. What are the rabbits like now?"

"Well, the dry spell has thinned them out, but present fur prices are high and gin-trapping pays well. The recent rain will cause 'em to start breeding again; and, as it looks like a good season ahead of us, they should be almost as thick this coming summer as they were last summer."

"I suppose you are hoping that they will be so?"

"Well, rabbits and foxes are my living. You –"

"Of course they are, Tom! For your sake, I hope they are thick. For my sake, I hope every rabbit and every fox dies soon. What concessions were you getting from Atlas?"

"Meat only."

"No scalp money? No tucker?"

"No."

27

For a little while Mayne pinched his chin and gazed vacantly at a near gum tree. "How long have you been in Australia?" he asked.

"Seven years, Mr. Mayne. I came out under the United Services scheme. But I couldn't stick wheat-farming. To me it was too dead a life. In the bush a man's always alive. I'm sure I could do much better with a truck. All that lost time travelling about could be saved."

Mayne's eyes suddenly lost their look of introspection and came to bear on the rabbiter's nose. He said, without smiling: "Was that you I saw with one of the maids last night?"

The blood flew into Tom Mace's fresh-complexioned face. "Ye – es."

Continuing to gaze hard at the man's nose, Frank Mayne said, still unsmiling: "I trust your intentions are strictly honourable."

"They – they are. Eva and me are going to be married as soon as we can get a place to live in, so that I can box on with my work and not leave here."

"Which is Eva?"

"Eva! Eva's the first housemaid, Mr. Mayne."

"Humph, you are a good picker! Well, Mr. Ching-wei's opinion of you is high. I'll advance you the fifty pounds, and I'll pay you a rabbit scalp bonus of twenty shillings a thousand, and give you station rations. Later I may be able to find you a house on the run, but any hanky-panky with Eva will result in your leaving Atlas. You see, the maids are my responsibility. You will please me by not keeping Eva out later than half-past nine."

For a space of three seconds they regarded each other with penetrating keenness. Then Mace said: "Half-past nine it shall be, Mr. Mayne. Thank you very much! I'd like to leave for Broken Hill on the mail-car to-night."

"Very well. Come for my cheque at eleven."

6

MACE'S business disposed of, Frank Mayne walked slowly toward the creek and the men's quarters beyond. Skirting the river bank, he noted how low was the brownish stream, more than twenty feet below him, and idly his gaze swept downstream, noting, too, the wonderfully even cut of the grey banks, appearing almost as though the huge ditch had been the careful engineering of man. At the men's quarters he visited the men's cook.

"Morning, Todd!" he said to a short, clean-shaven, fierce-eyed man about sixty years old.

Todd Gray rose from the table at which he was eating breakfast, revealing fully the speckless white trousers and the apron that covered his chest and fell to his knees. In a swift survey Mayne examined the long combined kitchen and dining-room. One bench was littered with used baking dishes, but of those utensils used by the men at breakfast he saw no sign. Already they had been washed and put back in their respective places.

Todd said: "Strike-me-dead! It's good to see you again, Mr. Mayne, 'deed it is. Have a good trip?"

"Splendid, Todd, splendid! I'm very glad to find you still on deck."

"Ain't I been on this deck for forty years? Course I have. A drink of tea?"

Todd went over to the wall at the end of his service table, and regarded for a second the three rows of enamelled pint pannikins, each hanging from a nail by its handle. The three pannikins at the end of the top row were half-pints in size. Above each was attached to the wall a short piece of tin and each piece of tin had a name punched through it. The pannikin beneath the name "Mister Frank", Todd took down to fill. Above the adjoining pannikin was the name "Mister Feng", and over the third "Miss Ann". There was no pannikin on the fourth nail.

"Still keeping those three pannikins clean, Todd?"

"Of course, Mr. Mayne. No one dare use 'em but their owners, but they gets washed with the others three times every day, including Sundays. Master Frankie's pannikin goes on that fourth nail. Gus is doing the name now. I got Mr. Feng to order the pannikin from Menindee yesterday. It should be here on its nail to-morrow."

Filling Mayne's pannikin from the big tea-urn, Todd brought it to the table, on which he set it down opposite his unfinished breakfast. Mayne took the form for a seat and added milk and sugar, whilst Todd continued his breakfast.

"It was Mr. Feng who started it," Todd said, as though making a complaint. "Used to run along here every time he could sneak away from old Mrs. Mayne, who was so dead frightened he'd fall off the bridge. And then he brought you along when you could toddle about, and you had to have a pannikin. No thought for me, who had to keep washin' 'em up. Oh no! When Mrs. Shelley died and old Mrs. Mayne used to have Miss Ann stay here for months, then Miss Ann must have a pannikin too. And all these years them three pannikins have had to be washed up, and me getting older and older. I'm getting wore out. Me blasted feet is that sore that I can't sleep o' nights. You know, Mr. Mayne, seven days a week, month after month, sets up friction and emphasises the sidereal influences, threatening to cause combustion in the mental chamber. What about a week off? I could do with a week's spell in Menindee."

"You'd start talking about the stars and forget to come home, Todd," Mayne said, with a show of indecision.

"I'd come back today week on the mail, for sure!'

"Very well," with seeming relief. "But you must first persuade Archie to carry on in your place."

"All right!" Todd grumbled. "He'll cost me a couple of quid, but I'll have to pay him, I suppose. Only lunatics take on cooking for a living. Archie will carry on for the two quid, and he promises to hang Master Frankie's pannikin on that nail directly it arrives. Can the youngster walk yet?"

"No, not yet," replied Mayne, smiling. Todd Gray had been his boyhood's hero, then a young man with a brilliant imagination to evolve an everlasting line of adventure stories. Well educated, Todd Gray's reason for undertaking station cooking always had been a mystery. The years had seen him degenerate into the free and easy bush manner of thought and speech, only alcohol pulling him back to those days when he had spoken culturally.

Cursed with tender feet caused by long spells of standing on floor-boards, his feet occupied his sober moments, whilst the stars occupied his mind to the exclusion of all else when influenced by whisky.

"Wot's it feel like to be back, Mr. Mayne?" he inquired, pushing away his plate.

"It feels good, Todd; darned good."

"You should never have gone all that time. The bush is a

jealous slut. You had to come back, didn't you, though?"

"Yes, I had to come back."

"Course you did! All dinkum bushmen has to come back to the Darling. Still, you shouldn't have stayed away so long. Like as not the bush will have her revenge. You look out! Be terrible careful when you're hoss-riding alone, and are well away from water on a hot summer day. You only need to make one slip, and the bush will see to it that you never leave her again. There was old Te –"

"Croaker!" Mayne chided, laughing. "I'll hear no more now. When you are in Menindee, never forget that I am expecting you back this day week."

Whilst Mayne walked to the shearing shed he could hear Todd Gray singing, in a cracked voice, a song in Latin.

CHAPTER III

OLD JOHN

1

AFTER leaving Todd Gray, Mayne, glancing at his watch, noted that it was nearly half-past eight, and remembered that his breakfast would not be served till nine. It was a nice hour to breakfast. He had become quite used to it; and yet, in passing over the creek bridge, he could not but mark the incongruity of a sheepman breakfasting at nine. Why, the day was then half sped!

Approaching Feng's bungalow, he saw a strange woman stoking a portable copper near the back door; and, seeing her jabbing at something beneath the rising steam, wondered why his friend's washerwoman was not doing the work in the homestead laundry, where there was every convenience. When the woman stooped to push a billet of wood into the fire beneath the copper, the revealed width of her hips engaged his interest. Her huge arms, bare to the shoulder, were whitened with suds.

After pausing before the opened front door of the bungalow, he entered and called loudly: "Hey, Feng! Are you up?"

Feng answered from the interior of a shut-off room at the precise instant that Mary O'Doyle surged along the passage to the hall wherein stood Mayne.

Confronting him, Mary at once fell into one of her fighting attitudes, standing square on her feet thrust into elastic-sided stockman's boots, hands on hips, her large red face thrust forward, the button of a nose twitching, the brilliant blue eyes unwinking. "Who might you be, raising hell at this hour of the morning?" she demanded.

"My name is Mayne. Who are you?" he replied, with difficulty keeping amusement from his face.

"Oh!" Mary O'Doyle's fighting attitude relaxed. "Morning, Mr. Mayne! I didn't know, for sure I didn't. Me, I'm Mary O'Doyle, born in County Clare when the grand John Redmond was in his prime. Was you wishin' to see Mr. Feng?"

"I was."

A door was opened. Resplendent in a rose-hued dressing-gown, Feng smiled at them impartially. "Come in, Frank. Mary, a cup of tea for Mr. Mayne."

"I've already had two cups.' the squatter protested.

"An' a third'll go good," emphatically stated Mary, turning back to her kitchen.

Within his friend's bedroom Mayne stood looking about him. The old severe plainness had given way to luxurious comfort.

Feng said: "When I had your house redecorated and furnished, I took the liberty of removing the old furniture that did not harmonize with the new period scheme. You see here some of it, added to pieces I bought with yours. How do you like my bedroom?"

"I like it well. I am glad you launched out. Europe taught me the meaning of luxury, and when we can afford luxury, why the dickens can't we have it in the bush of Australia? By the way, Ethel is most pleased with your taste in furnishing. The interior of the house quite surprised her."

"Ah! I am delighted. I had some little fear that my taste would not meet with her approval."

At this point Mary entered with Mayne's tea, and lingered for a moment to fuss with the cup and the plate of biscuits.

When she withdrew Feng asked: "How does work appeal to you?"

"Good! I'm as keen as anything. By the way, we expected you

to dinner last night."

"Thanks! I thought, however, that Mrs. Mayne would like time to settle down. Er – you see, Frank, one cannot now be too unconventional. Not as we used to be in the bad old days. Which is why the coming of a mistress to Atlas will do us both much good. I think, too, that you both will benefit by enjoying a degree of privacy, even during meals. I know, were I married, I would not relish always having other people at my table. Already I am thinking that I've secured a jewel in Mary O' Doyle, and I am enjoying immensely the – well, the independence of my establishment."

"Excellent! I was afraid you might feel out of it now I've brought home a wife. Feng, we want no one, not even a wife, to come between us, do we?"

"Of course not, Frank," replied Feng Ching-wei, once again noting Mayne's trouble of spirit. "Of course not. It would be unthinkable. To insure against such a remote happening, I refurnished this house and installed Mary O'Doyle. Naturally, I'll be delighted to accept an invitation to dine as often as your wife sends me one. I hope to invite Mrs. Mayne and yourself here sometimes."

"A good suggestion!" agreed Mayne, smiling again. "It will break routine, and I must never allow Ethel to become bored with routine. We are giving a house-warming dinner to-morrow night. We are sending word to Ann and Cameron, and I intend walking down to Sir John after breakfast. That reminds me to ask you, what kind of a fellow is Cameron?"

Feng was placing a used match on the bronze ash-tray, and Mayne did not see the slight contraction of the eyelids over the black eyes. But there was no change in either expression or voice when Feng looked up, saying:

"He's a good sheepman – above the average. In appearance, smart. Possesses culture of a kind. He was managing a place in Central Queensland before coming here. A little too partial, possibly, to women; no snobbery where they are concerned. There was some difficulty last year with a maid, I believe. Has his good points, of course."

"Humph! Well, we will see the fellow to-morrow night. My wife met his uncle, the shipping man, somewhere. Neighbour, you know, and all that. Where are you to spend your holiday?"

Feng laughed in his soft, chuckling way. "I am going to spend it here, and enjoy a real good loaf," he said. "There are several pictures I want to finish, and two I wish to paint."

2

LATER in the morning Frank Mayne set off to visit Old John. When he came out through the main gates in the paling fence, facing westward toward the office and store buildings, he turned to the north, and, walking round the fence corner, followed it almost to its end at the edge of the steep river bank, when the beaten path he trod branched away to continue along the bank.

Save for a single line of small puff-cloud the brilliant sky was clear. The south wind caressed Mayne's neck with cool touch and, with a sound like the distant hiss of many snakes, rustled the leaves of the red-gum trees beneath which he passed. Occasionally the kookaburras burst into apparently uncontrollable laughter, and with high-pitched screeches a roosting flock of galahs impertinently gibed at a passing school of the big black cockatoos that replied in a lower, more raucous tone.

Elsewhere than at the bends the river in many places was easily fordable. Here slabs of granite forced the stream to flow swiftly through a channel at the foot of a stretch where the bank was grey mud; beyond, the stream expanded to the width of the bed to flow sluggishly into a rock-girt hole many feet in depth. Cranes flapped awkwardly up and down the river course level with its banks; shags stood high on dead branches, wings outstretched to dry; whilst finches hopped and chirped among the branches of the grandest avenue of trees in Australia.

Following the narrow man-trodden path, Mayne walked on till he came to the edge of a belt of lantana bush, which was on a much lower level than the surrounding flats, and accordingly was flooded when the river was moderately high. A quarter of a mile wide beside the river, it spread to several miles in width two miles westward, where a bank of sand-dunes prevented further expansion.

The path wound sharply downward to the lantana belt, there to wind in and out among the giant masses of tangled, cane-like bush. Down here among the lantana the sunlight seemed to wane and thin, and at the moment of entering it was as if the sun was suddenly masked by a cloud. Midway across, Mayne came to a little natural clearing, where lightning first had killed and a windstorm subsequently had uprooted one of the gums. Beyond the clearing the path re-entered the lantana, and the river was not again seen until the higher flats beyond were reached. And then, after walking a third quarter of a mile, Mayne could see the Australian seat of Sir John Blain.

The house was built on high land, immediately behind a point composed of snow-white, large-grained sand, round which the river flowed into a very cavern of a hole where lurked the forty- and fifty-pound cod when the stream ceased to run. The dwelling was constructed of sheet-iron nailed to a wooden frame. Facing east, its front was protected by a walled shed, or veranda, built entirely of cane-grass, a shed almost as large as the house itself, and used by the tenant as a dining-room and a kitchen. Within the hut a window faced west, a window without glass, a wooden drop-shutter being raised on hinges when light and air were necessary.

This small bush home was surrounded by a well-kept kitchen garden, the whole being securely net-fenced against rabbits. The exterior of the hut – the garden and ground adjacent – was kept scrupulously clear of rubbish; an oasis set amid a trackless desert littered with leaves and dead branches flung there from the great gums by the winds of the season. A splash of red rose from the south side of the grass shed and almost covered its roof, formed by the countless little flowers of a creeping vine, the name of which none knew, not even Sir John, who years before had brought the cutting from Adelaide.

Although he was seventy-two, Sir John was one whose forces appeared never to have been sapped by the follies of youth or of middle age, one whose youthful strength obviously had been extraordinary. Despite his years, his back was straight and his legs steady. Six feet one inch he measured in his socks. Snow-white hair and a full snow-white moustache with drooping ends, wide, clear grey eyes that gazed steadily from beneath pent white eyebrows, a firm, dominating mouth, and a square chin made him appear as one of those patriarchal Vikings whose descendant unquestionably he was. A stern, unbending character at one's first casual observation, it was when one came to study carefully the extraordinarily vital face that the single contradictory feature explained his past history and his present. Even the full moustache failed to hide the lines of his wide mouth, revealing tenderness – nay, weakness.

He was seated on a sawn length of red gum rolled to within a few inches of the rough-made garden gate. A dried sheepskin hung over the fence, making a comfortable back seat. His feet reposed on a board, for the ground was damp, and two yards beyond the board the ground fell sharply to the river level, thirty feet below.

On Atlas he was known to everyone as Old John. In the near township of Menindee, in Adelaide twenty-five years before, and in the South of England twenty-five years before that, he was known as Sir John Blain, Bt., of Blain Chase, near Winchester.

This morning Old John was dressed in dark-green gabardine trousers, and a frayed and faded Norfolk jacket. On his feet were elastic-sided riding boots, about his neck was a white silk handkerchief, on his great head was set a battered, weather-stained felt hat. He surveyed with the calm eyes of age a resilient gum sucker, six feet in length, thrust firmly into the river bank near the water. From it stretched a white fishing line, the stick acting as a springer which would automatically hook and play a fish. He sat as the artists depict King Canute commanding the sea to come no higher. He looked as ancient, as sturdy, and as defiant as anyone of the trees forming the thousand-mile winding avenue down which flows the "Gutter of Australia", as the Darling River is often endearingly called.

3

THE crackling of leaves and small twigs awoke into vivid life a small fox-terrier that scampered away round the corner of the garden with short, staccato barks. Old John demanded to know the reason of "Beelzebub's" sudden departure in a voice that boomed as that of a sailor, then slowly he rose to his feet, stood erect, and turned about. He saw, approaching, Frank Mayne.

With shrewd, puckered eyes the old man appraisingly examined the visitor, noted how the slightly bowed legs carried the lithe, supple body with the springy step of the horseman.

When Mayne rounded the corner post of the fence Old John was quick to see the unusual paleness of his face, lit now with the strange fire of the wanderer at long last returned home.

"Why, Frank! I'm glad you have come," he said heartily. "Feng told me the other day that you were expected, but I did not think to see you so soon. Sit down, my boy! Sit here beside me and spin away at all your adventures."

"To do that would take me a week, John," Mayne said, conscious of the undiminished strength of Old John's hand on his own. "You are looking not a day older. You are looking splendid."

"Looks often lie, Frank. I have never been ill in my life, but my heart is getting tired of work, and sometimes complains. Beelzebub, to heel! Silence, sir! But never mind me, Frank. You are married! Well, well, well! Feng tells me that you married the second daughter of Dean Dyson. I have been wondering. Does the Dean come from the Dysons of Tavistock?"

"Yes, he does."

"Then I know him. He was in the second form when I was in the sixth at the old school. Strange – strange! I saved him from a hiding one day, and the little beggar wanted to divide a hamper from his people he received the following week. The jumping Nabob! How time flies! Tell me of her, your wife."

"She's a wonderful woman, John," Mayne said quietly.

"Of course she is. I don't want the obvious. Is she a brunette, like all the Dysons? How old is she?"

"She is twenty-five – taller than I am. Yes, like all the Dysons, she is dark; black hair and brown eyes, and a complexion like rose-tinted cream."

"Enamelled?" Old John asked dryly, chuckling.

"Of course not. Ethel doesn't paint."

"The heir? Is he a Dyson too?"

"No, he takes after the Maynes. Now his hair is long and curly, and the colour of ripe wheat. His eyes are wide and deep blue. When he laughs I hear Old Man Mayne, and there was seldom a man who laughed more heartily than did my father."

"How old is he now?" asked Old John, gazing fixedly at the fishing-line springer.

"Eleven months."

"Can he run yet?"

"No. But it won't be very long before he does."

Old John continued to look down on the sun-reflecting river and his line for nearly half a minute, but the scene before his eyes was not the scene viewed by his brain.

"You must let me see the lad, Frank. You must bring him along one day," he said slowly at last.

"As a matter of fact, we want you to come along to dinner to-morrow evening. Will you?"

"It isn't quarter day yet. Won't be for another seventeen days."

"I am aware of that," Mayne countered. "To-morrow evening we are giving a little house-warming party. There will be Ann Shelley, and the new man at Thuringah, Feng, and, if you will come, yourself. Ethel wants to meet you."

The old man pondered with knit, bushy brows. Then: "You'll let me see the boy? You will not have him tucked away in bed?"

Mayne laughed indulgently. "No," he said. "You'll come?"

"Yes, I'll come."

"Good! I'll send the car for you about six. Dinner will be at seven, so that you will have an hour to get acquainted with my two people. I also have some photographs to show you."

"Photographs! Of what?"

"Of Blain Chase," Mayne replied with twinkling eyes.

Old John swung round to face the younger man. His eyes were clear and strong with light. His voice was a roar.

"Then why the devil didn't you bring 'em with you?"

"I intended to use them as a bait."

"Be damned!" came the roar. "Your son is bait enough. Did you go there? Did you have a look-see at the old place?"

"We did more. We found the Sheffields delightful people, and they invited us to stay a week-end. We duly paid the visit last September. Oh John, John! What a place! What a home!"

Old John did not speak again for several minutes. Mayne, seeing the old man's reverie, refrained from breaking the silence. When Old John did speak his voice was low, in it a faint tremble.

"England, Frank!" he whispered very slowly. "Blain Chase is the trebly refined essence of England. Oh, God! How my heart always has hungered for Blain Chase! If any man knows what Adam suffered after being flung out of the Garden of Eden, I do."

Again silence fell between them, and once more Mayne refrained from breaking it.

Then: "Where did you sleep?" came the question wistfully.

"In the right wing. You go up to the first landing lighted by the great stained-glass window, then take the right-hand passage, and it was the first room."

"The first room? Are you sure?"

"Quite. We slept there three nights."

"Did you know that that room was her room? That it was the room in which I found her – and him?"

Mayne suddenly stiffened. His right hand gripped Old John's right forearm. "Was that the room?"

"It was that room. Strange! Strange that you went across the world to Blain Chase to sleep in that accursed room, when there are twenty-two undefiled bedrooms. Your wife slept there too?"

"Of course."

"Humph!"

"Why did you ask that – about my wife sleeping there?"

"Nothing."

After that abrupt reply there was silence for a long time, the old man staring with eyes that saw scenes of long ago, Frank watching idly the fishing-line and Beelzebub, who was racing along the water's edge. The invigorating breeze rustled the leaves of the giant river trees and whipped the surface of the stream above the sand point into what looked like frosted glass. Now the sky was mottled with tiny clouds like balls of wool – balls of wool littering the floor of a vast shearing shed.

Presently Mayne spoke. "The sundial you described so accurately and so often is still on the lawn opposite the terrace steps. Mr. Sheffield explained it to me. He made a suggestion about that sundial."

"Indeed!"

"He thought that, perhaps, you might like to have a little piece of Blain Chase, and said that if you wish it he will send that sundial out to you."

"Remove the sundial! Certainly not, Frank. Blain Chase would be incomplete without that sundial."

"Mr. Sheffield made a second proposition. As they have no children, and go into society very little, he would find it quite agreeable to let you the entire west wing, with full use of his domestic service and the grounds. Oh, John, Wouldn't you like to see it all again? To live there?"

Old John's hands were clasped tightly together. For a moment his face was as that of a saint regarding heaven. Then quickly the eyes became moist and his chin sank to his massive chest. He said: "It's quite impossible, my boy. Sheffield is a square man, and you must write and thank him for me. No, it is impossible now. How is Sheffield keeping up the old place?"

"First-rate. It was the most beautiful place I saw in England. I wonder no longer at the Englishman's love of the Old Country."

"It is the finest place in all England, Frank. It was first built by Sir Hugh Blain in 1717. The cost almost ruined him. His son, Sir Richard, made a fortune in the West Indies, and really founded the family fortunes. I wonder how long they will call it Blain Chase after I'm gone. If only Dick had survived the War! If only his mother – Damnation!

"Frank, when one becomes old, one becomes weak and sentimental. Yes, I'll come to the dinner, and thank you. Have those photographs to show me, and that son of yours too. It is fortunate that I knew your wife's father. That will provide a chain of interest between her and me. Did you say that Alldyce Cameron was also dining with you?"

"Yes. We have not yet met him. Neighbour, you know. Must ask him."

"He's a flash, Frank," Old John said sternly. "He reminds me of – you know. Easy talker, easy mannered. Expressive eyes and a silver tongue. The kind that can recite poetry to a pretty woman when the moon is up. Poetry! Faugh! However, I'll be polite to the fellow."

"Good!" said Mayne, chuckling, seeing the old man regain his habitual buoyant good-humour. "Be ready at six. How has Feng been looking after you?"

"Thoughtfully, as always. You two are good boys. You are like your father, Frank, in more ways than in looks, and Old Man Mayne knew what he was doing when he picked up Feng. I am indeed fortunate. Now, you be gone! I have valet's work to do. I am a better man than any of the Blains, because I can valet myself."

And, when the old man lost sight of the figure of Frank Mayne among the trees, he looked down on the log seat and found there a package of photographs of Blain Chase and its grounds.

CHAPTER IV

THE MANAGER OF THURINGAH

1

ETHEL MAYNE dressed with care late in the afternoon for the house-warming dinner. She had selected an evening gown of black *crepe-de-Chine*, unrelieved by any colour. Surveying herself now and again in the full-length mirror, she for the first time felt a thrill of thankfulness that her father's financial standing had not permitted the services of a lady's maid for his three daughters; for now, when the services of a good maid were impossible, her practised reliance on herself stood her in good stead.

The gown clung to her slim, well-moulded, youthful figure, accentuating the soft curves, and throwing into relief the cold, lovely face, on which emotion was so seldom pictured, crowned by the shining, cropped black hair. Undoubtedly her greatest accomplishment was how to dress. She knew she was beautiful, and was pleasantly conscious that her choice of dress made her strikingly so.

She wanted this evening to create surprise and admiration. Her guests, excluding Feng Ching-wei, were two Australians, a man and a woman. Of the man, Alldyce Cameron, she had learned a little from a conversation with Feng, who drank tea that morning with her and her husband, and what the little Feng had said in his suave, guarded manner was sufficient to fire her lifelong passion for sexual conquest. Coming to realise thus early that her social world here at Atlas was so limited, she felt that of necessity she must make the best of every opportunity.

Then there was the woman, Ann Shelley, mistress of a run almost as huge as Atlas itself. Of her, Feng's veiled reticence, added to her husband's less diplomatic statements, aroused in Ethel Mayne a growing desire to know more of past history and

precisely what part in that history had been played by her husband
and Ann Shelley. Old John then was of no interest to her. She had
forgotten him, a broken-down baronet living on Atlas charity.

The third daughter of the Very Reverend Dean Dyson, the
whole of her pre-married life had been lived in the somewhat
narrow social atmosphere of a cathedral city. Hers had been the
unenviable lot of the youngest daughter in a *ménage* where
money, or, rather, the lack of money, was of paramount
importance. The Dean's stipend, plus a small private income, was
drained by many pipes, the largest of which was that supplying
the Dean himself, who was an ambitious man of extravagant
tastes.

It had always been the Dean this, and the Dean that. Or: "You
must remember, dear, that your father has his responsibilities and
his position to keep up. We simply cannot increase your dress
allowance." And again, when Agatha, the eldest, was to be
married: "Agatha's wedding will be most frightfully expensive,
remember. The Dean simply cannot permit a quiet, inexpensive
function. We must consider the Honourable Edward's people as
well as ourselves. No, you must go to dear Aunt Emily this
summer."

Scrape, scheme and plan everlastingly to make a crown go as
far as a pound note! It had been sickening, and even her shallow
soul had at times revolted against the hollow pretence of
affluence. And into that world of make-believe riches, where the
skeleton of poverty lurked behind every peal of laughter, every
tinsel colour, there entered one day Frank Mayne.

They had met at a garden-party whilst he was the guest of the
Bishop. It was the Bishop who in all innocence later described
Atlas and Old Man Mayne, when he, the Bishop, had been on
mission work in New South Wales; and consequently when, after
a friendship of only three weeks, Mayne proposed marriage, the
whole Dyson family was aware of the precise acreage of Atlas
and the probable value of the property.

Here plainly was a golden avenue of escape from her small
world of horrid pretence, parsimony, and genteel poverty so
cleverly dissembled. Mayne's impulsive declaration astonished,
although it pleased; for in Market Wallop he was already regarded
as a prize, a rich Australian squatter around whose head was the

aura of gold and power. Were not by tradition all Australian squatters wealthy and powerful?

To be sure, marriage with Frank Mayne meant being a good deal in the wild back-blocks of Australia; but, with his three-quarters of a million acres of land, and some seventy thousand sheep, he could provide her with a decent dress allowance, whilst almost certainly they would move in Vice-Regal circles three months of every year.

After a proper show of maidenly hesitation, she accepted this Colonial Midas. She liked his well-bred, if easy, manner. She liked his boyish impulsiveness, recognising in it the certainty of her easy ascendancy over him as his wife. Yet his passion for her did not fire her blood, and cause her pulses to leap beneath his touch, and because no man had fired her it is not to her discredit that she married less for love than for worldly things.

Followed her acceptance of him, a whirlwind courtship, a period spent in a sudden rain of gold, for Frank Mayne showered gifts on her worthy of the fabulous Colonial millionaire. They were married at the end of a month. The golden shower continued. The magic carpet of gold carried them around Europe, some way into Asia, through America, back again to England, where she had her baby, then to proceed at a slower rate, till finally it stopped at Atlas.

The solidity of Atlas pleased her, solidity and security. A tour of the homestead conducted by her husband was a revelation. She had expected to see a log-built ranch-house and roughly constructed out-buildings, her mind having been coloured by the vivid word pictures portrayed by the most popular American and Canadian novelists. She found her bush home to be well built, spacious, set amid an oasis of fresh green vines, plants, and trees, beautifully furnished, lighted by electricity, and staffed by a woman cook and four maids, supervised by a housekeeper who relieved her of all household worries. The men's quarters, she saw, were roomy and comfortable for mere hired hands, each compartment containing but two iron bedsteads.

The huge shearing shed, with its long row of pens on one side flanking the board on which twenty-four men could shear, the wool-sorting room, the great presses, and the maze of yards and runways outside further impressed her. The carpenter's shop, the saddler's shop, the blacksmith's shop, the poison house and the poison carts, the stockyards, the store-rooms, and the most important looking office, as well as the barracks in which lived the bookkeeper, and the jackeroos – a completely independent establishment – all spoke of solidity, all proclaimed that Atlas was founded securely on gold produced by the thousands of sheep scattered over the vast territory she presently was to see.

The old hatefully dependent life was far behind her. No longer had she to defer to others: people deferred to her. She had but to command to be obeyed. In her own small rosewood *secretaire* lay a cheque-book and a bank pass-book. Every quarter-day her bank account was enriched by three hundred pounds. Lying in her chests and hanging in her cupboards were costumes, gowns and lingerie of which she always had dreamed, but never possessed until she had married this rich Australian squatter.

Solidity! Security! Power! All were hers. All were given her lavishly, without stint, without question. They were given her as tokens of love, rendered her in rightful expectation of her love in return, and, deep in her heart, Ethel Mayne knew that the recompense she made for these gifts was unworthy. At intervals – very far apart – she recognised that she did not love her husband with the fire, the passionate devotion with which he loved her; recognised, too, that sometimes he was disappointed by her coldness and lack of response. Ethel Mayne had hitherto loved but one person, and that was Ethel Mayne; but now she loved two, herself and Little Frankie.

2

NOTWITHSTANDING her selfishness, her pride, and her passion for luxury, Ethel Mayne was not indifferent to the duty she owed her child. No doubt had entered her mind that she always would be a good wife and mother. Her happiness on attaining worldly success was at first darkened by the arrival of Little Frankie, because the incident of child-bearing had so spoilt her figure and had compelled retirement from the excitements and the pleasures which were her right as the wife of an Australian squatter. Not maternal love, but repulsion did she feel at first sight of the baby. It was only latterly, when the child began to bloom into real loveliness, when her figure again was lithesome, when the child so evidently was a credit to her, that she came to love him. It was the beauty of the child and not love of its father which inspired that love.

A knock on the door of her room announced her husband. Turning from the mirror she saw him surveying her, one hand still on the door-knob behind him, his eyes lit with the admiration that in any man's eyes thrilled her to consciousness of her sex appeal. Whilst his eyes swept over her she incuriously wondered at the power her body held over this man.

"Do you like me in my black frock?" she inquired coolly, as though questioning another woman.

"You look – you look just superb," he replied haltingly. And then, with quick, restrained earnestness: "Ethel, you are wonderful."

"I shall become wonderfully vain if you go on in that strain. Still, I am glad you like my frock. I want to look nice to meet our neighbours."

When he left the door and approached her, her alabaster lids drooped, shutting away the light that came into her eyes as the slats of a blind turned down will shut out the light of day. In her husband's face she saw his hunger for her, but felt no responsive warmth.

"Don't touch me, old boy! I've taken lots of trouble with my toilet," she cried out protestingly.

"Very well, dear."

Mayne stiffened into immobility, standing still to study her face feature by feature: first the semi-closed, languorous eyes, then the rather long, straight nose, and finally the perfect mouth and the slightly pointed chin. Lovely though she looked to him at that moment, he wondered how still more lovely she would look if only her face was flushed with passionate love. He said: "Sorry, sweetheart, but you are so adorable, and I – I love you."

"I know you do," she told him, a thrill of satisfaction in her low, rich voice; now, in privacy with him, free from the affectation learned in the elocution class. "Yet I mustn't be pulled about. You are not yet dressed. Do hurry!"

"Indeed, I must. I popped in to tell you that Old John is in the drawing-room playing with Little Frankie. I wanted to introduce you before the others arrive."

"He – he is all right? Dressed, I mean."

"Come and see for yourself. I think you will approve."

He held open the drawing-room door for her to enter, and her first sight of Old John was of him on his knees facing the babe, who clung to a chair but two yards distant. And, even at her soft entry, Little Frankie suddenly left the chair and staggered on his stocky little legs across the adventurous sea into the safe harbour of the old man's arms.

"Why! He walks!"

Her voice was raised in ecstatic surprise. Her face lit up with an inner light that for the moment melted her cold beauty into ravishing loveliness. Thus it was that Old John, with Little Frankie in his arms, first saw Ethel Mayne.

"Madame, Boy Blue has the makings of an international athlete," boomed the deep voice of the old man when he stood up, still holding the child.

"But he has never walked before!"

"He has been waiting for encouragement – to gain applause."

"Ethel, this is Sir John Blain," Mayne interposed. "John – my wife."

She smiled into the old, strikingly handsome face of this big man, correctly dressed in evening clothes cut in the fashion of nineteen-ten, and her mind began at once to battle with the items of news she had heard of him, and proceed to obliterate some of them as untruths. The affectation of the elocutionist was strong in her voice when she said: "I am glad you came, Sir John – early. I am delighted to know that you are our near neighbour."

"Your welcome gives me great happiness, Mrs. Mayne. When I heard whom Frank had married I knew he had married rightly. Now, having seen you, I venture to add that he knew precisely what he was doing. And, and not only has Atlas obtained a royal mistress, it also has got a royal heir. Madam, this child of yours is worthy of Atlas."

"I am glad that you approve of us, Sir John," she said, laughing softly. "But isn't it wonderful that Little Frankie can toddle? You know, I was beginning to think he was backward."

"Backward! Not he! My boy didn't walk until he was thirteen months old, and he grew into a fine lad nevertheless. Very well, young fellow, you shall try again."

The child was struggling to be released from the steady, encircling arms, and the old man set him down on his feet beside the chair. Mayne, still standing near the door, watched the scene with a surging heart, saw Old John fall on his knees, saw his wife standing near him with an expression of rapt joy – an expression which caused him to think that he never had met this woman before. Old John called coaxingly, his face lit by an astonishing light, and again Little Frankie essayed the journey, this time with less success although with not less confidence. Without speaking, Mayne quietly withdrew and went to his room to dress.

"Your father! Is he in good health?" Old John asked, still on his knees, and addressing Ethel when she became seated.

"As well as *can* be expected, Sir John. His nerves are in rags, but he *will* work so hard. Every *moment* of his day is occupied by *something* or other."

Her emphasis on particular words jarred him. He could find no excuse for the daughter of Dean Dyson, who had mixed all her life with gentlefolk. It did not even amuse him, as such affectation in the speech of the ignorant would have done. Her good first impression on him already was wearing thin.

"It is a great thing to enjoy a busy life," he boomed. "Your father and I went to the same school, and I remember him as a thin little fellow anxious to please everyone. You will feel a little homesick for a while, but that is a phase which will be cured by time. I said just now that your husband had chosen well. Without impertinence I say now that you are a fortunate woman, for not only is Frank a fine man, but this estate which you share with him is well worth the co-rule of any woman. As an inheritance for your boy I know of none finer, save, of course, Blain Chase."

"Have you been here long?" she asked unsmilingly.

"Twenty-five years. A somewhat sordid incident drove me from Blain Chase. Doubtless you have heard of it from your husband. In certain circumstances men sometimes are very foolish. My son then was seven years old. I sent him to school and came to Australia, where I met Old Man Mayne, who persuaded me to stay. Now and then I went home to see my boy, and settle details regarding his education and subsequent career in the Army. After he was killed in action at Mons I felt no desire to go home; and have, with my own hands, built a little place of my own where I can fish and garden and dream away my closing years."

"Are you not lonely all by yourself?"

She saw him smiling at her with a suggestion of wistfulness.

"No," he said firmly. "My ghosts are my companions. There is the ghost of my woman who, to me, died many years ago; and there is the ghost of my dear boy. He is ever with me, and I am truly comforted."

No emotion was either visible on his face or audible in his voice. The matter-of-fact tones were strangely in dissonance with the subject of his words. He asked for, and expected, no sympathy. It was his simplicity that awed her.

He spoke again. "Old Man Mayne was my friend, and a very staunch friend he was too. I know something of the long, long battle he fought to make Atlas what it is. He was justified in his pride of possession, because he loved the bush as few men do, and he grew to love Atlas with a love transcending even a woman's love. When he died, not only did he transmit the property to his son, he also left him his pride of possession and his love for Atlas. I hope – with all my heart I hope – that you will come to love it too."

"I hope so," she said. "Do you know, I think I shall." But she thought that Old John was over serious, not understanding how anyone could so regard a tract of land and a few buildings.

3

FROM the hall voices drifted to Ethel Mayne and Old John. They became louder as their owners neared the drawing-room door. She recognised her husband's voice, and heard also a strange voice that was musical and vibrant with strength – a voice that had a pleasant sound in her ears. The door was opened, and there stepped into the room a man she had not before seen. She noted how his eyes widened when they stared straight into hers. The light of the room softened with colour.

Her husband said: "Ethel, meet Mr. Alldyce Cameron."

At pause just within the doorway stood a man six feet tall, with broad shoulders, slim hips, well-proportioned legs, and small feet. His evening clothes, of the latest fashion, fitted and became him to perfection. His square, clean-shaven face was tanned to the colour of mahogany, a colour that brought the brilliant blueness of his eyes into startling relief. Now the eyes were wide open. They bored into those of Ethel Mayne, speeding to her across the breadth of the room open, undisguised admiration. Her gaze was held – it seemed throughout an eternity – by the gaze of this stranger, so that but dimly conscious was she of his dark, wavy brown hair, and the flashing white of perfect teeth revealed between parted lips. Almost as a bird fascinated by a snake, she watched him cross the room to her, accompanied by her husband. "I am delighted to make your acquaintance, Mr. Cameron," she found herself repeating parrot-wise.

"My wife, Cameron," put in Mayne, realising that the introduction was not complete.

"To meet you, Mrs. Mayne, marks a milestone in the life of any bushman," Cameron said, his voice low and richly vibrant – the attractive voice she had heard coming from the hall. "As there are so few ladies in the district," Cameron went on, "your coming is to be regarded as a most important event. I trust that you never will be disappointed in us." There was slight emphasis on the last word.

Ethel found herself mentally striving to prevent her gaze wandering about his face, and to make her now semi-veiled eyes look directly into his. And then abruptly her habitual self-possession returned. "I am sure I will not, Mr. Cameron. Sir John, and now you, are both very kind in welcoming me to the bush. In a way, I feel like an interloper in this big, open-air world of yours."

"Rest assured, madam. You are one of us," boomed Old John, also emphasizing the word "us".

"Ah! Evening, Sir John!" Alldyce Cameron, turning a little, smiled. "Thank you for seconding me. As an amendment, may I be permitted to point out that Atlas, now having gained a mistress, will be pre-eminent among the stations of the Western Division of New South Wales?"

"Among the stations of the Continent, sir."

"Agreed! I stand reproved. Mrs. Mayne, tell me, do you not think Atlas a wonderful place?"

Alldyce Cameron again was smiling on her, and at the back of her brain an imp whispered: "Look at his mouth – look at his mouth!" For the fraction of a second she did look at the firm, parted lips and at the smooth, chiselled chin. She said lightly: "The most wonderful place in the world. So far I haven't been beyond the homestead boundaries, but Frank promises to take me out when lamb-marking starts. I went –"

Tiny hands tugged at the hem of her gown, and the group, which had entirely forgotten the child, followed her gaze to see him pulling himself to his feet. His frail weight temporarily threatened to affect the fall of her dress, and, frowning, she stooped to put the boy from her. Then large, white, blue-veined hands swept into the arc of her vision, snatching the boy away; and, when she stood up, she saw him held by Old John.

"You little rascal!" the old man exclaimed with laughter in his voice.

"Coo! Daddy! Mine daddy!" Little Frankie began to struggle toward Mayne.

"My! What a fine boy! How old is he?" Cameron demanded.

"Just over eleven months. He walked for the first time this evening."

Cameron's eyebrows lifted just a fraction. It was Old John who gave the information when he passed the energetic child to his father. Ethel, who saw the faint indication of surprise, felt annoyed, for did not Sir John take matters too much for granted?

4

AGAIN the door was thrown open. Into the room came a vision in pale yellow, followed by the immaculate Feng, whose lid-shrouded eyes swept over the group about Ethel Mayne.

"Hallo, Frank! Why, you haven't altered a wee bit, in spite of all your travels. Later on, you must whisper to me the secret of youth. Welcome home, and all that!"

"Neither have you altered, Ann," Mayne said, whilst holding her hands. "There is no need for me to impart to you the secret, because you have it too. Allow me to present to you my wife. Ethel, this is a friend of long standing, Ann Shelley, of Tin Tin."

Ethel found herself rapidly examined by dark-grey eyes, widely spaced and steady. In this fraction of time she knew she was being judged, and decided that she did not like Ann Shelley. The woman was familiar, and she detested familiar people.

"Ever since I heard that old Frank was bringing home a wife I have been wildly curious about you," Ann said, smiling but cool. "I have been guessing your colouring, and I've guessed right. I knew Frank would choose a brunette. Welcome to Atlas, Ethel! You will let me call you Ethel? And you will call me Ann, won't you?"

"I think we shall be friends – Ann. As neighbours we must be, must we not?"

Again Old John noted the peculiarly precise enunciation. It was as though Ethel Mayne wished to show herself superior to the Australian bush girl. And then Ann Shelley saw Little Frankie, again on the floor where Mayne had put him on her arrival.

"Oh!"

For an appreciable space of time she stared down on the sturdy figure and at the upturned cherubic face in which wide blue eyes looked upward with baby directness. Feng's eyes blinked. He knew what Ann Shelley was thinking and feeling now that she gazed on Mayne's child.

"Oh, you darling!" she cried, and fell on her knees before the boy, regardless of dress. "Why, you are a miniature angel!" Her hands flashed to the bosom of her blouse and produced a silver whistle shaped like a bird. A tiny ring was attached, and through the ring was run a narrow ribbon of gold silk. Gently Ann Shelley blew on the whistle, and hearing the liquid, throbbing note the boy left the supporting chair and with a short rush staggered into her arms. With one slightly trembling arm round the little boy, Ann Shelley taught Mayne's son how to blow the whistle.

Feng turned to Old John. "Children are much like puppies and chickens," he said softly. "So very interesting whilst they remain young."

"They are, Feng, they are! They are interesting, too, when they approach man's estate, for then their characters are forming."

"You will soon have to pick him out a pony," Cameron said laughing.

A faint trilling announced Little Frankie's first successful effort. Then there came a more sustained result, followed by delighted, gurgling laughter. The whistle occupied the baby's mind to the exclusion of everything else, and Ann Shelley rose to her feet. Feng saw how her eyes were shining.

51

"He's the loveliest child I've ever seen," she said. "Aunty Joe must be wild about him." Her eyes were passing from one to another while she spoke, and she was quick to see the haughty gleam in Ethel's dark eyes, and the troubled look in those of her husband.

Old John went on talking with Feng, and Feng knew Old John talked with reason.

Ethel said: "The aboriginal woman is not to be my child's nurse. I cannot bear black people anywhere near me. They make me shiver, and I shall not feel comfortable until Frank has moved them on. I have a young girl coming up from Wentworth on the mail to-night."

"Ah well! We cannot help our antipathies. I have a horror of snakes. I hope you will get over your antipathy towards Aunty Joe, because she is a dear old soul. She was Frank's nurse, you know."

"Yes. But I will not have her, or any other black person, near me."

5

A gong of Burmese brass sent forth its deep note. Mayne offered his arm to Ann Shelley. Cameron stepped forward to Ethel Mayne, but Old John was before him, bowing with courtly grace. She smiled up into his fine old face, yet was conscious of a feeling of disappointment. Whilst crossing the hall to the dining-room Ann Shelley noticed the tall, black-gowned figure of Mrs. Morton, the housekeeper, standing near the drawn curtains at the entrance to the covered way leading to the kitchen. Mrs. Morton now was relegated to the background. In former days, when Feng ruled Atlas, Mrs. Morton was treated as an equal.

The dining-room was plainly furnished, more indicative of the owner's character than was the drawing-room. The electric chandelier shed subdued yellow light on the napery and the silver and glass of a perfectly appointed table. Dark yellow velvet curtains masked the three pairs of French windows. An expensive Chinese carpet covered the floor. Above the high, wide mantle of one fireplace hung a coloured photographic enlargement of Old Man Mayne, and above the other a similar likeness of the late Mrs. Mayne. There were several oil paintings by Feng Ching-wei of pastoral subjects, and a spirited portrait of Pride of Atlas, the famous race-winning filly of the 1912-13 season.

Ann's dress of rich yellow, Ethel's of unrelieved black, and the men's faultless evening clothes – all, without doubt, were repeated at hundreds of tables in London, Paris, and New York; but outside this warm, silent, and peaceful house lay stretched the vast slumbering bush, the bush with its body of beauty, its voice of music, and its soul of calm indifference to man and his efforts to subjugate it.

Old English service custom was maintained, governed by convenience. The Atlas domestic staff was extremely good for a bush homestead, made possible only by high wages; yet Ethel Mayne was dissatisfied by the absence of a butler, the services of whom she determined to secure at all costs. At the head of the table Frank Mayne filled the soup plates that were set before the diners by the maid, Eva, the sweetheart of Tom Mace, the rabbiter. After the soup the host served cutlets of Darling cod, and later carved the roast mutton; dishes of potatoes, tinned peas, and asparagus being offered each guest in turn. It was not as Ethel Mayne would have liked it. Cameron guessed that.

"Doubtless you find our bush ways unfamiliar, Mrs. Mayne," he said, his gleaming eyes resting on her snow-white shoulders before rising to meet her own. "I trust that you will not become homesick for the slick service of hotel and restaurant. For myself, I prefer the more direct and personal service found in the Australian bush. Do you not think, Sir John, that when a host himself serves his guests it proclaims a warmer personal interest in them?"

"Assuredly. The modern fashion places a host outside the link that joins his guests to his *chef*," Old John agreed. "I have no sympathy with modern methods of service, or of governing an estate. In my time, when at home, I knew personally each of my tenants, the names of every child on the estate. Yes, and the names of their dolls and dogs. Nowadays a landlord leaves everything to his agent – he is too busy combating Socialism to look after the everyday welfare of his people."

"Changes which have come to the English countryside have also occurred here," interjected Mayne. "Save for Atlas and Tin Tin, and three other stations, all, or nearly all, our present properties are governed through managers by boards of directors living in the luxury of a city and knowing little of the employee who produces the dividends. I know three managers who control absolutely the properties owned by individuals in Great Britain, but the others are merely mouthpieces. The unfortunate result is that there is everlasting niggling warfare between city employer and bush employee. Tin Tin and Atlas and those stations governed by real managers seldom suffer labour trouble, but the city director-controlled manager almost always has trouble, especially at shearing time, because he cannot – even if willing – act without his far-distant directors' consent. It is a great pity the old-time squatter no longer exists."

"Well, this is a land of strikes, isn't it?" cooed Ethel.

"Not more so than any other country, I believe," Mayne replied. "Unfortunately for Australia, overseas newspaper editors appear to think that Australia can offer no subject of interest but a strike."

"Still, there are always strikes in Australia," his wife persisted. "They call this country a Working-man's Paradise, and I suppose it is thought that decent people should not live out here. The root of the trouble is that the upper classes here have permitted the working-man too much liberty. England is quickly going the same way. Presently we shall be expected to eat with our workers. Papa often says that he hopes there is not Socialism in heaven."

Old John's sudden laughter, booming through the room, cut off the hint of bitterness. Chuckling, he said: "Then the Dean has not altered much since he was a boy, my dear Mrs. Mayne. He was always a theologian, even at school. I remember him expressing to me the same hope, adding: 'If there is Socialism in heaven and a properly constituted monarchy in the other place, I may decide against heaven!'"

"Perhaps I, too, will make the same decision," Ethel said more lightly. "What will you do, Mr. Cameron?"

"Start a counter-revolution in heaven, dear lady."

"You may not be eligible," Old John suggested dryly.

"In that case I should start a general strike in the other place. I believe that any untroubled political system produces national degeneration."

"I do not agree with you, Mr. Cameron," countered Ann.

"Agitators ought to be killed off. If you and I should arrive at the same place, I shall certainly recommend your extinction."

"Ah! Then it is certain that – er – hell will finally receive me; because, arriving at the gates of heaven, I shall have to ask St. Peter if hc has admitted you, and, learning that he has, it would not be wise for me to accept his invitation to enter. Of course, Miss Shelley, St. Peter might say that he had directed you elsewhere."

"Knowing you, Mr. Cameron, St. Peter would say to you: 'Be pleased to step right in.' And when you were safely in, St. Peter would say to himself: 'Now, Mr. Cameron, look out for Ann Shelley, who most certainly will keep an eye on your political manrœuvres.'"

"Quite logical – as always, Ann," murmured Feng.

The conversation veered to horse-racing, as it had to in this Australian home; but the subject was quickly dropped when it was seen to bore the hostess. It was Alldyce Cameron who first scnsed that Ethel Mayne knew nothing of horses, and wished to continue to know nothing.

"Have you subscribed to a library yet, Mrs. Mayne?" he inquired; and, receiving a negative answer, proceeded to argue the advantages of several in Adelaide and Sydney.

"But can we obtain the books we want?"

"Well, not always, unless one keeps to the best-sellers. There is nothing here to equal Mudie's, you know. Still, the range of books is fairly large, and the postal service quite satisfactory."

"I must see about it," Ethel concluded. "I shall so miss Mudie's. Already I am feeling an exile, for it does seem so strange not having seen a *Tatler*, or a *Graphic*, for weeks."

"I shall be pleased to send along the *Tatler*. It comes to me every mail, posted by Lord Henry Lowther, whom I met during the War years."

"Were you in the Army?"

"Oh yes! I had the honour to command a battalion."

"Did you?"

And Alldyce Cameron found himself surveyed with fresh interest.

The dinner proceeded to its destined end, and, after a quick glance at her husband, who nodded, Ethel addressed the company with what was really a short speech.

"Having become an Australian by adoption," she said gaily, I am going to suggest that Ann and I be permitted to drink our coffee with you gentlemen at this table. Do you not think, Ann, that that would be properly democratic? I do. While the men smoke their cigars, we will smoke a cigarette and lounge in our chairs, and listen patiently to the masculine gossip."

"A great idea, Mrs. Mayne! Thank heaven that you, too, are a rebel against society's conventions." Turning directly to Ann, Cameron continued: "Surely you agree, Miss Shelley, that the custom of the ladies retiring while we men smoke and gossip is really prehistoric?"

"It may be, Mr. Cameron. Thank you, Ethel, for your suggestion. If I cannot have my cigarette immediately after a meal, I become very nervy. I am afraid I am such an ordinary home-bird that real society would bore me to death."

Ann Shelley was the first to leave that evening, but before Feng escorted her to the powerful single-seater car she insisted on paying a visit to the sleeping Little Frankie. She shook hands with the mistress of Atlas, and nodded a laughing farewell to Mayne. Feng held open the door of the car for her, and tucked the rich fox-skin rug about her whilst she drew on her driving gloves. A black boy climbed into the open dicky. He was her gate-opener.

"You are going to have a cold drive, Ann," Feng told her, noting the steam of their breath in the reflection made by the brilliant headlights.

"Nevertheless it is going to be lovely, Feng, old thing. What has become of Aunty Joe?"

"She is camped with King Bill's crowd at White Gate Bend."

"Then I am going to send for her to come to Tin Tin at once. It – it – Oh, how *could* Frank have let her go from Atlas?"

Feng's voice was soft, yet even. He said: "Happy marriages are based on diplomacy, Ann. As time passes, Mrs. Mayne will become less antagonistic to the blacks."

"I trust so." She pressed the starting-button, and the well-tuned engine broke into a hum. There was a catch in her voice when she spoke, leaning outward towards him. "She's lovely, Feng, isn't she? And the little boy! He – he is – Good-bye, Feng!"

The car shot away, leaving Feng Ching-wei gazing after the

red tail-light, the pain at his heart stab, stab, stabbing; for Ann Shelley had gone with tears in her voice.

CHAPTER V

THE CAMP

1

SLIM JIM WESTER'S philosophy was well-nigh perfect in a world where the virtue of generosity is carried almost to a fault. He did not believe in working that he might eat, because to eat did not mean having to work.

During but two periods of the year did Slim Jim labour: at the annual lamb-marking and at the annual shearing. On Atlas the lamb-marking averaged four weeks of the fifty-two, whilst the shearing extended from five to seven weeks. The remainder of the year was lived as a Darling River Pirate, a life of unlimited freedom and boundless leisure, of walking without haste from station homestead to station homestead along one side of the river and down along the other side, with interposed breaks now and then of a week or a few days at work when a rest from constant travelling could be appreciated.

"Why work?" was Slim Jim's pertinent inquiry. "I carry my swag up the river on the east side, camp where I like, fish when I like, call on a station cook for tucker when I like, sell a fish out of the river to a township pub or a squatter for a few plugs of tobacco, do the same when coming down the west bank, and engage as a lamb-markers' cook and a wool-presser for money enough for me 'olidays. And at the end of twelve months I am just as well off as you blokes – who work all the year round. Work! Coo! Only suckers work!"

Thirty years as a Darling River Pirate had enabled Slim Jim to become thoroughly acquainted with every squatter and station cook from Wentworth to Burke, as well as every fishing-hole in that thousand-mile river course. To the squatters he was a man possessing two good points: he could cook well with the primitive utensils of a shifting camp, and he could be relied on to turn up on time if engaged for the lamb-marking six months previously.

Visualise, please, a man weighing fourteen stone, measuring six feet in height, possessing a face like a multi-split tomato, and a voice with the carrying power of a foghorn. His day at the lamb-marking camps of Atlas started when the alarm-clock rang at half-past five. A greater autocrat than the overseer, who was boss of the camp, Slim Jim occupied a tent in which were stacked the stores, and when he had dressed in spotless white drill trousers and cotton shirt, and had buttoned up a ragged overcoat, he stepped out into the brilliantly starlit, frost-gripped night, rolled toward the uprights and crossbeam which marked the fire-site, seized a rod and raked among the domed heap of white ash till he had bared the still glowing embers of wood billets he had so carefully buried in the depth of the fire before going to bed. Upon these embers he tossed an armful of twigs left in readiness, and, when the twigs caught fire, added log after log till, presently, a huge column of flame brought out of the darkness the white shapes of half a dozen tents expertly erected on frames.

Quite near was a round, galvanised iron tank of water, and from it he filled a pint billy-can which he hung over the fire, low, and in the centre of the flame column. In a minute it was boiling. Then Slim Jim removed his overcoat, and when he had made himself tea he sat on a box and sipped from the blackened billy-can whilst he smoked his first pipeful of strong, ink-black tobacco.

Himself refreshed, he examined his bread dough. Removing first a sheet of iron weighted by a log, he rolled away a sheepskin, when there was disclosed a round hole, and within the hole a large bucket covered with a cloth. When the cloth was removed it could be seen that the dough in the bucket was "ripe". For fifteen minutes he punched this dough on a table built of a door laid over a rough bough frame, and when the dough had been once more placed in the bucket he set it near the fire, and carefully protected the far side from the cold night air with the sheepskin.

From another tent, which was his larder, he removed the mincemeat balls he had made up the night before, and placed them in two large iron camp-ovens, beneath and on which he shovelled red embers. Above several shovelfuls of red wood coals he hung the wire-netted grill, which he proceeded to cover with about ten pounds' weight of mutton chops, which also had been cut in readiness the evening before.

Like the shroud of a ghost the eastern sky was shimmering whitely. Slim Jim was a kind cook. He set against the back of the fire two four-gallon petrol-tins of water before setting out on the long boarded table beneath the tarpaulin roof loaves of yeast bread, tins of jam, bottles of sauce, and heaped plates of slab brownie, or eggless cake. In the big iron boiler, half filled with boiling water, he made the oatmeal burgoo.

The stars were being quickly washed out by the dawning day. The camp was pitched, as now could be seen, on the bank of a waterless creek lined with box trees. Galahs, parakeets, and finches became active in their daily search for food, whilst five hundred yards further up the creek the baaings of many sheep drifted from a maze of low-built yards. It was two minutes to seven when Slim Jim looked at the clock in his tent.

Now with a grin of perverse pleasure he took up two short pieces of bar-iron and began a tattoo on a headless oil-drum used sometimes for carting water. The quietude of that sylvan scene was shattered by pandemonium. The galahs fled away over the plain beyond the creek with screeches of protest, the parakeets fled up along the creek, and the many finches ceased their food hunt to crouch motionless till the storm of sound subsided.

First to emerge from one of the tents was the horse-tailer. He should have been after the musterers' horses long before this, riding the chaff-fed night horse; but no amount of pleading and argument would induce Slim Jim to call him at daybreak. The cook's contention was that his alarm-clock would wake any ordinary man within five hundred yards, and if the horse-tailer, who slept in a tent a bare forty yards distant, could not hear the vicious bell, well he, Slim Jim, was not paid to call him. Two minutes later the tailer was being whirled away on the night horse, which lived only for these morning gallops.

When the uproar of thumping iron sticks on an empty oil-drum ceased, it was continued by the dozen dogs chained to near-by trees. A man staggered out into the crisp morning air, rubbing his eyes and blenching from the cold. During normal periods of the year he was the Atlas bullock-drover. For three minutes and twenty-two seconds he cursed the dogs – in lieu of the cook – with a string of words very seldom repeated.

2

"YOU'RE a nartist!" Slim Jim said admiringly, standing with his back to the fire.

"The ruddy dogs yelpin' like that gets on me quince," stated Fred, the bullock-drover, with emphasis. "This water fer us?"

"Yus. Nice warm water to sponge yer tender dial with. Just fancy, now! 'Ot water for measly station 'ands. Coo!"

Fred, a long lank man of forty or so who slouched in his walk so that his middle appeared to follow his head and his feet follow his middle, glared at the cook, opened his mouth, concealed by a bushy, unkempt ginger moustache – then succumbed to mental lethargy, not being properly awake, and refrained from addressing Slim Jim as he had addressed the dogs.

Slim Jim, who had expected another artistic treat, felt let down.

The other men – fifteen all told – hovered about in the warmth of the fire, loth to leave it to wash, even with the warm water provided.

"For Gawd's sake, get out of me bleedin' way!" Slim Jim roared, moving unnecessarily about his fire. "Come on, now! You'll never get to work to-day. 'Oo wants burgoo? Come on, you burgoo-eating Scotchmen! Now, Fred!"

"None of yer pig-feed fer me."

"Naw! You're a good Aussie, you are. Chops for you with the blood drippin' out of 'em. Well, 'ere yer are. Now, Mister Andrews?"

"Porridge, please."

"Porridge! Wot's that? Oh, yer means burgoo! Naw – nar! You ain't in a droring-room nar. Burgoo it is. 'Ere y'are. Git that down yer swan neck. Now then, next! Oh! Yous want yer chops well done, eh? Orl right. 'Ere's yours done to a cinder. Take 'em away. Morning, Mister Noyes! Will you partake of por – no, burgoo – this morning? Yes? Mud on the liver this morning, eh? Well, you're here for Kerlonial experience, and, by Gawd, you're a-getting of it! Ah! 'Ow do, Mister MacDougall? No need to ask if you'll 'ave any burgoo. Men a bit dopy. Slept in too long. Work 'em 'ard to-day, Mister MacDougall. Exercise is wot they want. Kerlonial experience! Give 'em Kerlonial Hexperience. That's wot they're 'ere for."

There were but few better sheepmen in New South Wales than Angus MacDougall. Descended undoubtedly from Scottish ancestors, he was short and dapper, ungainly on his feet, bowlegged, long-armed, and round-shouldered. There was nothing braw about this Australian Scotsman, not even in his speech.

"Plenty of gab this morning, Jim," he said in a soft, drawling voice, which did not disguise long acquaintance with command of men.

"Yus, I'm feeling good," Slim Jim admitted. "These nice fresh mornings livens me up. You don't see me rubbing me eyes and looking like I been on the booze for a month. You see –"

Angus, who had placed two meat chops on a huge slice of bread, carried this in one hand, with the plate of porridge in the other, across to an empty ration-case, and began his breakfast as though he had forgotten the existence of the cook. After the first serving the men became less lamb-like.

Fred the bullock-drover, said: "Gimme some chops, and gimme less yabber, you river pirate!" Three evil-looking teeth became bared in what was supposed to be a smile of affability.

"Wot, just woke up?" ejaculated the astounded Slim Jim, whilst loading into an enamelled plate four of the fattest chops which he knew would find approval.

After this, conversation became more general. Whilst Slim Jim was by no manner of means tactful in his speech, he was thoroughly appreciated as a cook. When one man liked his meat underdone, he was sure to have his taste suited. Another man, who liked his meat well done, invariably was offered meat well cooked.

A rumble of hoofs announced the arrival of the musterers' horses. A cloud of fine dust swerved outward when the bunch of horses raced into the roughly built stockyards, the tailer's horse right on the heels of the last of them. The men began to stack their utensils on the end of Slim Jim's cooking-table, then to separate, some walking across to the sheep-yards; others, the musterers, carving their lunches from loaves of bread and cold roasts of mutton set out for them.

Angus and Noyes went into short conference, the overseer directing the jackeroo, who was boss of the musterers, where to

61

drive the sheep in the pass-out yards, and which paddock to muster that day for sheep that would be dealt with on the morrow.

In his ungainly manner Angus MacDougall walked to the yards whilst the horsemen were saddling their hacks. Within the yards were some five thousand ewes with their lambs. The uproar increased with the coming of the markers. Two horsemen galloped out wide of the yards, and the gates of the pass-out yards were opened wide. A stream of dun-coloured wool poured outward in a long column, finally halted by the two riders and their dogs until the flock of some three thousand began to mill in a huge bunch, whereupon three riders urged them gently across the southern plain to the mulga timber. Four other men were riding north on jogging mounts, blue tobacco clouds floating out behind them in the clear air like ladies' blue silken scarves.

At the gates at the end of a runway Angus began to draft the two thousand ewes with their lambs. Men "yowled" and waved their hats to force the sheep into the runway; and, when they reached the drafting gates, Angus saw to it that the lambs entered one yard and their mothers a second yard.

The bleating of lambs parted from their mothers, and the baaing of the mothers for their lost lambs, became intensified. Men climbed into the yard containing the hundreds of lambs, each seizing a lamb and holding it with its rump resting on a rail. A knife between his teeth, Angus MacDougall moved up and down the line of lambs presented to him, followed by Andrews wielding ear-markers and tar-brush. These two wore dungaree overalls. Very soon after the start of the day's work the overalls became streaked and spotted with the crimson blood.

It was an easy day, this day. Only fifteen hundred lambs winced at the sear of the knife.

3

AT about the same time that Angus MacDougall started work, Frank Mayne left the homestead in the big station car on his first trip of inspection since his return from Europe. Beside him sat his wife, with Little Frankie, coated and capped and gloved, sitting on her lap. In the tonneau of the car were stored a hamper and thermos flasks containing milk and coffee. Quickly Ethel Mayne's face was stung by the cold, frosty air, whilst the child glowed with health and fidgeted with vigour.

With his eyes half closed – it is remarkable how habit so quickly reasserts itself – Mayne drove the car at a fair speed along the track twisting over the river flats. The flats were wide, grey-brown in colour, utterly bare of vegetation, save in sheltered places beneath the spreading branches of the gnarled box trees. Here, protected from the frost, the wild carrot, parsnip, and spinach were shooting up, forming distinct circular green carpets.

After a little more than a mile they came to a gate in a wire fence, beyond which the river flats abruptly gave place to red sand-dunes on which grew the drought-defying mulga and pine trees. This day his own gate-opener, Mayne was obliged to open it and close it again after he had driven the car through.

When once again the car sped forward and had crossed the belt of dunes, they emerged on flat red-sand country harder than the flats, and studded with fifteen-foot scrub, beneath which, sheltered from the frosts, the tussock-grass was sprouting and the wild barley already was three inches high. The river country now left behind was banished from mind by this totally different class of land. In a good year, when herbage covered the river flats, the wide-spaced trees and the unbroken carpet of green made a picture not unlike an English park; but in this mulga country, where grass was still absent on the unprotected parts, the shorter scrub gave it the aspect of a boundless orchard of plum-trees.

A run of twelve miles brought them to the second gate, and when they had passed through, Ethel asked: "What station is this, Frank?"

"Atlas," he replied and, looking at her, smiled with the pride of possession.

Little Frankie, now between them, was content to croon a baby tune, to the accompaniment of the purring engine. Ethel fell back on her meditative silence, whilst her husband became fully occupied in mentally noting the condition of the country and planning improvements to fences and buildings.

If his wife guessed correctly precisely what did occupy Mayne's mind, he never thought to guess of what she was thinking. Actually she was going back to the house-warming dinner, recalling every action and word made and spoken by two people. Since the dinner those two people had been constantly in her thoughts.

Of Ann Shelley, Ethel's first impression remained. There were occasions when Ethel Mayne was remarkably honest with herself and, without consciously colouring her judgment of Ann Shelley, she frankly admitted that she admired Ann's well-moulded figure and beautifully formed features, made lovelier by the transparent purity of her mind.

What was it in Ann Shelley that Mayne's wife disliked? She disliked the cool, steady gaze of the wide-spaced fearless grey eyes. The personality of this Australian woman, like her colouring, was the antithesis of Ethel Mayne's. The wife's nature was to gain a point by devious paths, by subtlety; it was Ann's nature to reach a point by proceeding straight to it. Ethel was, or could be, an apt disciple of the great Machiavelli; whilst Ann would not bother to waste time, or think it worth while to plan or scheme to obtain anything by subterfuge.

Ethel recognised at the first moment of their meeting that she and Ann Shelley were as clay and sand. It was merely that which aroused her antipathy, whereas a less self-centred woman would have assessed the advantage of being the subtler of the two. In beauty she felt she was not inferior; in brainpower she decided she was Ann's superior. Certainly she was superior to Ann in cultural attainments and experience; and, in consequence, having nothing to fear, she decided to tolerate her romantically powerful neighbour.

Presently she was aroused from her meditation by Mayne pointing out several kangaroos that were taking long, loping jumps away from the passing car. They were the first kangaroos she had seen outside a zoo, but she could see no beauty in their physical grace or movement; and once more she relapsed into silence.

She thought of Alldyce Cameron, and already recognised the significance of thinking overmuch of this man; but she was not a woman to banish thought or memory of anything she knew was not healthy to think about or remember; rather she preferred to analyse her impressions and her feelings, for the scorching fire of deep emotion never yet had been presented to her for analysis.

The picture of the man gazing steadily at her whilst he stood just inside the door of the drawing-room was indelibly photographed on her mind. That she was tremendously impressed by Cameron she honestly admitted. Never before had she met a man so vitally alive, so magnetic, so masculine. Turning back the leaves of the book of life, she found in it no man better-looking than he, and but one only who came near the standard Alldyce Cameron set. His culture was evident, even before he spoke, and Ethel Mayne considered that culture was ingrained by birth and education.

All this she could dispassionately examine and dissect. What she could not analyse was the peculiar colouring of the lights at her first sight of him, the lightness of spirit his impact on her life had caused, and the reason why her mind constantly conjured his picture, especially his mouth and chin. This she could not analyse because such experiences never before had entered her life; for, despite her upbringing by clever, ambitious parents, despite her life lived on that social stratum wherein few illusions remain after the twentieth year, she failed to recognise that, despite her cold and stately physical aspect, she was but a butterfly in imminent danger of being scorched, if not consumed, by fire.

"What are you thinking about?" Mayne asked abruptly.

Without hesitation she replied: "I was thinking of Ann Shelley. Does she live alone at Tin Tin?"

"Oh no! The homestead is just about as populous as ours. Ann has a companion of her own age living with her ever since her mother died. She has a housekeeper as a further safeguard against the inquisition of Mrs. Grundy. A manager – his name is Leeson – lives in a bungalow quite near the Government House. But Ann is boss. A very efficient woman is Ann."

"You seem to be on quite familiar terms with her, and she with you," Ethel murmured. "Accepting the fact that you have known each other since early childhood, do you not now think it were better to address each other more formally?"

"Maybe," Mayne answered doubtfully. "I never thought about it. I have always called her Ann, and she has always called me Frank. Feng and she and I have always made up – what shall I say? – a triple alliance. Does such familiarity annoy you?"

"Dear me, no! But it does strike me as unusual. Perhaps it is coming among a people so very democratic which over-emphasises a custom to an Englishwoman. As your wife, and as one having known Miss Shelley only a few days, you must excuse what must appear to you an unwarrantable objection. Oh, look!"

They were passing through a thick belt of pines, when two emus appeared as from the ground and raced along the track ahead of them. The diversion gladdened Ethel Mayne, for the subject of their conversation had reached a point when it was better for the seeds it contained to take root in her husband's mind.

Mayne increased the car's speed. Ethel watched the flying legs of the two birds, and wondered why neither used its wings, not knowing that an emu's wings never develop. On being lifted up, Little Frankie clapped his gloved hands and viewed the race with wide, sparkling eyes.

The speedometer needle quickly fell to thirty miles an hour. Mayne held the car at thirty-five miles an hour for ten minutes. Gradually the machine lessened the distance. A short burst at forty miles an hour brought the car to within two yards of the fern-like tail feathers, when now the giant striding feet flung dust and sand against the wind-screen. Still faster sped the car. The speedometer needle hovered a fraction over forty-three miles an hour before Frank Mayne saw that he had conquered the speed of the fastest running creature on earth.

The birds were becoming winded. Their beaks gaped wide, whilst from side to side they moved their heads to eye the monster purring behind them. Now Mayne slowly slackened speed, ever slower until they were travelling no faster than fifteen miles an hour. Yet over a further mile the silly birds ran before suddenly diving into the bordering scrub and disappearing from sight.

"My! Can't they run!" Ethel exclaimed, thrilled out of her cold reserve.

"Without doubt," her husband agreed. "I have estimated that thirty-six miles an hour is about the top speed of the average bird. Of course their speed is based on their physical condition. Only once have I driven an emu over forty-six miles to the hour, but when they are in poor condition their speed drops to about ten."

"Can one eat them?"

"They are rather rank and oily," he said, chuckling. "The blacks are very fond of them, however, whilst the emu oil possesses exceptional penetrating qualities."

Ethel became avid for information about emus. Purposefully she kept her husband's mind from recurring to what she had said about Ann Shelley.

4

QUITE suddenly the road debouched on a small plain, on whose further side could be seen the several white tents and the fire-smoke of the lamb-markers' camp, with the yards a short quarter of a mile apart, from which slowly drifted a slanting column of dust. Whilst they crossed the plain Ethel discerned the figures of men at the base of the dust column, and the white-clad figure of the cook near his fire. A minute later they were stopped but a few yards from the camp, when Slim Jim sauntered towards them.

At this red-faced giant of a man Ethel looked with interest, noting the livid mark down one cheek which gave his face the appearance of a split tomato. His bare arms were weather-stained and hairy. Only when he stood close to her husband did he remove the blackened clay pipe from between the few remaining teeth in his mouth.

Without touching his forelock, he said: "Good day-ee, Mr. Mayne! Good day-ee, marm! Hallo, younkers! By gosh, you're the dead image of Old Man Mayne!"

For Slim Jim this was studied politeness. Unabashed by the leaping haughtiness in Ethel's eyes, the lamb-markers' cook proceeded without the fear of the angels: "He's a beaut, for sure. Old Man Mayne would have been proud of him, marm. 'E's got the old bloke's mouth and eyes. I'll bet when 'e grows up he'll let out a laugh just like Old Man Mayne's roar. Are you stopping for a cup-er-tea?"

Frank Mayne looked at his wife. He said: "I must have a word with MacDougall. We'll be here half an hour at least. If you care to accept Jim's invitation, by all means do so."

How her husband's familiar reference to this common, brutal-looking man did sting! She was about icily to refuse, when she recalled the cook's reference to Old Man Mayne, which denoted that he was not a newcomer to the district. Suddenly she smiled. "I think I would like a cup of tea, Jim," she said in quite a friendly tone. "The baby will perhaps drink a cup of milk. Frank, find the

67

milk thermos, please."

Oh, why wouldn't her husband see the absurdity of his Christian name almost coupled with that of this ruffian grinning at her and her child? But Mayne, having secured the flask, handed it to Slim Jim, smiled at her, nodded casually at Slim Jim, and as casually left them, strolling away toward the sheep-yards.

Carrying the thermos flask, Slim Jim gallantly conducted his guest to the long table beneath the tarpaulin roof, where he reached for a packing-case, which he placed in position, dusted, and bowed her on with ludicrous politeness. From this open-air dining-room Ethel surveyed the camp with interest: the tents, the water-cart, the huge iron ovens, and the large open fireplace over which hung petrol-tin buckets and large billy-cans, and in her heart approving the outward cleanliness of the cook.

She became seated at the table, with Little Frankie on her lap, whilst Slim Jim produced what was almost unheard of in a lamb-markers' camp, a china cup and saucer. Little Frankie drank his milk from an enamelled pint pannikin, and seized on a slab of sponge-cake, as the eternal child will do to denote that at home it seldom gets anything to eat.

"We bin lucky, marm," Slim Jim remarked, leering at her in pouring tea from a billy-can. "The musterers brought home nine emu eggs yesterday."

"Are emu eggs suitable for cooking purposes?"

"You bet, marm! One emu egg is equal to a dozen hen eggs. When you make your next bread batter, beat in a dozen hen eggs or one emu egg. You'll be surprised how it will improve the bread."

Suppressing a shudder, Ethel Mayne lightly said that she would accept the advice, adding: "Are you an Australian?"

"No, marm. I come from Pommyland. I bin in this country twenty-seven years," replied Slim Jim, seating himself at the opposite side of the table.

"Pommyland? Where is that?"

Slim Jim revealed astonishment at her ignorance. He searched for his pipe, remembered the importance of his guest, rubbed his hands on his spotless apron.

"Why, Hengland, marm. The Orstralians call all Englishmen Pommies. It's a way they 'ave."

"Pommy! What a peculiar name! What does it mean?"

"Bless yer, marm, I don't know," Slim Jim candidly admitted.

"You don't know the meaning of an Australian expression after having been in the country for twenty-seven years?" Ethel exclaimed in calm, cold surprise, so cold and disapproving that the cook thought he had undone all the good impression he had been so careful to make.

Almost he gasped. "That's a fact, marm," he said. "Wotever it does mean, it's got two meanings. If a bloke calls you a Pommy and you know he's chiacking you, you take no notice; if a bloke calls you a Pommy and you see that 'e is serious, well, you bash 'im on the nose."

"I see," Ethel said slowly, although she didn't. "What does 'chiacking' mean?"

"Oh, that means kidding – er, you know, teasing."

"Oh, I shall have to memorise these quaint Australian words." She added further milk to Little Frankie's pannikin, and dusted the crumbs from the front of his jacket. Quite abruptly she looked straight at Slim Jim's winking eyes, and he now appeared as a victim of an examining inquisitor.

"I suppose you know everyone in this locality. Have you ever worked on Tin Tin Station?"

"Plenty of times, marm. Old Baldy – I mean Mr. Leeson – is a good boss. So's Miss Shelley. If a bloke is sacked by Mr. Leeson an' 'e ain't just ready to leave, Miss Shelley will put 'im on again if she's asked proper. Anyway, a bloke 'as to be pretty tired for old B – Mr. Leeson – to put ' im orf."

Now sure of his ground, Slim Jim warbled on, unconscious that Mrs. Mayne was taking particular note of what he said.

"Yes, Tin Tin is a good place. Old Shelley retired years ago, having made tons of oof" – Ethel did not know the meaning of the word "oof", but refrained from interrupting – "but I reckon the bush got 'im 'ard and fast, 'cos 'e had to come back from Adelaide to shuffle orf on Tin Tin. The bush 'as got Miss Ann too. I was diggin' up the garden one day, and she told me 'erself she wouldn't leave Tin Tin for all the tea in China. I can't say nothink against that, 'cos I've bin roaming up and down the Gutter for twenty-six years, and never bin orf it – and never will."

"What other stations have you worked on?"

"Me? Lots, on and orf, as the saying is. Durlop, up Burke way, was a good place before the War. Albemarle, above Menindee, ain't bad either."

"Have you ever worked for Mr. Cameron?"

"Yes, marm. For three days." Slim Jim had reached thin ice, and knew it.

"Only three days! That is quite a short period, isn't it? Why did you leave?"

"Me and Mr. Cameron 'ad a kind of disagreement." Slim Jim stated, actually flushing. He knew he could never dare explain to this "'aughty tart" how he had inadvertently discovered Alldyce Cameron flagrantly flirting with one of the Thuringah maids, and in consequence had been paid off the following morning with a bribe of five pounds silence money.

He said: "Yes, me and 'im 'ad a nargument. 'E spoke kind of sharp, and my tongue ain't slow of a cold morning. Anyway, there's always plenty of work for a cook, marm."

"Yes, I suppose there is," Ethel concurred, wondering why the man lied. It was unfortunate that her husband returned just then.

5

AGAIN speeding westward, they passed two huts built near a tall windmill set over a well, Mayne explaining that the two stockmen usually camped there were now at the lamb-marking camp. Beyond this place, known as White Well, they left the mulga country and entered on a great stretch of rolling plain country covered with tussock-grass, which appeared blackened as though by fire, the new shoots not sufficiently conspicuous to tinge the expanse with green.

Red sand-dunes appeared far to the north, among them a windmill and hut, and a huge surface dam known as Karl's Dam. To the south a line of black-looking mulga marked the horizon. The wind tore at Ethel's hat and whipped her cheeks to colour. Her mind was awed by the vastness of space about them, but she felt no thrill when her husband told her that just north of the mulga belt was the south boundary fence, and that far beyond the northern sand-dunes lay the north boundary fence.

Up and down over the gentle swells of the ground the car sped at an even forty-five miles an hour. The low, dark smudge of westward scrub so very slowly grew into sharp relief that it seemed as if they hardly moved at all. Beyond the scrub belt the land rose into a range of low hills, blue-black in colour at the foot of the azure sky.

Twelve miles, and they had crossed the plain. Now the car approached a camp called Mulga Flat and, as White Well, deserted. The iron structure of the hut appeared to the woman as the work of a crazy man whose materials were battered iron sheets, hessian bagging, and bare poles. Miles still, whilst steadily the track lifted them up to the summits of the rock-strewn, mulga-coated hills. And then abruptly, when they swung round a spur, Mayne stopped the car and sat silent whilst his wife looked out over the western limits of Atlas.

Nestling in a gully almost directly below were clustered the iron-roofed buildings comprising the Atlas out-station called Forest Hill. The large, stone-built building with the single wide veranda was the home of Angus MacDougall and his wife. Beyond that gully the hills were lower than the point of the track at which they were halted, and beyond those lower hills, stretching to the horizon, lay a vast, flat, grey sea of salt-bush. From north to south stretched the salt-bush plain; north-west to the foot of the gigantic blue rocks lying along the horizon as rocks towering above the sea, rocks that were the distant Barrier Range, among which the enormously rich lead mines of Broken Hill were situated; west and south-west to the clear-cut horizon, as distinct and as even as the horizon of an ocean. Somewhere out on that vast salt-bush-covered plain, running north and south, was the west boundary of Atlas.

It was very pretty, Ethel thought, but rather uninteresting. A river or two, and a cathedral surrounded by oaks and elms, would have added beauty to the scene. She was rather hungry, and said so.

Frank Mayne could have sat an hour gazing out on that mighty panorama, he who was thrilled by the magic of those almost limitless spaces; the waves of dark green in the foreground, the even sweep of grey beyond, and the brilliant azure of the sky. They were sixty-three miles from home and still on his own land.

"Shall we have lunch here, or shall we go on and get Mrs. MacDougall to give us lunch?" he asked, conscious of a tinge of disappointment at the obvious failure of his wife to appreciate what he felt.

"We will have it here, please. I don't think I want to meet your overseer's wife to-day, Frank."

"Very well," he answered, with his habitual deference to his wife's wishes.

So it was they picnicked within sight of Forest Hill, and later, when Mayne turned the car for the homeward run by different tracks, he pondered the words he would say to excuse their not calling on Mrs. MacDougall, who assuredly would have seen the car and wondered why, when so near, he had not called and presented her to the new mistress of Atlas.

Almost against her will, Ethel Mayne absorbed a little of the vastness of Atlas, coming to understand the extent of an Australian sheep-run. Yet long before sundown she was wishing she were at her new home, and wondering which of her dozen gowns she would wear at dinner that night. At sunset they were crossing the river flats, and she roused sufficiently to ask her husband the meaning of the word "Pommy".

Mayne chuckled and smiled at her sheepishly. "It is difficult to decide the origin of the word," he said slowly, and she knew he was choosing his words carefully. "Some say it is derived from the word 'Pomegranate', applied to new-chums on account of the freshness of their complexions. Of latter years it is not nearly so much used by Australians, and much more used by English people themselves."

"Is it not used in a derogatory sense?"

"Sometimes, but only by those Australians whose parents did not originate from the British Isles. For centuries people have traduced poor old England and her sons. In some respects, some of us are ridiculously narrow-minded."

They had travelled about one hundred and forty miles that day without ever touching a boundary fence of Atlas.

CHAPTER VI

THE SHEARING

I

SHEARING officially began on the last Friday in July. Actually, work in connection with the shearing started on Atlas the previous Monday; started and proceeded strictly governed by routine perfected over many years. With Angus MacDougall, Frank Mayne toured the run and inspected the flocks and the paddocks, as might a corps general inspect his troops accompanied by his chief of staff.

It was quickly seen that the grass and herbage brought up by the June rain was retarded in growth, first by the frosts, and secondly by the lack of further rain. MacDougall of the hatchet face, the ham-like hands and the bow legs, stated that despite the lack of feed growth the sheep were gaining wonderfully in condition, and that the lambs were rapidly gaining strength. Yet to Frank Mayne these pre-shearing conditions were far from satisfactory.

"If it doesn't rain in August we shall have to start scrub-cutting," he said whilst they ate a cut lunch by the track-side. "This season has me bluffed. Do you think we are in for a bad drought?"

"Well, it's hard to say until we see what September brings us in the way of rain," replied that quiet, almost taciturn Australian Scot. "Pity it can't rain to-day. An inch now would give us whips of feed all summer. The small men are feeling the dry pinch already."

"I wish it would rain, Mac. We've still got those nine thousand wethers, last year's hoggets. I was hoping the market would harden, but it won't if it doesn't rain next month. And now, having marked seventeen thousand lambs, we are in a bad position to face a dry summer. We're carrying too much stock."

MacDougall refilled their pannikins with tea from the billy-can before replying. "Well, it's no use jumping before we reach the hurdles. If it rains good and hard next month, Atlas will do well out of them wethers and we can cull the flocks heavily for fats. Remember, nineteen-twenty-two was like this year, and that year we had a wet spring, and knee-high grass all through to the following winter."

"That is so." Mayne lit his pipe with unconscious carelessness. He was beginning to dread the possibility of having to apply to his wool brokers for an advance – a position he would be obliged to accept if he could not dispose of his surplus stock.

The first decade of this century had given a bitter lesson to the squatters on the major fault of overstocking their holdings. During those years, and before, the majority of stations had carried flocks in almost every paddock on the runs, so that when drought gripped the country there was no reserve of land, which meant reserve of grass and herbage, and fearful losses were incurred, Old Man Mayne having once lost sixty thousand sheep over a period of eighteen months.

Following that lesson, overstocking was the nightmare of the careful sheepman. As a margin of safety Mayne, and Feng immediately before him, had kept seven great paddocks empty of sheep; and now, instead of seven, in three months time Mayne would have but three. The mention made by MacDougall of the difficulties already felt by the small men was instantly appreciated by his employer.

"How many is Westmacott running on his place?" he asked.

"He reckons he'll shear eight thousand."

"Phew! Eight thousand on twenty-seven thousand acres!"

"Yes. Like Mr. Feng, he hung on to his hoggets expecting the market to rise."

"He'll crash this year if it doesn't rain."

"Decidedly – unless he does what Chidman once did."

"What did Chidman do?"

"He went over one of his stations, and he saw that the three thousand head of cattle were getting mighty poor on account of the dry season. Nineteen months it had been without rain. He says to the manager: 'Give all your men guns and ammunition. Get out and draft off two hundred of the best breeders and six of the best bulls, and have every other beast shot. You can then sack all your men and carry on with one blackfellow. We can buy more steers and breed 'em when the season changes, but we can't grow scrub-trees in less than a hundred years, even if we plants 'em; and if we go on carrying them three thousand beasts, in twelve months time, even if it does rain, the place won't carry five hundred. So shoot 'em!' That's Westmacott's only chance. Get out and slaughter three thousand five hundred of his eight thousand sheep, if he can't sell 'em at any price, or even give 'em away."

"You're right, Mac. He can't safely carry more than four thousand five hundred on his place."

On the Tuesday before the shearing the flocks began to move into the key paddocks precisely as battalions taking positions in the line before a battle. The ewes and the lambs were to be the first to go through the shed, for the first shorn would be the first to travel to the western paddocks over country not quickly eaten out by moving flocks. The shortage of feed now had become an urgent problem. When the shearing was in full swing the flocks would travel almost over the same ground once they passed White Well, where was the strange bottle-neck caused by the resumption of land by the Government for closer settlement. Before the shearing was half through the scarcity of sheep feed between the bottle-neck and the shed would be acute, because the preceding flocks of sheep travelling to and from the shed would have taken it all. That bottle-neck, caused by the bite being taken out of Atlas to form the small holding owned by Westmacott, had always been a source of worry.

Feng Ching-wei cut short his holiday to relieve Barlow of the ordinary office work, thereby permitting the old accountant to concentrate wholly on the records connected with the shearing.

On the Wednesday the Government House cook decided that no longer could she put up with "the highfalutin ways of the missus, who ought to know better than interfere in the kitchen, 'specially when there was a housekeeper". She left by the mail-car that night, and only after Feng himself had used persuasion did Mary O'Doyle consent to cook for Government House.

"Orl right, Mr. Feng, as you ask me I'll go. But you tell 'er to pass in a menu she wants put up, and tell 'er that if she comes into my kitchen and cuts red-'ot cakes like she did to Emily Johns, I'll pick 'er up and sit 'er down on the 'ot stove. I takes my orders from Mrs. Morton."

"It will be all right, Mary," Feng said in his suave manner.

"We'll get a cook for Government House as quickly as possible. I'll ask Mrs. Mayne not to interfere. We must make due allowance for her inexperience of bush ways."

Thursday saw the arrival of the shearing contractor and the wool-classer. They were quartered with the bookkeeper and the jackeroos, and were cooked for by Todd Gray. Later that day two cars and two trucks arrived, crammed to capacity by shearers and shed hands. Henceforth beyond the creek all was noise: the shouts of laughter of men certain to earn good cheques, the cynical hoots of the whistle on the huge steam-boiler that would drive the machinery and was in charge of one Gus Jackson. A meeting of the men was held in the long dining-room of their quarters, and after prolonged uproar a cook was elected, as well as representatives to act for them in case of dispute with the management. That night from their quarters came the sounds of many accordions and mouth-organs.

The work started the following day, the morning being devoted to sharpening the shear combs, men casting lots for positions along the "board", and getting the hydraulic presses in good order. The actual shearing started after the noon rest-hour, undertaken as a trial run; for, whilst the shed hands were paid by the week, the shearers worked by contract at two pounds five shillings per hundred sheep shorn.

On Saturday morning came a real burst of activity, followed by quietude that afternoon and Sunday. Monday the shearers started practising for the highest individual tally. The receiving pens inside the giant shed were full of sheep. The outside yards were full. Snow-white, dazed sheep, minus their fleeces, began to trickle through the outlet doors of the shed. They were almost the first of a vast army. The presses whirred and thumped, and tumbled out iron-hard packs of compressed wool, each weighing some three hundred pounds. The men now were working like galley-slaves, not driven by the whips of slave-masters, but by the competitive urge of amassing money quickly.

2

THE river of wool flowed slowly eastward to the shed. Men on horses mustered paddocks west and south of Forest Hill, gathering the sheep into classified flocks, moving a flock at a time eastward to the hut and yards at Mulga Flat, when the riders stationed there took charge of it and moved it to White Well, whence the stockmen there stationed delivered it to the shearing shed, and returned with a shorn flock that eventually was passed along the run into one of the western salt-bush paddocks.

Calm, brilliant weather, diamond day succeeding diamond day, night by night frosty and indescribably silent. All day long, save meal and smoke hours, the huge shed vibrated with whirring machinery. From the adjoining yards and pens the complaining bleat of sheep mingled with the rising grey-brown dust. Driven by yelping dogs and bellowing horsemen, sheep in their hundreds arrived full-fleeced and slow. The same horsemen and the same dogs departed, driving hundreds of sheep snow-white, but marked by the tar covering shear wounds and with spirits lightened as their bodies had been lightened. Every day that first week twenty-four shearers passed twenty-four hundred sheep through the shed.

Todd Gray now rose at four o'clock every morning. He had some fourteen men as well as the occupants of the barracks to cook for, with now and then a party of stockmen quartered on him for a night. He baked bread for Government House, an excess of duty, to lighten the work of Mary O'Doyle, who had to produce for the fastidious Ethel dishes requiring much time.

Barlow was kept busy mostly adjacent to the shed. He had to check, brand, and weigh the bales of wool for dispatch to the railway by motor-lorries and two camel-drawn wagons. Feng Ching-wei worked on the station books and issued stores. Naked to the waist, Slim Jim, with a mate as herculean as himself, laboured at the wool presses, steadily piling up a cheque. Mayne was everywhere. They saw him in the shed. The branding men and yard men saw him among the sheep outside the shed. His car flashed over the outback tracks, and the men with the travelling flocks were visited.

It is doubtful if there was a man within the shed or out on the huge run who felt or visualised the inner romance of this annual period of feverish activity. Sheep – tens of thousands on Atlas; tens of millions throughout Australia – were being stripped of their fleeces. There is romance in lumber and in wheat, but they are dead commodities. This industry was a living one, for every eight to eleven pounds of wool came from the back of a living

animal, on whose breeding thousands of pounds of money had
been expended, and both money and thought lavishly spent on its
care and upkeep.

Frank Mayne now was seldom at home with his wife and boy.
As his father before him, he was no drill-clothed veranda squatter.
With Little Frankie, now able to walk short distances, often Ethel
and the child wandered about the homestead lawns and orange
grove, and sometimes out among the homestead buildings,
looking in on Feng, who took them into the ration store and
permitted Little Frankie to discover preserved ginger or a box of
candy procured especially for him. Twice they crossed the bridge
over the deep creek, now quite empty of water, and visited Todd
Gray whom, of all her husband's employees, Ethel most favoured.

The short, fierce-eyed cook both times came limping toward
them from his sizzling stove, set before them a little lunch of
cakes, and from a nail beneath Little Frankie's name took and
filled a half-pint pannikin no man dared to touch. The pannikin
was the child's badge of representation among the men. And
always, whilst they were seated at the long table, Todd Gray
waited on them without deference, but with obvious regard for
Little Frankie, to the great amusement of his mother. Ethel Mayne
was beginning unconsciously to adapt herself to her new life.

At both visits Todd Gray said: "He's a star of the first
magnitude, madam. He's brighter than all the Cepheids, 'deed he
is!"

"The Cepheids!"

"Too true. They're the stars having a luminosity ten thousand
times greater than the sun."

This caused Ethel's eyes to open, but she refrained from
comment. Todd's reference to the stars, as well as mere hints of
knowledge of other equally recondite subjects, created slight
disapproval in her mind. It seemed wrong that a common
working-man should have knowledge of such an order; but, like
many other things she had discovered in Australia, human ethics
were topsy-turvy. How hateful was the phrase, "Jack is as good as
his master"! Already she suspected that, in this land of her
adoption, some Jacks were superior to their masters.

Only once did she pay a visit to the shed, where she was
escorted from end to end by the "Boss of the Board". She was

introduced to the wool-classer. Slim Jim, appearing as some monstrous gargoyle, grinned at her, and him she snubbed in a manner that failed to hurt him because he did not understand it. Amid the long rows of shearers beneath the overhead running gear, she was silently introduced to the "gun" shearer.

"What are you going to do to-day, Blue?" shouted Ethel's escort.

Blue showed even white teeth in a smile. "I'm taking it easy to-day," he said. "It'll be about a hundred and fifty."

"How many can you shear in a day?" Ethel ventured.

"Oh, round about two hundred. I once did three hundred in one day to win a bet."

She smiled at him when she left. She thought he deserved it. Just a common man, she knew, but rather good-looking. She knew she had made an impression on him.

3

ON August 26th there came a break in the diamond days, a break that had been long and eagerly sought. The shearing had proceeded smoothly, for the few complaints the shearers' representative had laid before Mayne had been quickly settled to the satisfaction of both sides.

The 26th fell on a Sunday, and very often, on this day of the week, Frank Mayne sauntered along the river bank and climbed to the Seat of Atlas, high in the giant gum tree on the high ground below the homestead. This afternoon, when he seated himself on the sawn square of red-gum, his mind was conjuring memory and forming pictures of the long ago, when Old Man Mayne occupied the seat and he, Frank, played about on the floor of the rail-protected staging.

From the dim past the strong voice of Old Man Mayne sounded in Frank's ears: "Bring your troubles to the Seat of Atlas, lad. Here you are far above the world, to look down on it as one of the Gods of Olympus. It's surprising how small troubles become when you look at 'em from a height."

Abstractedly Mayne filled and lit his pipe, then stared out over his kingdom. His pipe had become all the more valued a companion since to please his wife he had given up pipe-smoking in the house, where, however, he could smoke expensive cigarettes in some of the rooms.

The dark carpet of the bush stretching to the horizon was almost unbroken by the plain. The far distant windmill was not revolving for lack of wind. Apparently just the near side of it, but actually several miles distant, a column of red dust rose high, steady and persistent. It was not one of the sudden dust columns caused by a miniature "willy-nilly"; it was, as he well knew, caused by a flock of sheep which had left White Well that morning for the shed. To the south-west, and much nearer, a second dust column indicated the position of a shorn flock which had left the shed that morning.

After weeks of clear sky, that afternoon a belt of cirrus clouds, so light that the sun was seldom dimmed, drifted slowly to the north-east. A whispering north wind, hinting of the tropics, rustled the gum-leaves and brought to Mayne's nostrils the haunting perfume of gum-wood burning on the fires of the Atlas homestead. He could hear the voices of men shouting whilst they fished in a deep hole farther down the river, guessing that one of them had hooked a big fish. Sometimes a dog barked, sometimes a swooping flock of galahs or cockatoos screamed at him, whilst almost continuously the kookaburras from far and near laughed and cackled and chuckled: the devil himself in their mocking jeers.

This day Mayne's chief worry was the state of the Adelaide meat market, and the sheep market in general. The nine thousand wethers that Feng had not sold at the beginning of the year were, luckily, still in fair condition, and now the wool was off them he was prepared to sell at fifteen shillings per head. But the current price was about eleven shillings, and if it rained within a week or two the price would be almost sure to jump again to eighteen or nineteen shillings. If it rained! That was the kernel of his problem. If he held, and the rain did not come, the price would drop further still.

At normal times there was no difficulty in disposing of the surplus ewes and rams of the famous Bungaree stud to the small station-owners and selectors; but now none dared buy, even if money was available, and all wished to sell, uncertain of the climatic prospects of the summer. To Mayne, as to Westmacott and others, to slaughter sheep to save the bulk of the flocks when rain might come at any hour was unthinkable then and always. Chidman's drastic methods might suit cattle-owners, but would not find favour with sheepmen whose backs were hard-pressed against the wall of ruin. Mayne was now faced with selling his surplus stock at any price offered, or holding on the gamble of rain within a month.

As a point in his favour against a generally vexing position it was certain that, despite the dry summer, autumn, and winter which were passed, despite the poor condition of the flocks, the percentage of lambs had been extraordinarily high. Atlas would shear this year a post-war record number of sheep. This was truly significant, since reports from Bradford and Continental wool centres hinted that the prices for this season's wool would be higher than had ruled the year before.

The situation indicated to Mayne that what he might lose on the roundabouts – otherwise surplus stock – he would gain on the swings of increased wool production and higher prices. Of a certainty his wool cheque this year would be large, and if only he could sell off his surplus sheep it would obviate what was coming to appear the necessity of seeking an advance from the wool brokers if rain did not fall soon. The twenty-one thousand pounds to the credit of Atlas at the beginning of the year had shrunk to three thousand. The annual labour costs amounted nearly to five thousand pounds, taxes about four thousand, the shearing contractor would require nearly three thousand, and his ration account would quite reach that figure. Rent, rates, insurance, motor expenses, and horse feed would account for the balance. If the coming spring proved to be rainless, he would have to start hand-feeding the flocks, and then his expenses would mount in earnest.

For all this the problem was not one of life or death. If even the previous year's wool prices were maintained, the value of the present clip would more than cover his future expenses. It was a problem almost too common, one repeatedly presented to a pastoralist, and finally solved in accordance with the personality of the sheepman to whom it was presented.

As his father before him, Frank Mayne had the gambling streak in his soul. The father never would have made Atlas if he had been a cautious man, and the son would not have retained the great property had he been faint-hearted. The Australian industries of wool and metals have been created by gamblers, fearless men always ready to take a chance.

Mayne decided to take a chance.

4

A problem of less urgency, yet still demanding a solution, was one nearer his heart. It was nothing less than the gradual dispersion of the illusion he had cherished regarding the continued and continuous happiness of marriage. Two years now it was since he had married Ethel after a whirlwind courtship. From the first moment he saw Ethel Dyson, looked into the dark pools of her inscrutable eyes, felt his man's nature attracted and thrilled by her femininity, he had loved her with so great a passion that all which had gone before in his life was wiped out.

Yet, even so, marriage with Ethel had not been quite what he had expected, hoped for. Never once had his wife accepted his embraces without reserve, or with abandon. Time after time he sensed that she held him, if not at arm's length, at half arm's length. Finding her cold, unresponsive, all his fire failed to warm her. She had changed even from the woman she had been. Whilst not positive, he inclined to the belief that the change dated from the coming of Little Frankie. Never demonstrative, Ethel, before that terrible hour, had evinced a restrained, gay insouciance brought out by the wonder of their honeymoon and the shower of gifts he rained on her.

For a while his mind dwelt in that beautiful past, and idly, hardly conscious of the observation spurred by habit, he noticed how the cirrus clouds were now showing a south-western edge, beyond which the sky was clear.

Yes, the change in his wife, if change there was, had occurred when the boy was born. The change had been so imperceptible that until quite recently he had failed to notice it. Her new attitude towards him was a kind of drift, as though she floated on a raft slowly pulled seaward by the current, leaving him behind her on the land, helplessly watching her go ever further from him. And she, looking back across the widening water, seemed to regard him curiously, puzzled why she ever had given herself to him.

An hour passed whilst he occupied the commanding Seat of

Atlas, brooding, thinking how best he might break down her reserve and the barriers her reserve surely was building between them. That he loved her he was certain. There was never a doubt about that. But her excuses to put him off! It was her new frock; or fear of her hair being disarranged; or a headache; or just plain mopes. Too sensitive to battle against these excuses, too civilised to trample them under foot in the approved sheik or "he-man" style, he mentally strove to discover a path along which he might reach her and claim her.

Tentatively he considered the idea of making full confession to Feng Ching-wei, seeking guidance from this inexhaustible fount of wisdom. Had Feng been married, Mayne would not have hesitated, for Feng was – indeed, always had been – the depository of his troubles. And, thinking thus, it was almost as though Old Man Mayne stood there beside him, uttering one of the many truisms his grim nature approved: "You must lie on the bed you've made, son. If you gamble and lose, don't whine. Gamble again."

But had he lost? He stood up and threw back his shoulders. Had he really lost? Was it not possible for him to have been more attentive to his wife since their arrival home? Had he permitted Atlas to reabsorb him too much? In his heart he admitted how powerful in its influence over him was this land, this piece of the vast Australian bush, confined by boundary fences and named Atlas. It was a part of him and him of it. Its many vibrations, the rustling leaves, the whispering winds, the silences, the bird cries, the scents – all were in exact tune with the vibrations of his being. The bush had called, and from the other side of the world he had come.

As his spirit entered the shadow of doubt, so did the material world enter into a cloud-cast shadow. His eyes sought for the cause of the dimming of the material world, and his mind temporarily forgot the cause of that spiritual dimness. Across the north-west arc of the sky stretched from horizon to horizon a knife-edged bank of even-coloured cloud.

5

RAIN! The zephyr wind still blew gently and warm from the north. It was a wind favourable for rain. The cloud bank, coming as it did from the north-west, also favoured rain. Long did Mayne stand gazing at the cloud-belt steadily rising to the zenith, observing with satisfaction that along the far north-west horizon there was no light to indicate thinning clouds. Rain! Two inches, two hundred points of rain would fill all the surface dams and assure Atlas of sheep feed right through the summer. To him such a fall would be worth precisely fifty thousand pounds. And it might fall. August was a favourable month for rain.

With joy in his heart he walked rapidly from the ancient tree to the shearing shed. He found there Noyes with two stockmen yarding a flock of wether sheep for the next day's "run". The shearers and the hands were occupying their leisure in a dozen ways: a party playing the national game of two-up outside the dining hut, in which a larger party was playing banker! The clink of money drifted to Mayne in passing. Arrived at the shed receiving yards, he beckoned Noyes to join him.

"Get as many as you can into the shed pens, Mr. Noyes," he ordered. "It looks like rain, and we must give the shearers as long a run as possible to-morrow."

Should rain fall during the night, only those sheep within the shed would be shorn, for wet sheep cannot be stripped of their fleeces. Noyes was a fair-headed, fresh-complexioned youth in whose brown eyes danced the mirage of the bush plains.

"It will be a jolly good thing if it does rain, sir," was his opinion. "All right! We'll jam 'em in."

Noyes went back to his work. Mayne's critical eyes examined the milling, dust-raising, bleating animals. They were some of the nine thousand surplus wether sheep. He would be better able to judge their condition after they had lost their wool.

It was a little after four o'clock when he reached the office, there to find Feng writing letters. On entering the doorway one came parallel with a short counter on which business with the hands was done. Directly beyond the counter stood Barlow's table, flanked by a set of cupboards in which the books were kept. On the further side of the large room stood another table used by both Mayne and his lifelong friend. A safe and a press and several Windsor chairs completed the plain furnishing. The walls were adorned with large-scale maps of New South Wales and South Australia, showing the stock-routes in red, and photographic enlargements of rams and ewes, of several race-horses, and a large framed picture in oils of the Atlas homestead done by Feng from the Seat of Atlas.

"It looks like rain, Feng," Mayne ejaculated before sitting down at the table opposite his friend.

"Rain! Does it, indeed?"

Mayne nodded. "If it rains an inch before morning," he said, "many of our troubles will be solved. If it rains two inches, all our troubles will be at an end."

"They will be," agreed Feng, smiling blandly, yet with black eyes that twinkled with affection. "We want rain badly enough."

"Who are you writing to?" asked Frank, with the freedom of long friendship.

The smile on Feng's face broadened. Leaning back in his chair he regarded his questioner through eyes that were almost concealed by their lids.

"I am writing to a lady, a lovely lady, the most beautiful lady in Australia," he said.

"Not to my wife, surely?"

"The letter will be addressed presently to Miss Ann Shelley." Mayne sighed with exaggerated relief.

"I am glad to hear you say that," he said, laughing. "I was so sure it was Ethel whom you so accurately described. Ann Shelley! I wonder, Feng, whom she will marry."

"Sometimes I wonder too." Feng's smile now was less broad. "However, it is none of our business till she chooses to tell us. I am writing to suggest that I go along to Tin Tin once every week to paint her portrait."

"Good idea, old man! But I remember you saying in one of your letters to me that you were then painting her picture. What happened to that?"

"I destroyed it. I was not satisfied."

"Indeed! But then, Feng, you were always your severest critic." Mayne got to his feet. "It's tea-time. Before we go, I'll ring up MacDougall, who happens to be home to-day."

A few minutes later he turned back to Feng, saying: "MacDougall says it is raining at Forest Hill. That's good news, isn't it?"

"The very best," Feng cordially agreed.

After drinking afternoon tea with Ethel, they spent an hour with her in miscellaneous gossip in the drawing-room. Eva, coming in to draw the curtains, shut out the fast-falling night and attended to the fires, announced that it was raining. Impulsively Mayne opened one pair of French windows and, followed by Feng, stepped out on the veranda. They could just see the gleaming drops that fell to patter on the cinder path and on the leaves of the shrubs beyond it. The perfume of the thirsty earth met their nostrils, carried to them by the west wind.

"Great!" Mayne sighed, inhaling deeply. "Dear God, give us a hundred points at least!"

"Amen!" murmured Feng, so solemnly that Ethel, standing between them, wondered.

At eight o'clock it was raining lightly but steadily. At eleven, when Mayne went to bed, it was still raining. Ethel was asleep, and he refrained from waking her to tell her the good news. For an hour he fidgeted, unable to sleep, and at midnight he went out quietly to the veranda to hear the rain falling.

But the rain had stopped. The wind was blowing coldly from the south, from which quarter rain seldom came. The sky was ablaze with stars.

Going out to the rain-gauge, he removed the measuring glass, struck a match, and saw that eleven points only had fallen.

CHAPTER VII

THE SECOND PHASE

1

THERE were shorn that year on Atlas the highest number of sheep since the year 1911. Sixty-six thousand sheep passed under the shearers' hands, and the wool clipped from them filled eighteen hundred and sixty bales. By the end of September every bale had been carted to the railway and dispatched to the wool broker's warehouse, there to await the first series of wool sales.

The eleven points of rain which fell in August freshened the growing grass and herbage, and the twenty-one points that fell during September helped it at the most needed time. The two falls, however, were not heavy enough to ease the market; and, believing now that a dry season was inevitable, Mayne instructed his agents to find buyers for his surplus stock.

Eventually the agents quoted seven shillings a head for his wether sheep, but were unable to quote any price at all for his culled ewes. All one night Frank Mayne sat in the office weighing the pros and cons of this offer. Ethel never knew that he spent that night out of his bed, and failed to remark his heavy eyes at breakfast the next morning. The Governor-General with his suite were touring the Western Division, being scheduled to spend two days at Atlas – a prospect that possessed Ethel's mind to the exclusion of all else.

Despite Feng's counsel to sell, Mayne did not close with the agents' offer of seven shillings. He considered, and justifiably so, that if he lost fifty per cent. of the wethers the remainder would compensate him when the rain did come to send prices soaring again. As for the culled ewes, they must take their chance.

Neighbouring stations were in worse plight, whilst the position of the selectors was becoming desperate. Although under modern conditions Atlas was now overstocked, had outrun that margin of safety dictated by bitter experience in the past, it was by no means singular in this respect. Where Atlas was in a slightly better position was in the inclusion within its boundaries of much plain country covered with the low grey salt-bush, better able than grass to defy the long dry period. Nevertheless, the many square miles of this hardy shrub did not give sufficient margin of reserve, even had the sources of water supply been more numerous and unlimited in volume.

The Vice-Regal visit cost Atlas three hundred pounds. The expenditure was due almost solely to the ambitious Ethel, who insisted on the engagement of a *chef* from Adelaide, and an experienced butler from Sydney. Both these men she wished to keep, but they were unable to find happiness so far from the cities. The single-seater car she set her heart on – secretly to vie with Ann Shelley, but openly to permit her to take Little Frankie on short excursions – cost eight hundred pounds; whilst the general upkeep of Government House was now two hundred per cent. higher than ever it had been.

These extra expenses caused Mayne no uneasiness. Atlas was

free of mortgage, whilst his personal fortune, sadly reduced by his three-year overseas trip, was nearly twenty-two thousand pounds.

Until his wife had thoroughly settled into her new life, he was determined to grant her every desire in order to lighten, if not keep at bay, that terrible malaise suffered by the new-chum after the first novelty of the life has worn off. Nevertheless, the season and the prospect of a dry summer meant very close attention to his business.

No rain fell during October, but early in November there fell thirty-six points, which started green shoots in the tussock-grass and germinated grass and herbage seeds the earlier and lighter rains had failed to do, but fell too late to benefit the scanty grass and herbage, stunted in growth and already ripe. The wished-for following rain did not come; instead, there arrived the first heat-wave of summer. A hot north wind and a scorching sun in six hours whitened the green shoots and killed them, sucked up the little moisture in the ground, and blew away tons of edible sheep feed.

The heat-wave lasted two days, being broken by wide-spaced thunderstorms, from which little rain fell and that in narrow strips, the heat of the ground evaporating the moisture by the next sunrise.

There came one afternoon to Atlas Harry Westmacott, owner of the resumed land that took a bite out of Atlas, spoiling its shape, making a bottle-neck which to Mayne always was as an open wound. For this he did not blame Westmacott. It was due entirely to the State Lands Department, which could have cut off the area from Atlas on one of its western corners, thereby not so disfiguring its shape. Mayne talked with his visitor in the seclusion offered by a cane-grass summerhouse at the foot of the garden.

"What I'm wanting, Mr. Mayne, is agistment for about three thousand sheep," Westmacott said without needless preamble. "My son, young Harry, off-sided by a nigger, started off last week with two thousand wethers for the public roads of northern Victoria. By keeping 'em down there, picking up what they can, he'll be able to pull them two thousand through this blasted summer and bring 'em back when the feed is good after the first autumn rain. Still I'm left with five thousand, and to-day my place won't carry five thousand. I got to get rid of three thousand of them."

"I am sorry, Harry, but I haven't the paddocks to spare. Like yourself, I'm overstocked too. Why don't you sell two thousand of your sheep for what they will fetch?"

"For the simple reason that no one will buy 'em."

And therein lay Westmacott's tragedy, and the tragedy of the majority of the small sheepmen.

"If you were to cull heavily, how many culls would you get out of the five thousand you've now got on your place?" Mayne questioned.

"Not so many. I've culled heavy in the past, and, as you know, I started with good Bungaree stock from Atlas. Will you take two thousand off me for three shillings a head?"

"Short of money?" asked Mayne.

"No! Short of feed," come the fiercely spoken reply.

Mayne knew his visitor for a careful man. For years before Westmacott got his selection he had worked for Atlas. Mayne knew Mrs. Westmacott, a frugal Scotswoman. No, it was not money of which the man was actually short, as he had said. He desired to get rid of the sheep so that the remainder could be pulled through the summer.

"Well, I can't take 'em, Harry, not if you were to present them to me as a gift," Mayne said, to add more deliberately: "But I will give you seven thousand pounds for your place as it is. You know how it bottlenecks Atlas, spoils Atlas. If you sell to me for seven thousand, you could take a job till the dry spell breaks, and then buy another place."

But Westmacott shook his head vigorously. "I couldn't sell," he said. "Why, me and the wife have made Nardoo. She helped me to build the flamin' house, and you remember how young Harry rode here with me when he was only five years old and helped me drove the first mob of sheep home. No, no, I'll never sell!"

Mayne sighed. He understood Westmacott.

2

THE second heat-wave came in the first week in December, at the time Mayne was compelled to order the removal of his breeding ewes from several of the western salt-bush paddocks in which the half-filled surface dams had gone dry. Those sheep were brought in to the river paddocks to be partly hand-fed with a ration of one ounce of maize per head, with a little pressed lucerne. Since the two Atlas trucks were required for the actual working of the station, the maize and lucerne were brought from the railway by contractors at the price of one shilling per mile per ton.

Four extra hands were put on lopping the mulga, cabbage tree and sandalwood branches in the paddocks between White Well and Mulga Flat for the wether sheep to feed over; the culled ewes, the weaner lambs and the hoggets remaining in those salt-bush paddocks where there still was water in the dams.

Against his forthcoming wool cheque, which promised to be for a large amount, since the first portion of the Atlas wool had realised twenty pounds per bale, Frank Mayne had obtained an advance of ten thousand pounds.

During these trying spring months he had spent much time out on the run, being absent from the homestead repeatedly for several days. He came to believe a little in that old saying, "Absence makes the heart grow fonder"; for, on his return from those trips, he discovered Ethel to be more attentive and affectionate. But the following morning, invariably was she again barred from him by her chilly reserve. It seemed that the flame his absence created in her burned out at his touch.

Her silence one meal-time maddened him to protest. They were alone, Feng being again served by Mary O'Doyle in his bungalow cottage, and all through the meal Ethel had refused to answer his questions, or to speak one word, sitting opposite him and stonily looking down at her plate. Pushing back his chair, Mayne regarded his wife with drawn brows, rage smouldering to fire in his heart, the cave-man desire growing ever stronger to spring on her and beat her into warmth and submission.

There never had been a wish he had not gratified. There never had been an instance when he had spoken sharply, upbraided her, or consciously given her offence. He had deferred to her, studied her wants, figuratively laid himself down for her to tread on, loved her slavishly, even worshipped her. And why she was silent, why she refused to speak one word, he had absolutely no remotest idea.

Keeping yet a grip on the reins of impulse, he said calmly: "Won't you tell me what is wrong, dear? If I knew, I could help, possibly."

She made no reply to his entreaty. Her eyes gazed steadily at her plate. The seconds passed with ominous deliberation. Quite still, the knuckles of Mayne's hands gripping the arms of his chair were white. Added to the worry caused by the dry spell, the domestic situation was intolerable. Ethel gave him one swift look, when he saw the sneer disfiguring her mouth. It was that which ended his self-control.

His face white beneath its new-won tan, his eyes now blazing with a strange green light, he rose abruptly and, crossing to the door, locked it and slipped the key into his pocket. When he recrossed the room and locked the first pair of French windows Ethel rose to her feet, watching him with a faint smile of contempt and mockery. When he closed and locked the second pair she said: "You are becoming quite melodramatic." And when he fastened the third pair of windows: "Are you going to cut my throat?"

"It is about time, I think," he said in metallic tones that gave the woman a first thrill of fear. He added, "I will, however, be merciful."

At the farther end of the room stood Old Man Mayne's favourite writing-table, each end of which was fitted with spacious cupboards. These cupboards now contained all the valued relics of Frank's father, and from among them he took out a beautifully plaited kangaroo-hide stock whip, measuring from thong to short handle butt twelve feet and three inches. Gathering half the length of the whip in the hand that held the handle, there was left a striking length of about three feet. This adjustment occupied his attention whilst he walked the length of the room, coming to stand close before his wife. When he spoke Ethel did not recognise his voice.

"In dealing with *his* recalcitrant wife the despised aboriginal displays real wisdom," he said, his voice as cold and hard as his facial expression. "For the last time, what is the reason for your present mood? There must be a reason, because you are not mentally deficient. If by continued silence you refuse me an explanation, I am going to thrash you until you do give it."

Across the space of a few inches their eyes met and held with unwinking steadiness, ice-cold fury in his, haughty amazement in hers. At first the crisis was so astounding to one of her high culture that fear was non-existent. Common women, she knew, were sometimes beaten by their husbands; but she – Ethel Dyson! Yes, she was about to be ignominiously thrashed by the infuriated man now glaring at her – no longer docile, submissive – after all, not weak as she had thought, but whose patience and long-suffering she had strained to their limit.

Climax was followed swiftly by anti-climax. Mayne saw the white mask confronting him melt as though from heat. The corners of the red mouth descended, wrinkles leapt into place either side of the long, straight, sensitive nose. The blazing dark orbs became swamped, extinguished by tears. Ethel dropped into her chair, her arms swept forward over the table, pushing away the china and the cutlery, and on them her head sank in a burst of violent sobbing.

The black man's wisdom was forgotten. The black man's strength of mind became as water. Almost stupidly Frank Mayne looked down on the crouching figure of the woman he yet loved. From his fingers the whip dropped soundlessly on the carpet. On his knees he fell beside his wife, and one arm stole round her slender waist. "Tell me, old girl, just tell me what's wrong," he urged softly, his voice trembling, the soul of him undecided, wanting to reach hers and comfort it, fearing to be rebuffed. A long minute pregnant with emotion slipped by. Another passed before Ethel's sobbing began to subside. Then, as suddenly as she had fallen into her chair, she turned to him, placed her hands on his shoulders and, with eyes still streaming tears and voice choked, burst out into speech long pent:

"Oh, I am so sick of this awful life! There is nowhere to go, nothing to see. Doesn't the eternal silence crush you down? Doesn't the eternal sun become hateful with its searching glare? Cannot you understand how I miss the cold, and the rain and the fog; that my soul aches to hear the roar of the traffic and see the rushing people? What is there here? Nothing, nothing, nothing! The silent house, the wretched garden, the lonely tracks, the mockery of a river! That is all I have, and it all is an emptiness, a nothingness. Oh, I can't stand it – I can't stand it, I tell you!"

Her hands were beating on his shoulders. Repeating over and over again, "I can't stand it," she buried her face once more in her arms when she again fell forward over the table.

Mayne was aghast, astounded, because unable to understand. England, and all that for which England stood, was all right for a little while, a period of holiday. He could not understand, and, being an Australian, never would be able to understand, how an exile from Europe could be sick, soul-sick, for lack of the climatic vagaries peculiar to the country in which the exile was born and reared. There was no climate superior to that of Australia, nor was there a country superior to the Island Continent. Sunshine! Open spaces! Freedom from cramping conventions! What more could man or woman possibly desire? Yet really it is no more difficult to understand the British exile's craving sickness for rain and fog and snow than it is to appreciate the longing for sunshine in the heart of a South Sea Islander exiled in Scotland during the long winter months.

Ethel was living through the dread second phase of the new chum's life in the Australian bush, one only in every fifty sufficiently determined to stick it out, ultimately to find a deep, complete happiness in the mysterious lure this bush reserves for its initiates.

Frank Mayne recalled Feng's sage counsel, given when they were on the Seat of Atlas. He felt the urgency of Ethel's case, whilst understanding it not at all. There and then he decided to take her to New Zealand for the rest of the summer, show her new scenes, introduce her again to gaiety and action. There were matters he would first have to settle, when Feng would be able to drive Atlas as a well-tuned motor-engine. Say in two weeks' time.

An hour later, when he left his wife, she was radiantly smiling and happy.

3

THREE days after the scene in the drawing-room, Frank Mayne went outback again to join MacDougall on an inspection of the western salt-bush country. The weather was hot, calm, and clear. At noon the thermometer hanging from a nail driven into the shady side of a post registered one hundred and ten degrees, one hundred and fourteen degrees at two o'clock, falling to one

hundred and five at six, and to ninety seven just before dawn.
These readings did not much fluctuate over a period of six days.

Ethel could not escape the heat, and she did not appreciate the
fact that her position in Government House was extremely
favourable. She tried to obtain lower temperatures by having
every door and window open one day; and the next, acting on
Feng's suggestion, having all the doors shut and the blinds down,
finally discovering that the coolest place was in the cane-grass
bower-house flanked and shaded by date-palms at the bottom of
the garden. Here, with Little Frankie to take up her attention, or,
when he slept, with books loaned her by Cameron, and
needlework, to amuse her, she spent most of the daylight hours
while her husband and MacDougall and the hands blistered in the
sun and drank vast quantities of lukewarm water to fail in
quenching a quenchless thirst. It was the fourth day of her
husband's absence, and the fifth day of the heat-wave, when that
happened which strict obedience to convention all her life, the
possession of refined, deeply rooted culture, clear reason, pride in
loyalty, and an hereditary sense of honour, all failed to prevent.

In the bower-house she reclined on a cushioned rustic settee.
Little Frankie lay asleep on a folded rug on the floor. Outside in
the heat of mid-afternoon not a bird broke the silence. She heard a
man's footsteps crunching on the cinder path before his shadow
fell across the entrance, and her heart told her who had arrived,
her pulses yet remaining normal. Her expression was one of calm,
friendly welcome when she rose to meet Alldyce Cameron.

"Good afternoon, Mrs. Mayne!" spoke the full-toned musical
voice. "I was riding down the far bank of the river, and decided to
cross by a fording place which invited me, and try to cheer you
this excessively hot day. How are you weathering our Australian
summer?"

"Not very well, Mr. Cameron, I am afraid," Ethel said, smiling
into his big, handsome face, which she saw was cool and without
trace of perspiration. "Won't you sit down and tell me how you
got home after our little card party last week?"

The settee was long, and, sitting herself, she occupied one end.
He saw that he was expected to be seated at the other end, where
Ethel had pushed a silk-covered cushion.

"Whew! It is hot in the sun, and this is delightfully cool."

Cameron flicked a handkerchief, slightly scented, across his massive brow and stretched his elegant legs, encased in English riding slacks. The silver, goose-necked spurs glittered at the heels of his polished and dustless boots. The romantic, wide-brimmed felt hat – romantic because the brim was unusually wide – was tossed aside.

The drawling voice began again. "You know, Mrs. Mayne, this is not a white man's country during the eight summer months. Really it isn't. The people who boast about Australia's climate are those who would die of fright beyond the confines of a city. Doesn't this heat make you long for a good old London drizzle?"

"Yes, it certainly does."

He saw that she was looking beyond the entrance of the little house with narrow-lidded eyes which peered across the world. He knew, did this astute man, exactly what it was dragging at Ethel's heart. How lovely then did she look in profile! So cool and slim, her face and figure as though carved by a master sculptor. Woman! And woman to Alldyce Cameron was as the scent of aniseed to a horse.

"My uncle, old Josiah Bannerman, the shipping man, whom you once met, wrote me by the last mail, and his letter was full of complaints," Cameron said conversationally, drawing her gaze to him. "He is an indefatigable first-nighter, and says the new season's plays disappoint him. He's worth pots of money, and more than once I have told him to buy a theatre and put on plays he himself likes. Then he found fault with London's first real fog because his new chauffeur got hopelessly lost carting him to the Savoy, where he was to dine with Lord Wantford and Lady Rose, the daughter. Good God! Fancy writing about plays and fogs and things to a man who is sweltering in this fearful country!"

"But are you not an Australian?"

"Oh no! I was born in Londonderry, and came out here to Queensland it was – when I was twenty-two. How many years, do you think, that means I have been out?"

He was smiling at her with all the magnetism of his personality in his smile, smiling at her as he had smiled at other women who had been conquered by it. Ethel smiled in return, whilst frankly examining his features to guess his age; her eyes, as the eyes of other women had done, for one long final second, gazing at his mouth and chin.

"I – I find it hard to guess. Is it fourteen years?"

"And plus two," he corrected. "I am not an old man yet, am I?"

"No-o!"

Cameron shifted his position as though it irked him. Now he was sitting more square, and a little closer to his companion. With the damp handkerchief, not the scented one, he had previously dipped in the river water with which carefully to remove traces of perspiration, he negligently mopped his brow, on which perspiration beads were gathering. It was an occasion when a man must not perspire.

"May I smoke?"

Ethel started as though his request recalled her wandering thoughts. She bowed her head permissively. Cameron produced a case and matches. He offered the opened case, and she accepted a cigarette. He struck a match and held it out for her. He was intently watching every tiny movement of her face, electric fire coursing through his veins. Now – now! With all the force of his mind he exerted his power. Above the flame of the match their gaze met, held.

She saw his brown eyes, wide and warm, compelling and penetrating. His masculinity swept over her as a cool sea breeze, and her body began to tremble with exquisite feeling. Here was man to her woman. The impressions and all the little secret thoughts a dozen social meetings had created appeared to gather into one momentous onrush of rainbow light which flooded her whole being, made her heart to pound and yet suspend her breathing.

Watching her as no cat ever so intently watched a mouse, Cameron saw the flush dyeing her face and the soft cameo light spring into her now wide-staring eyes. He thrilled with the joy of anticipatory conquest. The match expired, burning his fingers, which parted to drop it without feeling the hurt. Holding her with his will, slowly he moved nearer, nearer still, until at last with gentleness his arms reached out, his hands touched her, and the next second she was being strained to him and was wildly returning his burning, ecstatic kisses.

"I love you – I love you – I love you!" came his low, whispered words. "Oh, my sweet! I want you for my very own, for always and always!"

She stopped his words with her kisses, and then with gentle force he tilted back her head and kissed her throat and neck. From his lips there poured into her body, electrifying it, a feeling no man before him had ever awakened within her.

A fallen twig on the cinder path snapped with a tiny report. Ethel stiffened. Memory swept back into her stunned brain. Determinedly she thrust Cameron back from her, but it was not difficult to free herself, for he rose quickly, and as silently as a shadow moved to the entrance and looked out.

He did not see Feng Ching-wei concealed by the trunk of a date-palm, Mayne's friend having entered the garden in search of Ethel to consult her regarding a household matter.

"I thought I heard someone," Cameron said softly, turning to her, to see her standing, her face aflame, her hands pressed to her bosom.

"Go!" she whispered with difficulty. "Go! Please go!"

"Very well – at once!" was his swift consent, satisfied with what he had already obtained from this peerless woman, and too wise to hurry the climax. Picking up his hat, he drew close to her, holding out his arms. "*Au revoir!* Only *au revoir!*" he whispered thrillingly.

But seeing his invitation, she shrank back against the settee, her face now white as death, her eyes big with self-reproach and revulsion. "No, no! Go – do please go!"

Alldyce Cameron smiled his bewitching smile, bowed, and walked away. Once he turned from her, once he had passed out of the cane-grass house, he permitted the flame of triumph to surge to his face. He had cast his net, and he had at last caught the fish, the loveliest, the most glorious fish even so expert a fisher of women as himself ever had caught.

Until the gong sounded calling her to her solitary dinner, Ethel Mayne lay full length on the settee in the bower-house, alternately crying and venting little moans, whilst hugging the boy to her in a tempest of self-accusation. By tightly shutting her eyes she tried to banish memory of the vision of his parted lips drawing ever nearer to her own. With all her might she tried to cast from her the memory of that leaping fire rushing throughout her body. Yet those memories she could not put from her, even when she hugged and kissed her husband's child with feverish abandon.

The carefully cooked dinner was almost untouched. The minutes were as long as hours whilst she waited for the stroke of nine, when she rang through to Feng at the office and asked to be connected with Forest Hill.

"Is that you, Frank?" she said, unable to keep the tremor from her voice. "Oh, how are you, old boy? When are you coming home? Yes? But come home soon – please, please come soon. Oh, yes! I know. But do hurry through the work and come home. I am distracted with – with loneliness, and could scream with boredom. You must come back soon. Do you hear? Come at once! Yes, Little Frankie is asking always for you. We want to get away, far from Atlas. All right, Frank. Good night! Hurry back! Good night – good night!"

Until the ring announced the conversation at an end, permitting him to break the connexion, Feng Ching-wei lay well back in his chair, his face upturned, his lips pursed, allowing perfect smoke-rings. His eyes were almost closed. There was a ghost of a smile about his lips.

GRIPPED BY DROUGHT

PART II

THE SECOND YEAR

CHAPTER VIII

THE PICTURE

1

IT was the last day of the year. Dressed for dinner, the manager of Atlas Station reclined in a wickedly luxurious chair on the east veranda of his bungalow, slowly smoking a cigarette, and gazing with the appreciative eyes of the artist across the track, beyond the lip of the river's near bank, across the hundred-yard-wide empty channel to the farther bank gilded and blotched with amber by the light of the setting sun. The two stately red-gums in alignment with his position appeared to emit from their shivering leaves the greenish orange of opal fire, glinting and winking against the background of the agate-grey sky of early evening.

There came to Feng Ching-wei his housekeeper-cook-guardian – and benevolent tyrant – Mary O'Doyle. Her greying hair was drawn back severely into a "bun" situated at the corner of her large cannon-ball-shaped head. She wore a skirt of thick brown serge surmounted by a white muslin blouse with open V-neck, and the sleeves rolled to the elbows of her mighty arms. On her outsize feet were elastic-sided riding boots; in her face the look of one bowed beneath the yoke of pain. Her weight forced complaint from the veranda boards. On encountering Feng's soft smile her expression changed to one of strange wistfulness.

"That blackguard av a Todd Gray has only just started to make the pastry for them mincepies he promised to do for me," she said belligerently. "I took special care over that mincemeat, an' he'll hear me tongue if he's late in cooking of it. If he was my ole man, I'd put life into him, for sure I would; anyways enough life to make 'im forget his pore tender feet for once."

"There will be time, Mary," Feng murmured, smiling up at her. "I cannot yet hear the Tin Tin car, and Harry has only just left to fetch Sir John."

Mary O'Doyle bent forward as far as her rigid corsets would allow, to say: "Is Sir John leaving to-night for another bender?"

"If the word 'bender' you use is a synonym for business, yes,

100

Mary. He goes to Menindee, as you know, at the end of every quarter to transact certain business."

"Humph! The kinda business me late lamented – I don't think – husband used to – to transact. Well, Sir John won't fall beneath the wheels av a table-top wagon. I 'ope not, any'ow. He's a decent old pot, a proper gintleman an' all. Would you come an' take a bird's-eye view of the table, Mr. Feng? I ain't much of a 'and at layin' la-de-da tables, and I mayn't have got it just right."

"Very well, Mary. But we need not be too particular, you know." Feng rose.

Mary turned in her own length and, with the stately majesty of a liner leaving a wharf, led him to the dining-room, where the square table was set for three with polished cutlery, glinting glass, and snowy napery, revealed by the low-hung, crimson-shaded cluster of electrics. There were a few minor adjustments needed to the table, but not for the world would Feng point them out. After the examination he stated that everything was perfect.

"I'm glad av that. For sure, I'm wanting to do me best this night," Mary said, her face suffused with a flush of pleasure.

Feng was listening intently. "That must be Miss Shelley coming now. I will ring, Mary, when I want dinner served."

"You won't keep it above half an hour after now, will you?" inquired Mary, looking at the mantel clock.

"No. I will keep note of the time."

Feng was standing at the gate to welcome Ann Shelley when her car slid to a stop before him.

"Hallo, Feng!" she cried, laughingly squeezing his hand with the affectionate *bonhomie* of long friendship. "Do you know, I just love you in a dinner suit. Thank you for asking me this evening! Miss Watts has a headache, so I did not press her to accompany me. Bold, am I not? Unconventional, and all that stuff?"

"'Stuff' is an apt word, Ann. But come, let us go in. May I offer you a glass of wine? A cocktail? No? Iced coffee, then?"

"Iced coffee? Where did you get the ice?"

"We have here an ice-making plant now. Mrs. Mayne insisted on it."

"You lucky man! I am going to have iced coffee, please."

Seated in Feng's studio-drawing-room, Ann sipped her coffee

and smoked a cigarette in the reflected glow of the sunset. Feng, who sat with his back to the light, dared a harsh Fate to twist the knife in his heart whilst steadily he examined the lovely Saxon face.

"Have you heard from them recently?" asked his first guest.

"You mean Frank and his wife? Oh yes! They left Sydney for New Zealand last Friday. Frank said that already the change was benefiting Mrs. Mayne."

Ann Shelley, looking hard at her host, tried to penetrate the shadow lying across his face. She said impatiently: "I did not know that Ethel had been poorly."

"Not exactly ill," Feng said precisely. "The heat, however, tried her nerves severely, and, I understand, there were moments when she was almost hysterical."

For a little space neither spoke.

Then: "Feng – I can't help it, really – but I am sometimes saddened by a little suspicion that old Frank has made a mistake," she said softly.

"Let us hope not," he said defensively. "We must allow for the effects our lonely living must have on one who always has been used to city life."

More emphatically impatient, Ann said: "You speak as though Ethel Mayne is singular in leaving England to live here. What of the thousands who have come to Australia and settled on the land to make for themselves farms or a living here in the bush? What of Eva, the house-maid, Tom Mace the rabbiter, Mrs. MacDougall, my Miss Watts? Since being in Australia have they had hysterics? A wife to such a man as Frank, with a station homestead to occupy her time, should have no time for hysterics. She is not an invalid. I can see nothing deficient about her."

"Doubtless it is a matter of breeding," murmured Feng. "We are not so highly strung as Mrs. Mayne. You and I cannot view people and things from her angle. I have read of those cathedral city societies, and if what I've read is true to life, we certainly must appear to Mrs. Mayne – well, let us say, difficult. Assisted by time, she will come to accept our valuation of things. When once she can value a man and a woman for what they are rather than for what their parents were, she will fit better into the Seat of Atlas with Frank."

"You are wasting your time at Atlas, Feng."

"Indeed!"

"You could be of great service as a diplomat in a foreign capital."

"You flatter me, Ann."

"Not a bit. You seat me here so that you can watch my face, and seat yourself so that I cannot see yours distinctly. Then you calmly array a lot of excuses in defence of Ethel, who has hysterics when she should be busy and happy in the well-being of her angel of a boy and her husband. It won't do. Why does Ethel have hysterics?"

"I did not say that she had hysterics, Ann."

"Do not let us split hairs. What's wrong with Frank's wife?"

"I do not know,' Feng replied calmly, "if you decline to accept my explanations."

"Then I will tell you." Ann selected and lit her second cigarette. "You know me sufficiently well, Feng, to be sure that I am above petty jealousy. Ever since we heard that Frank was married I have been honestly glad that he was happy. I could be jealous of no woman who made Frank happy. Since they returned to Atlas I have dined here six or seven times, and I have been forced to the conclusion that Ethel is not making Frank so happy as she could do. You see now all my cards. Show me yours."

For three seconds Feng remained quite still. Then he got to his feet abruptly and moved his chair so that he, too, faced the light. He laid his hand over the back of hers which rested on her chair-arm.

"Even as Frank's greatest friends we cannot discuss his wife too intimately," he said quietly. "I agree with all you have said. But, even so, we must be tolerant. Ethel has not been long enough on Atlas to prove herself. Even as you, Ann dear, I am not jealous of Ethel, but I am jealous for Frank's happiness"

Ann sighed deeply. "I cannot understand the type of English mind which persists in regarding us as uncouth Colonials with whom it is an act of condescension to mix," she said thoughtfully. "That type will admit nothing of good in Australia, and seems to take a perverse delight in comparing us and this country to the English and England to our disadvantage. What such people expected to find in Australia I don't know; but, really, they are dreadfully boring. I do hate unintelligent people, don't you?"

2

"HOW is Atlas going on?" Ann Shelley asked, when Feng Ching-wei offered no further comment about Ethel Mayne.

Feng leaned back in his chair the better to observe the deepening light falling about the tresses of Ann's brown hair. How well he loved this woman, with her clear mind and her musical voice, who had just expressed without reserve the thoughts of disapproval she was too honest to keep hidden!

In reply to her question he said: "As well as can be expected. We shore over sixty-six thousand sheep. Too many! I have been constantly regretting not having sold those wether sheep at the beginning of the year."

"I urged it."

"I know. Yet I did not think that the winter would be dry."

"Never mind! Conditions will improve later this summer. Fortunately, I sold all my wethers last March, and had I not done so I should have been overstocked. Mr. Leeson says that Tin Tin is in a good position to face a dry spell. By the way, is the Atlas domestic staff being kept on?"

"No, excepting Eva, who remains to look after the house. Mrs. Morton, you know, left last month. She felt she could no longer occupy a servant's position."

"I think that Mrs. Morton, like Aunty Joe, was treated badly."

Feng was quick to note the gleam in her grey eyes. Silently he concurred, but was naturally more reserved than she was. The arrival of Sir John Blain in the Atlas car was, he felt, opportune. Ann rose, Feng stood beside her, then followed her to the wide creeper-covered veranda, via the French window. When she placed a slim hand on his arm the frown was gone and she was smiling.

"Feng, please don't talk banalities for long," she whispered. I am dying to see my picture."

Sir John alighted from the Atlas car as once he would have alighted from his carriage at the portals of his London club. Over his dinner-suit he wore a fawn-coloured raincoat. A light silk muffler was flung loosely round his neck. An immaculate top hat was set at a semi-rakish angle on his head. Whilst he walked the

104

short distance from gate to veranda steps, a gold-headed ebony stick under one arm, he elegantly removed the kid gloves from his work-hardened hands. His booming voice floated away across the empty river.

"Good evening, Feng! My dear Ann, as always, you look superb. Every time my eyes are pleasured by the sight of you, I wish profoundly I was a modern Dr. Faust."

"Surely you would not pay M'sieur Mephisto's price?"

"When you look at me as you are now doing – yes, and be damned to Mephisto!"

"Sir John! You will spoil me with your flattery."

"Tut-tut! Whoever heard of anyone spoiling a bush aristocrat? I put it to you, Feng. Is it possible?"

"Certainly not. But come in, Sir John. Come in, both of you. I want to show you Ann's portrait, which I have just finished."

"Ah! You capture my interest. This will be the second?"

"Yes," Ann interjected. "Feng was dissatisfied with the first and destroyed it."

"Destroyed it, Feng! I am surprised. I considered that other portrait exceptionally well done. It was lifelike. Well, well, well! You might have given it to me, Feng."

"It was not satisfactory," Feng said suavely whilst conducting them to a shallow, curtained alcove. He turned down an electric light switch and quickly drew aside a curtain, to reveal a picture lighted by cunningly placed bulbs.

For almost a minute no one spoke. Neither Ann nor Sir John Blain were art critics. They knew nothing of the jargon of the studio, and valued a picture only according to the success of its photographic reproduction of life. They looked on the head of Ann Shelley. There was the sheen of gold in the carefully arranged brown hair. In the eyes was Ann's fearless outlook on life, direct, frank; the lips were daintily curved as her lips were curved when her mouth was in repose. The contours of cheeks and chin were alluring. The whole picture was an artistic triumph.

The living subject sighed. She turned to Feng quickly, impulsively. "Thank you, Feng! It's wonderful."

Evidently her soft voice aroused Sir John. "Excellent! Excellent!" he boomed. Turning to Feng he added: "My boy, it is a striking portrait. It's – it is a – a camera study in colours. Yet –

pardon an old fool criticising – I liked that other best."

"From the artist's point of view, this pleases me much better," Feng stated crisply, himself continuing to gaze at the picture. "This does not create in me the feeling of disappointment that that other did. You like it, Ann?"

"I think it just great. You have caught my face as it is, and not as sometimes I would like it to be."

Again they fell silent. The old man stood with beetling white brows, his big hands clasped behind his back, his monocle screwed into his left eye as though failing to render the assistance it was intended to do, the tall straight figure now bent forward from the hips. Old John was puzzled, because in the picture before him there was a vital something lacking which Feng's first picture possessed. On this point he could not appeal to Ann, for she had not seen the first picture. Still puzzled, he regarded Feng shrewdly, but made no further comment.

3

AT dinner, with Ann Shelley seated on his right and Sir John on his left at the small square table of rosewood, Feng Ching-wei entertained his guests with the polished grace of a mandarin of the first degree. Eight hundred miles from Sydney, four hundred from Adelaide, surrounded by hundreds of miles of virgin bush, the voices of the night-birds drifting in upon them on the balmy air, Sir John decided that, save for the lumbering Mary O'Doyle, he might well have been dining at Shepheard's Hotel, Cairo. The table decorations were right, the lights were right, the wines were right, his fellow diners were right.

"You will be going to Menindee to-night, Sir John?" Ann inquired lightly.

"Yes. Yes, I have business at Menindee at the end of every quarter," replied Sir John briskly. "I shall have to reprimand Trench for not sending me my account for the last quarter's stores. There are the four old-age pensioners who have now come to look for me and a Treasury note four times a year. And, of course, I must pay my usual visit to Mrs. Longfellow."

"She always makes me sad, yet I feel I must see her when I go to Menindee," Ann said soberly.

"She is a wonderful old lady. Her husband lived in Menindee

when Burke and Wills, the rash explorers, went through on their last fatal expedition. Always waiting for that doctor son of hers to come home. Always so full of news of his progress in Adelaide. It is strange how she should suffer illusion on but that one point. Yet she receives a measure of comfort. Lying paralysed and blind, it is her only sustaining joy – that she will one day hear the steps of her son coming along the passage."

"Young Mrs. Longfellow ought to take the picture of him from the room, don't you think? Supposing the dear old soul recovered her sight!"

"It is most unlikely, Ann. Anyway, it is not the picture itself which would give her a shock," the old man pointed out. "If, after all these years, Mrs. Longfellow were to recover her sight – if, after many years, during which she has suffered the delusion that her son was doing well in his profession, she were to read at the bottom of the picture: 'Richard Longfellow, killed in action, Gallipoli, August 1915' – the shock, I'm sure, would kill her. But the daughter says that if she attempted to remove the picture, the sightless and helpless old lady would know instantly."

"You always have been so kind to poor Mrs. Longfellow, Sir John. Will you tell me just why?"

"Well, her helplessness appeals to my sense of chivalry, Ann, for one thing. And, for another, Robert Longfellow in the picture is much like my own son."

"Will you be absent long?" interjected Feng, sensing that the spirits of his guests were becoming shadowed.

"About the usual fortnight, Feng," Sir John said a trifle sharply, as though he resented the question as too personal.

Mary O'Doyle's mincemeat embedded in Todd Gray's famous pastry provided a pleasant interlude. The small, stick-like pies recalled to Sir John the days of his boyhood at Blain Chase, and of that Lady Blain, his mother, whose absorbing hobby had been cooking. "Demnition fine!" was his vocal verdict. "You are to be congratulated, Feng, on a jewel of a cook."

Which praise caused Mary O'Doyle, then hovering about the service table, to remember only that her mission in life was to feed men unaided by "la-de-da" tables. Thrusting a dish before Sir John, she said: "They're as good as me gran' mither ever made 'em. 'Ave another?"

The old aristocrat, leaning back in his chair, gazed upward at the round weather-beaten face, showing many of the scars of life. What he saw now in the twinkling blue eyes prompted his suggestion: "Thank you, Mary, I will. I would really appreciate a few of them to eat on the journey to Menindee. Would you make me up a little parcel of them?"

"Shure an' I would, Sir John. What about you, Miss Ann?"

"Just one, please. I have never before tasted such divine mincemeat."

Mary had her reward.

Later Ann Shelley smoked a cigarette with the men. In mental power and in poise there was a lot of masculinity in the very feminine Ann. She could so talk that men forgot their masculine superiority, and were able easily to admit her to their level. What greater terror for men is there than that of the clever woman compelling them to recognise her cleverness? Whilst Sir John discussed the results of recent excavation work in Crete, with Feng and herself interpolating intelligent questions, her mind now and then dwelt on the exact business that was taking Sir John to Menindee that night, as it had done about every quarter day for many years, seeing in that "business" the pity and the shame resultant from the tragedy that had ruined the life of this lovable old gentleman.

Afterwards she played the piano whilst Sir John and Feng reclined in chairs on the veranda. From his position Feng now and then was able to steal a glance at her, at those moments when Sir John's attention was given to his cigar. They three each had their vision – Ann Shelley seeing pictures of Mayne's child, Feng thinking of her, and Sir John deciding what a demnition shame it was that Feng Ching-wei just happened to be a Chinaman.

Presently, from across the river, beyond the moon-silvered gums, came the growing hum of an approaching car. Ann thought that Sir John was just a trifle too ready to leave his chair. Barlow came to the garden gate, carrying the mail-bag over his sloping shoulder. Mary O'Doyle brought out Sir John's hat and stick, coat and gloves. She brought, too, a small wicker basket containing a half-bottle of port, a glass and several of her pies wrapped in a doily. Himself carrying his suitcase and the wicker basket Sir John departed with Barlow, his voice booming back to them: "*Au* revoir, my dear! *Au revoir*, Feng! And thank you for a delightful dinner."

Reseating themselves in silence, they could hear distinct voices from across the river, could hear the voices of Sir John and old Barlow whilst crossing the dry bed above the great hole directly below the Atlas garden. The car-engine burst into a roaring hum five minutes later, died with the changing of gear, broke out again, died and lived a third time, then grew imperceptibly softer whilst the mail-car continued on its way to Menindee with mails and passengers.

Five minutes – to Feng, golden, living minutes – and Ann went in to get her hat and Feng to take down the recently completed picture, wrap it in cloth and secure it in the Tin Tin car.

"It is very good of you, Feng," she said when settling herself behind the steering-wheel, and when the black boy gate-opener was climbing into the dicky. "I shall prize that picture as no other. When – when do you expect them home?"

"Not until April, I think. Good night, Ann!"

"Good night – and thank you again!"

As always, he stood quietly watching the tail-light of her car till it disappeared, thoughtfully then to re-enter the drawing-room. He switched on the mantel light and his face was revealed, calm, without expression save that habitual one of bland suavity. Below the light hung an oil painting of the Darling River in flood, and at this he gazed for some few moments. The frame of the picture was very deep. It was a double frame, holding two pictures back to back. When he reversed the frame, the picture he now gazed on was that of Ann Shelley, the portrait he so often had said he had destroyed.

With arms resting on the mantel, for long he looked up at the face he worshipped. Very slowly, as though the act caused agony, he turned the double picture. His head sank on his arms. A curlew in its flight down-river vented its terrible, haunting scream. He wished he could scream like that ghostly night bird.

CHAPTER IX

FUR

1

SINCE the War Great Britain has sent to Australia three classes or types of emigrant. By far the biggest class in point of number comprises those who are content to slave all the daylight hours for farmers, with the ambition of ultimately owning their own farms and slaving all the daylight hours for themselves. In point of number the second biggest class comprises those men and women who, having been tricked by immigration propaganda into believing Australia to afford an easy living to all and sundry, stowaway on home-bound ships or write letters to the home papers describing their sad experiences. This class is as useless to Australia as it must have been to Great Britain. The third class, small in number, may be called the aristocracy of the immigration movement. It consists of those men who, having the wanderlust deeply rooted in their hearts, are not satisfied with the narrow confines of farm life, and needs must push into the interior of the country to live the freer life of the station hand, the drover, the prospector, the sandalwood cutter, and the engineer.

To this last class belonged Tom Mace. He came to Victoria direct from the Army in India. The Ex-Service Migration Association which sponsored him guaranteed him work on a wheat farm, and he had not been on that farm long before he began to wish himself back in the Army. Fortunately, an avenue of escape presented itself in the person of a bushman carrying his swag back to the bush from Melbourne, where he had "gone broke" after the spending of a two-hundred-pound cheque.

Said the bushman: "Cripes! Fancy working for a cocky! Not me, thank you. I'm on me way back to the stations, where ordinary times a man don't work until it's too dark to see."

"Let me come with you," Mace pleaded.

So Mace left the farm. He asked for the wages due to him, four weeks at thirty shillings a week; and, the farmer demanding a week's wages in lieu of a week's notice (to which he was not entitled), Mace told him to keep his money, and dragged his suitcase and two blankets out to his new-found friend who was waiting on the road.

"Wot are you gonna do with that flash suitcase? You can't hump that about with you. Here, layout your blankets like this. Now empty out your case. Arrange your shirts and spare clothes like this. Now fold over the blanket edges so, and now roll up hard like this, so that you've got a swag. Never mind the towel yet. I got some cord to spare. We tie the roll in two places and join the ties with the towel loose like this, so you can sling the swag over the shoulder, the towel not cutting into it. See? You got a bushman's swag now. What are we gonna do with the blasted suitcase?"

"This!" cried Tom Mace, and, taking a run at the suitcase, kicked it over the fence into his late employer's horse-yard.

"You'll do!" the bushman said admiringly. "Now, if you just take notice of what I tell you and not try to teach me how to suck eggs, I'll show you a hundred better ways of earning a living than working for a cocky, or a sweating factory boss. How any man can be such an utter sucker as to work in a factory or on a farm when there's life and freedom to be had almost in the next street, as it were, beats me."

They walked to the border of New South Wales and one hundred miles into that State. Mace learned how to bake a damper loaf in the camp-fire ashes. He learned the best approach, first to a farmer's wife and eventually to a station cook, to secure the three main items of food – flour, tea, and sugar –with the addition of mutton once they entered the pastoral country. He was taught bushcraft; his initiative was developed to a point when he lost that dreadful fear of losing a job, yet still was not content to be without work.

For twelve months he worked on a station near Rankin's Springs, starting as a homestead roustabout and leaving one day when he was the bullock-drover's off-sider. He left with his swag rolled and slung from one shoulder, because he wanted to peer into the great north country.

It was early winter when he reached the township of Lake Cargelligo, on the edge of this splendid permanent sheet of water. In a hotel he met one who called himself "King of the Rabbit

Trappers". The king leased camp equipment and traps, found trapping ground and collected skins and carcasses with a motor-truck from his lessees, who worked on a very fair percentage.

"Is this trapping hard?" Mace asked.

"Too hard for you!" replied the King of the Rabbit Trappers.

"Don't be too sure of that. I'm a trier, anyhow!"

"All you Pommies say that. You can do anythink, can't you?"

"I've caught rabbits at home with my old mother's sewing thread."

"You 'ave? How do you set a snare?"

Mace demonstrated with a piece of string and a pencil. "Damned if I don't give you a go," the king decided.

And so for another twelve months Mace caught rabbits with gin-traps on a percentage basis which returned him more money per week than ever he had earned before in a month. During that year he saved enough to purchase a horse and dray, camp equipment, and the necessary two hundred gin-traps. He left Lake Cargelligo for the River Darling, someone having told him the rabbits were thick on the Gutter of Australia.

2

OF medium height, and now toughened to the resilient yet enduring qualities of kangaroo hide, Tom Mace had by great good fortune found his country and his occupation. Mentally high-strung, physically endowed with untiring energy, imbued with ambition to make money, he fitted into the scheme of things like a well-oiled cogwheel.

At the beginning of the drought he was thirty-three years old. The elements were stamping his features, making the formerly round plain face lean and rugged, and giving to it a hint of the hawk that existed also on ground animals. Grey-blue eyes peered from beneath sun-drawn brows, whilst the mouth had gained firmness and was becoming slightly suggestive of one of his own gin-traps.

The beginning of the second year of drought found Tom Mace trapping hosts of rabbits which came to the surface dams on Atlas nightly to drink. He did not use the gin-traps now, but wire-netting. The great heat-wave found him at Ware's Tank, five miles south of White Well. Each succeeding day added to itself a further meed of heat. The sun rose mighty and of bronze, moved with infinite slowness across a sky of haze, finally to set in a sea of blood. Day – by day – by day. Never a cloud to mask for a moment the celestial furnace and cause men to thank God for the shadow.

For thirteen hours daily the sun blazed on a forty-by-forty-yard square of water lying in the bottom of a man-made hole, daily sucking from it in invisible vapour four inches of water – precious, priceless water – in a land rapidly becoming a desert.

The huge, scooped hole in the ground, situated where surface water from rain might flow into it, was surrounded by a ten-foot rampart of the earth taken from it. Of necessity the dam lay in a ground depression between two lines of sand-dunes divided by a half-mile flat of red flour-fine dust, soil pounded and repounded by the hoofs of thousands of sheep, the feet of two thousand kangaroos, and the paws of ten thousand rabbits coming every night to the dam to drink. Black, stunted pine and mulga, growing, or struggling to grow, on the sand-ridges, dotted the country beyond. The plain surrounding the dam was an unnatural plain: no phenomenon of Nature had made it a plain where once had grown the stunted scrub-trees. It had long been cleared of every tree, every bush, every bleached wisp of grass by sheep, rabbits, and kangaroos which were loth to go far from the water.

On the farms the larger numbers of settlers on smaller land areas are able to cope with the rabbit and control its depredations, if not entirely destroy it; but on the huge pastoral areas it has been proved that huge expenditure on poisons and fumigation has hardly any appreciable effect. There is good in every ill phase of Nature, and drought will do what man, despite all his efforts, cannot. At the beginning of a drought the land is in fair condition, and the rabbits, being widely "spread" over the country, do not appear to be notably numerous. It is after a dry period, when no moisture remains in the herbage and grasses that the rabbits, coming to congregate in the vicinity of the man-made water-catchments, amaze by their countless numbers.

It was the second week in January. Mace had erected a fence of wire-netting one yard from the edge of the square sheet of water, so constructed that at two places along each side the fence sharply turned in to the water in the shape of a V, the point of the

V but four inches from the water, thus:

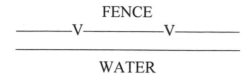

FENCE

————V————————V————

WATER

At the V-points, two inches from the ground, Mace had made holes just large enough to permit a rabbit to squeeze through to get at the water, whilst at opposite corners in his fence outward pointing V's led into stoutly constructed trap-yards.

At this time Mace was in undisturbed possession of Ware's Dam – so named from the contractor who sunk it – for at any moment of the day the shallow sheet of water might magically disappear. The sheep had been removed from those paddocks the dam supplied, and Mace's only enemies were the kangaroos.

He had taken a meal of baking-powder bread and salted mutton, accompanied by draughts of black tea, when the sun, a flaming crimson, went to bed behind the distant scrub, the while he walked over the mullock rampart carrying a billy-can of tea, a water-bag – the water in the dam was undrinkable and luke-warm – a shot-gun, a haversack of cartridges, and his skinning knives. Watching him were nine kangaroos, halted by his appearance a quarter of a mile away.

Mace set down his gear on the level ground between the

mullock rampart and the bank of the dam, thence to proceed on a tour of the holes at the point of each V in his fence, and assure himself that a selvage of the netting lay flatly on the ground inside the fence, or that side nearest the water. His final preparations completed, he returned to his gear, seated himself on his hat, for the ground was still too hot to sit on without adequate protection, and, after making a cigarette, loaded his shot-gun.

The sun-stored heat, radiating upward from the earth, struck on his face and naked arms. The metal of the gun was almost too hot to touch. The moisture of his mouth was difficult to maintain, and was only kept fluid by constant sipping from the billy-can. That day he had drunk so much that he felt unwell. Despite his having an hour before poured two buckets of water over himself and put on clean undervest and trousers, his body felt as though it had been bathed in gum. Everywhere his clothes touched his skin the material stuck to it.

His world was plashed with amber and with crimson. The water was like a sheet of aluminium. The sky above was the tint of cadmium. In the west it resembled the walls of a slaughter-house. Twilight was slowly darkening to indigo the eastern sky. It was so silent and the air was so still that it seemed as though the sun had congealed the air so that sound could not penetrate. Mace's tobacco-smoke rose straight above his head in a thin column five or six feet high. The brilliant crimson of the dreadful western wall was fading as blood with age, whilst night pushed its blue-black curtain over westward, downward to the horizon. Stars appeared, winking, almost violently dancing, in the heat haze – golden stars like windfalls from some vast orange grove.

Arrived abruptly the vanguard of a mighty host, shadows on the ground revealed by the last of the lingering twilight. A rabbit appeared on the summit of the rampart, paused for half a second to sit up and stare at him, then ran down the rampart, passed him but a yard from his feet, sped on down to the balking fence. Ten seconds later three rabbits were coming over the rampart. The main host had left the scrub a quarter of a mile each side the dam, moving purposefully, determinedly, without fear. Ten seconds after the first rabbit appeared, Mace saw three, and two seconds later he saw a dozen. After that he was unable to keep count.

A rabbit frantically running along the outside of the fence

came to one of the V's pointing to the desired water. Into the V it went, quickly to reach the hole in the netting at its point. There it hesitated, its twitching nostrils not four inches from the water it must drink. A little fearful, it edged to the V-hole, ready to dash back, but the water magnet proved too strong. Overwhelming desire suddenly banished timidity. It must drink. Resolutely it pushed through the hole its head, its shoulders, and drank and drank, lapping like a cat. Its period of hell was temporarily over.

A second rabbit entered that V behind the first. Seeing and hearing the first rabbit drinking, knowing that the first rabbit had found a hole in the fence and was blocking the hole, the second rabbit bit the first on the rump. The first rabbit, determined not to wriggle back till it had swelled its stomach with water, fearing to wet the fur of its paws, twisted through the hole, yet remained on the inch or two of dry ground between the V-point and the water, and came to greater space between the water and the fence itself, there to continue drinking; and ultimately was unable to find its way back to the V-point through which other rabbits were pouring.

Like all successful hunters, Tom Mace was a born naturalist. He thrilled at this, the most wonderful natural phenomenon Australia can offer. With him familiarity did not lessen the fascination. An army of rabbits, a hundred quickly following a hundred, followed by yet more hundreds, ran across the flat summit of the rampart, sped down to the fence. No human being could count their multitude. The faint whispering of their feet on the uneven ground was like the sigh of water deep in the earth. Already probably a thousand rabbits were racing along the *outside* of the fence.

Mace could not now see the fence, but he knew that through the hole at the point of each V the rabbits were passing as drops from a dripping tap. Hundreds of rabbits now were racing along the *inside* of the fence, their bodies swelled with water, frantically searching for a way back through the fence, finally finding a way – the hole at the V-point which enticed them into one of the two trap-yards.

A shape, grotesque, monstrous, slowly appeared on the west rampart, outlined on the ribbon of dark silver sky. This vision of a hybrid horror, a cross between a spider and a crab, with the ancestry of a beetle and a horse, for a second remained motionless, then slowly rose and, gradually shedding its horrific appearance, took to itself lines of wondrous beauty and grace; until, balanced by its tail, holding its forearms close, its baby hands across its chest, there sat a kangaroo alternately staring with suspicion at the motionless man, and with desire at the forbidden water. The long curves of its body mounted to the outline of a noble head, with long, gently moving, leaf-like ears.

Unable now to see his gun-sights, yet practised to work without such aids, Mace fired. The 'roo crumpled, thrashing the ground with its broken legs and its tail. Above the sounds of its final struggle came the undiminished sound of racing rabbits. Vibrating thumps were made by a sentinel 'roo's tail far beyond the rampart, warning others, now halted by the gun report, sitting up like bronze images, mystified, a little frightened. Yet they, too, must drink or perish, and soon were down again on forepaws creeping toward the dam as horrors from another planet; whilst others, leaving the scrub-lands, bounded across the narrow plain more gracefully than our racing thoroughbreds.

One kangaroo reaching Mace's flimsy netted fence would have made a breach and liberated hundreds of rabbits. With straining eyes he sought for them, discovered their almost invisible outlines against the now dim steel of sky-line, and fired again and again.

A fox ran over the rampart too quickly to be seen. It saw the ring of rabbits balked by the fence, saw the fence, the water beyond. Nothing in all the world mattered to the fox but to lap and lap and lap the water it had craved for fourteen dreadful hours.

Mace heard the increased humming roar set up by the rabbits in frantic effort to give passage to the fox. Yet the fox did not disturb him. Its catlike spring to the top of the fence and over did not threaten its stability. It was the creeping, persistent kangaroos, a perpetual menace to his fence, which fully occupied his attention: his sight, his hearing, and his gun.

The sky no longer reflected the past terrible day. It was ten o'clock. Still the earth radiated the sun-stored heat, still the air felt as though congealed. No cooling night wind reached Mace to relieve the strange mental lethargy that possessed him. His eyes burned. His lips felt as though cracked, and the cracks as though filled with salt.

An hour later he lit the hurricane-lamp and went down to the fence. Bordering the outside of the fence, ringing the four sides of the dam, was a compact mass of animals, here a foot in width, there three feet in width. Through the V-points they still trickled. At places long rows of rabbits were drinking. Only those rabbits that had drunk their fill and were trapped inside the fence dashed along it before his approach.

Reaching one of the six-foot, stoutly built trap-yards, he lifted the lamp above his head and gazed down on a block of rabbits eight feet square, and averaging eighteen inches in depth. Impossible now for any further rabbits to squeeze in. Those below the surface of the mass were asphyxiated; those alive on the surface were bunched in heaped-up masses at each corner.

Now and then from the dam came a soft "plop", marking the moment when a rabbit, maddened by the imprisoning fence, sprang from the shore. Tiny gurgling sounds denoted its death by drowning. What the lamp revealed was unimaginable save by one who has witnessed that scene. Low, tiny sounds, mysterious and sinister to the uninitiated, encompassed Tom Mace. Beyond the dam the silence of the void. It was as though the tragic drama going on below the ramparts of the dam was being enacted on the dimly lit stage of some enormous theatre, watched silently, entranced, by the red, winking eyes of an audience of stars.

From each of the two traps Mace took and killed four hundred rabbits. He skinned them at the rate of three a minute, tossing the carcasses into heaps, and, when he had done, bagging the balls of fur. He proceeded then to lift the netting of the fence at several places, permitting the rabbits at the water to escape with concerted rushes through the masses pushing to get at the water. Save those killed the next day by the heat, the eagles, and the crows, every rabbit would return for a drink the following night. When he left the dam for his camp, each trap-yard still held approximately two hundred rabbits.

He had been gone but a minute when the dam ramparts were alive with creeping and crawling kangaroos and slinking foxes, all passing through the army of rabbits as though it did not exist, to reach the water every living thing must drink to survive the coming day.

3

MACE again was astir when the dawn first lightened the eastern sky. He boiled the billy, made and sipped hot tea then carted the rabbit carcasses on his truck to a place one mile distant from the dam, there to dump them where some thousands of carcasses already were dried hard and blackened by the sun. With the rabbit carcasses he carted and dumped the carcasses of the kangaroos he had shot, not bothering to skin them, the prices of 'roo skins being low. When the sun had heaved but half its bloody mass above the horizon, its heat scorched the land and raised shimmering heat-waves to roll over the ground.

Picking up the bagged skins of the animals he had killed early that night, as well as those remaining in the traps, and skinned before carting the carcasses, Mace retired to his camp. Of the camp it could be said only that he was in occupation of the ground below the dam-site. It was quite unnecessary here and in this climate to erect a tent in which, day or night, it would be impossible to stay long.

The box tree, one of the Eucalypti, possesses leaves wider and larger than the many species of wattle which cover most of the bush-lands. Its shade, therefore, is of the best, yet poor compared with that given by the river gums. Beneath this tree was Mace's camp: a camp stretcher, on which was a flock mattress only, for sheets and blankets were as unnecessary and as unbearable as the tent. A heap of wire bows – lengths of stout fencing wire bent to form a U over which the skins were stretched – a number of chaff-bags in another heap, three wool packs filled with skins and one partly filled, the camp fire but a little way from the truck, and the truck itself carrying the rations, the tucker-box, the small iron water-tank, and serving for a dining-room safe from the ubiquitous ants, made up Mace's bush camp – a camp and conditions which would have horrified a hard-bitten explorer.

Twelve hundred skins Mace slipped over the U-shaped pieces of wire, the points of which he stuck in the ground so that the skins would dry clean of dust and grit. It was nine o'clock when he lay down on his stretcher, covered his face with mosquito netting to keep off the flies, and tried to sleep. Six hours of fitful, tormented half-sleep, after which he rose to make up the fire, proceeded to remove the now board-hard dried rabbit-skins from the wires and pack them in the unfilled wool bale, and then bake damper bread in a camp-oven and boil a piece of hard and mildewed mutton in a kerosene tin.

Many a time has the gold fever been described, how men energized by the fever pushed into the North American wastes to perish of cold, and penetrated the deserts of Australia to perish of thirst. Man's frenzied labour whilst he collected the precious gold, labouring till he dropped from fatigue, we also know; and much akin to this terrible gold fever is the fur-getting fever, varied and intensified by a different set of circumstances. The gold-hunter really need not hurry, for the gold will abide passively in the earth; but the fur-hunter, whose trade is governed by seasons and animal life-cycles, must ever race against time.

Perhaps during three months, or but one month, of one summer in a decade, will rabbits mass to drink as now they were massing to drink at the dams on Atlas. In this year at this time the price per thousand skins obtainable in Sydney was fifteen pounds. The average earnings of Tom Mace were fifteen pounds every night. It was made possible by the heat, the scarcity of surface-water, and the absence of moisture in the dead herbage and grasses. With ordinary gin-traps such nightly hauls would be impossible; and, whilst the rabbits came to drink in their thousands, Mace must tackle the flow of fur with all his might; for at any hour a thunderstorm might fill the clay-pans and allow the rabbits again to be scattered thinly over all the land.

Had Mace been a god, had he been able to live and work without sleep and muscular rest, he could have killed and skinned three thousand rabbits every night. They were on the land bordering Ware's Dam to which they came to drink – and be trapped. Already that summer at one dam he had taken eleven thousand, at another fourteen thousand. At Ware's Dam, during his nineteen days trapping, he had taken nineteen thousand rabbits; and yet there remained, he estimated, a probable six thousand.

Day by day the heat increased. At the Atlas homestead the thermometer registered 121° at two-thirty in the afternoon of this day, which proved to be the peak of one of the worst heat-waves experienced on the Darling.

The Atlas thermometer was in shade – real shade. Near it were huge red-gums casting real shade in which the air might cool. Mace in his comparatively shadeless camp, and the sheepmen in the shade of their red-hot iron humpies, lived in conditions far removed from the luxurious comfort of a station homestead.

Mace sought peace and rest and found them not. He lay on his stretcher-bed, a piece of cloth in his hand, ever battling against the swarming pestiferous flies attracted by the moisture exuding from his heated skin. About him was no faintest movement of the air, hot enough now to blister him, burn his eyes, and send the blood to his head to hammer at his temples.

Impossible to sleep, though his brain ached for sleep, the sleep cut down, rationed by the demands of his trade, the inescapable urge to seize the fleeting skirts of Opportunity. Impossible to keep still, impossible to imprison himself within a mosquito-net wherein he would suffocate. The muscles of his arms screamed for rest from the hopeless task of keeping at bay the flies.

The shade was a mockery. At noon the sun cast the shadow of a man's head almost on his boots. There seemed little advantage to be gained by keeping in the shade, for the air in shadow was almost as hot as in sunlight. The ground radiated heat as if it held volcanic fire.

Mace rose and drank from a canvas water-bag hanging by a wire hook from a branch. At once the water oozed from his body through the pores of his skin, giving momentary coolness. He rolled a cigarette and, producing a wax vesta, laid it against the blade of a skinning-knife, when it immediately burst into flame. The galah cockatoos that morning had spent much time by the water in the dam, and now about fifty of them were perched in the branches of the three box trees. For an hour in the forenoon they had singly flown from tree to tree seeking the coolest shade, but for two hours not a bird had dared to leave the shade they had. Ten of them were perched above Mace's camp, curved beaks wide open, throat feathers throbbing, whilst they gasped for air. From some point a crow almost fell into the tree in its haste to escape the sun, managed to cling to a branch, gained secure perch after much wing-flapping, when the sound of its gasping, tortured breath reached the man.

Escape! There was no escape. He and hundreds of men, most

of them a little more favourably circumstanced than he, were held
prisoners by the heat, as by the dust-storms of spring and the cold
winds of winter. Unable to keep still, unable to rest, unable even
to concentrate his mind on a paper, Mace was unable to find any
task to which he could apply himself.

Seated on a folded bag on the running-board of the truck, he
buried his face in his arms in a fruitless effort to escape the flies.
Whilst thus he sat there reached his burning ears a "swishing"
sound ending in a soft thud, and, raising his head, he saw at his
feet one of the galahs – dead. Beyond it, beyond the tree, over all
the miniature plain, rolled wave after wave of shimmering heat. It
was as though on the plain lay slowly moving water-waves
scintillating as the wings of dragonflies. The waves beat on the
camp, on him, on the birds, and presently another galah fell from
the branches – dead.

That most wiry of all birds, the crow, was sorely tempted to fly
away, but fear of the hell of sunlight overcame its age-long fear of
man. Even when Mace walked round and round the tree-trunk,
wildly waving a cloth about his head to keep off the flies, the
crow remained.

For several moments panic gripped Tom Mace. He thought
that were the temperature to rise by only one degree, he would no
longer be able to bear it. He was tempted to start the truck-engine
and drive to the river, twenty-four miles distant; but resisted,
knowing the danger of tyre blow-outs, when his situation would
be far worse. He saw the grey streak from tree to ground when a
galah in the next box tree fell from it, suffocated; and half an hour
later the crow above him gave a gurgling "caw-aw", fought
upside-down to maintain its hold on the branch, and only when it
died relaxed and fell.

Men would talk of the heat of that day for years to come. It
became a terror to Tom Mace, there alone amid the heat-waves.
He had heard of the birds falling dead from the trees, but this was
his first experience of such heat. His seared eyes swept the
southern sand-dunes, and then examined the dunes to the north
for no reason save the search for something to occupy his mind
for a second. He saw at the foot of one long sand-ridge a low but
thick-growing bush that promised real shade; and, because he
knew that if he did not do something he would go mad, he

decided to walk to the bush and ascertain if it did cast real shade that might be cooler than in his camp.

With a length of calico over his head like an Arab's burnous, Mace walked across the plain, with a flaming hell filling the sky above and below, a roasted world burning him through the soles of his boots. Reaching the outer fringe of sparse bush, he saw that every inch of shade was occupied by a rabbit's live body, and that on ground over which the shadow had passed there lay the swelling carcasses of many dead rabbits. At his approach many of the living rabbits left the shade cast by one bush to run staggeringly to the shade of another. Some ran for three or four yards, a few reached their objective, but the majority was halted by the sun. They leapt upward with a short sharp squeal, to fall dead.

In that one day the sun killed more rabbits than the eagles, the foxes, poison baits, netting fences, and Man could destroy in twelve years.

And when the terrible sun at long last had been swallowed up by the blackened bush, Mace watched the survivors of a host come to drink. He trapped one hundred and nine. He would have trapped one hundred and twelve had not two foxes killed three.

When Tom Mace reached Menindee with his four wool packs filled with rabbit-skins, the heat-wave had subsided to moderate summer weather. He brought back to Atlas a drink-sodden man who had completed his quarterly business.

CHAPTER X

MONEY

EARLY in February the second heat-wave of the year was broken by a week of thunderstorms even more trying than the fiercer, drier heat. The storms that massed and rumbled daily dropped a total average fall of nearly an inch of rain, putting many feet of water into the dry or drying-up surface dams, but coming at the wrong time of the year to maintain new grasses, which would inevitably be burnt off by the hot sun unless additional rains fell during the month and in March. When Mr. Rowland Smythe came to Atlas the weather again was clear, but less hot than it had been.

Smythe was the manager of the financial department of Messrs. Boynton and Reynolds, stock and station agents, wool brokers, and station financiers, not of one particular city, but of all Australia. Half-yearly he paid a visit to every pastoral property in which his firm was interested, or was about to become interested, in every State save Western Australia. It could be said with truth that of all men engaged in the wool industry he was the most expert, his sensitive finger ever laid on its fluctuating pulse.

Upon his advice, under his direction, the wealthiest financial concern in Australia advanced money on property mortgage, on wool clips in bales, and on wool still on the sheep's back. His firm bought and sold stations, floated companies to control stations, owned huge wool stores at every Australian major port, and was interested in a fleet of cargo carrying ships. In short, Messrs. Boynton and Reynolds carried the pastoral industry as the various State Governments carry the farmers.

Mr. Rowland Smythe came to Atlas in a roomy eight-cylinder-engine car, accompanied by much luggage, and driven by a chauffeur. Over a plain suit of tweed he wore a dust-coat of the cheapest make, and on his head he wore, as a dove on its nest, an eleven-and-sixpenny trilby hat. His appearance and his bank account did not match. Short, tubby, and close to sixty-five, his red face irresistibly suggested a shining apple: his small blue eyes always gleaming with good humour, one found difficulty in appreciating his granite hardness in finance until engaged with him in a business deal. With him money was governed by cast-iron rules that could never be broken without disaster.

He was given the quiet room in Feng Ching-wei's bungalow, and sat down to dinner as immaculately garbed as his host invariably was when he entertained. They talked of foreign politics, of pictures, and of books, rigorously eschewing the subjects of wool and finance. Afterwards, in the cool, balmy night air, they lounged on the wide veranda with cigars and whisky between them, within hearing of ten thousand frogs lifting up one tremendous song of thanksgiving for the recent rain.

"The fall appears to have been fairly even over all the Western Division and the south-west of Queensland," Smythe observed when he had secured the acme of comfort. "Conditions were beginning to look blue, many of the small men being hard up against it. Times like these prove my contention of many years that when the country is cut up into small areas of about thirty thousand acres the holders of those areas should be compelled to co-operate with each other, and should at all times be strictly limited to the number of stock each holding should carry. To-day the small man is as prone to overstock as the big man was two to three decades ago. Artificial feeding quickly ruins the small man. It is the greatest money-thief of all."

"Yet artificial feeding is now recognised to be very necessary."

"Agreed, Feng, agreed. How many are you feeding here?"

"About sixteen thousand on maize and lucerne. We are cutting scrub for a further twenty thousand. Or, rather, we have been cutting scrub. The rain has enabled us to stop that."

Smythe pulled at his cigar. His voice when next he spoke was a little harsh, as though it had not properly recovered from the abuse it had undergone when as a young man he had auctioned stock.

He said: "The next lesson the pastoralists have to learn is that it doesn't pay to have paddocks as large as they generally run to-day. Ten-by-twelve-mile paddocks are too large, unless water is to be had at both ends. As you know, a large number of sheep watering at one dam or well quickly eat out the feed in the vicinity, and have to travel miles from water to grazing and from grazing to water. Five-mile-square paddocks are large enough, holding a fourth of the number of sheep in the big paddock. The less sheep are compelled to walk about, the longer sheep are able to keep condition in dry times."

The financier paused to sip his whisky. Since Feng offered no comment, well knowing that what his guest said was true, Smythe went on: "Quite apart from the dry spell, however, which even now is not definitely ended, it is up to all of us to go very slowly, and look hard at every pound before parting with it. This country is facing a deuce of a bump. Our incessant borrowing in London cannot go on much longer. The evil practice of our politicians – even a generous man could not call them statesmen – in borrowing money with which to pay interest on money already borrowed, would be amusingly naïve were it not presently to be

so tragic. Do you know that since the War the six Australian
States alone have borrowed nearly three hundred millions?"

"Yes. I read something about it the other day," admitted Feng.

Smythe grunted. He was used to people regarding hundreds of
millions as a mere current account, and even his host did not
appear to appreciate the enormity of the swollen national debt.

"Our Australian trouble is that we regard politicians as cinema
actors. We send men to Parliament who neither are clever enough
to make much money for themselves whilst the chance is theirs,
or stupid enough to be hopelessly unable to balance expenditure
with the income of their weekly wages. As I said, the bump is
coming with the inevitability of Fate. John Bull is going to wake
up from a long snooze, and discover that he has been quite an
ordinary sucker swindled by quite common confidence tricksters.
It is revealed, when we study the psychology of the sucker, that
when once the sucker is sucked he is a most frightfully jealous
guardian of his cheque-book. When are Mayne and his wife
coming home?"

"Next month. They are in Melbourne now."

"Been away nearly four months? Been to New Zealand?"

"Yes."

"Humph!"

Between them a silence. In the half-darkness the red ends of
their cigars glowed, died down, glowed again. Away across the
creek someone was tunefully playing an accordion. The low
murmur of voices – those of Mary O'Doyle and Eva – reached
them. Feng was thinking of Smythe's thoughts, or probable
thoughts. His "Humph!" had been so expressive following his
brief discourse on Australian national finance.

After a while the money genius said: "From memory, the
balance of the Atlas wool cheque, after the overdraft had been
deducted, was a hundred or so above four thousand pounds,
wasn't it?"

"Yes, that is so," replied Feng, congratulating himself on
having accurately guessed the other's thoughts.

"Humph! Well?"

"Well?" Feng parried, shying at putting into words the thing at
which Smythe balked.

Then Smythe burst out with unwonted vigour: "Damn it, man!

Four thousand pounds won't carry you on until next shearing, will it?"

For the merest fraction of a second Feng hesitated. "No," he regretfully admitted. "Our annual expenses are about eighteen thousand. Above that we now have the expense of artificial feeding and scrub-cutting. I wrote Mayne about shortage of cash early last month, and he has written me that he is applying to you for an overdraft of twelve thousand against this year's clip. Even that amount will not be sufficient to meet all our expenses, but the Atlas credit is good enough to get us through the coming winter, which surely cannot be as dry and rainless as last winter."

"How do you or Mayne or I know that it will be better or worse than last year, Feng? After one dry year it isn't safe to gamble on the second year, or even the third year, being wet. I shall, of course, recommend the overdraft. Rain coming now augurs a better season this year; but, my dear Feng, sound as is Atlas, it will not long stand the drain Mayne is placing on it. Three years on a world tour, spending at the millionaire rate, and, almost immediately afterwards, a four months' tour, also, I presume, at the millionaire rate, is unreasonable to ask of any property, dependent on the seasons, to give."

"I think it likely that when they return they will settle down in earnest," Feng countered loyally.

"Well, to use an old English phrase, they'll have to draw it mild. I understand that the wife is a good-looker?"

"Exceedingly so."

"And doubtless expensive?"

"She has become used to the best, Smythe."

The financier sighed, and said no more until he had lit another cigar.

Then: "It is a little easier to convince individuals than it is to convince nations that living above income ends only in one thing – perdition," he said deliberately. "As you know, I knew Old Man Mayne for years, sometimes advising my firm to assist him with finance. He was a tough old bird, and as game as any the Old Country ever exported. His son suffers from a very natural disability. As the majority of men with rich fathers, he is apt to regard money as something to play with rather than to work with. Frank takes after his mother in many respects, but she, not less

than the old man, valued the pence. Talk! She could talk a
kookaburra into speechless silence. But to revert. I have known
Frank and you since you were toddlers, and I may claim to be a
little warmer than a business acquaintance. For Frank's sake,
whisper a word of warning into his ear."

"But matters are not as bad as all that, surely?" Feng
expostulated.

"How much is the Atlas reserve fund?" Smythe demanded
sharply.

"There is no such fund."

"I knew that; but why? Why, after many post-war boom years,
hasn't Atlas a reserve fund of at least fifty thousand pounds?
Does a farmer owning a good milking cow decline to breed heifer
calves to take its place when age dries up its milk? Frank has
thought that Atlas is an immortal milking cow, and now that
conditions are bad he hasn't a young heifer, in the form of a
reserve fund, with which to carry on. No, matters are not really
very bad. They could be much worse – and, Feng, they could be
much better. I am not imputing that Atlas is financially unsound.
To-day it is worth, lock, stock, and barrel, close on two hundred
thousand. When, however, I say that Australia is not sound,
despite the stupid mob-catching political cries about our great
future, our great natural resources, and all the other greats, I
merely state a common, but unappreciated, fact. When John Bull
does wake up, he will even burn his cheque-book, so that he will
not succumb to the temptation to keep a poor relation. And then
Atlas will withstand the almighty shock if, and if only, it has a
reserve of strength."

"Are you not now a little pessimistic?"

"Everyone says I am," Smythe grumbled. "Even my principals
accuse me of pessimism. I may be getting too old for my job.
Time will judge. Between friends, it is a pity Frank didn't marry
an Australian bushwoman. It is a darn pity he didn't marry Ann
Shelley. However, in a roundabout way, I am telling Mayne to cut
his cloth with the scissors which fit his pocket. The recent rain
might mean the end of a dry period, or the beginning of a longer
one. By the way, did you know that Thuringah fellow, Allwise or
Alldyce Cameron, has come into a fortune?"

"No. I haven't seen him since before Christmas."

"He has. His uncle, the shipping man, slipped his anchor and left him a quarter of a million. Lucky devil! I had an uncle who died worth a hundred thousand, and he left it to a Dogs' Home or something. Money! Everyone has –"

"Ah!" Feng Ching-wei remembered Cameron holding Mayne's wife in his arms. Surely now he would leave Australia for good to claim his fortune?

CHAPTER XI

LABOUR

1

ON their return to Atlas the Maynes were accompanied by a visiting English family whom they had met in Melbourne. There was Sir William Vaux-Middleton, knight: short, pompous, red-faced, monocled, having the appearance of the traditional retired Indian Army Colonel, but actually a London bank director. There was Lady Vaux-Middleton: fair, fat, and forty-five, placid, and, on the surface, subdued; whilst Ursula and Freda Vaux-Middleton were smart young women of twenty-four and twenty-five, who invariably dressed exactly alike. The young ladies were always charmed by the romantic Colonials reputed to be rich, and at all times blissfully unconscious of those Australians who were not rich. Sir William talked incessantly of Australia's natural resources, which appeared strange in a banking man; whilst his wife said, over and over again: "Yes, father; no, father"; and from long practice ably kept from her features, but not from her eyes, the laughter supplied to her soul by her husband and her two daughters.

Feng Ching-wei, who charmed the daughters and pacified the father, quickly penetrated the mother's armour, discovered her delightful sense of humour, and thoroughly enjoyed the visitors' three weeks stay at Atlas. The twenty points of rain which fell early in March had lifted the depression created by a long, dry, and hot summer, and the resources of Atlas were organised to provide the Vaux-Middletons with unflagging pleasure. There occurred only one regrettable incident, and that was the meeting

of the Vaux-Middletons with Ten Pot Dick, a meeting which, in
the absence of Feng, only Lady Vaux-Middleton appreciated to
the full.

Ten Pot Dick was so named by reason of his habit of years
which asserted itself every time he reached Menindee after a long
sojourn in the bush. Never had he been known to deviate one inch
from the straight line between the vehicle that deposited him at
the township and the bar of the nearest of the three hotels. Not
once had he altered his demand for ten tankards of beer – known
as pots – to be set down in a row before him to be consumed one
after another with amazing speed – in order, so he was careful to
explain, to banish from his throat the alkaloids and other
impurities in the surface-water on which he had been living.

He was one of those men who scorn to expend time and money
on personal appearance. If he shaved at all, no one ever saw him
clean-shaven. His whiskers seemed to have stopped growth after
about seven days, and those grey whiskers were so sparse, and
stuck out from the flesh so stiffly, that they were not like ordinary
whiskers. In age he might have been fifty, or possibly seventy. No
one knew, since he himself did not know his age.

At this time he was feeding three thousand ewes with a two-
ounce ration of maize. The maize was carted by truck and
dumped at his camp five miles up the river, and every morning he
set off with the day's supply loaded on a dray drawn by one
horse.

Mayne drove the Vaux-Middletons out to see the hand-feeding
of the best of his breeding ewes the third or fourth morning of
their sojourn at Atlas. It was a warm autumn day, and beneath the
trees tiny grass shoots struggled to defy the burning sun.

Two miles from the homestead they were met by four
thousand sheep that were awaiting the arrival of the feed-truck.
They had become used to being fed regularly on a particular area
of clay-pan country by men tipping from the back of a slowly
driven truck a stream of maize, and on hearing and seeing the
approach of the car rushed towards it with joyful baas. Mayne
slowed up before the oncoming flock and began to sound the
klaxon, but the noise of the horn only swelled the uproarious
welcome.

Normally this flock of sheep would have rushed wildly away

at the sound of a horn and at sight of a car, but artificial feeding had very quickly tamed them to the docility of domestic cats. They crowded in a compact mass about the halted car, blaring forth their demand for food, refusing to budge, voicing protest at delay, every one of the four thousand heads turned directly to the car.

The ladies, though set coughing by the fine grey dust of the river flat, yet gurgled their delight. Sir William began to discuss the rise in recent years of the value of Australia's wool clip, and continued his speech, despite the fact that if he had shouted the words at the top of his voice no human ear could have heard him. In low gear Mayne sent the car very slowly through the press, gently pushing a way, until he at last managed to win clear, whereupon for the first hundred yards four thousand sheep chased the car protestingly.

His real reason for taking his guests to see the sheep in charge of Ten Pot Dick was that this flock was the cream of his breeding ewes. Arrived at Ten Pot Dick's camp, the absence of horse and dray denoted that the sheep-feeder had started on his daily trip to the paddock that enclosed the flock; and, having proceeded some four miles west of the river, they found Ten Pot Dick standing over a bag of maize on the dray, and permitting a stream of grain to fall to the ground behind, whilst the old horse trudged on between two ramparts of low sand-dunes.

The car was stopped, and Mayne proceeded to explain that, since the natural food was almost all swept away by the winds of summer, and since the heat had burned off the slight growth of new feed brought up by the recent rain, either maize or lucerne was given in this way to help repair the lack. The Vaux-Middletons could not see anything at all on the country for the sheep to eat, and wondered how well two ounces of maize daily kept the sheep alive. Sir William asked how much per day per thousand sheep the hand feeding cost, and was informed that even if the cost eventually equalled the value of the sheep by the time the dry spell ended, it was money wisely spent; for otherwise the losses at the end of the dry spell would probably take several years to make good by breeding, whilst making good the losses by purchase would be almost impossible, since all would be buyers and no one a seller.

2

TEN POT DICK had laid a ribbon of maize almost half a mile long, finishing the ribbon by encircling the station car and shouting at his horse to stop when but thirty yards distant. The Misses Vaux-Middleton affected not to observe the man clambering down from the dray to the ground, when was revealed a large patch of red flannelette partly covering the seat of his blue dungaree trousers. Lady Vaux-Middleton shook visibly, but no tell-tale smile irradiated her maternal and plebeian features.

On reaching the ground Ten Pot Dick struck a match on that strikingly coloured patch, lit his pipe, and shuffled towards the car, his watery eyes gleaming dully, a sheepish grin fractionally widening the space between each dirty grey bristle. With the nonchalance of long habit he expectorated, reached the car, placed one foot on the running-board and his bare and hairy forearm on the front door; proceeding then to speak to his employer, he drew noisily at his ill-favoured pipe across the stern and haughty front of Sir William.

"Good day-ee, Mr. Mayne!" was his drawled greeting. "Weather keepin' 'ot late this year."

"Morning, Dick!" replied Mayne, oblivious of the horror created in the breasts of Sir William and his daughters. "Where are the sheep this morning?"

Ten Pot Dick chuckled and again expectorated. "I gotta trick the cows," he explained with a casual glance at the frozen faces of the others, a glance that unashamedly admitted them to his confidence. "You see, it's like this 'ere. I feeds 'em 'ere one day, and over beyant another day, and away back for a change the next day. I got 'em that flummaxed that they don't know where I'm gonna feed next. You see, if they spots me coming, they crowds around and don't give old Wall-eye a chance to move 'is feet."

"But if they don't know where you lay out the feed, Dick they might very probably miss it altogether. That won't do," Mayne objected.

For the third time Ten Pot Dick expectorated, a long, thin, nicotine-coloured stream. Once more he lit his pipe and enveloped Sir William in a cloud of smoke from tobacco that must have been entirely a brand of his own. It was too much for the bank director, who smoked Triple-Duplex Havanas, and between coughs he muttered his intention of alighting and stretching his legs. But either Ten Pot Dick did not hear Sir William, or he was obstinately decided to expound his methods of "tricking the cows" before he budged, for he made no effort to move from his drooping position over the door.

Still chuckling, he said: "That's all right, Mr. Mayne. Don't you worry. They gits their tucker regular; leave it ter me. They're never that far away they can't hear me a-calling of 'em. You watch."

He returned to his cart and, again exhibiting the flannelette patch, clambered aboard with a hoarse injunction to the horse to stand still. Sir William descended from the car with a slight show of haste, and his lead was accepted by his daughters, who fanned themselves with three-inch squares of lace-edged cambric. Mayne, whose thoughts were centred on his sheep, failed to notice Sir William's irritation, or the faint indignation apparent in two pairs of blue eyes. Neither did he observe Lady Vaux-Middleton's ample bosom shaking as a rocked jelly. The sheep-feeder, standing up on the dray, cupped his hands and roared with extraordinary volume:

"Ya, ho-ee! ya, ho-ee! Pea-nuts! pea-nuts! Ya, ho-ee! Pea-nuts! Roast pea-nuts! Salt and peppah! Ya, ho-ee!"

For a while he kept still in an exaggerated attitude of listening. Then abruptly he turned towards the astonished visitors and grinned triumphantly, a grin that spoke as loudly as his pea-nut call, "I told you so."

Came to the Vaux-Middletons a low, far-off rumble of sound rapidly rising to a dull hum, which burst into a roar when five thousand ewes hurtled over the crest of a sand-dune and raced down to the ribbon of maize with a blare of baaings.

The dust rose straight into the air, churned and scattered by twenty thousand hoofs. Light red in colour, as fine as flour, it swirled about the Vaux-Middletons, the car, and blotted out Ten Pot Dick, until he appeared coming through it as some wonderful object appearing on a developing photographic plate. Almost at once the baaings ceased, the sound to be replaced by one most resembling a thousand machine-guns in action a mile distant – a sound caused by five thousand sets of teeth cracking maize grains.

Slowly the dust drifted southward. Mayne, still oblivious of his discomfort, still thinking of his sheep – for sheep were his world and the dust but a floating speck in it – idly watched Ten Pot Dick standing near, his hat half-filled with maize. No one, apparently, saw one ewe detach itself from the long double line of sheep marking the corn stream, and rush towards the group standing by the car.

It was unfortunate that Sir William was the unit farthest from the group, and as unfortunate that the ewe was no respecter of persons. It butted the unsuspecting Sir William, sent him sprawling on his hands and knees, and began determinedly to nuzzle the Birthday Knight's expensive Panama hat.

"Hey! Wot cher doing of?" shouted Ten Pot Dick, and Sir William thought that the question was addressed to him. The voice differentiated the humans in the mind of the sheep, which rushed on the feeder, who permitted it to eat the grain in his hat. "She's a funny cuss, she is. She persists in eatin' 'er tucker outer me 'at."

The man's voice evinced affection and pride. He saw no humour in Sir William's wild scramble to his feet and quick stoop to snatch up his ruined panama.

Of them all only Lady Vaux-Middleton fully appreciated the spectacle, and doubly appreciated her husband's remarks addressed to a genuinely astonished Ten Pot Dick. She choked when Ten Pot Dick said aggrievedly: "Strike me dead! 'Ow was I ter know Little Mary was gonna bunt you?"

It took Frank Mayne the whole of the drive home to banish Sir William's ill-humour. More than once during the drive the Misses Vaux-Middleton regarded their mother with suspicion.

3

A few days after the departure of the Vaux-Middletons the station car and the truck were dispatched to Mildura on the Victorian border to bring to Atlas half a dozen people the Maynes had met in New Zealand, together with their luggage. This party was timed to stay two weeks, and, unlike the Vaux-Middletons, the members of it were of that peculiarly obnoxious Australian monied class which considers a high falsetto voice and ridiculous emphasis on certain words are the hall-mark of English culture. Mayne was irritated almost beyond bearing, and Feng, who kept aloof with the excuse of much work, noticed that Ethel Mayne's speech became more affected than usual. Other parties were to follow, and it was borne in on Feng Ching-wei that Ethel Mayne had planned relays of visitors throughout the autumn and the coming winter, and he wondered if this plan was evolved to defeat nostalgia, or something more subtle and consequently more dangerous – the approaches of Alldyce Cameron.

During the remainder of March no rain fell. Not unduly worried, Mayne proceeded to nurse his giant holding back to the prosperity indicated by the rain that had fallen early in the month. He schemed, directed, sometimes laboured, a secret gladness in his soul that once again he was home, again overlord of his ancestral kingdom. He felt once more a whole man now that this earth and those tens of thousands of animals were within sight of his eager eyes. Ethel could have her jarring visitors. To him remained the freedom and the quiet peace of the real Atlas.

Throughout the first half of April, each day warm, each night cool and calm, he and the rugged MacDougall inspected all the back country of Atlas. In his overseer Mayne had implicit trust, and between them they reached decisions to be put in force immediately winter vigorously tweaked the tail of summer. For fourteen days, using an old Ford truck on which were carried water and rations and swags, guns and two kangaroo dogs, those two had roamed the vast paddocks, roughing it almost as severely as did Tom Mace when he was rabbiting, cooking their own food, shooting kangaroo, a steak of which grilled on a wood fire was Mayne's secret delight, and camping wherever they might be when the sun set.

The morning he left Forest Hill, the out-station, for the Atlas homestead, the sky indicated a coming weather disturbance. Mrs. MacDougall, very large, very jovial, her face weather-beaten and her accent Scottish, herself saw to it that his tucker-box was filled with her good cooking, and safely stowed on the floor of his car, and that the canvas water-bag, hung from the spare tyre, was also full. With her husband she accompanied him to the waiting machine. They had been at Forest Hill eight years, and he had come to regard the great-hearted couple with affection.

"Wind!" MacDougall said, looking up at the sky.

"Yes, and perhaps rain, Mac."

"Every drop a pound to the squatter, a shilling to the overseer, and a penny to the station-hand," Mrs. MacDougall said with a deep laugh.

"You will be right, Mrs. MacDougall, bar the overseer and the station-hand, who will get respectively more than the shilling and the penny. Well, *au revoir*, and thank you, Mrs. MacDougall!"

He left Forest Hill at nine o'clock. The sun, now rising in the north-east and setting in the north-west, already glowed with uncomfortable heat through a high, almost invisible haze which covered the sky with a ghostly white veil. Without doubt that haze presaged the coming of wind and rain, rain and wind that would banish the long summer and introduce the splendid invigorating winter.

Nevertheless, he drove at an easy twenty-five miles an hour. There was plenty of time. Feng did not require his immediate presence on any important matter, and Ethel would be occupied with her new sets of guests. He sighed, remembering the MacDougalls, eighteen years married, and blessed with three children all away at school; remembered, too, the little sly glances of affection he had seen so often pass between them.

For two miles the car descended the winding track twisting among the low hills, presently to come out on the gently undulating country, plain chiefly, excellent grass-lands, but bare now save for the almost invisible green shoots thrusting upwards from the tussock-grass roots and mutely crying for rain.

Reaching Mulga Flat about ten o'clock, he was received by the senior of the two riders stationed there, examined the well, decided to send a man to renew some of the white-ant-riddled timber, and obtained the riders' mail and ration list.

"It seems ter me," the rider drawled in careless speech, "that that crook heat-wave we 'ad in February killed all the rabbits, and now that the foxes ain't got too much tucker they're going to play up with the coming lambs."

"Yes, Archie. That is what Mr. MacDougall thinks. Any of the lambs appearing yet?"

"Nope."

When Mayne left Mulga Flat the wind was noticeably

freshening. It came from the east of north in a peculiarly steady pressure, recalling to Mayne's mind similar conditions in other Aprils and other Mays which had been followed by abundance of rain.

Whilst he drove eastward his speed countered the wind force, the machine making hardly any air disturbance. The flies, able to keep pace with him, tried to drown themselves in his eyes and crawl into his ears with irritating persistence. Midway between Mulga Flat and White Well he left the main track and travelled northward for fifteen miles to a hut near a dam named Karl's Dam, after the contractor who had created it. Here he found Tom Mace who, when his living at rabbit-trapping was destroyed by the first heat-wave, had applied for and was given a job. Here he was managing the petrol-engine that fed drinking water from the fenced-in dam to receiving tanks that fed drinking troughs in two paddocks.

"Well, Tom, how are things going here?" Mayne asked the highly strung, alert Englishman.

"Aw – all right, Mr. Mayne. Bit of a change from the rabbiting. I've made up for a lot of lost sleep."

"The money is not so good though, is it?"

"N-no. But the work is not so hard," Mace pointed out, from an innate sense of fairness.

"How are the foxes?" was Mayne's next question.

Mace offered a suggestion. "Let's go along to the troughs. The sheep haven't been to water since last night. We'll see the tracks."

Together they left the hut, passing the iron shed that housed the engine, then the dam, and so to one, the nearer, of the two long lines of troughing. They returned by skirting the sheet of water in the dam, and everywhere they cared to look they saw on the ground countless impressions of fox-pads not yet obliterated by the rising wind, tracks so numerous that it was as though during the night the foxes had come to drink in a close flock, like sheep.

"All the sheep drinking regularly, Tom?"

"Y-yes, Mr. Mayne. Harry says that the last rain wasn't heavy enough to fill the gilgie holes in these north paddocks."

"Ah! Of course! The country here is too porous to hold surface water. The foxes coming here proves that. What about you dealing with them?"

Mace considered. Then: "Well, it's a bit early," he said. "The fur won't be fit for the market till next month."

Pinching his chin with forefinger and thumb, it was Mayne's turn to consider. He recognised this fox menace created by a succession of good years. The good years had enabled the rabbits to breed with their astonishing fecundity. Because the rabbits provided quickly and easily won food for foxes and eagles, both eagles and foxes in their turn had bred rapidly. The eagles were a degree less to be feared than the foxes. Over all Atlas he had seen fox-tracks. It was the eternal cycle, Nature's adjustment of the scales. First the good years with their abundant gift of life, then the bad years when Life is reaped by Death, to be followed by the ousting of Death by Life, and so on and on.

"Well, Tom, the foxes must be dealt with," Mayne decided, thinking of his sheep. "What about you starting operations right away if I pay you station wages and tucker and give you a scalp bonus of half a crown, till the fur comes in and you can skin for the market?"

For yet a further spell Mace considered. The proffered terms were most generous. Yet, for all that, his objection was the legitimate objection of every trapper. It was to him almost criminal to kill a fox out of season, as it were, before its pelt had grown to prime.

Quite suddenly he appreciated his employer's viewpoint. "All right, Mr. Mayne."

Mayne smiled a little grimly. He, too, appreciated Mace's viewpoint. "Very well, Tom," he said. "I'll send a man out to relieve you to-morrow." They walked over to the car. "Shall I mention to Eva that you will be in to-morrow night?"

Mace flushed scarlet.

When in the car, the engine running, Mayne spoke again.

"You stick to me, Tom, and you'll discover that I'll stick to you," he said seriously. "When this dry spell is definitely broken, if one of the married couples' houses is not vacant, I'll build you a house near the homestead."

Again Mace flushed scarlet. "Th-thanks, Mr. Mayne!" he managed to say.

4

When Frank Mayne again reached the east-west track the wind was rising to a gale. Maintaining its steady, even pressure, it swept up the surface dust, laying over the ground a foot-thick reddish blanket. The sun, now almost at its zenith, shed surprising heat, heat that the wind did not temper, for the wind itself was hot against the driver's face.

It was two o'clock when Mayne reached White Well, twenty miles out from the Atlas homestead, and experience had convinced him that White Well was a most unpleasant place during a windstorm. The two corrugated-iron buildings, the near-by well and windmill, and the sheep-yards in the distance formed the centre of a circular plain rimmed by sand-dunes that rose forty feet above it, like a line of huge whales cast up along the shore. Now the plain was as bare of herbage as the summits of the dunes, and lay beneath a dust pall varying from six to sixty feet in thickness.

Imperceptibly the wind moved to due north, its velocity increasing, its temperature unpleasantly hot. It hissed through and thrashed the branches of the solitary half-century-old pepper tree that grew beside the living hut, and, sweeping between that hut and the kitchen dining hut, put a face of pure sand on the low wall beyond the buildings. A dozen hens crouched in the shelter of a roughly made dog-kennel, whilst the dog, with sand-rimmed eyes, looked out from its interior, too uncomfortable and wretched to bark.

Mayne, having telephoned the solitary rider stationed here to remain in to meet him, descended from the car and was almost forced into a run by the wind whilst making for the dining-kitchen door. It was latched, opened outward, fought to keep shut, slammed shut when Mayne slipped through. Within the dim, dust-filled interior he found Fred Lowe, the youthful, lithe, crack stockman of Atlas.

"Phew! What a day, Fred!" he said, gasping.

"Ya-as. It's a hell of a day all right, Mr. Mayne," the rider agreed, having now laid aside a Nat Gould novel, putting billets of wood under the swinging boiler in the great open hearth. "An' this is a hell of a place to be in on a hell of a day too."

Dark eyes peered at Mayne through the murk. A wispy black moustache emphasized the whiteness of perfect teeth when the man grinned at his employer with unconquered cheerfulness.

"It is not a nice day, certainly," Mayne said. "But if the wind brings rain we shall soon forget the dust and heat and flies. While you are making a drink of tea, I'll telephone the homestead."

Two minutes later he was talking to Feng Ching-wei from the instrument in the living hut.

"It is blowing big guns out here, Feng," he said with voice raised to overcome the rattle of the roof sheets. "But it looks mighty like rain. Two inches now would assure a good season and end our worries, eh? Yes. Ah, well, I'll be in in an hour or so. Put me through to Ethel, will you?"

He heard his wife's voice a few seconds later. "Hallo, Frank!" she said in her calm, cold manner.

"I'll be home about four o'clock, sweetheart," he told her cheerfully. "It's a beast of a day, but let us hope it will end in a good rain. How are all the people?"

"All locked up," Ethel replied. "Mr. Wilkins and Miss Jefferson and the two Rawlings are playing bridge in the drawing-room. The others are in their rooms resting, but we have to have every door and window shut, and consequently the heat is horrible. Even here in the house the air is full of sand and everything is coated with dust. Really, Frank, this Australia of yours is a terrible country. I had no idea we'd have this dust and heat at this time of the year, or I would not have asked these people to come. It is most unfair to subject them to such hardship."

"Well, well," he said soothingly, "the wind will die down by sunset, and it'll then become cooler. Anyway, you are really lucky. This hut is surrounded by sand-hills, and inside it is almost as sand-fogged as it is outside."

"That makes it no better here," Ethel told him, a trace of tartness in her carefully modulated voice.

Her emphasis on the word "no" irritated her husband. "I'll be home about four. Keep smiling till I get in, old thing. *Au revoir*!"

Mayne waited for a return "*au revoir* ", but heard only the click of Ethel's instrument being replaced on its hook. He sighed, and for a moment gazed with unseeing eyes at Fred Lowe's bunk, its calico covering deeply reddened with sand. For weeks small faint voices had been striving to command his attention, and, whilst he stood there in the red murk, with every sheet of iron in the building rattling beneath the vicious wind, one voice did make itself distinctly heard.

The voice told him that his wife hated Atlas.

Regret lasted fully a minute, to be followed by anger. Memory recalled scenes and conversations between them before they were married. He remembered how careful he had been to describe to her the several bad points that were so much outweighed, to him, by the good points of the climate of Central Australia. He had been so careful, so meticulously honest in describing the disadvantages of living so far from civilisation. But never had she made any demur, or weakened in her determination to accept him as her husband. And now, having married him, having accepted Atlas as her home, the least she could do was cheerfully to make the best of things.

A little tight-lipped, he rejoined Fred Lowe. The young man was not so good a cook as he was a horseman. The slab of cake he produced from a calico bag was hard and leaden. There was tinned milk in lieu of cow's milk, and whilst he stirred his tea Mayne remembered the hamper so carefully packed by Mrs. MacDougall.

"Slip out to the car, Fred, and bring in that box of tucker you'll find on the back seat," he requested. "And, Fred, let the dog loose and bring it in here. Out in the flying sand it can hardly breathe."

Mayne shared the contents of the luncheon hamper with his rider, and whilst they ate the thought occurred to Mayne how grossly unfair it was that he should enjoy the comforts of life merely because he was begotten by Old Man Mayne, and his men should exist in the conditions he found here at White Well. Was it any wonder that the bush was rapidly being emptied of bushmen, who were coming to realise the absurdity of living, as Fred Lowe was living, almost as primitively as the aboriginals, starved of ambition, the chance of marriage and winning a home almost as remote as winning a prize in a sweepstake?

"Ole Westmacott met up with a bit of trouble," Fred was drawling whilst lounging at the table, minus cloth and smeared with sand particles.

"Oh!"

"Ya-as. Met him yesterday along his boundary. 'Member young Harry, helped by nig, taking twenty hundred wethers down to the Victorian roads last year?"

"Yes. Westmacott told me."

"Appears the old man gave him legal authority to sell at ten shillings a knob. Young Harry gets the sheep down to Swan Hill. Leaves Sampson, the nig, with the sheep whiles he goes into town for a spree. Falls in with a barmaid who sools a bloke on to him to sell at four bob a knob. Tells young Harry she'll go to Melbourne with him on the cheque. And young Harry bites. The bloke gets 'em at four bob a knob, and gives the tart a diamond ring for doing her work in the deal. Whiles young Harry was hanging about for the barmaid to go off to Melbourne with him, he loses all the four hundred quid gambling."

"Silly young ass!" Mayne said.

"Ya-as. As the old man said to me, if young Harry 'ad come home, a tongue-lashin' was all he'd have got. There was no need to drown himself in the Murray."

"Drown himself!" Mayne echoed, startled into bolt uprightness. "Ya-as. It's knocked the old bloke rotten. He says the old lady does nothink but screech."

"Good God! That's dreadful. I didn't know. When did Westmacott hear?"

"Police told 'im about it yesterday."

Shocked into silence, Frank Mayne thought of the Westmacotts and of their long, hard struggle on a selection which, like almost every pastoral selection, was too small in area to support a family through bad years that came with the inevitability of Fate. There were Sanders and Wills on his south boundary, both now facing ruin. Sanders had asked for employment on Atlas, intending to leave his two daughters to look after his flock, but Mayne had sufficient men for his needs. He felt he could not put off a man to give Sanders a job, because the man would work for Atlas in the good years when Sanders would not.

Yes, the small men were already becoming desperate. If the coming winter did not prove to be marked with good falls of rain, their case would be hopeless.

Telling Lowe not to come out to the car, Mayne battled with the wind to reach it, started the engine, and drove slowly across the small plain, instinct assisting him to keep to the track, now wiped from vision by the moving sand. He could not see the surrounding sand-dunes until he arrived, by good luck, at the point where the track passed through them, and then he dared not look toward those on his windward side. He knew that their summits smoked as the stacks of battleships, and that every ten minutes their shapes were completely changing. The sand-grains flayed his left cheek, compelling him to keep closed his left eye. He could have fastened the car's side-curtains, but considered that they would be torn away. The car was buffeted so that it rocked.

The sun appeared now as a huge ball of blood. The scrub-trees he passed screamed in torture, their branches thrashing wildly. Gradually the sand fog became deeper red in colour as it became more dense. The wind veered to the north-west and blew harder. Surely rain was behind that wind!

He had gone but four miles from White Well when he decided that until the wind dropped he could go no farther. Arriving at an open clay-pan covered space, he swung the car round, so that its back faced the wind, and pulled up. When he got out and stood on the ground, he could hear the water in the radiator boiling, the effect of the labour of the engine. Putting out his hand gently to unscrew the cap, two-inch blue electrical sparks flashed from each of his fingers to the metal cap. Sand grains and wind had stored in the metal parts of the machine electric static. When he was climbing on the back seat preparatory to covering himself with a rug, a spark from the metal hood rod gave him a second shock.

With his head enveloped in a rug he sat inside the car for hours – till the sun went down and the wind fell to a light breeze coming from the south. And the sky, when the sand wrack thinned, he saw to be quite clear of clouds.

CHAPTER XII

THE DOOMED

1

THE western sky was pink. The air was cold and still, and vibrated with the harsh cries of many galahs returning from a dam, which they had visited for a drink, to the gum trees beside a dry creek wherein they roosted.

On the bank of the dam sat Tom Mace, reflectively smoking a cigarette, and wondering how many foxes he would secure that night and skin on the morrow. Beside him was set a large, roughly made wooden tray, covered with small pieces of raw meat sprinkled with powdered strychnine crystals. Near the tray lay a split-open sheep's head to which was attached a length of rope.

His activities at this time were producing amazing results. Undoubtedly his success in catching foxes, like his success in rabbit-trapping, was based less on downright slavish labour, although this aspect was by no means unimportant, than on a paradoxical love of all wild things – a love that demanded and received an intensive study of the habits of the animals he slew.

It is remarkable that when the mating season starts foxes will not take a poisoned bait, whether of meat, fish, or butter. Obviously, Mace thought, they must eat something. Inquiries of old hands and other trappers failed to produce the solution of this mystery, a failure that put an end to fox-trapping at a period when fox pelts are at their best. Undeterred by failure, he held a post-mortem examination on a fox he had caught in a dingo trap, which revealed the fact that Reynard was subsisting on centipedes, scorpions, and trapdoor spiders.

His surprising catches this winter rested also on one other thing. During the three months of his foxing operations on Atlas it rained but once, and then only seven points. The absence of surface-water compelled the foxes, with the sheep, to visit the comparatively few dams and wells. They came to Mace, instead of his being compelled to seek out their favourite natural watering-places.

When the last lingering watchful crow had followed the last galah flock to the distant gum trees, Tom Mace dragged the sheep's head at the end of the rope completely round the dam outside the mullock embankment. The mark on the ground made by the passage of the head was distinct, but the darkness was fast making it hard for him to follow when over the mark he laid a complete line of poisoned baits about two feet apart.

His preparations now complete, he walked the few hundred yards to his truck, parked beneath a wattle-tree, against which was his camp. On the fire he threw thick dead timber, and then proceeded scrupulously to wash his hands clean of possible poison crystals, as well as to scrub his finger-nails. Later, when the leaping flames made the walls of night draw close about the camp, he grilled mutton chops on a netted wire grid, and ate them with hearty relish to the accompaniment of buttered damper, for now winter was come the luxury of butter was made possible.

Not an insect of any kind moved over the surface of the windswept, sand-ribbed ground. It was too cold to sleep on his camp-stretcher, and he scorned to erect the tent. Unrolling a mattress of straw, he laid on it his blankets, and at that end nearest the fire set his pillow so that when he lay down the fire provided ample light.

Drawing at a cigarette, the stars claimed his idle attention. Familiar with that celestial jeweller's show-window, recognising all, yet able to name but a few of those marvellous, distant worlds, Mace, as he always did, dreamed of Eva and the now rapidly approaching time when he could offer her a home of her own.

Already this season he had secured more than six hundred foxes, four hundred of which he had skinned and for each pelt would receive something like eight shillings. Whereas the rabbits had provided grains of gold, the foxes now were providing small gold nuggets. The total of his banking account already reached three hundred pounds, and before the mating season put a stop to his foxing activities he hoped to increase it by another hundred at least.

Eva! Pretty, trusting, innocent Eva! She was now kept constantly busy by Ethel Mayne's succession of house parties.

She saw the arrival of a real *chef* from Sydney, a butler from Melbourne, a chauffeur to drive Ethel's single-seater, a boots, and a kitchen help, in addition to three extra maids from Broken Hill. The butler was young and good looking. There were moments when Tom Mace feared that butler, and at the same time lashed himself for doubting his Eva.

Lying on his blankets, the "quok-quoks" of quarrelling foxes came to him from the direction of the dam, and sometimes a fox's barked "whorl-whorl" or softer "quok-quok" from an animal coming from far to drink.

Early Mace turned in. Once – at two o'clock – he was aroused by the cold to replenish the fire with wood. Not trusting his own time sense, his alarm-clock roused him at half-past six, and, until the day gave requisite light, he ate a little breakfast and smoked cigarettes.

When the coming day had lit the sky, yet before the darkness had lifted from the earth, he carried a dozen chaff-bags and an empty tin to the place where his poison-trail began and ended. There he waited, beating the cold out of his hands by slapping them against his legs. Overhead a crow flew with swishing wings and a mocking "caw-aw", determined to be early and to steal a feast – if possible, to alight on a dead fox and tear its pelt with its beak.

The light came slowly. Carrying the tin and several of the bags, Mace began to walk over the trail to retrieve the baits not taken by the foxes, which, if left, might months later constitute a menace to stockmen's dogs. Now it became a race between the crows and himself. He found but seven of the estimated two hundred baits. The light, strong and revealing, showed him the bright, reddish brown bodies of foxes; some lying close beside the trail, some on the dam banks, some away out on the clear, smooth sand-patches. At a jog-trot he gathered fox to fox, and covered them with the chaff-bags to defy the crows, and whilst doing so he counted his catch. Thirty-four were easily gathered. He found five at the edge of the water in the dam where, the poison eating at their vitals, they had gone to drink – and to die the sooner. Hurrying in ever widening circles round the dam, he found fox after fox, some hidden in the inequalities of the ground. For three hours he quested, as far distant as half a mile from the trail. Small knots of crows, settled on red sand like ink-drops on red blotting-paper, revealed to him the position of yet other foxes, and to those he raced to rescue the precious pelts. Lastly he looked to the crows to find for him any remaining carcasses he had missed.

By ten o'clock he decided he had found all he was likely to find. They numbered sixty-one. It was June. The pelts, long and silky to the touch, would average in the Sydney fur market eleven shillings.

For the rest of that day he was occupied in carefully skinning his catch. Although he ran a poisoned trail that night, he secured only eight the following morning. The skins he tacked with short pieces of wire to hard clay-pan country to dry, and covered them with bags for protection against the crows and eagles till he should return for them from a night's poisoning at another dam or well.

The fur fever burned in Mace more fiercely than could the gold fever. He had no thought but of money and Eva.

2

TO Frank Mayne his home had become a populous hotel in which he felt himself to be an intruder. The incessant clamour, the rushings about, the excursions, he did, however, emphatically refuse to allow to distract him from his work, and for many days at oft-repeated periods he escaped to the peaceful solitudes, working with the hands or accompanying MacDougall.

He denied his wife nothing.

July came in, dull and cold, trying to rain, yet the threat of rain a mockery in face of the cold south wind. Mayne was riding home across a river paddock late one afternoon whilst small black puff-clouds passed slowly eastward beneath the higher dun-coloured unbroken cloud-mass. He rode with a light heart, because this day the wind blew fitfully from the north, which indicated rain.

But, when two miles from the homestead, he saw that which contracted his brows. He was crossing grey river flats, and abruptly was met by a bunch of very young lambs which had been sheltering in the lee of a newly fallen tree-branch. Bleating pitifully, seeming as lost children in the woods, they ran to meet him, and, when he reined in his horse, stood looking up at him still bleating woefully, little flanks tucked inwards with hunger, weak legs trembling. The sight of them weighted his heart with sadness.

For he knew why these lambs were there, far from the flock of mothers – knew they were doomed to die, prey of the eagles, of the foxes remaining from Mace's hauls, and the crows. In every paddock now occupied by ewes and lambs, there would be other abandoned lambs, tens and twenties together, totalling in all many hundreds.

They were the outcasts, the Ishmaels, the abandoned of mothers who had not sufficient milk for twins. The lack of green feed kept the supply of milk very low, and the ewes with twins knew that the supply of their bodies was sufficient to nourish one only of the twins. Those mothers, therefore, had hunted away from the udder the condemned, who, weakening from lack of nourishment, were left behind by the flock, thereafter to gather into small parties, pitifully weak and frightened, watched by the insatiable crows in neighbouring trees and the giant eagles circling low in the sky, to be attacked immediately they lay down and devoured alive.

Mayne counted twenty-two lambs in that party, and passed a second gathering of deserted lambs numbering eleven before he reached the stockyards, when he unsaddled and freed his horse. With his face cast in thoughtful lines he hesitated outside the garden gate, heard the high treble of a woman's voice, sighed, and turned back to the office.

"Have you completed that rough half-yearly balance-sheet I asked for, Barlow?" he said to the old accountant.

"I am working at it now, Mr. Mayne. I will have it ready in twenty minutes or so."

Mayne nodded and, before seating himself at his desk, took from a wall-hook the weather records for that year. Moodily he filled his pipe, turned a sheet, lit his pipe, and fell to studying the sheet devoted to the past month of June.

The total rainfall had been seventeen points. Nine points had fallen on the twelfth, and eight points on the thirteenth. Three days had been overcast and two cloudy. Twenty-five days in this month, a month preceding mid-winter, had been cloudless. Turning back this sheet, he studied that for May. The rain had been nil. Two days had been cloudy, twenty-nine cloudless.

"God! What a season!"

"I beg your pardon, Mr. Mayne?" inquired Barlow politely.

With bitterness Mayne laughed. "I was not aware I spoke my thoughts aloud," he said. "I was thinking what a devil of a dry winter we have had, so far."

"It certainly has been very bad," Barlow agreed, and again attacked his masses of figures.

Mayne rang up Forest Hill. "That you, Mac? How's the weather looking out your way?"

"Good. Very good. It might rain."

"It is not raining yet?"

"No – worse luck," MacDougall replied regretfully. "Anyway, it mightn't rain here first. The disturbance appears to be working directly south, and if so, it will begin to rain at both ends of Atlas at the same time."

"The ewes are deserting one of their twin lambs, Mac. I came across two deserted bunches this afternoon."

MacDougall's voice came in a low growl. "I've been expecting that. If only we had had half an inch of rain in April, it would have prevented the sun burning off the green shoots started by that March rain. It's a pity, because even if it rains to-night it won't save the abandoned lambs."

"It will strengthen the others, though, and the sheep in time for shearing," Mayne pointed out. "We want about three inches."

"Let's hope we'll get it," MacDougall grunted. "When do we start lamb-marking?"

Mayne considered, his gaze on a calendar in a silver frame on the desk before him. "Better make it Monday, July 21st," he said slowly. "Lamb-marking will occupy us only a fortnight this year, by the look of things. And if it does rain to-night there will be time for the ground to dry a bit. So long! I'll ring up again about eight."

3

WITH Barlow's rough balance-sheet in his hand, Frank Mayne left the office and walked along to Feng's bungalow. From Government House there now came the sound of gramophone music. His wife and her guests would be lounging in the drawing-room, drinking afternoon tea, careless of time and money,

149

oblivious of the opening phase of the battle with drought, unaware of the worry eating into his brain, the awareness of which would have astonished them. They thought Atlas to be a perpetual gold-mine.

With the freedom of an old friend, he walked straight into Feng's sitting-room-studio, where he found Feng seated before a leaping fire, reading a novel and sipping tea.

"Going to rain, Frank?" asked the Australian Chinaman, pulling an easy chair to the fire for his visitor.

"May do – hope so, Feng," was Mayne's view when he slumped into the proffered chair. "That buttered toast smells good."

"Mary will bring you some," Feng said in his quiet, restful tone of voice, and having rung for Mary O'Doyle, that woman of parts appeared. "Mary, tea and toast for Mr. Mayne, please."

"Shure! An' it's a day for toast and tay," Mary said warmly, and ambled away.

"You look worried, old man," Feng observed.

"I am worried. The ewes are deserting their twin lambs."

"It was to be expected."

"Still, it is heartbreaking to see them and to be unable to do anything. Affairs are looking blue. Have you any idea how far I am behind at June thirteenth?"

"Well, I have and I have not," Feng replied. "I suppose Atlas is behind to the extent of fifteen thousand."

Mayne's mouth was a thin red line. For nearly half a minute he continued to stare at his lifelong friend.

Then: "Adding the cost of artificial feeding to our normal exes, we're behind close on nineteen thousand pounds. And only half the year gone, and our average annual exes over ten years only seventeen thousand three hundred." Mary entered with Mayne's tea. "Take a look at the balance-sheet while I appreciate Mary's toast. Thank you, Mary!"

Silently he sipped the tea Mary O'Doyle poured out for him.

The night was crowding into the room and Feng was reading by firelight. Mary switched on the electric and drew close the curtains across the windows before withdrawing. When Feng Ching-wei spoke, it was as though he owned Atlas.

"I see that our ration account has exceeded three thousand

pounds for the first six months of the year," he said, "and, if I remember rightly, three thousand pounds has been our annual average. Our motor expenditure has gone up. Horse feed, of course, is bound to be heavy. We cannot save anything on the artificial feeding and the scrub-cutting. And you will have noted, Frank, that this half-yearly statement does not include the shearing expenses, which an annual statement would do. From a casual glance our expenses appear to have jumped to over double our ordinary average expenses. Even the wages account is almost double."

For a few minutes Frank Mayne made no comment. Then: "Blast the drought! I thought that March rain meant the end of it. If only it would rain in floods to-night!"

"Rain or not, Frank, we've got to face the position," Feng said in soft, yet steely tones. "In nautical parlance, we're sailing too close to the wind. We've got to cut down the wages bill. Petrol consumption must be cut down to set off the extra expenditure on horse feed, and the ration account must be substantially lowered."

Mayne's friend was now very earnest. He was leaning forward, a forefinger tapping each of his points on the balance sheet with a hollow sound.

"Forgive my plain speaking, Frank," he went on. "I do it, remember, as a pal of long standing. You're a better sheepman than I, but I am a better financier than you. We have got to recognise that in present conditions Atlas cannot stand the expense it is being put to, to entertain Mrs. Mayne's successive relays of guests. The increase in the ration account is due entirely to Government House, as, too, is the increase in the wages account. A *chef*, a butler, a kitchen man, a boots, and five housemaids, as well as a chauffeur, is a staff beyond the reach even of Atlas, when it has to face artificial feeding to preserve the breeding flocks. In short, I must repeat that it cannot go on."

Another and a much longer silence fell between them, Feng gazing steadily at Mayne and Mayne gazing as steadily into the fire.

Presently the squatter vented a deep sigh of mental weariness. "I must talk it over with Ethel," he said, rising abruptly. "Thanks for the tea. See you later."

Feng heard him pass out, heard him cross the veranda and

heard, too, the wicket-gate creak. Then he heard rapid steps recrossing the veranda. The room door was flung inward. Round the edge of it appeared Frank Mayne's transformed face. He was smiling.

"Feng, old lad, it's raining!" he almost shouted.

4

THE manager of Thuringah, a property of half a million acres, surveyed himself in the long bevelled mirror standing in a corner of his dressing-room. He saw a splendid soldierly figure, an inch above six feet in height, most certainly a man of distinction both in face and form. Even when not consciously observed the face was full of magnetic power, the expression a blend of ruthlessness and gentleness. The gleaming white of his shirt-front and collar emphasised the high colour of his complexion, which might have been mistaken for sun-tan, but was the result of bodily indulgence. The brilliant blue eyes looked out of the mirror candidly, appraisingly, and for nearly half a minute the chiselled features practised the slow breaking smile that was one of Cameron's most potent weapons.

Alldyce Cameron was one of those men who exert, without effort, a universal fascination for women, and who create in other men an equally universal desire to kick them. Strangely, this masculine desire to kick Cameron was produced less by jealousy than by his blatant self-assurance, based as it was on his undoubted gift for leadership. Despite the fact that a highly placed war general disliked him, it was due to that general's wife that Cameron rose so rapidly in rank.

Of his many ambitions, the highest, the most fiercely desired, the ultimate, was – Woman. Woman was Cameron's God. Woman was the sole spring and font of his life, the absolute director of his existence, and as to the possession of Woman his politics were purely socialistic. The youngest son of a Scottish peer, Woman had been the cause of his leaving Cambridge. His uncle, the shipping baron, took him into his office; but Woman drove him from London to a managership in Queensland, and again Woman had transferred him to Thuringah, New South Wales.

It was his over-socialistic politics regarding Woman which so disgusted his cynical father and his equally cynical uncle. To him, in desperation, said the uncle, a white-haired, handsome man, seated behind a magnificent desk:

"You have got to learn discrimination. You have to arrive at the thorough understanding that Woman and Wine are alike in requiring it. How on earth do you expect to appreciate good wine if you swill slush? With your breeding and your education, I fail to understand you. Damn it! Your discrimination is nil, your tastes plebeian and atrocious. You are an animal. You appear to have no appreciation of the joys obtainable from the chase, which to a man of your class should be far more exquisite than the actual conquest. If you do not use discrimination, you will end in a madhouse. Idiot! Read Aristotle! If you do not use discretion you will soon lie in a coffin. Queensland for you! Should you be alive at the end of three years and unattached to a black gin, should you prove yourself to be a business man, I will alter my will in your favour."

The old fellow had grinned delightedly, and with not a little affection for the young man who stood stiffly before him. There followed the affair on board the ship, when a man looked for him with a revolver. Cameron had coolly secured the gun. There had been the affair in Central Queensland, when a six-and-a-half-foot Australian-Irishman objected to his wife flagrantly favouring Cameron. No guns were used, but Cameron resided in hospital for six weeks. Where Cameron's father, his uncle, and several other relatives had failed, the Australian-Irishman succeeded. Cameron learned discretion, but not discrimination.

Thus he had managed to live, had resolutely kept clear of the gins, and had learned his business. True to his grim word, the uncle had left him most of his money. And now that it was possible for him to escape the bush, now freedom and opportunity were his to worship his god with fervency, he elected to remain the manager of Thuringah Station because the loveliest manifestation of his god, the most beautiful fish he ever had lifted out of the sea, lived a few miles down the river at Atlas.

5

LATE in the afternoon Cameron left the Thuringah homestead, driving the American car provided by his company. A gentle wind from the south met him with cold crispness. The cloudless vault of the sky, a wonderful blue at the zenith, was glowing with gradations of green, yellow, and pink, for the sun had set. The down-river track led him to a river bend, and to the towering avenue of big gums where he was mocked and jeered by the all-seeing kookaburras, as though they laughed at him, this fine-looking man, the worshipper of the god, Woman, on his way to worship.

Regardless of the birds' satanic laughter, Cameron drove on, passing with indifference a party of abandoned lambs, bleating at him pitifully, leaving a few yards to their rear a poor struggling baby with both its eyes plucked out by the attendant crows loth to roost. He did not see the fox crouched beyond the tree-stump, like a cat, waiting for darkness to fall before he slashed at red flesh in the grip of the lust to kill. Unrecognised by Alldyce Cameron, the Great Enemy was at his dreadful work, having at last conquered the Great Friend, and reigning supreme. Plenty lay defeated. King Drought, he whose heraldic sign is the picture of a bloody crow, had destroyed the rabbits, was destroying the seed-eating birds, would destroy the foxes escaped from the poison, was now destroying the lambs; was about to destroy the sheep, the cattle, the horses, and the kangaroos, even at long last many of the crows. The drama of this silent, terrible war was in progress, a one-sided war against defenceless things with the foul weapons of hunger, thirst, and pain. Cameron ignored it. His god was his all; it rode his mind and dominated his thoughts, whilst Feng Ching-wei and others were beginning to worry about the endless drought, and Frank Mayne was experiencing the horror of watching animals tortured to death, realising his impotency.

The manager of Thuringah stopped his car beneath an old gum tree opposite the Atlas homestead. With his usual care he made sure that his battery was switched off, for he was not the kind of man to risk a run-down battery, which would prevent his dashing start for home, probably heard by feminine ears if not seen by feminine eyes. Carefully he picked his way down the steep, annoyingly muddy bank of the river, crossed the now dry bed above the rock-lined hole below the homestead, and, climbing the opposite bank, reached the Atlas garden.

With infinite pains he removed the mud from his pumps with a

piece of rag brought for that very purpose. To sweeten his breath
he sucked a scented cachou. Dusk was now deep over the garden.
It was very quiet, very peaceful, very lonely in that darkened
garden. Presently he reached the cane-grass bower-house wherein
first he had tasted the dew on the lips of that wonder-woman, the
mistress of Atlas, since when he had but tasted once again, and
now was exceedingly athirst. When he came opposite the entrance
of the little house he was confronted by Eva, the affianced of Tom
Mace.

"Hallo! What are you doing in there?" he inquired in the silky
tone of voice used when in the presence of Woman.

A little breathlessly, Eva said: "I am looking for Master
Frankie's play-ball."

She recognised this tall, magnificent man, standing so easily,
so grandly before her, the man she so constantly was comparing
with her hard-working lover, the man who laughed so gently,
whose eyes were so expressive.

"Is that not a task for Master Frankie's nurse?"

"Yes, Mr. Cameron. I am now Master Frankie's nurse. You
see, Ella left yesterday without notice, and Mrs. Mayne offered
me the position."

"Ah! In that case the play-ball must be found," Cameron
murmured. "A light on the subject will help, will it not?"

Entering the bower-house, Eva following, he struck a match,
and soon discovered the ball beneath the rustic settee. Retrieving
the toy, Cameron handed it gravely to Eva, a now unnecessarily
lighted match revealing their faces.

"Your name is Eva, is it not?"

"Yes, Mr. Cameron."

Her reply pleased. Her voice pleased. Her really pretty face
pleased more. Her slight but well-covered figure pleased him still
more. The old fire began to course through his veins.

"I thought so," he said vibrantly. "I have noticed you many
times. Do you know what I think about you – Eva?"

"No," tremblingly.

"I think," he told her with deliberation, "I think you are much
too lovely to be a child's nurse. You were intended for something
so much better than a maid. You were expressly made for
happiness, for joy, for – this."

She felt one cool hand placed under her chin whilst the match died out on the ground. She felt another hand brush her neck, an arm, so firm and strong, slipped across her shoulders. She was drawn – drawn forward. She felt his lips against her own – firm, warm, scent-laden lips that kissed her without haste.

"I shall think of you – Eva," he whispered, his voice a caress, and – then – was walking toward the house.

Eva almost collapsed on the settee. As though the man had taken with him the oxygen from the air, her lungs fought for breath. Every nerve in her body was throbbing with strange fire. Her life, her past, Little Frankie, Tom Mace, all were blotted from her mind by the letters of flaming gold before her eyes which formed the astounding sentence: "He kissed me! He kissed me! He kissed me!"

And Alldyce Cameron reached the veranda steps, cool, unmoved, the incident within the bower-house docketed away in his mind for probable future reference – and advantage. Now, whilst he stood before one of the closed drawing-room windows and saw Ethel Mayne in conversation with a tall, white-haired man, his pulses began to throb with expectancy. Within that room was the loveliest woman he ever had held in his arms, loving him now, waiting for him, fearing her weakness because of his strength, surrounding herself with a protective barrier of visiting people.

Silly of her, really. As though she could for ever defeat Him!

CHAPTER XIII

THE SECOND SHEARING

1

AS MacDougall had told Frank Mayne on the telephone, the rain that fell that night early in July came too late to save hundreds of lambs abandoned by their mothers; but, by bringing up grass in the sheltered places, it strengthened the adult sheep and maintained the ewes' milk, which in turn gave strength to the lambs, as well as providing a little green food for them.

That rainfall also deferred the resumption of scrub-cutting and enabled Mayne to halve the artificial feeding costs, but his household and petrol bills did not diminish. Actually he made the rain an excuse to himself to defer, at least for the time, a conversation with Ethel which he foresaw would be fraught with difficulties. If he had but maintained that firmness exhibited when his wife had sulked for several days, if only he had been a tenth part the master of his house as he was of his run, it is probable that the agony and the terror that were to come would have been avoided. Where Ethel was concerned he was strangely weak.

House-party succeeded house-party, expense was added to expense. There was delivered to Atlas complete cinematograph equipment, followed by a bi-weekly exchange of films. Food delicacies found usually in only the very best of hotels were imported from Sydney. A constant stream of people came and went – people with whom neither Mayne nor Feng Ching-wei found anything in common – people who were not doing anything worthwhile in the world, of that class seldom heard of in Australia, but nevertheless in being, who live their allotted span in stupid idleness.

Feng Ching-wei waited and watched. These winter days he was a much puzzled man; and, whilst with his usual quiet efficiency he acted as Mayne's chief of administrative staff, drawing four hundred a year from Atlas, he studied Mayne's wife; and wondered, too, whilst he unobtrusively watched Alldyce Cameron.

The lambs marked this year were seven thousand below the number marked the year before. The lower percentage had been expected, and it indicated heavy losses among the flocks, especially those that were not being hand-fed.

The days of sunshine and nights of frost persisted. Big areas of land were as bare of grass and herbage as the seashore at a time of year when everywhere one looked it should have been covered with a carpet of green. The river had long ceased to run. Bird-life was low excepting along its banks.

Special precautions had to be taken before the shearing was timed to start, precautions entailing much thought on the part of Mayne, and labour on the part of his men. The drought had decimated his battalions of sheep and lowered to C3 the constitution of the survivors. Now completely retired from the trapping trade, which no longer existed, Tom Mace, with his truck, was stationed at White Well, where a dump of maize and compressed lucerne had been made. A smaller dump in charge of Ten Pot Dick was made at Mulga Flat.

The shearers came. Once more the huge shed vibrated with whirring machinery. Again the great army of sheep was on the move.

Whilst the comparatively robust maize-fed ewes and rams were being shorn, those flocks that had been fending for themselves were slowly and by easy stages moved eastward to the shed. On arrival of every sheep, either at Mulga or at White Well, it was given a ration of one ounce of maize and a little lucerne, with a second ration the morning of its departure. It was essential, this hand-feeding of the hoggets, the wethers, and the culled ewes, for they were so poor in condition when mustered in their paddocks that without artificial feeding the travelling losses were likely to be enormous.

Mayne and MacDougall did not spare themselves. Weeks were spent in the station car or the truck, and on the backs of horses, sleeping anywhere beneath the blazing stars on ground dusty and dry. To Mayne, Government House was become a place of pandemonium. Only occasionally did he encounter among Ethel's guests one sufficiently staid and serious to interest him. The noisier, the wilder her guests the more satisfied with life did his wife appear to be. It was a relief, thankfully recognised, to get away into the quiet of the bush with dour MacDougall.

Tom Mace was finding cause for worry too, although from a different source. The loss of his living, to be replaced, certainly, by that afforded by station work, was accountable only in part for the unease experienced by this go-ahead Englishman.

His chief cause of worry was engendered by the faint suspicion that Eva did not seem so keen on marriage as she had been. On neither word nor look could that suspicion be based; it was as though she herself was not aware of her changing heart, and, because of that, Mace was the more puzzled. Able to run into the homestead only about once a week, he might, had his been a jealous disposition, have sought for the solution in the right direction.

He was laying a trail of maize in readiness for a flock due at

158

White Well from the shed, when Mayne drew up and spoke to him. Mayne was dressed in old, serviceable clothes, and was wearing a soiled and dilapidated felt hat.

"Tom, I want you to leave at daybreak to-morrow with enough maize for thirty-five hundred sheep which will be camped to-night four miles on the Mulga Flat road. Mr. Andrews is in charge. There will be no time to give 'em a feed to-night. They should have got here for a feed before being put into the yards. Fred Lowe will take them over to-morrow and bring them on. If he has to leave any along the track, you truck the best of them here, and yard 'em with a little lucerne. Clear?"

"Y-yes, Mr. Mayne. Aren't they travelling too well?"

"Bad-very bad," Mayne admitted. "Well, I must go."

Mace watched him stride to his car, pondered over the lines of anxiety criss-crossing his employer's face, and felt glad he had not seized that opportunity of reminding Mayne about his promise of a house.

<h1 style="text-align:center">2</h1>

EARLY next morning three thousand five hundred sheep were freed from a roughly constructed enclosure built of long lengths of hessian stretched on stakes driven into the ground. Mace, who had arrived before sunrise, had scattered over a series of near clay-pans the ounce ration of maize, and now Mr. Andrews and his three riders shepherded and held the sheep to the clay-pans. At this point of their journey the sheep had become used to the maize-feeding, and for twenty minutes the cracking of the grain denoted keen appetites. But almost as soon as the maize had disappeared a number of them lay down.

Fred Lowe, with his three riders, reaching the temporary sheep camp half an hour later, sighed at the significance of sheep lying down after having been in a temporary yard all night. "Seems as though they're pretty tired," he said to Andrews.

"They are," the jackeroo agreed. "We started with forty hundred. About five hundred fell behind. We couldn't get them along. Mighty pleased you've taken over this mob. Did Mr. Mayne give any orders for me?"

"You are to go into Ware's Dam and muster the hoggets to-day and to-morrow."

"All right. We'll be getting along. We'll camp near the dam."

"An' we'll be getting a move on too. Only four miles, but by the look of them woollies it'll be dark before we get 'em to White Well. Darn the drought! Why in hell can't it rain sometimes?"

Sending a man to each wing, Lowe and his third rider, with three dogs, got the flock moving eastward. There was absent the wild, purposeless rush of good-conditioned sheep at the start of the day's stage. The leaders of the flock did make a half-hearted breakaway, but soon fell back to a brisk walk. They were yet strong, but the main body was too poor to maintain the pace they set, and the wing men were kept busy for an hour keeping the leaders back.

At the expiration of three hours Lowe had moved the flock two miles nearer White Well, and Mace, who followed with his truck, had picked up eleven "dead-beats". These he took on to White Well, dumped into a yard, and, returning, was obliged to pick up seven others that had fallen during his absence. They had lain down, and neither dogs nor men could force them onward.

By noon the flock had been moved barely two miles.

Lowe wisely halted the flock and decided on a two- hour camp. Within ten minutes hundreds of sheep were lying down, with the leaders placidly looking at them and making no attempt to wander. The men boiled their quart pots, made tea, and lolled in the lee of a ten-foot ridge of pure red sand, for the south wind was cold, eating their lunch and afterwards smoking the inevitable hand-made cigarette, whilst the horses stood near-by, held prisoner only by their bridle-reins hanging to the ground.

"How's yer voice, Bill?" asked Lowe.

"Crook, Fred, crook!" replied a lank man of middle age, whose narrow face was distinguished by an outsize nose. "I feels as though I couldn't ya-hoodle again for a fiver."

"Even my dogs can't yap no more," a man with a Cockney accent said. "An' I've worn me 'at out flailing 'em. Look at it! When they talks about the cost of living in the Arbitration Court, they never says any think about the cost of 'ats a bloke wears out on sheep's backs."

"Naw," Lowe drawled, pessimism clouding his usually cheerful face. "They're all too busy in the Court rushing through the business so's they can get out and enjoy theirselves on the workin' man's money. They're having the good times – judges, lawyers, and union bosses. We're only the bush mugs, without any say as to what's the value of our labour."

"There's one thing though," put in a tubby, red-faced, wild-whiskered man. "We are helping to produce wealth for the blasted country, while them politicians can only spend borrowed money and call theirselves statesmen. Statesmen! Coo! I could borrow a fiver any day and booze it up in Menindee, and no one calls me a statesman."

"No one ain't lookin' to fight you, Blue."

"Well, you can call me the Governor-General now. I'm too darned tired to fight. Me arms are near dropping off. It takes a sheep to rile a bloke proper."

"Well, we'd better get riled some more," Lowe decided, lurching to his feet and stretching his lithe body. "Come on or we won't get 'em to White Well till sun-up to-morrow."

When Mace had trucked two more loads of "dead-beats" to White Well yards he said, when he returned for the third load: "Look here, Fred! Just camp the mob here and I'll truck the whole darn lot."

"Wot about goin' into the homestead and bringing the ruddy shearers out here?" the lank man shouted, now walking and leading his horse, and "pushing" about fifteen sheep along.

"Ya-as! An' if they won't come, bring me out another voice," requested the tubby man.

The dogs were now useless, for the weary sheep took not the slightest notice of them. With dust-rimmed eyes and lolling tongues they continued their work, trotting up and down behind the sheep, but now made no effort to drive into the main body of the stragglers.

Only one man was needed to guard both wings and keep the now slow-walking leaders headed for White Well. The sheep walked with their heads low, as automata without consciousness. Even when a dog leapt across the backs of a press of them, there was no movement indicating normal fear. Three men, leading their bored horses, flailed sheep's backs with their hats, "ya-hoodled" with cracked voices, and constantly lifted sheep to their feet and urged them forward. Clouds of fine dust were wafted over them by the cold wind.

When the sun went down there was still half a mile to travel to reach the yards at White Well, for at three o'clock Fred Lowe had been obliged to let the sheep rest for an hour. The cook at White Well came and joined them in their work and his voice alone could be heard, and his arms alone moved energetically.

It was quite dark when the sheep were finally yarded for the night. The following day it was necessary to keep them shepherded in the vicinity of White Well, feed them morning and evening, and yard them again for a second night before attempting to move them nearer the shearing shed.

3

AS has been stated, White Well was situated in the bottleneck of Atlas caused by the resumption of an area of land by the Government under its Closer Settlement Acts. The boundary of Westmacott's holding lay within one mile of White Well, and to White Well one morning came Mrs. Westmacott riding a grey horse.

She was a small, wiry woman, about forty-six years of age, with a strong Scottish accent and large grey eyes that were the only handsome feature of her sun-wrecked face. Hearing the approach of her horse, the White Well cook went out to meet her.

"Are any of the riders about?" Mrs. Westmacott asked anxiously.

"Nope. They won't be home till sundown, missus. Anything up?" replied the cook.

"I don't know, but Harry never came home last night. I've been riding the paddocks since daybreak, and I can't find him. His horse came home in the middle of the night without the saddle, but still wearing the bridle."

"Musta bin thrown. Lying out somewheres, perhaps?"

"It looks like it," the woman agreed. "I was hoping Fred Lowe or some of the hands was here, and could come an' help."

"There's only me and Tom Mace, missus. Tom's at the yards there. You ride over and tell 'im to come in, and I'll make you a drink of tea time you an' him come back."

"All right. If anything's happened to Harry now young Harry's gone, it will –"

"Don't think about it, missus. Go and get Tom Mace," urged

the cook.

Mrs. Westmacott rode away to the yards on her weary horse, and the cook, after hanging a billy-can over the fire in the open hearth, rang up the Atlas homestead.

Feng answered the call, and heard the object of Mrs. Westmacott's visit. "Mr. Mayne is away, Jack. How many horses are out there?"

"Five, not counting the two colts."

"Saddles?"

"None spare."

"Very well, Jack," came the calm voice from the Atlas office. "Get Mace to run in the horses. Keep Mrs. Westmacott there. I'll bring out two men and five saddles right away."

"Goodo, Mr. Feng!"

Mace arrived at the huts, and left immediately on Mrs. Westmacott's horse to drive in the loose horses in the mile-square horse paddock.

Mrs. Westmacott was conducted into the scrupulously clean dining-kitchen-room, and made to sit in the cook's home-made easy chair to drink tea. "Don't you worry, missus," she was told. "Mr. Feng is bringing out a coupler 'ands, and, with 'im, that'll make five of us. We'll light on Harry in no time."

The woman, after the first sharp look at the cook, gazed fixedly into the log fire. She sipped the tea gratefully, but would not eat.

"Young Harry – and now his father," she said slowly and softly, over and over again.

"Don't you worry," urged the cook compassionately, while cutting thick meat sandwiches to be made into five packets to be tied to saddle-bows.

Mace brought the loose horses to the horse yards in the corner of the paddock with a thunder of hoofs, and watered and fed Mrs. Westmacott's grey in the almost wind-wrecked stable near-by. In this crisis he lost all nervousness in his speech. As the cook had done, he urged the bushwoman not to worry. "What time did Harry leave yesterday?" he asked, seated on an upturned petrol-case on the opposite side of the fire.

"About three o'clock," Mrs. Westmacott said dully. "He should have been home by dark."

"Where was he headed?"

"In a new paddock lying along the Atlas boundary we call North Paddock."

"How big?"

"Six miles by four."

"What work was he going to do?"

"He went out to cut the throats of the sheep that were down and dying, and skin them."

"Oh!"

After that there fell a long silence. The two men realised in those simply spoken words the long tragedy of the Westmacotts. Years of labour, of voluntary hardship, so that money with which to buy sheep might be saved. The good years when prosperity rewarded their efforts and increased the number of their flocks. The ultimate overstocking, the necessity of sending some of the sheep to feed off the roads of Victoria, the tragedy of foolish young Harry, an innocent, inexperienced boy. The withering of the sheep feed and its blowing away by the wind. The lack of money to pay for artificial feeding, the long agony of watching sheep die, and the final desperate wish to save at least the woolled skins.

A roaring truck brought Feng Ching-wei and two men. Mace met him outside the huts and gave him the necessary information he had obtained from Mrs. Westmacott.

"Do you know the Westmacott country?" Feng asked him.

"Yes. I trapped rabbits there two years ago."

"Wait."

Feng Ching-wei went inside the kitchen and found Mrs. Westmacott crying silently. The courage maintained for a year was breaking down. Feng said gently: "Mrs. Westmacott, it appears likely that your husband is lying out injured. When found it will be necessary to bring him straight in for medical attention. It might be necessary to take him to the hospital at Broken Hill. I want you to stay here, so that if your husband does require medical attention you will be able to go with him. You will stay here – alone?"

"Yes, I will stay here alone."

"Better still, will you go with Gus to the Atlas homestead and stay with my housekeeper, Mary O' Doyle?"

"No. I'll stay here. Harry might want me. I'll have hot water and things ready."

"Very well. Don't think too much. We shall not be long."

She was still sitting, silently crying, staring into the fire when they left her; but when the sound of their horses' thudding hoofs drifted in to her through the open door, she rose and put several kerosene buckets of water to heat at the fire. She wondered why Mace was driving his truck and not riding a horse.

Arrived at the south end of the Westmacott North Paddock, the four horsemen spread out to work the ground as though mustering for sheep, Mace following in his truck, the best way he could, a centre line, thus having two riders on each flank.

They found Harry Westmacott at a set of newly constructed sheep-yards. In the yards were some nine hundred sheep. Of the nine hundred a bare hundred were alive. Westmacott was singing whilst he cut the throat of sheep after sheep, and stacked the unskinned carcasses in a great heap. The sheep he was killing, and had been killing all through the previous night, were poor in condition, yet not dying sheep.

He was quite docile when they put him in Mace's truck and took him to Broken Hill, where, of course, he was certified to be insane.

4

THE shearing proceeded without interruption. All through the brilliant, sun-filled days the roar of machinery inside the shed vied with men's raucous "ya-hoodling" and the staccato barks of dogs without, distance softening the uproar, which reached Government House as the sound of angry bees in a hive. The nights were governed by frost, when Ethel's guests played bridge or viewed the latest films. In the shearers' quarters quietness was indicative of weary men lying asleep or reading.

One man in the Atlas employ was at work every day with a horse and dray. They called him the "Burying Party", an epithet that enraged him almost beyond endurance. He was a tall, cadaverous man of fifty or thereabouts, owning a very white face from which sprouted very black whiskers. Where-ever he went, about the homestead or near the shed, he constantly heard voices proclaiming: "Here comes the Burying Party!"

At the end of the last run every day, the shorn sheep were taken from the pens and herded into a small paddock bordering the river, where clumps of tobacco-bush and the river gums gave the utmost shelter from the frosts.

It was the duty of the "Burying Party" to drive his horse and dray into this paddock, and there feed the live sheep with lucerne, before collecting the dead sheep to cart them three miles away and burn them. The dead sheep lay in bunches, their snow-white, woolless bodies contrasting sharply with the grey earth.

Some mornings the "Burying Party" had to cart fifty sheep away to the burning place, where dry wood was plentiful; some days it was sixty or seventy sheep killed by the cold of the first night's exposure without their wool.

And so the work and the losses continued to the bitter end of this second shearing, when the day of reckoning came. Seated at his table in the Atlas office, Mayne chewed the stem of his unlit pipe, and pondered on the shearing tallies and those given him by the "Burying Party". Opposite him sat Feng Ching-wei.

Presently emitting a deep sigh, Mayne brushed aside the papers, straightened up in his chair and encountered his friend's eyes with his own. "Feng, old man, things are looking blue, but not as blue as they could be," he said with unusual slowness. "Of the 27,000 ewes shorn last year, only 21,000 turned up this shearing. Only 8,000 wethers came to light of the 17,000 shorn last year. We shore 17,000 lambs last year and only 7,000 turned up this year as hoggets. This year we shore 12,000 lambs instead of last year's total of 17,000. And the frosts have killed 3,271 sheep. At the close of last year's shearing Atlas ran 66,000 sheep. Now it has but 45,000. We've lost 21,000 sheep in the twelve months."

"Well – it cannot now be said that Atlas is overstocked, Frank."

"That is correct," Mayne agreed quickly. "And because we're no longer overstocked we should pull through. That half-inch of rain which fell last night will whip up the feed and give us a start for the early summer. If it rains during September it will certainly enable us to swim with the tide."

"That is so," admitted Feng, yet without conviction.

Mayne continued with increasing cheerfulness in his voice. He was like a man seemingly pleased at the prospect of successfully deluding himself.

"In consequence of our losses, naturally our output has fallen. Last year we produced 1,850 bales of wool; this year the total has fallen to 990. It is a good thing that the market inclines to rise above last year's prices."

"Your figures do not include the sheep and wool from Westmacott's place?"

"No."

For several seconds Feng's eyes bored into the very soul of the man sitting opposite him. Abruptly they became masked by tender good-humour. He said: "You're a likeable cuss in many ways, old man, but as a business man you suffer from fits of quixotic foolishness. You had the chance, you still have the chance, to buy Westmacott's place for three thousand pounds; and, despite financial stringency, I would have purchased, and now urge you to purchase, land which would wipe out the bottle-neck and add twenty thousand to the value of Atlas."

Mayne shook his head. "I couldn't take advantage of the woman's adversity to realise one of my life's dreams, Feng. Just remember! First they lose those sheep sent away with the son. Secondly, they lose the son. Thirdly, the man loses his reason and the woman the active support of her husband. As you know, I offered Westmacott seven thousand some time ago. To-day the place has no buyer. The sum of three thousand pounds placed on it by Mrs. Westmacott is absurd, and much less than half the proper value. She had to have money to retire to Adelaide, for she couldn't carry on alone. In the circumstances I think Old Man Mayne would have done what I have done – advanced her two thousand pounds, with a legal note to pay the balance of five thousand two years hence."

"Should we get a bad year next year you might well lose your two thousand."

"If we do, that sum won't save us; and, anyway, we have the use of Westmacott's selection meanwhile. Just now two thousand is two thousand; but I cannot afford to pay away seven thousand, and I could not afford to see anyone else get that property from a desperate woman who might accept one thousand for the place, lock, stock, and barrel. No. Times and the season will change.

They always do. This is a wonderful country to pick up after bad times. History has proved it."

"Still, it is well to assume that the change might be delayed another year, or even two years. Take my tip, and be cautious. The small Atlas profit of four thousand pounds last year will become a small deficit this year, that is certain. And now, even though the seasonal prospects are a little brighter, be advised and sell every butcher's carcass we have."

For fully a minute Mayne considered this.

Then: "No," he argued, shaking his head. "No. We might get seven shillings a head for the remaining fats, whilst if it rains good and hard in the near future we would get sixteen shillings and more by Christmas."

Feng attempted to argue back, but, as a mere friend, was unable to argue with force. Mayne was obdurate. He believed even more firmly than on his return from New Zealand that the dry spell was now at an end. He viewed the problem from the standpoint of one holding all he has for a market rise based on the occurrence of rainfalls that might come at once or be indefinitely deferred: being afraid, genuinely afraid, of having it on his conscience that he sold sheep at a panic price, when if he had held he could have sold them for at least double.

It is not to be doubted that Frank, like his father, was a gambler. As a foil to this characteristic was Feng's shrewdness. Feng did not believe that the dry period was at an end. There could not have been found half a dozen squatters in the Western Division of the State who would have agreed with him, but no arguments put forward by Frank Mayne could turn him from his conviction that Atlas faced an evil drought.

Feng advised, urged, implored Mayne to sell all he could of his sheep whilst the market remained at the slightly higher point; but Mayne was stubborn. The majority of the squatters, viewing the situation as he did, also held on. This was the critical decision that doomed Atlas and dozens of other stations as well.

"At least, Frank," Feng said in desperate earnestness, "cut down your household expenses. Reduce your petrol and oil expenditure and put off every man who can be spared."

"But why?" expostulated Mayne. "I decide to hold the sheep because the season is looking favourable; and, because that is so, there is no need to cut exes and sack men. If I follow your advice regarding expenditure, it is a tacit admission that I do not believe the coming season will be good, and am wrong by holding on to saleable stuff. I admit that we – that is, Ethel and I – have been living rather extravagantly, and I have made up my mind to persuade her to stop her house-parties. But, as for putting off men – no!"

He tapped the table smartly with an open hand, the action of an impatient employer with a too argumentative departmental chief. Yet, when he rose to his feet, he smiled cheerfully at Feng Ching-wei before passing out of the office.

CHAPTER XIV

SPRING-TIME

1

THIS year the seed-eating birds did not nest in the numbers usual to a normal year, but the carnivorous birds bred with unwonted fecundity, for their food supplies were abnormal. Long stretches of the river-bed were dry, and a selector above Wilcannia sowed a crop of oats along a mile stretch of sand-bottom – and reaped a harvest. Water in the holes at the bends mysteriously maintained its level, and in the depths lurked giant cod that preyed on the perch, which in turn preyed on the tiny fish that might have become giant cod.

Feng Ching-wei's life during these months of drought was far more independent than ever it had been. Before the coming of Ethel Mayne he had occupied rooms in Government House, which gave him all the privacy he desired, yet still kept him chained to the communal system presided over by a housekeeper in the employ of a man not himself.

With those conditions he was not dissatisfied. They had existed from the day he and Frank Mayne had come home to mourn Old Man Mayne and carry on the work of Atlas. He accepted them because he had known no other. Not until the furnishing of his bungalow did he appreciate real independence, and not until the coming of Mary O'Doyle did he experience that peculiar masculine satisfaction of being properly cared for.

Little links of confidence eventually formed for him the chain of Mary's harsh history, a chronicle of years of unwomanly labours unsoftened by the influence of real affection. Wielding a pickaxe, toiling at a windlass over a mine shaft, and yoking and driving a bullock team are not labours that help a woman to love or to be loved. The incredible conditions ruling the birth of her one child, which died a few weeks later, give sufficient proof of this. When she was heavy with child, she and her husband each drove a bullock team over the Broken Hill-Wilcannia track in the heat of early summer. They were nine miles from water when the pains came to Mary. She shouted to her husband to stop his team and keep an eye on hers whilst she went into the bush for an hour, produced her baby, brought it back to her wagon, and drove her team the nine miles to water.

Almost all her life she had worked as a man, and better than many a man. Frugal in her habits, she made money for her two husbands to squander on drink. All her life she had sought for love, and had found but poor imitations of it. When death took her baby it left her with nothing.

Looking backward from the security of Feng's house, her arrival at Atlas seemed like coming home from a stormy voyage. The conditions of Feng's household suited her independent spirit, which at several periods, never for long, bore with the oversight of a mistress. Here in Feng's establishment there was no "high-falutin', la-de-da, hoity-toity city woman" to order her about. Here she was mistress herself. Here, most wonderfully, she could mother a lonely young man, feed him, mend for him, guard him from discomfort, keep his house spotless. From the storms of life she found herself in the haven of peaceful anchorage. Feng she grew to love as she would have loved the baby born beside the track – as she would have loved either of her husbands had they been gentle.

All this Feng Ching-wei knew or shrewdly guessed, and because of it was the more astonished by the information imparted to him one morning by his cook-housekeeper-needlewoman-guardian. When she had set before him the tray containing the morning tea, she said, in unusually broad Irish: "Misther Feng, 'tis a worrd wid ye Oi'd loike."

170

"Very well, Mary," assented Feng, smiling into her round red face, in which the shining eyes and the shining button of a nose formed the points of a triangle. Rising courteously, he offered her a chair, which she accepted with hesitation. He observed her eyes to be dim with tears.

"Oi – oh, Misther Feng! Some'ow 'tis sorrowful Oi am to tell ye. But – but –" Mary burst into tears.

Feng waited in wonderment.

"Oi've served ye now nearly eighteen monse, Misther Feng," Mary sobbed. "All that toime ye've behaved like a gintleman, and now – and now –"

"You do not intend leaving me, do you, Mary?" Feng exclaimed in quick alarm.

"Oi don' be knowin', indade Oi don't. For shure Oi don' be wanting to, but that feller's been pesterin' the loife out of me, an' now he says Oi'm to go ter Menindee ter-morrer by the coach. Oi don' wanner go – yet Oi do wanner go."

"Please explain, Mary, why you want to go and do not want to go to Menindee," questioned Feng, now racked by the nightmare of living without the ministrations of Mary O'Doyle.

With great effort she dried her eyes by the application of a red forearm. When again she spoke her voice was steady and her accent less Irish. Volubly she burst forth: "'Tis that blackguard ava Todd Gray, the poor little runt. He's been a-courtin' av me these last six weeks, and then – him being in Menindee on a spree, as you know – he sent worrd to the sergint of police to marry us next Tuesday. That was close on three weeks gone. The banns 'ave bin posted outside the police-station, an' I've bin arguing with meself if I'd go or not. Now he's sint me worrd to catch the mail-car termorrer. Oh, Misther Feng! You must be a-letting me go, or he'll spind arl his money on the accursed dhrink, and come home like poor old Sir John."

"But –" Feng gasped, so intense was his astonishment, so terrible his fear of losing her. To be sure, Todd Gray often had been seen talking to Mary O'Doyle at her kitchen door, but courtship and marriage had never occurred to him. He began to make objections.

"But is Todd Gray going to make a home for you, Mary? Has he got a home ready for you?"

171

To which Mary countered with trembling indignation: "Make a 'ome for me! Not 'im! I wouldn't go in it if 'e 'ad. Till you be a-kicking av me out av this 'ouse, a hundred Todd Grays wouldn't be a-dragging of us asunder."

Observing Mary's bulk, Feng felt tempted to smile, but temptation fled before the seriousness of this affair, which yet was not quite clear. He said: "Then it is his intention, and yours too, to return to Atlas when married?"

"Shure," she said simply.

"As a married couple you intend carrying on your present occupations?" Feng pressed, with rising hope.

"You agreein', Misther Feng." Mary grew scarlet. "Todd could cart his dunnage from his room, and come and camp in my room here. It – it's big enough for two."

Feng's gaze dropped. For a little while he was silent. Then: "Supposing I could not agree to that, Mary?"

"Then it's a widder I'll be stoppin'. If ut's me choice, I choose me presint job, for I'm rememberin' 'ow it was you who picked me out av the Gutter av Australia."

"But I have no objection, Mary," Feng said, suddenly smiling at her. "If you want Todd for your husband, you shall have him. Besides your present room you shall have the one next it for a living-room or a sitting-room, whichever you prefer. There is no finer quality than loyalty. It was my intention to leave for Broken Hill next Tuesday in the station car, but we will leave to-morrow evening for Menindee, and I will stay over Tuesday and attend your wedding. If you like, Mary, I will give away the bride. Would that please you?"

For the second time Mary O'Doyle burst into tears.

2

THE township of Menindee on the Darling River, about 180 miles from that river's junction with the Murray, marks one of the oldest settlements in the west of the State. It was there when Burke and Wills passed through on their last ill-omened journey. And that was not so long ago, for an old resident there to-day describes their passage, and how common members of the party dared not dismount and rest their tired horses till the leader chose to command them to do so. With that kind of leader success was impossible.

Like many bush towns, Menindee to-day is but the ghost of its former self. In these years of drought it supported three hotels, a convent, a hall, several general stores, a police-station, and a school, besides some thirty dwellings constructed mainly of odd lengths of corrugated iron and many hessian bags. It is built on a belt of reddish sand which rolls toward the river from the wilderness round Lake Menindee, which is sometimes filled through a creek by the river when in flood.

To Menindee on the Monday afternoon drove Feng Ching-wei in the big station car, with Mary O'Doyle sitting beside him. In the Australian cities, or in any other country, what Feng had determined to do would have meant ostracism from his class. It did horrify Ethel Mayne, but she knew nothing of it till after it was over.

Arrived at Menindee, they discovered that Todd Gray was staying at the Menindee Hotel, and, consequently, Feng secured rooms for Mary and himself at the Albemarle Hotel across the sand-dune that constituted the main street.

The following morning, when Feng Ching-wei entered the dining-room, he found Mary O'Doyle already at breakfast, and he nonplussed a squatter, two jackeroos, and a director of a chain of stores when he smilingly declined their invitation to join them, and slipped into a chair facing the bride, who sat alone at a separate table.

Mary O'Doyle wore a black dress trimmed with grey velvet. Her hair now was ruffled in a style most unlike her usual "bun" affair, but which despite the greyness vanquished many years. Afterwards Feng discovered that on her heavy feet were elastic-sided riding-boots. But Mary's face was shining with suppressed excitement, her small blue eyes emitting a marvellous light.

"Well, Mary, are you quite prepared to face this important day?" he asked, before attacking lamb's fry and bacon.

"For shure, Misther Feng," she replied, smiling broadly. "Y'see, it'll be me thirrd weddin'. I know just wot to do to stop the confetti getting entangled in me 'air. But will ye be doing av me a favour?"

"Why, certainly."

"Then, whin I go along to the store to buy me one or two

173

things, will you dig up that blackguard av a Todd Gray, an' sober him up for the ceremony?"

"But surely he will not be intoxicated this day of all days?" expostulated Feng.

"Don't ye be believin' av it, Misther Feng. Weddin' days are a grand excuse for boozin' an' all. Don't I know it! Todd an' his cobbers will be starting out early, each seeing the other wan keeps sober. An' it'll be: 'All right. Only one now.' An' they'll say it that many times that they'll get as drunk as me uncle at a wake. Lor' bless you! He got that drunk he daren't lie down for fear he'd drown."

"Humph! Might be as well for me to go along and shepherd Todd," Feng conceded, a trifle grimly. "We are due at the sergeant's office at one o'clock. When you have completed your shopping, return here. The wedding breakfast is timed to start immediately we return to the hotel from the police-station."

"The weddin' breakfast! An' who'll be giving that?"

"I shall, of course, Mary. The giver of the bride always provides a breakfast."

"You will! Oh!" For three seconds of time Mary gazed at him before her lips began to tremble.

At last she said: "I – I never 'ad no weddin' breakfast afore."

And thus Feng Ching-wei came to understand that Mary O'Doyle never had become used to accepting kindness, and that, perhaps for the first time in her life, she was feeling the feminine comfort of leaning on one of the supposedly stronger sex. Her obvious and childlike gratitude delighted him. He felt both pleased and thankful that at great expense he had, over the telephone, induced a friend to bring that morning from Broken Hill a present for the bride and the largest wedding-cake procurable.

Breakfast finished, he parted from Mary O'Doyle, and, after completing arrangements with the landlady for the wedding breakfast, sought and found the bridegroom-elect drinking to his future happiness with Ten Pot Dick and several cronies in the bar of the Menindee Hotel. At his call Todd Gray came out to the veranda, where he was firmly invited to be seated on the long bench. Said Feng sternly: "I am told, Todd, that you intend to marry Mary O'Doyle this morning. Is that correct?"

"You bet, Mr. Feng," Todd replied, grinning sheepishly.

"Excellent, Todd! Let us discuss details. Mary told me that the arrangements for the ceremony have been made. Pardon my inquisitiveness, but I am to give away the bride. I suppose you were very drunk last night?"

Again that sheepish grin. Todd Gray's usually fierce grey eyes were flecked with red, but he was newly shaved and appeared clean and natty in a new suit. "Well, old Ten Pot Dick and me did have a few," was his admission.

"That I do not doubt. Still, as last night was your last as a benedict, over-indulgence was excusable. But to-day you owe it to Mary to keep perfectly sober."

Todd found himself being regarded by blue-black eyes boring inward to the secret recesses of his being. He began to fidget – which was not remarkable.

Feng's voice had grown steely in tone. "I want you to understand, Todd, that I take a great interest in your wife-to-be. I will not have you do anything to spoil the day for her. I am very serious about this. You will not take another drop till you are about to start for the sergeant's office, if then. Let Ten Pot Dick do as he likes. Who is to be your best man?"

"Old Ten Pot Dick, Mr. Feng."

Feng noted the flash of shame come and go in the other's eyes. He was aware that in the long ago Gray was well-circumstanced. Constant association with men of a lower educational level had slurred his speech, but never had vanquished a love for good books.

"I'll play the game," Todd said, and Feng knew that he would.

The rest of that morning Feng spent in the lounge of his hotel. He saw Mary come in and pass along to her room. His friend from Broken Hill arrived in a dust-covered, powerful car, when an enormous wedding cake was placed in the care of the landlady. At half-past twelve Ann Shelley drove up in her single-seater.

"Feng, you are a dear to 'phone me about this," she exclaimed when he greeted her in the hall. "But you did not give me much time, did you?"

Holding both her hands in his, smiling blandly into her expressive face, his pulses raced at the touch of her. If only he had the right to take her in his arms! If only it were his wedding day, and this lovely, fresh and pure woman was to be his bride! But thoughts forbidden! Master of himself, he pushed them down into oblivion with the punt-pole of pain.

"I did not know myself till Sunday morning, and did not think to invite you until this morning," he told her, now smiling in his inscrutable fashion. "Mary is in her room. It is number six. Some day I will recite her history, when you will, I know, agree with me that she is entitled to any little happiness we can secure for her." He glanced at his watch. "It is now twenty minutes to one. Will you go to her and talk to her nicely, and then bring her here for a glass of wine before we step over to the sergeant's office?"

Surprised, he watched her eyes blanketed in mist. Her voice was low when she said: "Of course, old boy! Your wife will be a lucky woman."

His wife! Turning, he watched her walking swiftly along the passage to Mary's room. His wife! If only–if–oh, hell–hell–hell!

Ten minutes, fifteen minutes slipped by whilst he lounged by the main entrance. He saw Todd Gray, wearing a bright-green trilby hat, accompanied by the wild-whiskered Ten Pot Dick, arrayed in new brown moleskin trousers and a coat of violent brown and black check, walk from the Menindee Hotel and trudge over the sand waste to the police-station.

For be it understood that Menindee' is a police-controlled town, and that the senior police officer is the registrar for births, marriages, and deaths.

Ann Shelley called him softly at last, and, turning, he found her beside Mary O'Doyle, Mary wearing now a fashionable hat and smart brown shoes.

"All ready, Mary?"

"Yes, Mr. Feng."

"Good! We will have a glass of wine before we go."

Mary O'Doyle tried to speak again, but failed. For a moment she clung to Ann Shelley as she might have clung to the mother she never had known.

3

THE invasion of his office by the bridal party gave Sergeant Brown quite a shock. Even though dressed in uniform, Sergeant Brown appeared more like a colonel in the Indian Army than the policeman he was. Matching his appearance were his duties, which were far more those of an administrator than an ordinary policeman.

The uniting of Todd Gray, whom he had known for many years, with Mrs. Mary Johnston, which was Mary's last married name, was an affair of no interest to him. The social position of the bridal couple was much lower than his own, and he was prepared to rush the ceremony through as quickly as possible. The appearance of Ann Shelley and Feng Ching-wei in company with a woman, obviously a bride, raised the importance of this affair many degrees, and his official austerity promptly melted.

He shook hands with the bride and the bride's escort. He actually smiled at the bridegroom and at Ten Pot Dick, whom the night before he had felt tempted to lock up and charge with the usual d. and d. formula. His front door and windows wanted painting, anyway. He placed the couple side by side before his desk, behind which he stood stiffly erect, and read portions of the marriage service. It went through with only one hitch, and that occurred when the sergeant put the question: "Will you take this woman for your lawful wedded wife?"

"Me! My bloomin' oath!" Todd Gray responded.

"Say 'yes', commanded Sergeant Brown, with quick sternness.

"Yes," said the groom with less fervour.

When they had signed the register, when the sergeant had presented Mary with the marriage certificate, Feng suggested that he would be a welcome guest at the breakfast. Realising now the interest that Ann Shelley and Feng-Ching-wei were taking in Mary Gray, he at once accepted, and, with Todd Gray on his one hand and Feng on the other, and with Ten Pot Dick, all hot and flustered, bringing up the rear, they followed the bride and Ann Shelley across the sand to the road and thence to the Albemarle Hotel. Several men on the veranda of the Menindee Hotel cheered; but, being in company with the elite, Todd Gray refrained from any sign of acknowledgment. Ten Pot Dick, however, believing it to be his duty as the groom's best man, opened his mouth for a responsive roar, caught himself in time, shut his mouth, and in silence wildly waved both his arms.

Within the spare dining-room of the Albemarle Hotel everyone was surprised at the sumptuous breakfast provided by Feng. Mary

O'Doyle – I shall continue to call her by her maiden name, because she always insisted on it – tightened her grip on Ann Shelley's arm, and drew in her breath sharply. Todd Gray's under-jaw dropped, whilst *sotto voce* Ten Pot Dick said: "Cripes!"

His face, aflame as that of a Dutch cheese, became suffused with the inner light of keen expectation, of fierce desire, quickly to be gratified. Abnormal distance of face surface separated each dirty grey whisker, whilst the twin red bottom lids of his eyes sagged away from the bridge of his nose. His washed-out, colourless eyes grew round at sight of the beer and wine bottles on a side-table. To the wedding-cake, however, he was blind.

The company became seated. Feng occupied the head of the table. The bride sat on his right with the groom next her. On his left sat Ann Shelley, with the Broken Hill friend beyond her, and beyond him the sergeant. Ten Pot Dick sat on Todd's right. The feast proceeded with mounting gaiety, and at last the maid brought in a huge carving knife, which was handed to Mary, who cut the cake with the delight of a child.

Feng rose to speak. "Friends, before we drink the health of the bridal couple, I wish to make them a small gift in token of my esteem. When you smoke one of these pipes, Todd, remember your oath to love and cherish your wife Mary, which oath you have made to-day." Laying before the groom a handsome case of pipes, he began to remove the wrapping from a small box, eventually revealing an expensive gold watch attached to a long gold chain. Slipping the chain over her head, he added in his soft tones: "Mary, may you have all the happiness you deserve! Now, please, drink to the bride and the groom."

They drank in silence. Then the sergeant, like a true sportsman, struck up: "For they are jolly good fellows!"

The chorus came to an end. Mary O'Doyle was weeping without sound. Big tears trickled slowly down her weather-beaten cheeks. With difficulty she said: "Todd – a speech."

"Wot, me?" gasped Todd.

"You – speak," and in Mary's voice was the brittle hardness of cast-iron.

"Well, ladies and gents," Todd began, having struggled to his feet, "I'm no speaker, silent water running deep, but on behalf of my wife and myself I beg to thank you all for your kindness, and the honour you have done us to-day."

Apparently Todd Gray found it less difficult to sit down than to stand up, but when he sat down Ten Pot Dick rose abruptly.

"As the best man I'd like to say a few words," he said, visibly refraining from expectorating through the open window. Pointing an accusing finger at the groom, he went on: "Todd 'ere sez 'e ain't no speaker. Don't you go and believe it. Last night he cornered me in the bar of the Menindee an' he talked stars and suns and universes for three solid hours. He kep' it up till he got stone sober. Talk! He make a kookaburra fall off 'n a branch. Don't ask him to talk no more, 'cos he might start on the stars and things again. Well, 'ere's 'ow to all of yous! I 'ope as how yous all have enjoyed theirselves as much as I have done." And alone he drank two glasses of beer with astounding celerity.

The breakfast was over. Mary O'Doyle impulsively kissed Ann Shelley and almost kissed Feng Ching-wei. The sergeant strolled away to his office. Ten Pot Dick disappeared into the bar. Ann Shelley and Feng stood on the porch watching the broad figure of Mary O'Doyle and the short, slight figure of her husband walk slowly to the Menindee Hotel.

Ann's voice was husky. "It has been glorious, Feng," she said softly.

"I am very glad, Ann. Thank you for being so nice to Mary O'Doyle."

"Why not? You were nice to her."

"Mary is my cook," he countered, smiling at her with eyes masking the ache in his heart.

4

THE newly-wed stayed three days in Menindee. It was a perfectly glorious time. Todd Gray and Ten Pot Dick removed successfully the accumulated alkaloids and other poisons contained in the water they had been drinking for many months, by the introduction of the counteracting poison of alcohol, and found the process pleasurable; whilst Mary O'Doyle, having decided to defer her husband's reclamation till their return to Atlas, made many friends in Menindee, and met several people who remembered her driving her bullock team and wagon to the river wharf, there to unload the huge bales of wool.

Came inevitably the day they were to start the return journey in Todd Gray's spring cart. Knowing that the journey of fifty miles to Atlas would occupy two long days, the first stage being at least twenty-two miles, Mary had everything in readiness to be packed on the cart first thing in the morning.

A dear father and two beloved husbands had given her a thorough insight into the psychology of Man at the moment Man has to leave the hotel that cheers for a further long period of dry privation. She gave neither her husband nor her husband's extraordinary friend any leisure after breakfast had been eaten, but kept them busy harnessing the horse and loading the cart with the many purchases she had made, besides food for the journey.

"Well, everything's on board, eh?" Todd remarked to no one in particular.

"That's so," agreed Ten Pot Dick absently.

"Well," Todd Gray repeated, looking slyly at Ten Pot Dick, "we better have a last drink and get on. Come on, Mary! A glass of wine will fortify you for the road."

In poor Mary's defence it must be stated that her husband had behaved himself very well that morning, that both he and his best man were then quite sober, and that her heart was as soft as a bride's heart should be. It was at this precise instant that Mary fatally weakened. She consented, and the three entered the private room at the rear of the bar. The drinks were served.

"One more!" Ten Pot Dick urged desperately. "'Ave another small glass of wine, Mrs. Gray. It won't hurt you."

Mary O'Doyle glared and consented reluctantly.

Then Todd said that Mary would have to "shout". Mary who, in the old days, had done much "shouting", relaxed from stern morality and did "shout". Anyway, it would not happen again, once she got the "runt" safely away from Menindee.

The horse harnessed to the spring-cart went to sleep. It slept for nearly an hour, and was violently aroused by Ten Pot Dick lurching into it. There was no need for him to grasp the bridle convulsively and hold it with great determination to prevent the horse bolting, since the horse was beyond the bolting age; yet he manfully did so whilst Todd Gray and two friends pushed Mary O'Doyle into the back of the cart, when she at once fell asleep on the several rolled swags. Those horrible men then slipped back into the bar, where they remained a further hour.

When eventually seated on the cross-board laid from side to side of the cart, with Mary O'Doyle sleeping peacefully behind them, Todd Gray urged the horse forward, and encouraged it whilst it strained and pulled the cart over the deep sand to the harder down-river track leading to Atlas.

Once clear of the town, the horse needed no driving. He knew the way home, knew that home was a desirable place. He lowered his head, pushed hard into the collar, and plodded, plodded ever southward.

The reaction of the human brain to alcohol is varied in a hundred interesting ways. The clever captain of a South Seas trading schooner made it a rule to get any new hand thoroughly drunk before permitting the new man to sail with him. He knew that alcohol will make visible the indulger's secret personality; and, therefore, by getting his new man drunk, the captain was able really to gauge the man's character. We may think we know a person thoroughly, but really we know only what that person chooses to reveal. Alcohol is the acid test of human character. It will bring out a person's evil or good, to be noted by those interested. A wise man accepts for a friend only him who has been so tested by alcohol, and found not wanting.

Alcohol will at first exhilarate most minds. Its action then will begin to vary. Some it will make lethargic, others will react with laughter and song, or with violence, whilst a few will find their minds stimulated to heights never reached without its aid.

The effect of half a dozen glasses of wine on Mary O'Doyle was to send her to sleep. Four times as many pots of beer produced the same effect on Ten Pot Dick. But, unlike fortunate Mary O'Doyle, Ten Pot Dick was unable to sleep because he was not permitted to sleep by Todd Gray, whose brain was fired by a mixture of beer and whisky. In his case alcohol cleared from his mind all the clogging veils of forgetfulness, so it had unbarred access to the vast store of knowledge gained from the books he had read and studied.

He began to talk about the stars. His voice now was clear, cultured, forceful, his real personality swamping the one superimposed on it by his life in the bush.

"There are millions of men like you, Ten Pot." he said. "Millions of men like you who live their little futile lives, blessed by ignorance – for, after all, ignorance is a blessing – and content to eat and swill, swill and eat, like pigs in their sties. Now hear me – don't go to sleep! I would like to show you a famous picture depicting an old man raking the muck in search of a lost jewel, while behind him hovers an angel offering a crown blazing with far better jewels. You and those other millions are like the man with the muck-rake. You never think to look upwards from the muck in which you stand, to gaze at the glories of our solar system, our universe about it, and the hundreds of universes beyond ours. Do you know how many stars have been actually photographed by the Americans with their great telescopes?"

"No," mumbled Ten Pot Dick.

"They have photographed a thousand million stars. One thousand millions. Hey! Get down and open the gate."

"Gate! Which gate?"

"You poor blind idiot! The gate you are looking at. There is only one gate."

Still undecided which gate to open, Ten Pot Dick managed to reach one of them, and was astonished to observe that when he pushed it open the other ninety-and-nine automatically opened at the precise instant.

"Have a look, and see if the girth-strap wants tightening," Todd commanded.

The wild-whiskered man fumbled among countless girth-strap buckles, and made sure each was in order, by unfastening the one. The result was that immediately Todd Gray urged the horse forward the shafts of the cart flew upward, and he, with Mary O'Doyle and all the loading, slipped out on the ground because he had previously forgotten to fasten up the tail-board.

It was an occurrence unsuited to the temperament of the horse, old though he was, and he was stopped only by the lightning spring Todd made to grasp his bridle.

"Pull down the shafts, you sot!" he shouted, and when Ten Pot Dick had obeyed he himself made sure that the girth-strap was securely buckled. His mind still fired by imagination and full of stars and universes, anxious to continue his discourse, he climbed into the cart via the step immediately in front of the wheel, and then urged the horse through the gateway and pulled up for his companion to rejoin him. Ten Pot Dick gazed around with a puzzled expression, closed the one hundred gates at the same time, grunted whilst he clawed his way to the cart seat, whereupon the horse was again urged forward and went on plodding, plodding along the downriver track.

"Missus –" said Ten Pot Dick.

"She's all right," countered Todd Gray impatiently. "As I was saying, Dick, the Americans have actually photographed a thousand million stars. And when they get their new two-hundred-inch telescope erected, they will be able to photograph another thousand million stars. Do you know how many stars there are reckoned to be by the latest calculations?"

"No," murmured Ten Pot Dick with closed eyes. Then his eyes opened wide for an instant, when he said: "Missus is –"

"I am not discussing my wife," interrupted Todd Gray grandly. "You keep awake now and listen to me. The latest estimate of the total number of stars is thirty thousand millions. The universe in which is our solar system contains only three million stars. The whole universe revolves on a mysterious axis at the rate of two hundred miles a second, and completes an entire vast circle every three hundred million years. Other universes are travelling through space at like speeds, universes beyond ours, comprising thousands of millions of stars, and beyond them are yet other universes.

"Your mind cannot grasp the number of the stars, and the distances each from the other. My mind cannot grasp it, nor can any mortal mind. The farthest star from us that we can see with the naked eyes is but a stone's throw away compared with the distance of the farthest star between it and that seen by the biggest telescopes. Do you understand?"

"No," Ten Pot Dick admitted sleepily. Then: "Er–yes, I mean. Your missus –"

"Leave my wife out of the conversation, please. To continue. I will honour you by revealing to you the secrets of space and time which Sir James Jeans, who wrote *Problems of Cosmogony and Stellar Dynamics*, which you should read, Ten Pot; Dr. A. S. Eddington, who wrote *Space, Time, and Gravitation*, a work a little beyond you; and the Master, Einstein, who states quite accurately that there is no straight line anywhere in Nature, have not been able to discover. They are men who have resolutely refused to admit imagination to their science. Their brains are fed by facts and figures. They do not drink like we do, Ten Pot, for they decline to permit their minds to become stimulated, fearing that under stimulation imagination will creep upon them. If anyone of those brilliant men got scientifically drunk, he would see at once the secret of Space and the secret of Time at the bottom of a pint pot. For, like all great problems, the solution of these seemingly insoluble secrets is absurdly simple."

"You don't say!" muttered Ten Pot Dick, with a quick flash of interest.

"I do say, Ten Pot. Now listen attentively. Hermes Trismegistus said of the universe: 'What is above is like what is below; what is below is like what is above.' If we take up a piece of rock we find that it comprises millions of electrons, some with attendant satellites, and space between them exactly in proportion to the space between the star worlds. In simple words, we have in our piece of rock a miniature universe.

"Now the astronomers, the mathematicians, and the philosophers all ask: What is beyond the farthest star? I can tell them. Beyond the farthest star, on and on, we come to the same star again. There is no end to the universes. Now, pay attention! Also there is no end to the atoms comprising this planet. Imagine an astronomer on one of the atoms in our piece of rock. He invents an enormously powerful telescope. With it he can see all the atoms in the earth. There is no straight line. To the man of intelligence that is definitely proved. Even vision is not straight. The astronomer on the atom, peering through his gigantic telescope, circles the whole world, and, if there is no atom of matter within his line of vision, he would see the back of his own head. It is, or would be, the same if an earth astronomer could use a million times super-telescope, and peered through it at the universe. Provided that no celestial matter blocked his line of vision, he would see the opposite side of the earth, because his line of vision would go out into space on a giant curve which would end at the back of his head, did not the earth on which he stood form the fatal blot of matter which would cut short his line of vision. Do you understand?"

"You bet! Go on!" Ten Pot responded in his sleep.

"The theologians are just as much at sea regarding the secret of life as the astronomers and others are regarding space," continued Todd Gray. "Yet the secret is as simple of solution as the others. The nearest approach to the secret of life, before I discovered it, was the Jewish conception of heaven: seven heavens, one above the other. When a scientist says: 'There can be no life after death because there is no proof', it merely indicates that he has not lived to see the bottom of a pint pot. You have observed the bottoms of many pint pots, but, like the man with the muck-rake, you are too ignorant to hold it against the light, as it were, and read. The secret of life is this. At birth a man's soul has arrived on earth from life on one of the atoms with which it is crammed. At death a man's soul goes on to the mighty universal world which is formed by the, to us, countless stars, which to that universal world are atoms. Do you understand that?"

"Yes," stated the atrocious liar.

"Well then, when those facts have become thoroughly established in your shrunken brain, get down and open the gate."

"Wot! Another one?"

"Exactly. We have arrived at the three-mile gate from Menindee."

"The missus —"

"Why harp on the missus? Open the gate."

With care Ten Pot Dick reached the heaving ground. With greater care he negotiated the distance between the cart-step and the several gates. The gate he grasped he opened wide, and then leaned against it and closed his eyes. Horse, cart, and driver passed through. Carefully Ten Pot Dick closed the gate. As carefully he completed the voyage to the cart-step. Todd Gray gazed down on his upturned, flaming face.

"The missus —" Ten Pot Dick managed to say, and stopped at that, because now he was becoming used to being cut short after he had spoken those two words.

Todd Gray sighed. "Well, what about the missus?" he said with the calmness of desperation.

"We left 'er back at the last gate."

Todd Gray turned round and looked down into the completely empty cart. His eyes winked, and, surprisingly, he came sober at that instant. "Strike me dead!" he said with the sibilant hiss of the astounded.

"I bin trying to tell yous for hours that she fell out when the shafts went up," Ten Pot Dick wailed.

Todd groaned loudly. The secrets of space and time no longer occupied his mighty brain. He said: "Open the blasted gate! We gotta go two miles for the missus, them stores, and that bottle of rum I slipped inside a swag roll."

CHAPTER XV

THE WARNING

1

IT was the third week in November when Mr. Rowland Smythe again came to Atlas, the sun then blazing with daily increasing heat, and the hot north winds blowing across the grassless wastes and raising from the corrugated surface clouds of red dust. The financial expert arrived about four o'clock, when Mayne happened to be on his way in from Forest Hill. Consequently Feng Ching-wei received him.

"Government House is full, Smythe. Would you not rather put up with me?"

"I would, rather," assented the red-faced, grey-haired, tubby man. "Someone somewhere told me that Atlas now has installed an ice-making plant. Good! I'll have a lump of ice dropped into a thin tumbler."

"Just the ice?" Feng said, chuckling.

"Well, you might pour a little Chablis over the ice and a dash of soda-water."

Feng ministered to the wants of his guest and led him at once to the spare bedroom, where Smythe's chauffeur was stowing several cases. Two minutes later the visitor was sighing and blowing beneath a shower. Twenty minutes after that he was drinking tea with Feng on the veranda. From Government House garden came to them high-pitched voices.

"Full house, you said, Feng?"

"Yes," Feng replied quietly. "You will have to meet them later,

I suppose."

"You speak as though meeting them would be an ordeal."

"It *will* be an ordeal," Feng said with slight emphasis. "You will meet Mr. Eric Tanter, who plays the piano very well. Tanter the pianist, you know. There are the three Singleton girls, resting after a season of revue. They are all right, even if their voices are too high-pitched and will fray your nerves. Mr. Bancroft is the famous Sydney engineer, a quiet, reserved man whom both Mayne and I like immensely. But his wife! I will not attempt to prejudge your opinion of Mrs. Bancroft."

"Oh!"

"Do you happen to know anything about the Russians?"

"The Russians! Certainly not – excepting that they are bloodthirsty and seldom wash themselves."

With difficulty Feng refrained from laughing. He said: "I don't refer to the present Bolsheviks. I mean, do you know anything about the great creative novelists of Russia?"

"I do not," replied Mr. Rowland Smythe firmly, regarding his host with suspicious eyes.

Feng sighed. "You soon will."

"But I don't want to know anything about them," Smythe protested. "Nat Gould is good enough for me."

"Your wishes will not be consulted. But, for heaven's sake, pray do not mention Nat Gould at dinner." Then, seeing that the discussion would be protracted, Feng said hurriedly: "Here comes Frank. I suppose you are going to talk sharply to him?"

"I am. But not until to-morrow. I've travelled two hundred miles to-day and I am entitled to relaxation. But about those Russians –"

"Please do not let us discuss them. I am sick and tired, Smythe, of Russians. If you won't talk about finance, let's talk about pictures."

So they talked pictures – which was Smythe's hobby – till Frank Mayne joined them, whereupon Feng offered him tea, which he accepted. From then on Mayne and Smythe monopolized the conversation, for it was the first time they had met since before Mayne had gone to England.

A few minutes before the dinner-gong was due to be struck, Feng conducted Mr. Rowland Smythe to the Atlas drawing-room.

Ethel Mayne and several of her guests were already assembled. The several pairs of French windows were wide open. Two electric fans circulated the air. The lights were blazing, although the sky beyond the windows still retained the sea-green of twilight.

To Ethel, who was wearing a frock of apricot georgette with an imitation black tulip pinned to her bosom, Feng said: "Permit me, Mrs. Mayne, to present to you Mr. Rowland Smythe. Smythe, Mrs. Mayne."

"I am glad you came to Atlas deciding to stay the night, Mr. Smythe. And so sorry that we could not put you up here. But really the house being so small, a few people fill it to capacity."

"It did not enter my head to complain, Mrs. Mayne. Mr. Ching-wei is treating me admirably. And I am, indeed, fortunate in meeting Frank's wife. You will allow me to call your husband by his Christian name? I am, to him, much like an uncle."

"Of course I don't mind," Ethel said, whilst Feng wondered if Smythe meant the allusion to the relative in a sinister sense. "Now let me make you known to my friends."

The three Singleton girls satisfied Smythe's sense of feminine perfection, and quickly pleased him with their vivacious camaraderie. Mr. Eric Tanter's hair was close-cropped, he was scrupulously groomed, but his voice was soft and languid. Mr. Bancroft was about forty years old really, but appeared to be nearer sixty. His hair was grey and scanty, his blue eyes were deep-set and steady. Three vertical lines were deep-cut between his brows. Like Tanter, he was perfectly groomed, but unlike Tanter his voice was deep in tone and crisp.

"Glad to know you, Smythe. Marlow of Younger Jones was talking to me about you a few weeks ago. Says you are the most travelled man in Australia. Vandyke Wilson, the author, is a relative of yours too."

"Yes. But, mark you, he claims the relationship, not I," Smythe replied, a note of protest in his voice.

"Why not? My wife thinks a lot of him. Here she is."

At the moment Mr. Rowland Smythe had his back to the pair of French windows through which entered a regal woman. The general conversation was stilled. Smythe caught one of the Singleton girls making a moue at Mr. Tanter, and then swung round. He saw surveying the gathering through rimless glasses a tall woman dressed in a severely cut gown of bright heliotrope. Her chin was square. Her mouth was large, straight, and grim. Her nose was long. Her hazel eyes were wide-spaced and magnetic, and her forehead was high and broad, revealed the more by the mode of hairdressing, which had drawn the straight, light-brown hair close across her head to the back. Feng distinctly heard him mutter: "My God!"

And then Smythe found himself being introduced, and heard a powerful, penetrating voice, which came from lips that hardly moved, yet was distinct.

"Ah! I have heard quite a lot about you from your nephew, Vandyke Wilson," Mrs. Leyton Bancroft said, as though she were a school teacher examining an insect brought by a pupil for her inspection. "For an Australian writer Vandyke Wilson is quite good. The influence of the Russian school is marked in all his work. There" – at the sound of the dinner-gong – "you must let me talk to you after dinner."

In spite of inward shrinking, Smythe heard himself saying that the coming talk would be an anticipated pleasure.

Throughout the meal he spoke seldom, although on his right sat the prettiest of the Singleton girls and on his left his hostess. The two uniformed maids who waited surprised him with their efficiency: the stiff-backed, perfect butler who hovered about the serving table created in him wonderment. He learned that in the kitchen reigned a *chef*, whose cooking vied with the best. The dinner comprised seven courses.

Over the wine Bancroft whispered to him: "Do you do much reading, Smythe?"

"Yes. Every week I read the contents of five financial journals, and manage to get through a couple of Edgar Wallaces."

At that Bancroft turned in his chair so that he came to face Smythe. Smythe's reply to Bancroft's whispered question was spoken in a firm, normal voice. Feng, then talking to Tanter, ceased, his interest at once arrested.

"You mean that you read the works of Edgar Wallace?" Bancroft inquired in surprise.

"That is what I mean," Smythe confirmed. "I think" – and now he took them all into his confidence – "I think that after a man has saturated his brain with market reports, company flotations, and wool sale prices, he is entitled to relaxation. I find relaxation in novels of the detective type. I read wholly for amusement. When I tire of amusement I go back to my financial journals."

"Surely you have read your nephew's books?" Tanter said, suppressing a yawn.

"He once sent me a couple. I find no amusement in pathological studies of morons and sexual half-wits." There was a hard glint in Smythe's bright blue eyes when his gaze became centred on Tanter, who was cynically smiling. "Personally, I prefer a good honest murder to the dirty morass of sex; hard-working, dangerous-living crooks, to the drug-craving, unnatural characters of the sex novel. Vandyke Wilson's work may please the Australian literati. It doesn't please me. I am one of the huge following of the writers of detective fiction. I go into a shop and spend seven shillings and sixpence on the novel I am sure is going to entertain me, and when I, and hundreds of thousands like me, buy a novel with hard cash, we are the masters of literature."

Tanter actually yawned in a polished manner. Mayne kept silent. Feng was experiencing unrevealed delight at Smythe's breakaway. But of them all, Smythe himself was the most surprised. Bancroft, then sitting next him, pressed his knee with secret approval.

Feng relieved the situation by introducing the subject of historical novels, and mentioned several of Dumas's masterpieces, in which facts were subjugated to his undoubted art. But worse was to befall the iconoclastic Smythe. As soon as he entered the drawing-room, Mrs. Leyton Bancroft led him to a corner.

"Mr. Smythe, I am going to talk to you very seriously," she said, with all stops out. "That clever nephew of yours should make you a proud man. It is regrettable that his financial position should keep him tied to a desk all day, and permit him to exercise his literary talent only after office hours, when he is consequently fatigued.

"It has been my pleasure to review his novels in an important Melbourne daily. I have given him encouragement because his work reveals profound study of the great creative Russian novelists. Privately he tells me that he adores Micheliski, and the immortal Dotski. In no uncertain fashion has he been influenced by Marcel Murnsivity. Your nephew's *The Progress of Lucien Halloday* is almost *the* great Australian novel we have so long been awaiting. Now – don't you see that you could serve literature in a most valuable way?"

"How, madam?"

"Well, cannot you see that if your nephew was relieved of the necessity of working in an office he could bring to his literary work a fresh, untrammelled mind?"

Since Mr. Smythe appeared a little dense, Mrs. Leyton Bancroft, the famous Australian critic, forbore to press the conclusion, but withdrew, circled, and attacked from a different angle. She continued: "It is a tragedy to Australia that so much encouragement is given to the crude, sensational novels produced by common bushmen and others. My life has been devoted to directing Australian literature, if not into, then parallel with, the immortal stream flowing from the Russian giants. Several young authors, among whom is your nephew, are influenced by the great creative Russian novelists, and I consider it the duty of every decent Australian to encourage them as much as possible, so that the modern trend in Australia should be swamped. It would assist the school of literary thought which I am directing if you were to make your nephew an allowance, so that he could give up the office work which is destroying his brilliant brain. Given the chance, he will become a second Carlplaty, a reincarnation of the mighty Dotski, a famous pupil of that wonder man, Alexander Micheliski."

"I'll think about it," temporised the exceedingly uncomfortable Smythe; but the only matter he could think about was the string of alarming Russian names owned by bewhiskered, wild-eyed men. And why shouldn't Australia have her own culture, her own homegrown literature?

Five minutes later he seized the chance to whisper to Feng Ching-wei: "Let's sneak across to your place for a spell. I want a breath of honest-to-goodness Scotch."

2

AT ten o'clock the following morning, Smythe, Mayne, and Feng Ching-wei sat in conference in the last-name's studio-drawing-room. Smoking a cigarette, the financier was seated comfortably in a leather-lined chair, at his feet an open shallow dispatch-box. For the moment, both Mayne and Feng felt as wayward sons about to be lectured by a justly indignant father.

Smythe said: "Last night you mentioned that Thurston, the English wool millionaire, stayed here for a couple of weeks. What was his opinion of the wool market?"

"He thought that the market was bound to fall a little," Mayne said quickly, even nervously. "Yet he was wrong, as the market firmed, and our national clip brought a record price."

"Precisely," Smythe agreed with a vigorous nod of his round head. "Thurston was wrong, though, only in regard to time. The future will prove him right about the falling market."

The financier tossed his cigarette-end into the ash-tray on the table with swift accuracy. He stiffened in his seat. As though wiped off with a sponge the usual look of benevolence vanished and was replaced by a grim sternness that appeared almost ludicrous on a face so red and round. The tone of his voice was metallic.

"It is like this, Frank," he continued with impressive distinctness. "Synthetic silk is going to have a slight effect, but the effect it will have on the wool market will be small compared with the effect to be caused indirectly, but no less certainly, by the feverish activity on Wall Street. It predicts the collapse of the long post-war boom in world trade. History proves that such trade collapses are always preceded by international gambling in stocks. Following the boom, inevitably comes the slump. To-day the world is crammed with goods which the mass of the people are becoming too poor to buy. I have to say, here and now, as I have to say elsewhere, that the present price of wool cannot continue, simply because the present trade boom cannot last."

"Well?" urged Mayne when Smythe paused to secure a sheaf of documents from the dispatch-box.

When the wool man resumed his voice was less harsh. "For the first time since nineteen-five my firm is interested in Atlas. Your last clip filled nine hundred and ninety bales, which averaged twenty-two pounds a bale, the total value of the clip being just over twenty-one thousand pounds. That was a drop of fifteen thousand on the clip before. As a personal friend, as well as on behalf of my firm, I warn you that, with the prospect of falling prices ahead and another dry summer facing us, you must, as a matter of common-sense safety, be most conservative in your future expenditure. Your wool cheque has failed to wipe out your overdraft with us to the extent of some five thousand pounds. Add to this the ordinary trade debts, and we will get at the total deficit facing Atlas."

"But you will stand by us for another year, surely?" Mayne interjected; to which Smythe instantly replied:

"Most certainly. Without any doubt. Both Old Man Mayne and you have been among our most valued clients. Nevertheless, there can be no sentimentality in business. My principals are quite prepared to see Atlas through this dry time, because Atlas is not mortgaged. As business men, using other people's money, they would hesitate to do so if Atlas was mortgaged. I can but concur with their views. Between us, and as a sincere friend, my opinion of Boynton and Reynolds is that they are the biggest financial octopus in the Southern Hemisphere. So watch your step."

"But why panic? What is five thousand or fifty thousand to the total value of Atlas?"

"Little, I know," Smythe agreed patiently. "What I want to impress upon you is the fact of the bad principle of being financially behind. The curse of this country is that ninety-five per cent. of all businesses, from factories to wheat farms, are loaded with a mortgage. Mortgages are the rule and not the exception they were fifty years ago. They are the very devil, but they rule in the hell of depression. Admitted, there are times when a business man cannot help seeking a mortgage, but there is no time when he cannot strive with all his might to lighten a mortgage. You made an advance on Westmacott's place, I know."

"Yes. When times change I'll pay the balance, and Atlas will be greatly improved by the elimination of the bottle-neck."

"You should have bought the place. It was yours for any sum."

"I couldn't take advantage of Mrs. Westmacott's desperate plight."

"As a business man my respect for your intelligence has gone down."

"I am sorry. I cannot help it."

"But my respect for you as a man has gone up," Smythe added

with a quizzical look. "Now, show me the extent of your indebtedness to outside creditors."

When Mayne had left to interview Barlow, Smythe said in low tones: "When I was last here, Feng, we discussed a certain matter. If you have rendered Frank the advice I suggested you should render, it does not appear that he has acted on it."

"He has not done so, but the situation then was not so disturbing as it is now."

"The general situation, do you mean?"

"Well, yes."

"And the wife, eh?"

Feng nodded, saying: "A spider woman."

"Then the wife must be brought to heel," snapped Smythe impatiently. "A butler! A *chef*! A chauffeur! Russian-mad guests! Ye gods!"

When Mayne returned with a statement of liabilities the financier examined them whilst pinching his under-lip with stubby forefinger and thumb. When he spoke his tones were kinder. "At the present date you are down to the extent of eight thousand pounds, Frank. Last year you showed a small profit of four thousand. Actually you are worse off by twelve thousand pounds."

"It is bad, isn't it?" Mayne admitted, frowning. "Our personal expenses have been heavy – too heavy."

How like Old Man Mayne was the son! was Smythe's thought. Another man would have emphasized the enormous expense of the artificial feeding. Another man would have made light of a deficit of twelve thousand pounds. He recalled to mind Old Man Mayne in those far-off difficult days, when he was obliged to borrow, and suffered loss of self-respect in doing so. And now here was the son also reduced to borrowing suffering in like manner, yet most obviously impotent to refuse his wife's demands. A spider woman! Begad! Feng was right. She'd suck the life-blood of her mate now that the mating was over.

"Yes, it is bad," he agreed with more cheerfulness. "It might have been worse, however; it might have been horse-racing. My principals, of course, will want Atlas for security, but the sum you will require to tide you over to the next shearing will not place Atlas in any danger – other things being equal. You will very soon have to continue the artificial feeding, because at all costs you must pull your breeding ewes and rams through this dry spell. My earnest advice to you is to plan as though you knew for a certainty that you will get no rain until next June. Stop all your improvement work. Reduce your labour costs. And – and –"

For a little while he was silent. They both knew that he was carefully weighing the words he intended to use. Then: "As you know, Old Man Mayne's favourite saying was: 'Look after the pence and the pounds will look after themselves.' You told me, Frank, that your private fortune totals about nine thousand pounds. You surprise me! I thought you would have been paying the fool Government's income tax on at least thirty thousand. Well, well! Doubtless you were a good advertisement for Australia whilst you were in Europe. Now you must set your mind on making up a depleted bank balance. As one having a long experience of finance, as one who is as much your friend as I was your father's, act on this advice. Cut – cut – cut! It is only one word, and a simple one. So easy to remember. Cut your household expenses. Atlas can't afford the great creative novelists of Russia these dry times. Cut your personal expenditure to the bone. Cut everything and everybody, bar pulling through this drought every sheep you possibly can."

Mr. Rowland Smythe heaved himself to his small feet in the manner of an old horse. His round, red face was now beaming, and his final strictures were sweetened with good humour. The papers he relocked in the dispatch-box, the box he laid on the table, whilst he took and lit one of Feng's cigars.

"What are you paying the butler?" he asked.

"Three hundred per annum."

"Equal to three thousand of these quite good cigars. Well, I'll arrange for twenty thousand pounds to be placed to your credit, and I will send on the necessary documents for signature. If you cut – cut – cut, you will pull Atlas through as easily as you have done before now, and as your father did many times before you. What are you paying your *chef?*"

"Four hundred per annum."

Smythe saw the pain in Mayne's eyes. He gripped Mayne's hand in a firm, strong clasp. "*Au revoir*, my dear fellow! You'll have a battle about the butler and the *chef*. Feng will help you fight it and win it. *Au revoir*, and the very best of luck!"

They escorted him to his car. He beamed on them both. The chauffeur awaited his signal. He leaned out over the side of the car, drew them together and close to him, and said, in what was supposed to be a whisper, for Mrs. Leyton Bancroft was emerging from the big house gate: "Cut–cut–cut!"

Then he was gone.

GRIPPED BY DROUGHT

PART III

THE THIRD YEAR

CHAPTER XVI

"SELL ATLAS!"

1

FRANK MAYNE sat on the Seat of Atlas. Around the edge of the spacious platform had been erected a low wooden balustrade to enable Little Frankie to romp or play with his toys on those occasions his father took him there. The child now was sturdy in physique and vivacious in spirit. Thirty-odd years before, Frank had been taken there by Old Man Mayne, to be shown his inheritance, to be given that pride of all pride – pride of the ownership of land.

It was an afternoon in early June, quiet, gently warm in sunlight, brilliant with diamond hardness. Since the conference between Mr. Rowland Smythe, Feng, and himself, more than seven months had passed with the wearisome slowness of time to a man tramping on the treadmill of frustrated hope. During those seven months and few weeks, eighty-two points of rain had fallen in one fall dated November 26th. Since that date no measurable rain had fallen anywhere on Atlas, although Tin Tin had benefited by two thunderstorms that dropped over an inch of rain in March.

To the Seat of Atlas Mayne came ever more often to fight the repeated skirmishes that were now becoming a general battle against adversity. The several dry spells that had ended in light rain, and which had lured him to the belief that a more prosperous season was definitely assured, were now become one continuous life-taking, shrivelling, choking drought. Day after day, week after week, month after month had passed – and no rain. It seemed that never again would it rain, that some vast natural disturbance had cut off the rain for ever, and that his world would quickly now be but a boundless dust-heap.

As Elisha of old he had sat on the Seat of Atlas and watched the cloud no larger than a man's hand – watched it remain the size of a man's hand. With hundreds of other anxious men he had observed, time and again, throughout the ghastly months, a knife-edged belt of dense clouds sweep from the north-west with

198

rumbling thunder and stabbing lightning, which let fall a few shilling-large drops of water, and sped on to the eastern mountains. The burning earth had steamed for ten seconds. During the whole of one afternoon in March he had sat watching terrestrial water-dogs coalesce over Forest Hill, and with hope surging through his heart and mind observed the forming of the resultant enormous black mass that began to move eastward towards the river – then to sweep southward several miles, describe a mighty arc, and with roaring anger and flaming breath let fall its treasure of water on the property of his neighbour.

Even though despair racked his vitals he did not begrudge Ann Shelley her stupendous good fortune, which delayed her artificial feeding some three months and filled many of her dams to the brim. And Ann had rung him up on the telephone, consoled him with brave words, and then had wept.

The first to succumb to the drought were the small men. They watched their flocks of three or four thousand sheep dwindle and vanish, helpless to save them, unable to meet the expense of artificial feeding. Millions could be found to finance the building of bridges and railways in and about the coastal cities, but nothing could be spared to save these heartbroken men and women, and relieve the agony of tortured animals.

Several of the selectors came to Mayne to implore him to give them employment, but he was putting off men who had worked for him for years. They applied to other squatters with like result, and finally many packed up and fled to the cities, there to secure employment in factories and on trams – never again to return to the accursed bush.

The recent summer had been long and hot. Throughout it he had not spared himself. The heat had bleached white his hair at the temples, had creased and varnished almost black his skin, had roasted into hard lumps the flesh at the corners of his eyes, so that they peered, this cool, cloudless, early winter's day, through twin slits.

He was now regretting that he had not instantly followed Smythe's earnest advice to "cut – cut – cut". After that last conference he had deferred the ordeal of acquainting his wife with the true state of the Atlas finances, and then the rain had given him fresh hope that the drought at last was ended. Not till the end of January had he come thoroughly to realise the seriousness of the position, and doubtless would still have procrastinated had it not been for Feng's outspokenness. At the time Feng both hurt and annoyed him, but now he knew that Feng had been justified in pulling him up to face hard and sinister facts.

His continued refusal to face facts – a refusal that came as a revelation to his friend, knowing him as one ever ready to look squarely on matters financial – lay in his deep-rooted love for his wife. He believed, and rightly so, that she would acutely feel the period of mental depression following the first period of delighted interest in the bush, and the chief reason he had taken her to New Zealand, and on their return had gratified her every wish, was that she might successfully live through the period of mental depression, to emerge into that lifelong content that is the reward of him or her who continues with determination to live in the Australian bush.

He was not then to know that Ethel's frantic desire to escape to New Zealand, and her subsequent passion for relays of guests, were based on something of much greater significance than homesickness. It was beyond the limitations even of his dreams that for twelve months and longer his wife had been honestly battling against an illicit passion for Alldyce Cameron. Even now, during the moments he sat on the Seat of Atlas, the personality of Alldyce Cameron did not intrude between him and the problem of his wife's coldness, dating back almost to the time he first had brought her to Atlas.

This worry and the worry created by drought were sending Mayne in upon himself. He found relief in getting away from the homestead and personally joining forces with MacDougall and the hands in their titanic struggle to pull the sheep through the summer. Those long, scorching weeks of incessant labour so absorbed his mind that not until he returned home did his worries descend on him with dreadful, soul-crushing weight. And the name of the weight was – Impotence.

"Cut – cut – cut!" had urged Rowland Smythe with utter seriousness.

"Cut – cut – cut!" Feng had almost snarled, his calm, controlled demeanour submerged by the desperate need of Atlas.

Mayne remembered every word of that interview with his

lifelong friend. Feng had begun: "The first cut we will make, Frank, will be my salary. Since your return from England I have been receiving four hundred per annum. While this drought continues my salary shall be cut down to-nothing. It is a lead you cannot refuse to follow. I have sounded Barlow, and I know he has saved sufficient on which to retire. Let him go. He must go. We can't even afford to feed him. His work can easily be added to my own. There are eleven men on Atlas employed as temporary hands. They must go. Even if they agreed to work for their tucker, which the law won't permit, we cannot afford to keep them. No matter how much it hurts you to put them off, they have got to go."

"But we needn't –"

Feng banged both fists on the table. His face was unnaturally white and unusually marked by emotion. "'Cut–cut–cut!' was what Smythe said. Smythe is no fool. I am no longer fool enough to go on watching you rush to the precipice. From now on to the end of the drought, you and I will work for nothing, and ten times harder. It will be up to your wife to make equal sacrifices. She must discharge her butler, her *chef*, some of her maids, the kitchen man, the boots, and the chauffeur. Object – go on, object! Refuse to face the plain facts – and you'll lose Atlas. Do you hear, Frank, damn you! Do you understand? You'll lose Atlas. Here, look at this. Here are figures which will prise open your eyes and keep them open, no matter how hard you try to close them. Read them! Read them again, and Cut – cut – cut!"

2

THE night following Feng's outburst had been the most dreadful in Mayne's life. He had taken the rough balance-sheet Feng had prepared to the office, and there had asked Barlow to get out, and had locked the door. He refused to answer the dinner-gong; he refused to open the door, first to Feng who feared suicide, and finally to Ethel, who blamed a bad temper. Until dawn he had wrestled with figures, thought and schemed for a way to avoid discharging those men and depriving his wife of her luxuries and pleasures. But there was no way out, and in the morning he had paid off the men, and afterwards had brokenly explained the situation to Ethel.

And Ethel had sneered and finally had sulked, even though she recognised that her husband was adamant now that at long last he had reached a decision. After that bitter hour when she had paid off the butler, the *chef*, the boots, the extra maids, the kitchen man, and the chauffeur – having assumed illness to bring her last house-party to an end – she faced her facts with dauntless courage, and saw that but two hair-like strands kept her from answering the persistent call of the first man she ever had loved, Alldyce Cameron, those strands representing her irreproachable father, and Little Frankie, her son.

For Ethel Mayne had character. Of that there could be no doubt in the mind of any person acquainted with her history. In common with her father and her mother, her career had been without blemish. Almost fanatically she had ever observed the tenets of strict morality and the iron conventions of her class. Her slightly shallow nature was less her fault than that of her social environment and upbringing. In love with love, inexperienced because she never had truly loved a man, she had found a happy release from genteel poverty in marriage with the legendary wealthy Australian squatter.

Came then into her life Alldyce Cameron to seduce her from loyalty to her husband, to quicken her pulses and fire her blood with his illicit kisses, to give her understanding of sexual love, which taught her that marriage with Frank Mayne was become a horrible bondage.

She desired and yet detested Cameron. There were moments when she loathed Frank Mayne and yet pitied him. Unacquainted with the conditions of Australian bush life, she could not appreciate her husband's heroic struggle to save Atlas when once he had consented to face the now serious situation. The abrupt cessation of visitors, the change from perfectly cooked meals to very plain fare, the quietude after months of gaiety, gave her opportunity for self-analysis and the study of her problem.

To her surprise Mayne, advised by Feng Ching-wei, suggested that she and the boy should return to England, and there stay till the drought ended and Atlas once more became prosperous. Her refusal was based not entirely on the lack of an adequate supply of money, which would compel her to go back to the scale of living she had known in her father's home. She was conversant with Cameron's improved financial position since the death of his uncle, knew that he remained at Thuringah merely because she lived at Atlas, and was sure that if she did go to England he would follow. Later, her husband had suggested her taking Little Frankie to Adelaide for the remainder of the hot weather, but she had declined this proposal on the same grounds.

Those twin, hair-like strands kept her from danger in the shape of Alldyce Cameron. She shrank from the certain hurt she would cause to her white-haired, selfish, but upright father, and her shallow, yet loyal mother, if she gave way to her wild longings; and, as well, she recognised the hurt her adored boy would suffer were she to sacrifice him on the altar of her passion.

She began to fight a good fight. She spent her leisure in keeping a diary and writing long letters home. She fussed over and played with Little Frankie every day, and during much of the day, knowing that thus she would strengthen the strands that would keep her from the abyss.

And all this time Mayne pondered on the now obvious failure of his marriage, blaming himself for its failure, yet quite unable to discover precisely where he had failed. It seemed as though the drought had withered his wife's love, even whilst it withered the life of Atlas.

If only Old Man Mayne had still lived!

3

THE homestead of Atlas was unusually silent. At the "boss'" table in the spacious office Feng Ching-wei was checking the bank pass-book with the cheque-butts of a used four-cheque-page book. To this quiet, unassuming, neatly dressed man the silence was accounted for by his knowledge that shearing was due to begin in seven days, and that every man of the reduced staff was with Mayne and MacDougall "edging" eastward the depleted flocks. Even the vegetable gardener had been pressed into the service. At the homestead now were Ethel Mayne and her child, her cook and one housemaid, Eva, Todd Gray, and Mary O'Doyle.

The door opened to admit the housemaid. "The missus says, would you care to have afternoon tea with her now?" the girl said, in tone and manner very unlike those efficient maids Ethel had been compelled to discharge.

"Thank you," Feng replied. "Kindly inform your mistress that I shall be delighted, and that I will come in one minute!"

With the closing of the door he proceeded to complete his task, the bland, unwrinkled face ably masking the thoughts running through his mind engendered by the financial position of Atlas at the end of July of the third year of drought. His nights were more sleepless now than those of Mayne. Mayne's love for Atlas was no greater than the love Mayne shared with Ann Shelley in the heart of Feng Ching-wei.

Well – they could not carry on with less labour than they were doing. Even before the coming of Ethel Mayne, Government House was staffed with four domestics. Last year they employed thirty-seven hands, but of these fourteen had been put off, leaving twenty-three to move starved and weakened sheep to the shearing. When Ethel was pressed to discharge Eva, she rebelled and kept her on, paying her wages with her own money.

Another rebel was Mary O'Doyle. Feng desired to discharge the Government House cook, install Mary, and eat his meals with the Maynes. The Maynes were willing, but Mary most emphatically refused to serve anyone but him. Feng decided to continue to pay her wages himself; but Mary, who had overheard the loud-voiced conversation between Feng and Mayne, when Feng had said that among the cuts his salary should be cut right out, again rebelled, saying: "Todd is gettin' wages wot he don't earn. I got a good home, Misther Feng, an' no wages will I take till the drouth is done."

"All right, Mary!" Feng had said, smiling – and forthwith opened a banking account in her name and paid the wages into it every month. Fanatic although he had become for economy, there were some cuts he could not accept.

Ethel Mayne he found seated at the table in the morning-room, the tea-things set out before her. She wore her favourite unrelieved black. Her face was creamy white, with scarlet lips. The dark eyes regarded him with calm scrutiny.

"Sit here, Feng," she commanded, indicating a chair opposite her, which placed him at a disadvantage in that he faced the light. "It is nice of you to come. I was beginning to be bored with my own company."

"It is nice of you to ask me," was his smiling acceptance. "Permit me to sit here. I am afraid the office work is telling on my sight," and he moved the chair so that their faces were both in shadow.

"Let me see – you do not take sugar? I thought not. A sandwich? Are you very busy these days?"

The question was asked conversationally. Whilst not even guessing its purport, Feng felt sure it preluded questions to answer which he had been invited to drink tea with Ethel Mayne. Till that afternoon their relationship had been governed by a coldness created in her by his resolute determination to stop her extravagance, and eventual success therein.

"Yes, I am fairly busy," he answered. "You see, in dry times everyone has to work harder."

"And you work so hard – for nothing?"

Over his teacup he regarded her with lowered eyelids. Then he smiled, a slow-breaking smile, saying: "Yes, for nothing. You see, Mrs. Mayne, in the good days Atlas paid me four hundred pounds for doing odd clerical jobs. When Frank was overseas my salary as manager was a thousand a year. It appears equitable, therefore, that when Atlas is hard pressed one should make sacrifices without thought of self. These hard times are bound to be followed by good times, when, I suppose, I shall again be handsomely paid for doing almost nothing."

"That does seem to be fair," Ethel agreed, watching him. "Do you know, you mystify me? I cannot understand one of your undoubted talents being content to live your life here."

"No?"

"No. Why are you content? You must think me impertinent."

"Not a bit, Mrs. Mayne. I will tell you why I am content to stay at Atlas. My father held a high position at the court of the Emperor Kuang Hsü, whose aunt – who ruled during the young Emperor's minority – he displeased by marrying my mother. They fled to Australia, arriving as poor emigrants, and went to the gold diggings of Tibooburra. There I was born, and there my mother died when I was about two years old. Heartbroken, my father came to Atlas and became the gardener. And then he died. He had lent Old Man Mayne two thousand pounds to help him through a drought. Old Man Mayne reared me, educated me, and when he died in 1918 he left me my father's two thousand pounds and twenty-five thousand pounds as interest. High rate of interest, wasn't it? Atlas always has been my home, and your husband my lifelong and greatest friend. I have no desire to desert Atlas, and as a matter of honour would not, even if I did desire it."

Surprised by his frankness, by what appeared to be an easy victory, she said lightly: "And these really are hard times?"

"I know no time more difficult in the past," was his reply, earnestly spoken.

They were alike, these two, in colouring. Their faces were naturally pale, and still unmarked by the rivers and creeks of age. They knew each other to be mentally strong and subtle, and between them existed respect for those qualities they themselves possessed.

"Will you be frank with me?" she asked him, knowing the folly of exerting her femininity on this man.

"Have I not always been frank?"

"Not always, Feng, but I want you to be candid with me now," she said seriously. "You see, my husband says that he is badly pushed financially. He says that we have ahead of us a most difficult corner to round. But he gives me no details, and I want the details. I want something definite, something more than bare generalities."

Feng pondered this request whilst again their eyes were in clashing gaze. Then: "Possibly it will not be outraging Frank's confidence in me if I do tell you a little of our difficulties. If you know them you will probably be able to forgive me my seeming antagonism to you in the past."

She made a deprecatory gesture with one slim hand.

"But yes! I have felt that you think my influence with your husband is, or has been, exerted unjustifiably, but it is not and never has been so; because, Mrs. Mayne, whilst he denied you nothing for love's sake, I could deny you many things for Atlas's sake, for your good, his good, and my good. Thank you!"

Accepting a cigarette, he held a match to hers, then lit his own, and, since she offered no remark, proceeded in his soft, well-bred drawl.

"Atlas, as doubtless you have come to understand, is something more than a mere tract of land. Originally, of course, it

206

was a mere slice of wilderness, a tiny part of a vast area of undeveloped country, before the coming of the white man. When white men did penetrate these far-western lands they took up huge grazing areas from the Government on lease. Old Man Mayne was not among the first settlers along the Darling River, but when he became established on one leasehold it was not long before he obtained others, and welded them all into the giant holding he called Atlas.

"Unassisted by Government loan money – nowadays every industry save wool is bolstered up with loan money – Old Man Mayne laboured, suffered privations and hardships, to unite his holdings with fences, roads, dams, and wells. He built up his flocks from one hundred ewes, and at one time Atlas ran as many as two hundred thousand sheep. That number was overstocking, even though Atlas then was larger than it is to-day. Its size has been reduced by the Government resuming land for closer settlement.

"Old Man Mayne married a woman of the bush, who never complained of the roughness of her life. I want now to emphasise a very significant point. Both Old Man Mayne and his wife possessed a highly developed land sense. Those early days in Australia were very similar to the feudal days of old England, with the slight difference that the feudal lords of England won their properties by military prowess and royal favour; whereas the Australian feudal lords gained their land and power by indomitable courage that rose above continuous set-backs and the opposing forces of Nature. The Maynes came west with many. The many returned to the coast settlements or went gold-hunting. The Maynes held their ground and won out, because of the deep-rooted land-love in both their hearts.

"The land-love or land-sense in them was transmitted to their son, your husband. Like them, he looks down on Atlas from his seat in the tree as any feudal lord looked down on his domain from the battlements of his castle. To Frank, Atlas is a real entity. It has a personality of its own. It claims his mind, his soul, as no woman and no child could do. You see, I know this, because I was reared by Mrs. Mayne and governed by Old Man Mayne, who imbued me with just a little of the same spirit of pride in the place, the crowning achievement of a dauntless man and a courageous woman. Shall I go on? Perhaps I bore you?" He saw that he had captured her interest.

"Yes, go on, please," she said.

"There is nothing discreditable in anyone not having that land-sense I have tried to describe," he explained. "To be blunt, you have so far given no evidence of possessing it. It is not because you are an Englishwoman. In the Australian cities you will find hundreds of women, the wives and daughters of Australian squatters, leading idle, useless lives on money which the Australian bush annually pours into their laps. You will read of their unedifying capers in the society columns, if you are sufficiently shallow-minded. But I do believe that one can acquire land-love, and pride in the possession of land, if one tries hard. If you want to try, get Frank to take you out on the run as often as possible."

"I will think about that, but I am afraid I never shall have that land-sense."

"Well, try, anyway. Now for figures. In normal years the profit from the Atlas wool averages about twenty thousand pounds. The unsophisticated will regard that amount as very large. Actually it is a low percentage on the money invested in the property, otherwise the value of the property."

"What is that value?"

"In good seasons a buyer could be found to pay anything up to two hundred thousand pounds for the leaseholds and every improvement and hoof on them. In a year like this it is doubtful if one could be found to offer more than half that amount."

"Well? Go on, please," Ethel persisted, now with one elbow on the table, her chin resting on a cupped hand.

Unhurriedly, coldly, Feng gave figures that shocked even cynical Ethel. "The year you came to Atlas it made a profit of four thousand pounds," he said. "Last year we had a deficit of eight thousand pounds. When I urged your husband to cut every expense to the bone, including household expenses, Atlas was beginning to slide down a steep hill. At the end of last month Atlas was in debt to the amount of thirty-two thousand pounds."

Watching her dark eyes widen with astonishment, Feng realised what a mistake Frank Mayne had made in not discussing finance with his wife long before. If she had not land-sense she had money-sense.

"Thirty-two thousand pounds behind!" she gasped, her controlled boredom for the moment vanquished.

He nodded. "Even so," he went on. "While the situation is grave, it is by no means disastrous, because the value of the property is big enough to carry double, in fact treble, that amount. Where we are most concerned is our standing at the break-up of the drought. When the drought is followed by the first of the succeeding good years, we shall pull up Atlas the more quickly the lower our debts are and the higher the number of sheep we have pulled through. It takes years to build up a flock of sheep, whereas a few months of drought will destroy it."

"Oh! Then Atlas is by no means bankrupt?"

"No," he told her, smiling quickly.

"Then was it really necessary to banish my guests, deprive me of my servants, stop petrol supplies for my car?" The question was calmly put, but the gleam in her eyes forewarned him.

The smile vanished. "Absolutely," he replied with grave finality. "I'll explain why very simply. Because no man can tell when this drought will end. A general rain guaranteeing future good seasons may come to-morrow, or may not come until six months hence or for another year, or even might be delayed for two years."

"Supposing the drought does last a further two years?"

"I would rather not think about it."

"But tell me. I insist, Feng."

"If it doesn't rain for another two years Atlas will be bankrupt, and Frank's heart will be broken."

A silence united them, she slowly drawing at her second cigarette, he leaning back in his chair, his gaze resting on the silver teapot. To them in the severe quietness of the room came Little Frankie's excited shouting in the garden. Feng became aware that she was regarding him intently. Lifting his face, his eyes encountered hers, dark, brilliant, forceful, and mysterious.

"Thank you, Feng, for being so good as to explain these things," she said thoughtfully. "You interested me with what you said about people having land-sense. I haven't got it, and I know I shall never have it, no matter how I might try. I hate Atlas! Sometimes I could scream for the cool feel of rain on my skin, or the tiny drops of moisture on my eyelashes when walking in a Scotch mist on glistening pavements. There are times when I simply cannot go out into the awful, eternal sunshine. I see a cloud with the wonder of a child, and at night I lie with aching heart and soul because I cannot hear wind and rain beating on securely fastened windows.

"Feng!" she was leaning toward him, and he marvelled at her tortured face, "You don't know, you can't know, you have no idea how I pine and pine for England. There are moments when, like Faust, I'd sell my soul to the devil for twenty-four hours in England. Land-sense! No, it is not in me. But England is, dear, dull, rain-washed England! Yes, lovely, green-painted England is. England is in my blood, a living, calling mother – dear God! – calling me day and night. And when I look ahead to the years I am doomed to live here, an alien in a strange country, I feel just as one must feel in prison, counting the dreary years before release. Feng, will you help me? Whilst not warm friends, we have always treated each other with the respect of good swordsmen. Will you help me?"

Surprised by her outburst, moved as never before had she moved him, Feng Ching-wei answered her warmly: "Of course I will, Mrs. Mayne. Of course I will."

"Then help me to persuade Frank to sell Atlas, and take me back to England."

The iron discipline of his features was shaken by this astounding request. His lips parted. For seconds he was unable to speak.

Then: "Sell Atlas! Frank sell Atlas! Why, he would sooner take Little Frankie to a river-hole and drown him. Sell Atlas! Good God!"

CHAPTER XVII

BATTLE SCENES

1

"BEHOLD a vast empty space!" Frank Mayne exclaimed cynically to his wife, sitting beside him in the station car. "We hear a lot about our vast empty spaces from our world-touring politicians who have never yet seen one save from the window of a railway carriage. We always shall have those vast empty spaces until God or a human genius makes it rain oftener."

They had left the main homestead-Forest Hill track five miles behind them and were running northward to Karl's Dam, where Tom Mace was pumping water for the flocks. Before them the road dipped into a shallow basin some four miles across. They were now in a world showing three colours only: the brilliant turquoise of the cloudless sky, the light, reddish-brown of the earth, and the green, almost black, of the scrub trees.

The colour of the sky was uninteresting. It was eternally the same every moment of the daylight hours. To Ethel Mayne the colour of the earth was refreshing to her sight after the slate-grey of the river flats, as was the dull tint of the sparsely set trees after habitually viewing the vividly hued, stately river gums.

The floor of the basin was a bewildering maze of hummocks carved into a thousand fantastic shapes by the wind: here a round knob, there a huge mass of hardened sand supported by a thin, wind-worn column, over there a twisting series of sand-ridges rising from a near scrub belt as waves leaping on dark rocks. About the edge of this natural basin sand-hills jagged and bumped into the blue: red, smooth, clear-cut in the motionless air. There were places near which they passed which reminded Ethel of a sand beach where a small army of industrious children had been playing with spades and buckets; places similar to scenes of the Rocky Mountains in miniature; and other scenes reproduced from those rocky, sand-blown hill-cliffs east of Cairo. Every desert, every wilderness in the world was represented here, yet this one was unique because of the scattered, wind-tortured trees.

They leaned at every angle, those trees. The scarcity of their blackened leaves revealed the gnarled nakedness of their poor, racked limbs, twisted and bent, some broken, with masses of red splinters at the break-trees that appeared as if stiffened in death after hours of atrocious suffering.

"A land of milk and honey! A Land of Opportunity!" Ethel sneered, unable to resist shuddering at the dark prospect.

"It is not always like this," Mayne told her, ever loyal to the land of his birth.

211

As a drunken man staggering across a street, a miniature whirlwind, sucking up a writhing column of red dust, moved across the flats in front of them. Of birds there were none, save three eagles sweeping in giant curves with never the flap of a wing.

Presently they passed a flock of some hundred sheep. Normally those sheep would have fled from the humming car. Now they stood with lowered heads, the heavy wool causing them to appear to the uninitiated in good condition. Ethel considered that there was something strange about their appearance, but could not define it. Their eyes were heavy and glassy. Their gaunt weakness gave them the appearance of great age.

"What on earth do they live on?" she inquired.

"Oh! Bits of sticks and roots, and odd stalks of dead herbage," Mayne replied absently. There was a man cutting scrub beyond the southern edge of the basin, and he made a mental note to send a rider to drive the sheep to the fallen scrub. Were they left there on those barrens, of a surety they would perish. The losses of stock this year would be enormous.

2

IN the rear seat of the car, barricaded on one side by stretcher-beds, blankets, tucker-boxes, and half a dozen necessaries, Eva sat with Little Frankie asleep beside her. She had overheard Mayne tell his wife that Tom Mace was pumping water farther along this road, and her thoughts now of Tom Mace were uneasy, made chaotic by persistent mental pictures of Alldyce Cameron. Cameron had but kissed her that once in the garden grass-house, and she had met him but once in that small clearing in the centre of the Poison Belt, yet she knew if Cameron called her she would answer, leaving all.

A long sand-ridge loomed before them, threatening to bar their passage; but the track, now faint on iron-hard clay-pan, turned east, skirted the ridge, rounded its flank, and by devious ways turned and twisted between hills of sand twenty feet high – hills of sand on which nothing ever grew. And then abruptly they were speeding across level country on which grew neither tree, shrub, nor grass. Against the edge of scrub timber a mile further, they could see the steel-grey blotch of an iron hut, revolving fans of two tall windmills, and lesser blotches of grey-blue iron, all of which danced in the air even on that cold, clear day.

To them it seemed long before they reached Karl's Dam, because, when first seen, the hut and mills looked only a hundred yards distant. Slowly on the screen of distance emerged two windmills separated by fifty yards of land, a dilapidated set of horse-yards, a newer and more efficient maze of sheep-yards beyond the hut, and what constituted an engine-house near the fenced-in dam.

In passing, both women examined the hut with interest. Its almost flat iron roof was kept firmly on the structure by the weight of several logs. A hessian bag, doing duty for a window, flapped gently in the breeze. The ill-fitting wooden door was open, and between the door-frame and the hut walls one could in places have put one's arm. Passing slowly, they were given a glimpse of the interior, saw a broken-down pine table, a camp-oven beneath it, several bag-mats on the earthen floor, petrol-cases in lieu of chairs, petrol-tin buckets, and a half-bag of flour hanging from a cross-beam away from the mice.

A barking kelpie dog rushed to meet them and scamper round the car, which finally was stopped at the engine-house. They could now see that two windmills, as well as the petrol-engine, pumped water from the dam into several great iron receiving tanks, from which lines of piping carried water to three long lines of troughing. For Karl's Dam provided water for stock in four paddocks, whose fences made a cross there. They did not know, however, that the mills were erected over wells that would supply water when that in the twenty-thousand-yard dam was all used.

About the nearest trough several sheep lay as though asleep. On the ground beyond the engine-house about a hundred sheep-skins lay with the wool undermost, drying in the weakly sun. The atmosphere smelt of wool and rotting flesh.

A man gained the side of the car next to Mayne. He was arrayed in torn dungaree trousers stained with grease and blood, an armless flannel vest, old elastic-sided boots, and a decrepit felt hat. His hands and forearms were foul with blood and grease. He had not shaved for several days. He was quite a contrast to the gallant, oiled cowpunchers of the cinema screen, whom at one time Ethel had expected to meet. He was Tom Mace.

"Well" Tom, how's things?" Mayne asked.

"So-so, Mr. Mayne," this caricature of a nattily dressed lover replied.

"Mills and pumps working all right?"

"Y–yes."

"You are not giving them too much well-water?"

"I don't think so. About one salt in three of fresh."

"That's right."

Mayne's gaze wandered over the wind-swept scene. The water in the dam was, of course, fresh water, but the water in the twin wells was as salt as the sea. Their water was added to the fresh water in the reservoir tanks for two reasons: first because the fresh dam-water was limited in quantity, and secondly because stock thrive better on brackish than on pure fresh water.

"Sheep coming in all right?" was Mayne's next question. "Y–yes, they're coming in all right, but a lot of them are staying in, Mr. Mayne."

Mace discovered Eva in the back seat and smiled. He saw her hesitate before she smiled back at him in a wintry manner. It was rough luck, her seeing him in his old skinning clothes. But she was thinking of the immaculate Cameron, whose face always was so wonderfully clean and shaven, and whose strong white hands were always so well kept. There were never any stains of blood and grease on *his* hands.

"Stopping in, eh!" growled Mayne. "You skinning them all?"

"Not all but most. I've had trouble with the engine. She keeps on konking out. I can't get the carburettor properly adjusted. And there's been no wind to drive the mills, so some nights I have to sit up with the engine to keep up the water-level in the tanks. The sheep seem to live only on water. Look at this mob coming in."

A flock of perhaps two thousand animals was approaching the nearest troughing. The leaders were barely fifty yards away, and through the slowly rising dust behind them the travellers saw that the sheep were marching in single file in several parallel lines, the rear not yet in sight, hidden by the distant line of scrub. The vanguard presently reached the water. With sheep after sheep reaching the trough, the body of wool grew dense, became ever greater, a swaying, bleating, dun-coloured patch beneath the dust rising in ever greater volume. The first to reach the water were the first to push back through the packed sheep behind. The watchers saw a sheep sink to the ground, and many others trample on it in their eagerness to drink. Another sheep fell, and yet others.

To the troughs Mace walked swiftly. The sheep gave way, but were strangely unafraid, although they had not been handfed with maize since the last shearing. Now enveloped in the red dust, Mace began pulling from the press those fallen sheep, assisting them to their feet, again picking them up when again they fell with very weakness, after staggering back into the *mêlée*.

The leaders now had reached the edge of the scrub and there stopped, looking behind them at those who followed and who halted in their places, every belly distended with water. About the troughs the press began to lighten, and now the leaders walked into the scrub-belt followed by long lines of sheep. There was less struggling near the troughs, but Mace was kept busy, pulling from beneath stamping hoofs the weaker sheep that had sunk to the ground.

Coming in through the long lines of outward-moving, water-filled sheep, isolated parties staggered haltingly towards the troughs. They comprised the "tail end" of the flock. Many of them lurched forward rather than walked, heavy-woolled skeletons, eyes dead and glassy, mouths partly open, tips of pink tongues protruding. Again and again some of these, the weakest of the flock, fell on their foreknees, their rear legs quickly giving out, their rumps collapsing. Several seconds' rest, and once again they were up and staggering toward the water. At the troughs sheep were drinking, drinking, their bellies distended as the bellies of gluttonous calves. The weight of water within them was beyond their strength to carry. One after the other they lay down, or rather collapsed, piteously bleating for the departing flock to wait for them a little while. Some there were whose heads rested on the ground whilst they lay upright on their knees, no strength left after that awful ordeal to reach the water.

Between the scrub and the troughs sheep stood still, gazing back after the departing flock, the instinct of follow-my-leader drawing them that way, thirst still urging them to the water. Many of these obeyed the instinct of follow-my-leader, and, after staggering towards the water for many miles, turned and staggered back without having had a drink – doomed, doomed to lie down for ever among the mulga and the pine-trees.

Half a hundred sheep lay about the troughs. Some presently would rise and lurch back into the scrub-lands, bleating, always bleating for the flock to wait for them. Some would never rise again. Even whilst the car party watched several struggled in their final agony.

And the wonderful, world-famed Australian sun shone on that scene of stark torture and death.

"More work for you, Tom," Mayne said lightly.

"Yes. There's no end to work. I'm skinning and carting away about forty every evening," Mace replied, smiling grimly.

Ethel Mayne could have struck him. Eva wanted to cry out. The lightness of Mayne's tone seemed to wife and maid stupendously callous. They did not know, and therefore did not remember, that these two men had seen so many precisely similar sights that as returned soldiers they cloaked their feelings with assumed cheerfulness that had become a habit, not a mood. Even the most terrible carnage will come to be commonplace. Month after month Mayne and his men had daily seen sheep lie down, struggle a little, then become very still.

3

SAID Mayne to Mace: "Tell Fred to take a ride through the Basin and muster the sheep back to the scrub-faller. I saw five small mobs coming across. Fred must keep his eye on Dead Man's Hole as well. That's a bad paddock corner even in a good year. I'll give you the mail and stores now. We must get on."

Whilst Mayne was thus engaged Mace edged back to Eva. "Having a nice trip, Eva?" he asked, smiling through the dust smears of oil and grease.

"Yes," she replied without an answering smile and in hardened tones.

Mace noted both and was hurt. He so badly wanted to talk to this pretty English girl, tell her how sorry he was she saw him as he then was, and explain how he had to labour from dawn till dark, oiling the engine and pumps, nursing the living sheep, and dragging away and skinning the dead sheep. He wanted to tell her about the bi-weekly dust-storms, and how the roughly cooked food was nearly always full of grit. With his soul behind his eyes he looked at her appealingly, failed to soften her, turned away, and accepted from his employer the box containing stores and mail. He raised his old felt hat to them when the car was being turned.

Only Mayne nodded a cheerful farewell. Holding the box in his blood-and-grease-stained hands, he watched the car until it disappeared, a tiny dot among the sand-hills at the northern edge of the Basin.

Once again on the main track, the squatter headed the car westward, to reach presently Mulga Flat, where they left mail and stores for the two riders stationed there, who then were out among the sheep. He drove mechanically and silently, his mind dwelling on the movements of those sheep being "edged" towards the river in readiness for the near shearing.

About Mulga Flat the country for miles was bare of grass and of herbage, the ground windswept, hummocked with sand, stretches of sand ribbed by the last wind-storm as sand left by the receding tide.

Blue sky, turquoise sky, hard, brilliant blue. Red land, barren land, windswept land. Dead land, lifeless. Trees that stood as dead trees, yet still bearing withered leaves; dying trees, gnarled, withered, tormented; trees with tapered, needle-pointed leaves, trees with greyish leaves, curled, brittle, sapless. And here and there heavy, slow-rising eagles and small flocks of fat, audacious crows, flap-flapping upward from the body of a sheep, mercifully dead, mercifully freed from the hell on this fair planet.

With unfading clarity would Ethel Mayne remember the panoramic scenes presented endlessly throughout this pre-shearing tour with her husband. There was the remnant of the station bullock team at one well, the well and troughing, as seemed usual, in the centre of a mighty dust-heap. Of the eighteen, seven only were alive – seven great gaunt beasts that stared at them with dreadful, expressionless eyes, and lowed plaintively after them whilst they sped away.

There were the ten or twelve horses they had passed in a wide pine and sand belt, horses that stood still, every rib-bone plainly marked falling from the skeleton backbone, hip-bones great knobs, skulls agrin above poor shrunken mouths. Mayne explained that they were the unbroken fillies. They never would be broken now.

They saw three, sometimes four men, each party accompanied by several dogs, moving flocks of several thousands of sheep: the men hot, weary, almost voiceless; dogs unable to bark any more and sore-footed. Ethel noted how sleek and well-conditioned were the chaff-fed horses of these stockmen, and with horror thought of those young fillies. She beheld Ten Pot Dick, arrayed in disgracefully patched trousers, scattering maize that later foolish sheep spurned with their hoofs because they were not accustomed to being thus rationed.

But it was the outcasts, the units that had been left behind the travelling flocks to take their poor chance of survival, which most moved her to horror or pity. There was the wether sheep lying close beside the track. Two eagles rose from it. They had torn the flank wool and skin away, and before they flew had been dragging out its entrails. Just when the car was passing the sheep lifted its head. And Mayne stopped, walked back, and cut its throat.

At a gate before which they stopped, a lamb, but a few weeks old, came staggering with infantile weakness across the barren, rippled land, attracted by the sound of human voices. Behind it hopped three crows like horrible black gnomes. One, more hungry or more daring than the others, flew up, alighted on the lamb's back, and dug its foul beak into the creature's shoulder. The lamb fell, the crow dropped behind. The lamb struggled once more to its feet and continued to advance, now guided by the purring engine. Blood oozed from its dirty-white, shrunken little body, dripped down both its cheeks.

"Oh, ma'am! Oh, God! Its eyes are pecked out," Eva wailed, and fumbled with the car door to rush to its aid. She felt Mayne's hand on her arm, and, through springing tears, saw his stern eyes looking down on her.

"You can do nothing, Eva. Stay in the car. I'll put the little thing to sleep."

The girl hid her face in her handkerchief. Ethel cuddled the wide-eyed Little Frankie, whilst Mayne picked up the lamb and walked behind the car.

"Frank, we can stand no more. Take us home at once!" Ethel implored, even her iron self-command now broken.

4

THE small morning-room was the warmest in Government House, and this had been converted into a sitting-room since the domestic staff of Atlas had been reduced. It was the evening of the day of the tour of the run which had been so ghastly a revelation to Ethel Mayne.

Now dressed with her usual scrupulous care in her favourite unrelieved black, she invited her husband to sit beside her on the becushioned settee drawn before the leaping log fire, prepared to fight one of her biggest battles. When she turned a little to face her husband her eyes were big, compelling. She said: "Frank, do you still love me?"

The question astonished him, so unexpected was it. "Of course," he replied quietly. "Why do you ask?"

Ignoring his question, she asked him another: "Do you know what I am feeling to-night?"

"No."

"I have felt as though I've lived in an enormous chamber, so big that the roof and the walls are beyond distance, in which were millions of weak things which were the subjects of an army of vivisecting devils. The horror of it all still presses on my brain. I shall never forget the sights I have seen. I feel befouled by evil."

"The workings of drought are, I know, fearful," he said gently. "You should not have gone. I am very sorry now that I took you. Even so, you must not take to heart what you have seen. All that is humanly possible is being done to save the flocks."

"I know that, Frank," she told him quietly. "But the fact persists in my mind that your money, all this elegance surrounding us, even the food we eat, is gained through the terrible torture of those poor sheep, horses, and bullocks."

He was about to speak, but she silenced him with her hands, whilst rushing onward: "It is no use. You cannot convince me otherwise. My illusion of romance in the 'abroad' countries, my illusion of romance attached to every individual Australian travelling Europe, has vanished, wiped out by the terrible reality. How I would hate you to-night were you fat and paunchy – excuse the expression! When I remember those politicians and wealthy retired squatters we met in England and Europe, all of them well-fed, like sleek cattle, my blood boils in my brain, for I now know that their fat has been gained by the starvation of those countless sheep. This wonderful Australia, those romance-clad sleek squatters, have become a hell and the devils who have amassed money through the unspeakable agony of helpless animals."

With growing dismay Mayne saw how big were her eyes, big blazing black orbs with ghostly flickers of crimson in their depths, like black opals from Lightning Ridge. Again he would have protested; again she stopped him with her hands. Her voice hinted at hysteria.

"Pain! pain! pain! All this vile Australia is one awful world of pain. It has become unendurable to me, something wickedly evil. You have no right, nor has any man the right, to rear sheep by tens of thousands to be tortured by Nature as never man was tortured by the Inquisition. Don't you understand the foulness of it? Cannot you see that the torture of hundreds of thousands of sheep is epitomised by that partly eaten yet alive sheep, and that sightless bleeding little thing of a lamb? The crows are not responsible, nor the eagles. You are responsible for breeding animals and being impotent to save them from a torturing death. You cannot blame the drought. You have had droughts before. You know fully what suffering the droughts bring, that you are impotent to combat this suffering, and you have no right, no kind of right, to have allowed that tiny lamb and those thousands of other dying animals ever to have lived to die as they are dying.

"No, no! Do not speak! Hear me! You have injured my soul by taking me with you. When I urged you to, you should have refused me. Since we came home I have been haunted by thoughts of those sheep dying at the water-troughs, those poor weary things which turned back to follow the flock after having crept so far to get a drink; of the lamb on which those foul crows were feeding; of those poor skeleton horses, and those nightmare bullocks. I keep seeing them, and hearing their pitiful cries for mercy. And you and I, and those other fat and wealthy people, stuffed our bodies with food this very evening. Oh, Frank! I'll never forget it."

And then came the tears – tears of horror, of sorrow, aye, of self-pity; because beneath her genuine outcry against the facts of drought Ethel Mayne knew that her accusations were overdrawn, that she was deliberately simulating hysteria to break down her husband's resistance to her wishes before she expressed them. She felt his arm encircle her waist, and permitted herself to be drawn close to him, feeling the surging triumph of success flooding her heart. She had not lost her power over him. She could feel him trembling. The moments fled. He made no attempt to speak, reckoning his physical closeness sufficient to calm her tempestuous mood. When finally she spoke again, her face was averted, and through real tears she gazed at the crackling logs.

"I – I'm foolish, perhaps, dear. I should not let such sights worry me. But I am no pioneer's wife. I haven't the grit and the endurance they must have had. I have been imagining, Frank, thinking of Little Frankie in the place of that tiny lamb. I cannot help it. I see him staggering over that awful sand country, screaming for me, followed by hopping crows, his wonderful blue eyes gone, plucked out, his –"

"For heaven's sake, stop!" Mayne commanded, his voice thin with horror. "Ethel, your imagination is running riot this evening. Pull yourself together."

"I am trying to, dear," she said, leaning against him. "I have tried, and you must be patient. I have been thinking of your offer to send the boy and me to England. But I can't go without you. We – I'd be lost without you. Besides, it would look so peculiar. Oh, Frank, let us go together! Let us go to England where the rain falls, and the grass is emerald green and as high as the knee, and the cattle and sheep are fat and sleek. Take me to England, dear, where we were happy before we came here. Let us get right away from this. Sell Atlas, Frank! Please, please, sell Atlas, and let us all go."

How carefully she had laid her big guns, how deliberately she had fired them! She waited a little breathlessly to hear the shells bursting on the objective.

"Sell Atlas!"

Her husband's words were the replica of those used by Feng Ching-wei. His expression was identical with that of his friend. To Ethel the two words sounded as though her bursting shells had stunned him.

"Sell Atlas!" No, the shells had not really stunned him:

221

surprised him rather. Again he said: "Sell Atlas!"

"Yes, sell Atlas and let us go back to England," she said with astounding calmness after the heat of the battle. And now, looking straight into his wide eyes, she knew she was defeated, knew that her ammunition had been wasted.

"My dear Ethel, what you ask is impossible. Atlas is my life. Atlas is me and I am Atlas. You don't understand, after all my efforts to make you understand."

The bitterness of defeat ate into her heart. "No, I shall never understand. Nor could any sane woman understand," she told him, her voice vibrant with rising anger. "You are ego personified. You are the King of Atlas, king of a barren dust-heap on which lie rotting carcasses. You care nothing for me. I can rot like your poor sheep in this lonely house, till I become a bedridden hag and perish. Oh yes! You are a feudal lord, a monarch, a great power in the land, but you can't stop your own animals from dying of starvation and thirst."

"Ethel!" he cried. "You are upset. Go to bed. To-morrow you will see things in a different light. Come, off you go! I have work to do."

This speech was meant to be solicitous, kindly sympathetic. To her it sounded more like bullying. Her face was like granite. Her voice was contemptuously weary. "Go to your office! Leave me in peace, for heaven's sake, or you'll make me scream."

She heard from him a sigh of pain. With her stony face turned to the fire she heard him leave the room, heard the door closed behind him. For a full minute she sat without movement, then rose abruptly and passed to a writing-desk beneath the window. With paper before her and ink-filled pen in her fingers, she hesitated before beginning feverishly to write:

Alldyce,

I give in. Come for me as soon as you possibly can. Take me away – take me back to England. I don't care what happens to me, but take me away. I cannot stop here another day, not for another day can I hold out. Oh, Alldyce, come to me quickly and make me forget all –

The door opened to admit Eva. "Please, ma'am, Little Frankie wants you. He simply won't go to sleep till you come for him to say goodnight to you."

Ethel Mayne drew in a long breath, slowly expelled it. Her voice sounded as though she were utterly exhausted. "Very well, Eva. I'll come in a minute."

For a little while Ethel Mayne sat very still, looking down on what she had written. When she rose to her feet and crossed to the fire she was sobbing quietly. Her appeal to Alldyce Cameron she dropped into the flames.

After all, Little Frankie had fired the heavier guns.

CHAPTER XVIII

THE THIRD SHEARING

1

AT mid-afternoon of the day the shearers arrived at Atlas, Alldyce Cameron was riding a powerful bay mare northward along the Thuringah side of the river. As always, he was dressed to perfection: now in English riding kit.

On arriving above the great hole at the foot of the tree bearing the Seat of Atlas, he urged his mount down the steep, evenly graded river-bank, and for a little distance rode along the dry, sandy riverbed, turning eventually up the bed of the creek, passing under the bridge, and then, riding up the less steep creek bank, came to level ground before the huge shearing shed of Atlas.

The man matched the horse. They made a wonderful equestrian picture against the background of vivid gum-tree foliage, and from the small crowd of men gathered outside the shearers' kitchen, engaged in balloting for a cook, one voice reached the rider: "Hey! There's the Turk. Where's 'is 'arem?"

The blood mounted to Cameron's handsome face. His blue eyes gleamed with anger. Tempted as he was to ride across to the group and thrash the impertinent man, he was wisely restrained by the knowledge that neither he nor Mayne could dismiss the fellow, since he was employed by the shearing contractor, and that almost certainly violence would be countered with greater violence. Within the shed he found Mayne talking with the shearing contractor.

"Hallo, Cameron!" Mayne said in greeting.

"Good day, Mayne! How's things?" Cameron drawled.

"So-so," Mayne responded. "I'll be free in a minute."

Cameron wandered through the great iron building, nodded condescendingly to big Gus Jackson, who was oiling the overhead machinery that drove the shearing machines, and from a doorway at the far end of the shed watched Mr. Andrews and another rider moving a flock slowly toward him. After several minutes he found Mayne at his elbow.

"How is your shearing going, Cameron?" he was asked.

"Bad, Mayne, bad. In fact, damned bad. We are losing a lot of sheep. Thank heaven, I'm independent of sheep!"

"Yes. You're lucky. When are you leaving us?"

Calmly Cameron eyed the shorter, slimmer man, noting the grey hairs at the temples, the crows' feet flanking the eyes, the three vertical lines between the brows: lines of concentrated thought, grey hairs of ceaseless worry, crows' feet of persistent introspection.

"I don't know that I shall be leaving, although I have got the old uncle's money at last," he replied. "Somehow this accursed country gets into one's blood, and I may be ass enough to buy Thuringah if the drought breaks the company."

"Do you think it will?"

"If it lasts another year it will bust every station in the western half of the State, don't you think?"

"Yes – if not all, then a big majority of them."

"Have you seen *The Graziers' Review* – the latest issue?"

"No. Have you?"

"I read it this morning," Cameron said seriously. "The editorial is somewhat disturbing. Says that the warehouses of the world are crammed with woollen goods: the people are either too poor or too flash to buy anything but imitation silk stuffs. It sums up by predicting a heavy fall in wool prices."

"H'm! Sounds bad. If we're hit with rotten prices on top of this drought, then, as you say, many of us will be in Queer Street."

For some few minutes they discussed the outlook, and then, since Mayne had several important matters to attend to, he urged

Cameron to go along to Ethel for some tea, saying that he would follow in half an hour.

That really was what Cameron had come for. With average good fortune it would be his first opportunity for having Ethel Mayne to himself, or, rather, his second opportunity. That other opportunity had been very brief. It had permitted him only one bare minute to draw her into his arms and smother her face with kisses – some of which she had returned after a brief and half-hearted attempt at resistance.

With a, "Thanks, old man!" a nod, and a covert smile of satisfaction, he left Frank Mayne in the shed, led his horse across the bridge, slipped a scent cachou into his mouth whilst passing Feng's bungalow, and finally passed the end of the bridle reins over the top of a fence picket near the main gate. Nodding coolly to Feng, then walking from store to office, he went through the gateway, stepped on the veranda, and knocked at the open door of the house.

"Is your mistress at home?" he asked the maid conventionally.

Inviting him into the hall, she left him waiting there whilst she sought out her mistress, returning presently in confusion, and ushering him into the drawing-room. Cameron's pulses began to stir. This room was so exquisitely feminine, the little things in it so characteristic of the woman whom he so much adored, the loveliest manifestation of his one and only god – Woman! Sudden stabs of electricity flickered through his heart muscles, sparking that organ into faster beating. And then he saw Ethel Mayne standing in the doorway, her eyes living black gems in a perfect cream-complexioned face, her lips slightly parted. So soon as she had closed the door he was standing near her, his arms stretched wide to her, his powerful chest inflated, his face tilted a little upward, the well-practised slow-breaking smile making him irresistible. He was a master of the art of rousing feminine passion.

"I can stand it no longer," he said with just the right degree of hoarseness in his voice. "Why continue to deny that you love me, you wonder woman? I know you do, while I worship all the inanimate things you touch."

"Not here!" she warned him sharply, when he would have swept his arms round her. Masterfully this strong silent man advanced, but she was no easy victim. She knew her strength because she knew her weakness. Until the moment he touched her she would be strong.

"Why don't you leave me alone?" she asked him. "You know I am not free. There are hundreds of women who would love you if you let them."

"I love none but you," he told her vibrantly. "If I may not touch you – and all my being screams for the touch of your lips – at least sit here in this chair where the light will fall on your dear face. We have but a minute or so, and then, I suppose, the maid will bring in the tea-things, and your husband will come in to – er – entertain us. Gad! How lovely you are!"

Seeing the adoration in his eyes, realising her power, Ethel Mayne for two seconds felt intoxicated. The splendour in which once lay a Cleopatra flashed across her mind in brilliant colours. She knew, and was thrilled by the knowledge, that she could make this big, godlike man do anything she wished.

"Why have you come?" she asked, her voice now less clear and firm. "Why do you persist in tormenting me? Why do you not go away, to England, now that you are independent?"

Seated opposite her, he leaned forward so that he could have touched her face. His eyes were blazing. "I have come here because I could not stay away one more split second," he said, his voice a growl, affectation and poise vanquished by his real passion for her. "I do not persist in tormenting you. If you are tormented, it is due to your hesitancy to accept what I offer. I offer you myself and all that I have, which now is not an inconsiderable sum. I offer you escape from this horrible country, from this flat, loveless life you are living; I offer to take you to Europe, to England, where it rains sometimes and the grass is always green and cool."

With quick roughness he demanded: "Answer me a question, if you can. How much is Atlas behind this year?"

"Feng says over thirty thousand pounds," she replied, not realising at the moment that she was betraying Feng's confidence.

"Oh! Thirty thousand, eh? And wool prices going down. And sheep dying in their hundreds. The drought and the coming drop in wool prices will reduce the value of this property by fifty per cent. Is Mayne offering you a trip round the world?"

"How could he do that?"

"Of course he could not do it, dear. What is more, he cannot offer to take you round the world for years and years to come. You adorable little fool! You are imprisoned here behind the bars of poverty, and you will not accept the key to your prison which I offer you. The key of gold is yours for the acceptance. You may step from your prison, and fly with me to the bright crowded world of luxury, gaiety, and – and love. Why, in heaven's name, why do you hesitate?"

For her life Ethel could not have told him. If he had picked her up in his arms and carried her away, if he had abducted her, she would have made no slightest struggle to escape. But when it came to putting the he-man's theory of feminine subjugation into practice, Cameron's nerve failed. He offered her all things but relief from responsibility for a fatal decision.

Ethel Mayne knew that she could herself never make that decision. She could not cast from her those scruples based on her love for Little Frankie and her regard for the white-haired ascetic moralist and prelate, her father. Whilst she struggled to conquer those scruples, to throw aside her hesitation and rush into those two strong arms, she knew that she never could abandon her child and strike down her father in shame.

She was saved the difficult task of confessing to her lover more than she would have wished by the entry of the maid pushing a tea-trolley, and by the time that the maid withdrew she was again mistress of herself.

"Your wisest plan is to leave Australia at once," she said quickly. "Travel! Undertake a world tour. Constant meeting with beautiful women will cause my image to fade out of your memory."

"Never! Never, I tell you."

"Mr. Cameron, in worldly wisdom I am a century old. Your trouble is that you have been in the Australian bush too long. You have met so few women, and so when you do meet a passably good-looking woman you fall in love with her. Travel, and you will meet really beautiful women."

"I shall not travel," Cameron said fiercely. "I am not a callow youth whose fancy is swayed by every pretty face." Hang it! why did he think of his uncle with his reference to wine and swill? "I shall stay at Thuringah, where I shall worship you and send to you my constant call of love until you can resist no longer, but come to me, and with me fly away to real life and supreme happiness. That is my determination, dear. You will lose your futile little fight. I shall win."

Later, when he was leaving the homestead, he met Eva coming through that belt of lantana called the Poison Belt. His resultant action became inexplicable even to himself, unless he really was like that connoisseur of wine who, as related by his uncle, when cast into prison avidly drank the coloured alcohol smuggled in to him. Cameron held Eva in his arms and kissed her again and again as though he suffered a great thirst.

2

ONCE again the great corrugated-iron shearing shed beyond the creek roared with machinery and hummed with human activity. Once again Todd Gray started working before day broke to cease only after night fell; now wearing easy boots on his wife's strict orders, for the habitual wearing of slippers had been the cause of his sore feet. This time for Feng Ching-wei it was a period of treble his routine work, and with his friend he spared not himself, the hours of his daily work sometimes totalling seventeen. Ten Pot Dick was imbued with extra energy, his duty being to feed all sheep in-coming to the shed, and to see that they were fed again before leaving for the long journey back to their barren paddocks.

The first eight days of the shearing offered no difficulties. The sheep that passed through the shed during this period were fairly robust, being the rams and the breeding ewes which had been handfed since early in February. Then began the shearing of all those sheep – the wether sheep, the hoggets, and the flocks of culled ewes – which in normal years would have been sold. The culminating horrors of the drought now began.

Knowing that this year but fifty per cent. of the sheep lived to be shorn, the shearers worked strenuously to shear individually as many sheep as they could; for, comparatively, this year's shearing cheques would be small. A shearer working to maintain a high daily average tally seized a sheep from the pen of sheep feeding his stand, then dragged it on the "board" beneath the gear from which a flex descended to his shearing machine. He pulled a cord, thereby putting his machine into gear, when the comb buzzed with speed, and, bending over the animal, began to strip the belly wool. It was then that the sheep shuddered and died.

Muttering an oath, the man went on removing the fleece, the carcass now relaxed and difficult to maintain in the desired position. When the fleece lay on the "board" as a patch of driven snow tinged with yellow, the shearer heaved the dead sheep through the chute into the pen that received his shorn sheep.

"'Ow do you like 'em dead, Jake?" inquired his neighbour.

Jake was an immense man who knew nothing of nerves, and thought of little else in life than piling up a shearing cheque.

"Me brother's an undertaker," he said calmly, walking to his feed pen. "'E got me to give 'im a 'and once sliding a corpse inter a coffin about a foot too small all round." From the pen Jake dragged another sheep. Then: "I reckoned when we boxed that stiff I was kinda out of me depth. Corpses, 'uman or sheep, I don't like. Hey, boss! what the hell are you giving us?"

He let fall the sheep he held, which was now dead, and glared indignantly at the boss of the "board", who answered his shout. "Hey! wot's this they're givin' us? This is a shearing shed, not a ruddy morgue."

"Stretcher bear – ers!" yelled a shearer further along the shed.

"Hi, boss! Call in the 'Buryin' Party'!" yelled another – a man as big as Jake. He held up the full-grown dead sheep by a hind leg as a man might hold on high a rabbit. "Hey! Tell 'em to draft in sheep. I ain't used to shearing bags of rattling bones."

One sheep in every eight died in the shearers' hands. One in ten died in the feed pens before ever the shearers could handle them. One in nine died in the receiving pens for shorn sheep. Their weakened constitutions were unable to withstand the shock of fright occasioned by the handling, or the noise of the machinery.

The nights were cold, a bitter south wind sweeping through the sheltered night paddock in which every evening Ten Pot Dick scattered maize for the sheep put there which had been shorn during the day. The exposure to the first night after their fleeces had been removed killed sheep as though the paddock had been swept with shrapnel.

The "Burying Party" visited Feng in the office. Mayne was

away on the run. The long, black, bedraggled moustache incessantly shivered as though a wind swept through it. There was rebellion in the black eyes.

"I wants six more 'orses and six more drays, and six more men to lend me a 'and carting away the dead 'uns," he said. "This ain't a shearing. This is a blooming slaughter."

"How many dead in the night paddock this morning?" Feng asked.

"Four hundred and seventeen out of eighteen 'undred. It's getting a bit thick."

"All right, Ned. I'll see about it. You carry on."

When the "Burying Party" had gone Feng's face was grave.

3

WHEN Mayne came to the homestead the next day he engaged a man owning a ton truck to transport the dead sheep five miles west of the river and there dump them. That man and the "Burying Party" worked hard for the remainder of this shearing.

"God! It's terrible, Feng," Mayne said, slumping into a chair in the office. "I have never known conditions to be so bad. The darned sheep simply won't travel. They lie down and refuse to get up. They kind of cussedly resign themselves to death, and make no effort to save their eyes from the crows or their innards from the eagles. To muster them into the shed is enough to break a strong man's heart. The shearers are growling, but they're a good gang, and know it's no man's fault. It is getting to be a nightmare."

"What sheep are they shearing now?" Feng asked.

Mayne stared across the table at his friend with eyes dulled by desperate misery. His face was lined by intense fatigue. Feng saw that for a long time he had had no proper sleep.

"What sheep?" Mayne echoed, and laughed unpleasantly. "Why, those nine thousand wethers – or rather what's left of them – that I should have let the buyers take at seven shillings a head."

"And that I should have let go at twenty-one shillings," Feng put in quietly.

"I'm not blaming you, Feng, as I have told you twenty times; I'm not blaming myself either. I gambled on rain and lost. And in the same circumstances I'd gamble again."

"Well, old man, we must accept the loss in a gambling spirit, and continue to play for a future win."

Feng leaned over the table toward his friend, and when he spoke after a slight pause he marked his points by softly slapping the desk-top with his open hand. "That you will not be able to do if you don't look after yourself. You look like a man who hasn't slept for a week. Stay home for a couple of days and take things easy."

"And hear nothing but English meadows with knee-high green grass, and running streams with trout jumping for flies, and busy streets lined by hurrying people, and unbroken clouds from which the rain falls for hours, and cultured society, and lords and bishops and deans and rectors, and old magnificent buildings – and – and – oh, hell!"

For a full minute the two men stared at each other, the brilliant sunlight falling athwart the desk, the rumble of machinery in their ears, with the sound now and then of men's varied voices and dogs barking. Then Mayne fell to rolling a cigarette, a simple common task giving sufficient proof to the observant Chinaman that his friend was at last revolting from the habits of English society imposed on him by his wife. Since his marriage he had smoked "tailor-made" cigarettes in an ebony holder, and never had smoked his pipe inside the walls of Government House.

"You know, Feng," Mayne said at last, "it is being borne in on me that I am the greatest fool in the back country. I fell deep. No man could fall deeper. I expected that oil and water would mix in the test-tube of love. Well, oil and water won't mix! Had I been a lord or something, or had Ethel been a housemaid, the result would have been all water or all oil."

"You always were impulsive, Frank; but, as Old Man Mayne liked to say: 'You've made the bed you must lie on'. You must go on trying to mix the oil and the water for your son's sake."

"I am not arguing about my mistakes or my fate," Mayne burst out. "But I am so damned tired of incessantly hearing about the beauties of England, and being pestered to sell Atlas."

"Sell Atlas!" exclaimed Feng, knowing now that Ethel, without his help, had proceeded with her intention of persuading her husband to sell.

Mayne sighed wearily, raised his brows, and repeated the now significant phrase. "Yes, sell Atlas. Sell Atlas! – sell Atlas! – sell Atlas! I'll rot before I sell my inheritance and deprive Little Frankie of his." Rising to his feet, he added: "I can do little here. Andrews is carrying on all right with the shed sheep. I'm off to give MacDougall a hand. We're criminally short-handed."

"But you've only been here a couple of hours," Feng protested. "Come, man! Give yourself a chance."

At the door Mayne paused, looking back. "All right," he agreed. "I'll have twelve solid hours' sleep – at Mulga Flat. *Au revoir!*"

Feng, pushing back into his chair with pursed lips and eyes gleaming through mere slits, heard Mayne's car roar into life before rushing away with a diminishing hum.

For a considerable time he did not work on his books, but sat and smoked cigarette after cigarette. It appeared to him that at long last Frank Mayne recognised the foolishness of his dream of happiness. Now it would be but a matter of time before he saw the stupidity of bringing to Atlas an untried Englishwoman when he could have won a woman whose land-sense was equal to his own, whose sympathies were the same as his own, and, most important of all, would have returned his love in brimming measure.

To this quiet, studious, unambitious, gentle-natured Oriental, born in an Occidental community, whose philosophy and ideas of personal honour were those of his father by inheritance, it seemed that what should have been in the first place would be in the last with the inevitability of fate. Long since had he known that his love for Ann Shelley, dating back to early adolescence, was, and would ever remain, a dream. Only if governed by unreasoning passion would she take him to husband, for she was as her father, as Old Man Mayne, as every wool-grower who was imbued with the ethics of breeding. She would regard marriage with him, if the thought ever occurred, as a sin against the science of eugenics of which she was a graduate.

With the eternal sunlight flooding his office, reminding of the drought, he felt that, as the drought was pursuing its way to its destination of ruin, so would the affairs of Mayne and his wife and Ann Shelley go forward to their destiny. Nothing would ultimately prevent that; and, accepting this, realising all he owed to Old Man Mayne, to Frank, his friend, and to Ann Shelley, also his friend, Feng Ching-wei determined to do all in his power to hasten forward that destiny.

He had seen Mayne's wife in Cameron's arms that day in the cane-grass house in the homestead garden. He had watched them during those occasions Cameron had visited Atlas, and he knew that Ethel loved the man who had "loved" many women. He knew, too, the reason prompting her frantic haste to escape Atlas and flee to New Zealand, as he knew the reason of those successive house-parties, which were to fence her against the fire of her passion.

But now that protective fence was gone. Cameron would have known its purpose, for he was a shrewd man. As he had desired women before, so he desired Mayne's wife. As before he had cast aside the playthings of an hour, so eventually would he cast aside Ethel Mayne.

"Sell Atlas!" She would sell Atlas. She would drag Frank away from his inheritance, leave some stranger in ownership of land that his friend and he regarded so justly as great. To her was debited part of the present financial state of Atlas; to her was debited part of his friend's worry; and to her was debited most of his friend's unhappiness.

Feng Ching-wei hated the woman. Her ingrained snobbery was an offence. He remembered the insult to Mrs. Morton and to old Barlow, the hurt loyal old Aunty Joe and several aboriginals, who had worked for Atlas since they were boys, had received when they were ordered off the run because Mrs. Mayne objected to their colour. Feng recalled the several domestics who had left, angered to fury by the cold superciliousness of their mistress. Nothing in Australia was good enough for her. In her sight the Australians were uncouth Colonials, born to serve, to follow, and to be patronised by the English governing class to which she belonged. Proud, haughty, disdainful, he would yet bring her to the dust, wielding the weapon she herself had forged, the weapon of her shameful passion for a he-man who had stepped from the pages of an ultra-modern sex novel.

He would free Atlas from a blight greater than the drought.

233

CHAPTER XIX

THE POISON BELT

1

OFTEN during the early spring days, which were calm and pleasantly warm, Eva took Little Frankie for outings, either up-river to pay Old John a visit, or down-river to the Seat of Atlas. At least once every week they visited the lonely old man, taking with them fresh bread and seasonable fruit, and returning always with a gift of a fine river cod or a brace of those black ducks that are almost as large as Indian Runners and decidedly more "meaty". Sometimes, if the wind blew hard, Eva pushed Little Frankie as far as the fallen gum tree in the clearing amid the lantana belt.

This day that they visited Old John, Eva appeared very winsome and fresh in a blouse of white poplin, and a fashionably short skirt of navy serge. Her imitation silk stockings, to wear which was sacrilege on a wool-producing property, were new and her shoes were smart. No hat concealed her light-brown uncut hair, and her hazel eyes sparkled with life.

Little Frankie in his fawn-coloured coat and brown felt hat, riding in a light push-cart, was a picture of childish health and joy in adventuring forth to meet that kind old gentleman who lived with Bells-bub and the tame birds.

It will be remembered that the lantana belt covered a roughly triangular-shaped area based on the western sand-hill country, its apex, more than a quarter of a mile wide, lying along the river. It was semi-floodland, lying lower than the level of the surrounding flats, and covered with the lantana peculiar to floodlands. The cane-like, useless bushes sprouted from the ground like giant wheat-sheaves, among which wandering horses and cattle and sheep had created a maze of paths, over which a stranger might wander till overtaken by death. The road to Menindee cut this belt half a mile back from the river, there being constructed of earth banked above a causeway of logs, for after heavy rain the Poison Belt was impassable by any vehicle and boggy enough to trap a

234

fox.

The man-made path along the river-edge was hard and easily to be followed. For no particular reason Old Man Mayne had named the lantana the Poison Belt, and in it the traveller seemed to be in a dim, sunless world, although the lantana bushes were widely spaced and seldom grew above ten feet in height. The countless openings, the short, twisting aisles, at this time of the year deep in shadow, hinted at ogres and dark mysteries, and Eva was always glad to reach that wide clearing in the centre of the belt where lay the trunk of a long-dead gum tree, on which she sat for a few moments looking down at the small fish jumping from the surface of a river-hole. The clearing she called the Rest House.

When they drew near Old John's dwelling Beelzebub, the fox-terrier, raced madly to meet them, and to scamper round the pushcart with much barking.

"Bells-bub! Bells-bub! Ooo – Bells-bub!" shrieked the child.

"Down, sir! To heel, you scoundrel!" Old John boomed, coming a little way to meet them too, in his baggy grey flannel trousers and a voluminous-skirted shooting coat flapping in the wind. "Welcome, Master Frankie! Good day to you, Miss Eva! Come along in – come along in, and tell me all the news."

And, turning, he led the way till they reached the garden-gate. There he assisted the eager child to alight, and gallantly bowed to Eva to precede him along the short garden path, he following with the child tugging at one gnarled old hand, and crying: "Where's birdies – my birdies? Ooo, Bells-bub!"

Arrived at the bush-roofed, creeper-walled veranda, Old John offered Eva a chair, himself sitting on a petrol-case near the table, and drawing Little Frankie to his lap. Whereupon the child eagerly reached for the sugar-tin, removed the lid, pushed it back to the centre of the table, and became immovable and silent, two wide blue eyes intently gazing at a pair of minah birds half hidden by the creeper leaves. Would they come down to the sugar or not?

"Don't talk!" whispered Old John thrillingly.

The suspense was becoming unbearable, when one bird, quickly followed by the other, swooped to the table, strutted sedately to the sugar-tin, and as sedately began to pick out the grains.

So absorbed was the boy that he did not observe the tame galah parrot climbing up Old John's back, assisted by beak and claws, finally to reach the broad shoulder and rub its beak against a tempting ear. "You ole devil! You ole devil!" it said affectionately.

Eva could not but laugh. Little Frankie's interest was immediately transferred to the galah, his blue eyes wider than ever. And there sat Old John, with his bushy white brows and long, drooping Viking moustache, gazing down at the rapt, upturned, vivid little face with an expression in his own that made Eva wonder.

The cat appeared, to receive the child's loving caress and a saucer of powdered milk. Afterwards Old John made tea in a billycan and produced a tin containing sugar-coated biscuits. And then, an hour later, having gravely accepted two loaves of fresh bread and a small basket of vegetables, and having bestowed a gift of a fine nine-pound river cod in the bottom of the push-cart, the host walked with them as far as the Poison Belt before wishing them bon voyage, and reminding them to remember him to the Maynes, and to Feng Ching-wei.

Those friendly little visits were red-letter days to Old John. They helped him to live through the long periods separating the quarter-days when, after having had dinner at the homestead, he would depart for Menindee, where he had business.

2

IT did appear, this last Sunday in August, as though the Gods mocked at Feng Ching-wei's determination to break the woman he hated with the weapon of her passion for the man for whom he felt nothing but contempt.

The shearing, with the additional work thrown on him, had interrupted the painting of a gum tree branch on which were perched a kookaburra with a writhing snake in its beak, and a galah with ruffled feathers and erected crest impudently defying the snake it feared. For his Nature subjects Feng relied a great deal on photography, and for the picture he was painting had found among his prints an excellent close-up of a laughing jackass, but no suitable picture of a galah.

The shearing this year had lasted hardly a month, but Feng

considered that he was entitled to half a day this Sunday to visit Old John and photograph Old John's pet galah, which would assume anger at sight of a teasing twig. With his reflex camera Feng left the Atlas homestead about three o'clock, and followed the river path always taken by Eva and others who had business with Old John.

A strong south wind swept along the bed of the dry river, tearing through scintillating gum-leaves of the grand old trees with a sound of sea-waves crashing over rocks. Through the wide-spaced western box trees, when now and then he could see the horizon, he noted how the sky above it was tinged with red, and from experience knew that over all that sand desert swept one of those unpleasantly cold dust-storms that later would recur often and last for days. All the bird life in the western half of the State appeared to be concentrated along the river, where water lay deep at every bend.

The sky was cloudless. Along the river the air was free from dust, and the birds provided interest. Soft-footed as all his race, Feng followed the well-used path down into the Poison Belt. Here the force of the wind was less, but the sound of it not diminished. Here in the shelter of the lantana it was pleasantly warm in the soft sunlight.

He came on Alldyce Cameron and Eva sitting on the fallen tree in the little clearing the girl had named the Rest House. They were close together. Cameron's right arm was about the girl's shoulder, his left lay across her bosom. Her head rested against his shoulder. Her face was tilted upward, eyes closed, to receive his kisses. Undiscovered, Feng Ching-wei slipped back behind a lantana bush.

His dream of confounding Ethel Mayne with evidence of her infidelity was wiped from his mind, for Feng could not conceive a man so base as to plan the ruin of two women at the same time. His was not the mind to fathom, and consequently understand, the astonishing action of Alldyce Cameron who, in his pursuit of Woman, had long since adopted the seafarer's slogan of "Any port in a storm", or that very old maxim that runs: "A bird in the hand is worth two in the bush", or even the old aboriginal saying: "Drink today, for to-morrow you may thirst."

The place Ethel Mayne had occupied in Feng's mind was

taken by Tom Mace, and Mace belonged to that category of men who on the surface are highly strung and reserved, yet are capable of dynamic action under stress. Precisely what purpose pictures of this love scene would serve, Feng then had no thought. Nauseated by Cameron's behaviour, he waited his opportunity. The wind sang across the tops of the lantana clumps, effectively drowning the "click" of the camera shutter when he made four exposures. Satisfied, he then withdrew from his inelegant position, and, making a wide detour, continued on his way, mystified and not a little disappointed.

He wondered how long this affair had been going on between Cameron and this fresh English girl whom every one liked. Knowing the kind of man Cameron was, he foresaw the inevitable result – unless he stepped in. Legally, neither Mayne nor he held any jurisdiction over the girl, but Mayne did have certain responsibilities towards an immigration society that had assisted Eva to Australia, and had placed her with Mayne on his application. Of this aspect Feng thought less than he did of the reaction of the situation on Tom Mace, and decided to wait and watch a little.

Old John's fox-terrier came running to meet him with joyful barks. He was patted, and then he ran back to the small garden-gate, where he stopped, still barking, as though anxious to escort the visitor to the door of the shack. There was no sign of Old John when Feng reached the gate. On his entering the garden the cat met him with tail erect. Beneath the roof of the semi-enclosed bush veranda the minah birds peered at him, and the galah he had come to photograph waddled in its absurd gait across the doorstep. On the floor lay a torn leg of mutton; in a shallow tin was almost a gallon of powdered milk; whilst on the table at least three pounds' weight of sugar was poured in a scattered mass.

"Where are you, John?" Feng called.

"'Allo! you ole devil!" said the galah. Met by silence, Feng entered the shack, then darkened by the far trap-door window being closed. At first he failed to distinguish objects; but, when he reached the trap-door window and was about to open it, he saw old John lying peacefully on his bed.

"Wake up, John! I've called for a yarn, and to photograph the galah," he said cheerfully, and, bending forward, looked closely at the old man. And then Feng felt a coldness at his back, for Old John was not lying in a peaceful attitude. Quickly Feng raised the trapdoor window, fastened it up, and returned to the bed, there to stand shocked into immobility, gazing down on the calm, majestic, dead face of Sir John Blain.

It was Sir John Blain who lay there, not Old John the hermit. The kindly figure of Old John had for ever vanished. Feng straightened the limbs, folded the hands across the breast, closed the eyes. Sir John Blain lay as several of his forebears lay in the church near Blain Chase, stone effigies of knights above their own sarcophagi.

The dead man was dressed in his slightly old-fashioned morning clothes, the clothes he invariably wore when on his business trips to Menindee. On the table, as though in readiness to be worn, were the well-brushed top-hat, the fawn-coloured kid gloves, and with them the ebony walking-stick. One stiffened hand held the picture of his beloved son, killed in battle.

As in life, the severe countenance was newly or recently shaven, because the hair had continued to grow since death. Sir John must have died suddenly, for his clothes appeared almost as though placed on the body after he had died.

The first shock having passed, Feng Ching-wei looked about the scrupulously tidied hut, and so found the letter on the table addressed co-jointly to Frank Mayne and himself. Standing, he read:

My dear boys,

As in the years passed I called you my dear boys, I fear I do so now for the last time. Since rising this morning I have been suffering acutely from a heart-attack, and now at nine o'clock to-night the pain has become worse and I have a premonition that I shall not live to see the coming day. My life is spent. For forty years it has been a broken life, yet on Atlas, thanks first to Old Man Mayne and finally to you young men, I have found peace and experienced many happy moments.

Believing that now the time of passing is near, I face the Beyond confident that I am to meet my dear son. I have dressed myself carefully in the clothes belonging to my real social station. It is not an act of snobbery, but rather of pride, a wish to die as a gentleman and not as a broken-down bush hermit.

Before dark I put out for my pets sufficient food to last for several days, in case no one should call. I desire that Beelzebub be given to Little Frankie. Perhaps Mary O'Doyle might consent to look after the faithful cat. The galah, I think, will be acceptable to Feng. The minah birds will be able to look after themselves, though they will miss the sugar.

Within a deed box in the chest are the documents relating to my estate. I have left the bulk of my personal estate, unfortunately amounting to only a few hundreds, to Thomas Mace, who has rendered me many acts of kindness, and whom I have found possessed of sterling courage, and imbued with the energy and the spirit which have made this blessed Empire.

Farewell to you both! May the drought quickly end, and prosperous years attend you!

John Blain, Bt.

Slowly Feng replaced the letter in the envelope. The cat was rubbing itself against his legs. The galah was trying to climb the smooth table-leg without success. The dog was standing on his hind legs beside the bed, endeavouring to awaken his master with a frantic paw. Reverently Feng covered the body with a sheet.

Well, a broken life had ended. It had begun so promisingly till tragedy overtook it. Lady Blain, after having been discovered with her paramour by Sir John, had run away with a neighbouring squire. Sir John had given to his wife a deep and an abiding love. He would have forgiven her her mad act, the hurt she had done to him; but he could find no forgiveness for her desertion of their son, then at Eton. The elopement ended as such elopements do. The wife became tiresome as a mistress. She sought forgiveness from her husband, but Sir John declined to receive her. On the railway passing Blain Chase, Lady Blain had laid herself down before an oncoming train.

Sir John Blain travelled the world – to stop finally at Atlas, persuaded by Old Man Mayne, whose rugged, proud character was so akin to his own. The son entered the Army, was killed early in the Great War. His death was the final blow that decided Sir John never again to see Blain Chase, where great happiness once had been his.

Old Man Mayne offered to build him a bungalow. Sir John declined, preferring to build himself a home far enough from the homestead to assure peace and independence, yet not so far as to be beyond occasional human intercourse. With his ghosts and his pets, Sir John became Old John –

The sun was setting, a drop of blood behind the western veil of red dust, when Feng, carrying the deed box, emerged from the hut. The galah already was climbing to its cage, whose door never had been closed. Calling the cat and the dog outside, Feng closed and fastened the door. Beelzebub would not follow when called. He lay before the door, his head resting on his paws, his nose against the narrow slit between door and step.

Down at the Rest House the lovers were gone, but of them Feng was not thinking. He was seeing a succession of mental pictures in which two mischievous boys, and often a merry girl, were sitting on the river bank, whilst a grey-haired man with a grey Viking moustache told them, in a strong, booming voice, the great stories of England's past.

Mayne was in the office when Feng entered.

"Sir John Blain is dead," Feng announced softly.

Frank read Sir John's letter several times. His eyes were moist on glancing from it to his friend. "He was a great gentleman," he said quietly.

CHAPTER XX

THE FALL

1

THE morning of September 5th saw Feng Ching-wei at work in the Atlas office studying, as he had studied a dozen times before, the shearing tallies. The figures made heartrending reading even now, those terrible figures that revealed the harvest of Drought, those same figures that had sent Frank Mayne with brooding eyes and sunken shoulders out into the wilderness to fight the cloud of despair in the shadow of which he moved.

The previous year Atlas had shorn forty-five thousand sheep, and the year before that sixty-six thousand. This third shearing in the great drought had brought the total shorn down to twenty-three thousand, and of that number over three thousand had died of cold after being shorn. At that instant, taking into account the sheep that had perished on their way back to the paddocks, it was doubtful if there were more than twenty thousand sheep on all Atlas.

Unstinted money had been poured out to save the flocks. The men had worked loyally and without complaint, ignoring the set number of hours per week laid down by the Arbitration Court. MacDougall had fought the drought as though the sheep had been his. Mayne had slaved as hard as MacDougall, whilst Feng had laboured no less. To no avail. From sixty-six thousand to twenty thousand! Of this number the great majority were the hand-fed ewes and rams, but by Christmas the total might well be reduced a further six thousand; by the end of the coming summer, if no rain fell, their number might have shrunk to five thousand – because the end of the stream of money was now in sight.

The wool clip had been transported to the railway at Menindee and dispatched to the brokers. It was, for a huge run like Atlas, a miserable consignment of six hundred bales, two-thirds of the number dispatched the year before, and but one-third of the number sent down the year before that.

To worsen the situation, the wool markets were rocking. Buyers from England, Europe, Japan and America awaited the opening sales, no one knowing what the cable advices they were daily receiving might contain, none being able to foretell to what maximum they would bid.

On Atlas the days passed with dull monotony to the wreck of a man driving a car or riding a horse over the desert that once had been a vast natural paradise: to the woman in Government House, disillusioned, racked by illicit desires, torn this way and that by taboos, affections, and longings; to the pale-faced man working at books and documents in the quiet station office, impotent to avert, unable to close his eyes to, the doom approaching Atlas.

September 12th fell on a Thursday, the day of the week the mail-car reached Atlas at eleven o'clock in the forenoon. Feng took the outward bag to the driver, and from him accepted the inward bag. With forced cheerfulness he asked the man how matters went with the people of Menindee.

"Crook, Mr. Ching-wei," the driver replied, rolling a cigarette. "The pubs are full of blokes spending the last cheques they'll make for some time, and the tracks are covered with blokes looking for jobs wot won't come to light till the rain falls again – if ever it does rain again, which I doubts. Isn't there a song which goes – 'It ain't gonna rain no more?' I bet an Aussie bushman wrote it. They tell me that Mornington Station has busted, and Myall Creek Station has sacked all hands and is leaving the sheep to take their chance. Boynton and Reynolds took over Thunder Downs, and offered Fairway, the owner, five hundred pounds and the station car to go away with. They found old Fairway in a water-hole the next morning. Well, I must get. No passengers this trip, and I've got to open and close all the darned gates myself."

So Mornington had crashed! It was one of New South Wales' biggest sheep-runs, and was considered the most solidly financed. And Boynton and Reynolds had taken over Thunder Downs from the owner, Fairway. Poor old Fairway! He had owned Thunder Downs for thirty years. Of course, other crashes would follow. The strain was too severe to be borne by any but stations governed by super-shrewd men or which, like Tin Tin, had been blessed by rain from chance thunderstorms.

Feng was followed into the office by Eva and Todd Gray, who conversed in low tones whilst he sorted the contents of the bag. Handing them the mail for Government House and the men, he was left with two private letters and the Atlas business mail. The first letter he opened was that which on the reverse side of the envelope bore the imprint of Messrs. Boynton and Reynolds, the brokers and station financiers. The contents acknowledged receipt of six hundred and two bales containing wool which would be included in the first of the series of sales that would start September 25th. The brokers added their opinion that the price would average thirteen pence per pound.

Thirteen pence per pound! Rapidly Feng figured the average amount each of the Atlas bales would bring at thirteen pence per pound. The resulting estimate was twelve pounds sterling per bale. And last year it had been twenty-two pounds per bale for nine hundred and ninety bales.

He rang up White Well. "Do you know where Mr. Mayne is?" he asked Fred Lowe, who answered the call.

"No. Haven't seen him for a week."

Ten Pot Dick at Mulga Flat announced that he had not seen "the boss" for "hell knows when".

Mrs. MacDougal thought that Mayne was with her husband in the paddock round Burnt Hut, and that they were camped there. Should she ring up Burnt Hut?

"Please, Mrs. MacDougall," Feng requested. "It is most urgent."

But it was not until nine o'clock that Mrs. MacDougall connected with her husband and Frank Mayne at Burnt Hut. She telephoned the information to the anxious Feng, since there was no through connection from Burnt Hut, and he requested her to take down a message and transmit it to Frank Mayne.

It ran: *Brokers advise wool to be sold September twenty-fifth. Forecast price at thirteen pence per pound. Shall I instruct them to withdraw wool from sale?*

Mayne's answer was: *Yes. We are not giving away the wool.*

So immediately the Menindee post office opened for business the next day, Feng wired the brokers to withdraw the Atlas wool until the first sale of the series showed the temper of the market.

To this telegram he received no reply, and was not unduly perturbed, for he expected none. The day continued with the heavy monotony of depression.

Mayne came in, stayed two days, and departed, and when he had gone Feng called seven men into the office, explained the position with frankness, and paid them off.

2

IT was Mary O'Doyle who shocked the anxious Feng out of the business depression into his former world of speculation regarding Alldyce Cameron and his love affairs. It was when he was sipping the after-dinner coffee that Mary had placed before him that she said dramatically: "There's some queer goings-on, I'm thinking, Misther Feng. Goings-on wot tickles me nose."

"Indeed! To what goings-on do you refer?" he inquired curiously.

"Well, from this here window I can look across to the far side of the Gutter," she proceeded impressively. "About a week ago I noticed that Eva went off with Little Frankie down the river, and, a moment or two after, she went off up the river. Why does she want to go up the river all on 'er own? She went up the river this afternoon when Eva and Little Frankie went down the river."

"She?" Feng asked blandly.

Mary O'Doyle jerked her head significantly towards Government House. "Her," she said, with utter simplicity.

"Do you mean Mrs. Emily?" Feng asked, referring to the cook.

"Not Emily. Her," Mary said, with what was meant to be cutting sarcasm.

"Oh!" The enlightened Feng tapped his coffee-cup with an apostle spoon. "Well, I suppose Mrs. Mayne is at liberty to take an airing if she desires to, Mary. Perhaps she goes to tend Old John's grave, for you will remember he was buried in his own garden plot, as he expressly wished."

Mary O'Doyle smiled scoffingly. She sniffed. Feng had heard that sniff before. So had Todd Gray. It indicated Mary's emphatic disbelief in a subtle way.

"Well, I 'opes she is enjoying av 'erself a-walking up the river all on 'er own – I don't think – when 'er own flesh an' blood takes an airing in the opposite direction. An' she says to Eva: 'Take Little Frankie to the Seat of Atlas this afternoon and show 'im 'is inheritance.' As though she troubles about Little Frankie's inheritance. She's a – a –"

"Mary!" Feng exclaimed sharply, just in time.

Again Mary O'Doyle sniffed, then rolled away with her laden tray. Left alone, Feng rose to his feet and walked to the window. Beyond, it was quite dark, and he could see nothing. The night-masked view held for him no interest then, for his mind sought an explanation of Ethel Mayne's stroll up the river toward Old John's deserted house, when she had instructed Eva to take Little Frankie to the Seat of Atlas to show him his inheritance. He felt inclined to sneer openly as Mary had done when the child's inheritance was mentioned as of concern to his mother.

Surely Cameron was not meeting Ethel when he was wooing Eva, the maid?

The thought flooded his mind as a coloured light. And what did Mary O'Doyle suspect? Trust a woman to be correct in her suspicions, whatever they might be! Even so, he could not very well ask her what precisely were her suspicions. But – he bit his

nether lip – should Cameron be wooing Ethel, even though he
kissed Eva, then the weapon Ethel had given him, Feng, and
which Eva in Cameron's arms had taken away – that same
weapon he would receive back again.

After considering these points for nearly half an hour, he
decided that he must know why Frank's wife walked up-river
when Eva and the boy had been directed to walk down-river.
And, obviously, the only method he could adopt to discover the
significance of this behaviour was to spy on Ethel Mayne. To
follow her, he must know when she went off, and this could not
be known without assistance, for it was impossible to spend the
whole of every afternoon in that room just to wait and watch
Ethel set out. For his friend's sake, for the sake of Atlas, aye, and
for the sake of the woman he loved, Feng Ching-wei decided to
spy on the haughty woman who hated Atlas.

He rang for Mary O'Doyle. "I believe, Mary," he said, when
that mighty woman appeared, "I believe, Mary, that you are a
woman of discretion. That being so, I know you will not ask me
what I am thinking about or tell me what you are thinking about.
That is, our thoughts regarding 'Her'. When next you notice Eva
and Little Frankie going down the river and observe 'Her' set out
walking up the river, please come to the office at once and let me
know. Now, not a word! And not a word to anyone – most
certainly not to Eva."

Mary O'Doyle's small blue eyes gleamed delightedly. She
opened her wide mouth to its utmost extent, and then shut it with
snapping teeth, so that her jaws became emphatically clenched,
and her lips were clamped into a straight line. Without speaking a
syllable she had conveyed to her employer her silent promise to
remain dumb on all matters concerning "Her".

3

SEPTEMBER 25th saw Frank Mayne about the homestead, a
silent, physically weary, spiritually depressed man. The post-
shearing work had been finished, the sheep having been
reclassified and placed in the best of the desert paddocks, with all
the breeding ewes adjacent to White Well, from which depot Tom
Mace and Ten Pot Dick hand-fed them with maize. The few
surviving lambs had been marked and the rams occupied a

paddock south of the homestead.

On Westmacott's old selection there was not a hoof. One could ride over it all day and not see a living thing, not a crow or an eagle. Of the two hundred horses a bare fifty survived to be drafted into one of the western salt-bush paddocks to which MacDougall now trucked daily sufficient water for them. In that same paddock the three surviving bullocks were also put. The country between the outstation, Forest Hill and White Well – tens of thousands of acres – was a vast stretch of river sand and dying scrub trees. It had not rained for eleven months.

"It is tough on those men being put on tramp, Feng, but you did right," Mayne said whilst he and his friend waited for the Adelaide telegram to be sent over the telephone to the Menindee postmaster. That telegram would give them the opening prices of wool in the first series of this season's sales.

"There was no help for it, Frank."

"No, I know. And now we shall have to dismiss two of the married men, as well as the teacher, if the wool prices are as low as the brokers estimate they will be."

Feng made no comment. He knew that never since the drought early in the history of the century had Atlas been unable to afford a teacher for the children. Not only three children of the married family to be retained, but also five others who rode horseback from as far as seven miles, would be deprived of schooling. Why comment on the dismissal of the teacher? The position was so hopeless. Until the rain came, Atlas and many other stations would be reduced to the position of mere selections.

The telegram arrived a few minutes before six o'clock, sent by a wool expert, acting for Mayne, who had attended the sale. It read: *Average price over day twelve pence halfpenny pound.*

Feng, who had taken down the dictated message, had turned his back to Mayne after giving him the slip. From it Frank Mayne looked out through the window that revealed the bare earth stretching away beneath the sturdy river-flat box trees. Pushing back his chair, he rose and passed out, and when the dinner-gong sounded he was on the Seat of Atlas.

4

THE blow fell on Atlas on the first day of October. It was struck by the Postmaster-General, when the mail-driver delivered the letter-bag. Mayne, being in the office, opened Boynton and Reynolds' long envelope and perused the contents. When he had read part he began again at the beginning, reading aloud to Feng:

As per our communication of recent date, the average price of wool over the first of the recent series of sales was a fraction below thirteen pence per pound. At the second of the series the average dropped fourpence.

Your consignment of six hundred bales was divided into those two sales and the amount realised after all expenses therewith deducted totals £4,985.

There is no evading the disturbing fact that the world's warehouses are overstocked with finished goods. As the financial outlook of all European countries and the South Americas is extremely bad, no rise in prices can be expected for several years. You will consequently readily understand that the depreciation of wool values will be instantly reflected in the values of station property and stock.

In view of these regrettable facts we were unable to withdraw the Atlas wool as requested, and the amount realised will be set against your indebtedness to us, the balance remaining of your indebtedness being at date forty-three thousand, five hundred pounds.

Governed by these circumstances, we must request you to dismiss all your employees save a cook and one maid for service in the house, to cease artificial feeding when present supplies of maize and lucerne are exhausted, and to turn the sheep into the best of your paddocks to take their chance of survival of this drought.

All future financial accommodation will have to be most carefully scrutinized, and our Mr. Rowland Smythe will be visiting you shortly to explain the situation fully to you. Whilst expressing our sympathy –

Mayne stood near the table looking blankly at Feng, who was seated. He was swaying slightly on his feet, his face drained of colour. His voice was hardly louder than a whisper.

"Oh, God!" he said. "They have got Atlas. They've got my

Atlas!"

"Frank!" exclaimed Feng sharply, alarmed by the despairing face of the man he loved. Springing to his feet, he passed round to Mayne and gripped his arm. "Frank! Brace up! It is not as bad as all that. Smythe will explain, and, if necessary, will find for us a way out."

Mayne's eyes seemed to be flecked with blood-spots. Across his dry lips moved the tip of his tongue.

At last he said: "Don't speak, Feng. Oh, God! Atlas! My Atlas gone!"

He stumbled once, crossing the office to the door. Feng, moved to the depths, watched him go, saw him pass the front window, and, when he looked out from the door, saw him crossing the bridge over the creek. He knew where Mayne was going, blindly, brokenly. To the Seat of Atlas where, before him, Old Man Mayne often had found peace, consolation, and inspiration. Feng Ching-wei followed.

As he had known he would do, he found Mayne seated on the squared block of wood, looking out blankly over the inheritance the drought now seriously threatened to steal from him, if already it had not done so. If Mayne was aware of Feng's arrival and his subsequent sitting beside him on the wood staging, he gave no sign. Neither spoke. Both recognised the hopeless situation of Atlas in debt to the extent of nearly fifty thousand pounds at a time when no man was likely to pay a price even as low as fifty thousand for a property that two years back had been worth two hundred thousand. He recognised, too – and herein lay the hurt – that Messrs. Boynton and Reynolds held them and Atlas in a cleft stick. The fate of Atlas lay in their grasping hands.

For a long time those two sat together in silence, their eyes blind to the drunken dust-columns swaying across the vast desiccated landscape before them, their ears deaf to the cries of the river birds, and the occasional sounds from the quiet homestead.

The sun went down, as now it went down always, an orb of dazzling fire in the cloudless sky. The shadow crept away from them to the far clear-cut horizon, dulling the twin colours of the earth into one great unrolled carpet of black plush, its further edge supporting the flame of the sunset. The light wind dropped to an unruffled calm. In stupendous silence – unbelievable silence to a city-dweller – unbroken by the twitter of a bird or the swish of a falling leaf, night came, took over command of the world from departing day, when lo! the silence was no more, banished by the hoot of an owl, the mournful distant cry of a mo-poke, the far-away scream of a curlew.

It was only then that Mayne moved. His left hand fell on the shoulder of the lower-sitting Feng, the fingers pressing as though seeking consolation from the faithful friend who had followed him into his Gethsemane. Reaching up, Feng placed a hand over the hand on his shoulder. When Mayne spoke his voice was steady. "Do you think they will give us a chance before the rain comes?"

"Why not?" returned Feng with assumed cheerfulness. "In spite of the fall in wool, the value of the property – real value, I mean – is threefold greater than the debt. We can but wait till Smythe comes. He must capitalise the debt, and we must pay the interest on it. In all decency they can't take Atlas before finding out how far we can go to meet them."

"They might not wish to meet us. They might demand their pound of flesh. My private fortune is now less than six thousand, and I have Ethel and the boy to think of. Then there is Westmacott's place – the instalment to pay to the widow."

Feng had to restrain an outburst against the woman who never for a single instant had considered her husband – who even now might be meeting her lover at the Rest House. He had been on the verge of offering his own fortune to form a dyke to keep back the flood-water of ruin, but mention of Ethel Mayne kept him silent on that point. She should not waste his money as she had wasted that of his friend.

5

THROUGHOUT the following morning Feng was busied making up accounts and drawing cheques. Mayne telephoned the men at White Well to hold themselves in readiness to come in on the truck he was sending for them, and to MacDougall to bring in the two men stationed at Forest Hill, after having instructed his wife to pack in readiness to leave in three days.

"It is the end, Mac," he told the dour Scotsman.

"Not it! Atlas will come again," MacDougall retorted.

At the pay-counter Mayne sat with the accounts and the made-out cheques before him. It was two o'clock, and all but those men then being brought in by MacDougall were outside waiting to be called. The spring sun poured its warmth on the iron roof of the building, heating the interior, but Mayne felt as cold as stone. He had refused to delegate the final act to Feng, who had offered to perform it, well knowing that Mayne felt as though he was to stab to death old friends, rather than pay off the supposed enemies of his class – the workers.

Dealing with the first five men, he spoke words of regret to them, checking the pay-cheque with the account, signing the cheque, and taking for it the signed receipt.

To Gus Jackson, the machinery expert, a clever man who could repair a motor-engine, build a house, and drive the shearing machinery, he said: "Well, Gus, the drought has busted Atlas. It comes very hard to me to have to pay you off after eleven years service. I hope you will find another place quickly."

"I hope the drought ends soon, Mr. Mayne, and you can offer me a job again," answered Jackson, tall, lean, efficient. "No one can carry on if it never rains, anyway."

To Fred Lowe: "I am more than sorry to part with you, Fred. I hope you will come back when the good seasons return."

"You'll find me camped in the shearing shed waiting for a job one week after the drouth ends," Fred drawled cheerfully. "We all 'as our ups and downs. I ain't grousing, 'cos I'm due for a down. Hooroo, Mr. Mayne! Hope I see you soon for a job."

The two jackeroos, Mr. Andrews and Mr. Noyes, both fourth-year men, he paid next, smiling with forced optimism whilst wishing them good luck.

Then came Todd Gray, his eyes gleaming. "You want to see me, Mr. Mayne?" he said, a trace of belligerency in his voice.

"Yes, Todd. After all these years we have come to the parting of the roads."

"Who says so?" Todd demanded.

"The Drought," replied Mayne simply.

"Oh, does it? I worked for Old Man Mayne through good years and bad years. I'm not taking the sack because of no bloody drouth. I don't walk off Atlas unless I walks off behind you, Mr.

251

Mayne, and you, Mr. Feng."

"There will be no more money, Todd," Mayne said, not daring to look from the documents before him, on the top of which were Todd's account and the cheque.

"I ain't exactly thinking of money, Mr. Mayne."

"Nor will there be any men to cook for, Todd."

"I ain't thinking of cooking. I'm tired of cooking, anyway. I'm thinking of all the bits of paper what will litter Atlas up, the garden that'll want watering, the ration sheep that'll have to be killed," Todd stated with emphasis. "You can stop me from camping in a hut, but you can't stop me camping on the river bank. I got a Miner's Right, and I'll peg out a claim outside this office before you'll push me off Atlas."

Mayne turned to Feng. His eyes were unable to meet those of his friend. "Are you keeping Mary?"

"Yes, Frank, I am."

"Very well, Todd. You may stay on, and to hell with the brokers!"

"Of course I'll be staying on," said a relieved Todd. At the door he paused, suddenly chuckling, and added: "And if the brokers come, just you leave 'em to me and Mary. Gawd 'elp 'em!" He vanished, and Mayne called Ten Pot Dick.

Through the open window Ten Pot Dick expectorated with wonderful velocity. "Don't you worry about me, boss," he said with hoarse laughter. "I've carried me swag that much that I've got corns on me shoulders as big as plates. I 'ope you 'as luck, Mr. Mayne. I'll be 'anging about when the drouth breaks."

Though his heart ached Mayne was obliged to smile. His men were leaving with courage to face a harder future even than the future he feared. They were leaving as his friends, and not because no more money could be made from their labour.

Three days later the MacDougalls arrived, their gear and one lad stowed on the truck they owned. It was the hardest parting of all. There were tears in Mrs. MacDougall's eyes when, the Atlas cheque in MacDougall's pocket, Feng entertained them and Mayne at tea in his bungalow.

"I don't know what we'll do or where we'll go," she said when about to leave.

"Write sometimes, Mrs. Mac, and when conditions improve I

will let you know, and you might like to come back," Mayne said. So long, Mac, and the best of luck!"

"So long!" was all MacDougall said before releasing the engine-clutch.

Atlas seemed deserted from then on. Tom Mace received permission to gather the wool from dead carcasses, thus being provided with a living for months to come. Todd became Mayne's companion on the incessant tours round the windmills that raised water for the sheep, most of which charged the car with loud baaings, now hungrily demanding the maize that never appeared.

Mr. Rowland Smythe came to Atlas. He went through the books, checking Feng's balance-sheet, which revealed a total indebtedness to all creditors of fifty-two thousand pounds.

"Well, Frank, it is easy to be wise after the event," he said before he left. "You know now how you failed. You believed the drought was ended several times when it was only just starting. That's not your fault. Where you deserve censure is in not starting to fight the drought a year earlier than you did. Still, you'll come again, Frank. So will Atlas. Carry on, lad! I'll try to capitalise the debt, and you'll pay the interest. Between us we'll keep Boynton and Reynolds at bay."

CHAPTER XXI

CONFIDENCES

1

DAILY the sun swung higher from the north. Cool weather periods alternated with hot, but with the advance of summer the cool periods almost vanished.

Central Australia was like a dust-heap stretching east from Mount Sturt to Roma in Queensland, and south almost to the coast. Over the western half of New South Wales, the north-west of Victoria, and the northern half of South Australia conditions had not been so bad since the drought of 1900-02. Hundreds of miles bore not a blade of grass or wisp of herbage on the rippled sand and cracked, iron-hard flats. The trees that had lived for a century were dying with dreadful slowness.

The equinoctial gales strengthening from the north, in veering westward swept to the east violent dust-storms which blacked out the sun on two occasions, creating pitch-darkness at noonday.

Frank Mayne had now become a working manager for Messrs. Boynton and Reynolds, assisted by one man only, the indomitable Todd Gray. The interest Mayne took in the remnant of the Atlas sheep was much more than was actually required of him. The wool brokers had said: "Let the sheep take their chance"; but Mayne was too good a sheepman, deep in the heart of him, not to do all he could to prolong the lives of the survivors.

Tin Tin also was now feeling the effects of the many rainless months; but Leeson, the manager, was a careful man, backed by a shrewd woman, and, unlike Atlas, Tin Tin had not been drained of its lifeblood–money reserve.

On her return journey from Menindee one night, Ann Shelley's car, which had been running perfectly, suddenly lost power and finally stopped in a way a car does when the petrol supply gives out. That was peculiar, because the twelve-gallon tank had been filled at Menindee. From a door-pocket she took a torch, and a cursory examination of the carburettor decided the matter. The engine was not getting petrol.

Quite efficiently this independent woman ran over the whole feed system back to the tank, and there she found that a portion of a branch or stick, sun-baked to the hardness of metal, had been driven up by the wheels against the tank, puncturing it. There was nothing else to do but walk on to Atlas, about two miles, and from Ethel Mayne seek shelter for the night. And, somehow, the prospect of receiving hospitality from Ethel was not alluring.

Switching off the car-lights, and carrying with her the torch in case of need, Ann Shelley set off on the unwanted walk, now and then pressing the torch-button to light her way over deep water-gutters and river billabongs. It was half-past eight when she left the car, and a quarter-past nine when she crossed the bridge between the men's quarters and the homestead.

There were no lights in the men's quarter. From them came no sound of men's laughter, of their accordions or mouth-organs. Of course she knew the plight of Atlas, knew that Mayne had been forced to payoff his hands. The faint, ghostly outlines of the

deserted buildings saddened her. That day, on her way from
Menindee, she had passed the deserted homesteads of two once
prosperous settlers. The light in Feng's sitting-room was the first
she saw to welcome her, and she obeyed the impulse to visit him
before turning in at the homestead gate.

Two dogs chained to their kennels in a corner of the fence
enclosing the bungalow barked as though they realised it was not
late enough to bark with vigour. Feng's front door was wide open,
as well as the French windows, which were uncurtained. Thinking
to give Feng a surprise, Ann Shelley trod the veranda softly,
reached the windows, and stepped in. And then she held her
breath.

Feng Ching-wei was seated with his back to her. She could see
the dark crown of his head above the top of the low easy chair. He
was facing the opposite wall, where two curtains hanging from a
portière had been pulled aside, and there was revealed in the
brilliant light a portrait of herself, Ann Shelley.

There was the portrait Feng so often had said he had destroyed,
a portrait that so much attracted her that unconsciously she crept
nearer to it. Why had he lied about this picture? Why had he spent
time in making another of her, so as to keep this one? The one he
had given her, the one she valued so much, was an excellent piece
of work; yet, in comparison with that she now examined, it was as
the work of a pavement artist to that of a Royal Academician. The
face was flushed, the lips just a little parted, revealing a fraction
of the pearl-white teeth. But it was the eyes that held Ann Shelley.
They were wide and sea-grey and misty, and yet the unshed tears,
instead of masking the soul beyond, revealed it plainly for all to
see. The soul behind those painted eyes, amazed, ecstatic, ablaze
with love: the eyes so misty, so full of longing love, full
unmistakably of the love-light. And, since Feng never had seen
that light in the eyes of the sitter, he had painted it there with the
genius of his imagination.

Quite suddenly she knew – knew Feng's secret love for her –
and found herself wanting to turn and run from the room, yet also
to creep closer to him who loved so hopelessly and console him
for the friend always he had been. Her body moved without
conscious volition. He heard the rustle of her dress, and was at
once on his feet facing her. For perhaps one full second she

looked into the man's unmasked face, before the black eyes blinked, became mere slits, and the mask again was in place.

"You gave me quite a start, Ann," he said, smiling.

"I crept in for that purpose," she told him a little breathlessly.

"You should not look into the forbidden chamber when Bluebeard is at home," he chided her gently, neither anger nor embarrassment in his voice. "I hope you like my new picture of you. I was admiring my own work when you surprised me."

The man's control was beyond belief. Calm and suave and courteous, none then could have guessed the strength of his emotion. Ann walked close, stood gazing at the picture, trying to control herself as he was controlled, trying to convince herself of his outrageous impertinence in painting that message into her eyes. And standing thus, against her will there came many mental pictures of herself and Feng and Frank holding parties at Atlas and at Tin Tin, riding together, hunting together, bound each to the others in comradeship: Mayne impulsively proposing daring escapades, Feng acting as a brake, always so solicitous for her safety and comfort. Feng, the boy who was and always had been Jonathan to Mayne's David; Feng, the man, shy, reserved, a little mysterious, invariably polished. And he loved her enough to paint and keep that picture – she knew it was the one he said he had destroyed – so that he could look at it in the quiet of lonely evenings and delude himself that the love-light was for him.

Swiftly she turned, holding out her hands to him, tears springing to her eyes. "Oh, Feng! Dear old boy! I'm so sorry!" she cried softly.

"There is really no need to be, Ann," he told her levelly. "I am sorry that you have found me out. I should have been warned by the dogs. But now –"

Switching off the *portière* lights, he drew the curtains across the picture. When again he faced her he was smiling quizzically, whilst he moved the chair he had occupied so that it faced the standard electric lamp, and drew close to it a crimson lacquered occasional table bearing cigarettes and matches.

"Be seated, Ann. Let us smoke, and you tell me then the answer to the fiction hero's question: To what am I indebted for the honour of this visit?"

"You mustn't hope, Feng," she said wistfully. "I shall never love anyone after he went away to England."

He was still smiling when he pointedly offered her the cigarette-box and held a lighted match in her service. He was smiling even when he said: "I know, Ann, I know. But even were that not so, even if your heart were free, neither of us could ignore the difference in race which would be an unclimbable barrier between us. I love you, but you must not allow my love to hurt you. I would have given everything I possess, even life, to prevent your learning my little secret. Please, Ann, do not let us talk about it ever again."

"But, Feng –"

"It will, I think, keep fine to-night," he said, still smiling, but in tones both metallic and final. He rang the bell for Mary.

2

WHEN Mary had departed, after setting before them a light supper, he said: "We will not talk about cabbages and kings, but about Frank and his wife. They are subjects that interest us both, and you and I will meet on the old and familiar neutral ground. I am in a quandary, and I hardly know how to proceed. Frank's marriage is a failure."

"Oh!"

"Frank's own description of his marriage is – the oil and water which cannot mix. That, unfortunately, is an apt description, Ann. I have long known the coldness of his wife towards him. Recently I came to know her unfaithfulness to him."

"Unfaithful, Feng!"

Feng nodded. He told her what he had glimpsed in the cane-grass house in the Atlas garden, described Ethel Mayne's frantic desire to get away from Atlas shortly afterwards, and the reason he suspected actuated her insistence on the successive house-parties.

"She fell in love with Cameron the first evening they met in the drawing-room over the way," he went on. "I saw it in her eyes during the dinner which followed. For months she fought against Cameron's influence, whilst he has been cleverly waiting, using every opportunity to attract her further. She is meeting him now in that little clearing in the centre of the Poison Belt – you know, where we three used to make believe it was a hunter's camp attacked by Red Indians. Cameron, at last, has won, and she, knowing it, is surrendering. The question is, ought I to inform Frank of all this?"

For quite a little time Ann pondered the question.

Then, shaking her head, she said: "No. Frank must find out for himself, which he will do eventually. No. He would not appreciate your telling him. He is not very hard-worked now, is he?"

"Not particularly so. All the sheep are in the White Well paddocks and towards the river. But Frank has been almost living out there. He and Todd Gray are cutting scrub for the sheep, doing all they can to help them through the drought. I rather fancy he is happier there than at home."

"The situation, Feng, is most delicate. If you do anything, poor Frank will probably never forgive you. You must let him find out for himself."

To this Feng made objection. "Let us look at it from this angle," he said. "Here we have two married people suffering acutely from a loveless life. The effect of this suffering on Frank is, I can assure you, greater than the effect on him of the drought and the bad position of Atlas. The position of Atlas would not have become so bad as it is had Frank's normal judgment not been clouded by domestic unhappiness, and I believe that the position of Atlas will become worse – even if it rains two inches to-morrow – should Frank's unhappiness be prolonged. And it will be prolonged up to the point that Atlas is rid of Ethel Mayne. Ann, tell me this, I beseech you. Do you still love him?"

He saw the faint flush rise in her face. Self was forgotten. He had a feeling of elation. He said: "Good! Assuming that Frank discovers grounds for and obtains a divorce, would you marry him?"

His directness distressed her. "Oh, Feng! You must not ask me such questions."

"But would you?"

"I – I might."

"Ann, don't, please, leave me in doubt. Frank's future, your future, my own, depends on conditions made clear between us now. Were he free, would you marry him?"

The power of his now blazing eyes made her tremble. She

could not disobey what amounted to a command. "Yes," she said, and hid her face behind her hands.

She did not see Feng cross to a bookstand and bring back a beautifully carved ivory box. Setting it on the table, he took from it a photographic print and laid it on the table before her. "Look!" he told her softly.

She took up the print, looked on it, and sighed. It was a picture of a man and a woman in such positions of abandon that only their lifelong friendship excused him for offering it to her. There was no mistaking Alldyce Cameron and Ethel Mayne, locked in each other's arms.

"Now this one," came the soft but inexorable voice.

She gazed on a picture, less flagrantly passionate, of Cameron clasping Eva and kissing her. And at this Ann Shelley cried out.

"Without these photographs it would be impossible of belief, would it not?" asked Feng, replacing the pictures in the box. Stooping, he brought his face level with and very close to hers, saying: "If I thought that Frank had the slightest chance of winning back his wife, I would shoot Cameron dead and gladly suffer the rope. But I know Frank has none. He was right when he said: 'Oil and water will not mix.'"

"It's dreadful – horrible! Why not show Ethel that print of Cameron and the nursemaid?" Ann suggested. "Surely that would sicken her of the man?"

But Feng was emphatic. "No. I will not consent to make the slightest effort to bring Frank and his wife together. The gulf is too wide. Far more than the drought she has been directly responsible for the ruin of Atlas. It was the Atlas money she loved, not Frank. When first she fell in love with Cameron he was comparatively a poor man, and she fought against her illicit love for him. Now that Cameron has come into money, and Frank is almost bankrupt, she is surrendering herself to Cameron. I cannot understand what is keeping her back on Atlas, unless it is the child. Whilst she remains Frank's wife, Atlas will never rise. She has been the curse laid on it. She hates it: she hates every one of us, we uncouth Colonials. Let her go! She must go. Not until Frank is rid of her, not until you have made him forget her, Ann, will he again be the old happy, courageous, far-sighted man he once was."

"Please, Feng, stop saying such things," she implored, pained at the accuracy with which he was expressing her little secret hopes.

"Cameron sends word to her when to meet him. I have found the place where they hide their letters, which I have taken the liberty to read. I don't know who delivers his letters to the crack in the fallen tree in the Poison Belt clearing. Are the blacks on Tin Tin?"

"Yes. The whole tribe are camped half a mile from the homestead. Aunty Joe lives in Government House. She helps the laundress."

"Then it can hardly be one of the blacks?"

Ann Shelley, reaching forward, gripped his hands. "Let the matter drop," she urged. "Things will all come right in the end. Believe me, they will. You can do no good by interfering."

"Perhaps not," he agreed a little doubtfully.

For a space they were silent. Then he said: "Come! I'll escort you over the way. It is ten o'clock. Remember – you have only just arrived at Atlas. In the morning, I'll run up and fix your car."

His eyes were masked. He was smiling in his old suave, almost mocking manner.

3

ANN'S MANAGER was approaching threescore years and ten, which is under the span allotted to Australian bushmen. He was tall, straight, supple, and, because he shaved, hairless. Known to the men as Old Baldy, Leeson was well up in the first dozen of Australia's shrewdest sheepmen. The only woman he loved was his wife, and the only woman he admired was Ann Shelley. The Saturday morning following her visit to Menindee, and later her one night's stay at Atlas, she was engaged, as was her custom on Saturday morning, with her manager.

The chief point of discussion this morning was if they should from then on maize-feed five thousand extra sheep – the best of the wethers – in addition to the breeding ewes. Leeson counselled it, knowing that when the drought broke the price of mutton would be high, and fat killers would fetch a good price; Ann demurred on account of the extra expense.

They argued for an hour, and finally compromised by putting

two flocks of ewes into paddocks where they could find a little feed, and reducing the ration of maize from one to half an ounce, with the proviso that should the ewes fall rapidly off condition the full ration should be restored them and the wethers must take their chance.

Now, when Ann Shelley left the Tin Tin office at one o'clock, determined to relax till the following Monday morning, she left behind her in the office the worries of the drought.

One of those mentally well-balanced young women, she was alive to the fact that nothing destroys good looks more quickly than worry. Her mental poise was reflected in her physical poise. Her body was in the perfection of health, and her mind was free from the neurotic trouble caused chiefly by idleness.

The afternoon was spent talking with her companion on the cool veranda about the fashion journals that had arrived by the last mail, and of those other matters dear to women – a delightful form of relaxation to one who throughout the week had talked and thought of little clse than sheep and wool and wool prices. At four she indulged in a cool shower, and then drank afternoon tea on the veranda with her companion and her housekeeper. Had not a telephonic communication been made a little before sunset, she would have spent the evening reading a novel. The week-ends found her very feminine: the week days, cool, efficient, slightly masculine in her mental outlook.

The house telephone-bell rang when the sun was dipping below the rim of the western scrub. When she picked up the instrument the book-keeper spoke: "Mr. Feng Ching-wei wishes to speak to you, Miss Shelley. Shall I put him through?"

"Please."

"Hallo, Ann!" Feng's familiar voice said to her. "I am glad I got you so easily. There is great trouble here. Little Frankie has been lost in the Poison Belt. Can you come at once and bring some of the blacks to track him?"

"Of course," she returned, consternation sharpening her tone. "Where's Frank?"

"He's out in one of the White Well paddocks. I can't get him before he returns to the White Well hut. You'll hurry?"

"I will. Good-bye!" She rang off, then rang again. The bookkeeper answered her. "Please run down to the men's hut at once and ask Charlie Morris to come immediately to me here."

She was dressing when the companion came in to say Morris was on the veranda. Flinging on a wrap, she hurried out to him.

"Charlie, get out the single-seater, and drive as fast as you know how up to the blacks' camp and fetch Abie and Ned. Little Frankie Mayne is bushed in the Poison Belt. If Abie is not in camp, bring Larry."

Fifteen minutes later the single-seater returned with Abie, Ned, and Larry. Five minutes were spent in filling the petrol tank and attending to the lubrication. Ann took the wheel. Beside her sat Aunty Joe. In the dicky were Abie and Larry. On the left running-board crouched Ned. Ten miles from Tin Tin the radiator sprang a leak.

CHAPTER XXII

THE GATE-CRASHER

1

FRANK MAYNE and Todd Gray employed themselves every day walking from two to three miles into one of the paddocks adjacent to White Well, and there cutting scrub across the line sheep would take to walk to and from water. Only at the far ends of the vast paddocks was there left a little scanty straw-dry grass and herbage, and to get at this the sheep had to walk six to nine miles from water. As Smythe had told Feng Ching-wei, the greatest cause of constitutional poverty in sheep was incessant walking between water and feed. Todd's and Frank Mayne's efforts were directed to lessening the distance between feed and water for seven flocks.

It had been a hot day in mid-November. When the sun rose, so had risen a stiff north-west wind which, aided by the heat, lifted up the sand and carried it over the land in dense cloud masses. That morning Mayne and Todd Gray had walked into different paddocks to cut scrub, each taking with him a roughly cut lunch, a billy-can and canvas water-bag, and this evening Todd Gray was the first to reach the White Well Hut. The ringing of the telephone-bell only met his ears when he entered the hut, for the wind still boomed and thrashed the branches of the solitary pepper tree.

He had drunk all his water and was thirsty. The three dogs who had been with him all day shepherding a flock of sheep on the scrub he lopped, were then lying in the water-troughs cooling their heated bodies and lapping. Gray with an oath quenched his thirst before going to the instrument, the bell of which rang imperatively.

"Hallo!" he called. The person at the other end of the line continued to ring with the perversity of a child, and the sound thundered at Todd's eardrums. "Blast!" he grumbled, holding the earpiece from his head. Then when the ringing stopped, he shouted before it could begin again. "Hey! Hi! Hallo!"

He heard a woman sob, struggling to cease her sobbing so that she might speak. "Frank! Frank! Is that you, Frank?"

"No, it's me. Who's speaking?"

"Me. Who are you?"

"Todd Gray. Is that Mrs. Mayne? Wot's up?"

"Is Mr. Mayne there? Is he?"

"No. He's not home yet."

"Where is he? Oh, God, get him quickly!" Ethel Mayne wailed. "I've been ringing and ringing for hours. Little Frankie is lost. He and Eva went out for a walk, and she's lost him. And it's getting dark, it's getting dark. Oh, Frank! Get Frank at once."

Todd Gray did a wise thing. He actually shouted: "Hey! Wot the hell's the matter with you? Take a tumble. Calm yourself. Wot's that about Little Frankie? Where's he bushed?"

"In the Poison Belt. Tell my husband. Tell –"

"That's enough, Mrs. Mayne," Todd roared into the speaker. "Where's Mr. Feng? Where's my missus?"

"He and Mary are down in the Poison Belt looking for my boy. But they won't find him. It's getting dark."

"Ain't there any nigs about? But no. Of course not. You 'unted them all away. Put me through to Menindee. Do you understand the gadget? Hurry!"

To ring up Tin Tin the connection had to be made at the Menindee exchange. The postmaster's daughter, the exchange operator, was at tea, the postmaster temporarily in charge.

"Mr. Ching-wei got through to Tin Tin half an hour ago.

Haven't they found the youngster yet?"

"No. Hey! Put me through to Thuringah. The Turk must send men."

"Mr. Ching-wei spoke to Thuringah after he broke off Tin Tin."

"Oh! All right. Thanks!"

So Feng had rung up Ann Shelley for the blacks. By that time Cameron would be in the Poison Belt with some of his men. Todd passed outside. The wind blew dust in his face, but it was cooler and less strong. Heat and wind! The wind would have prevented the searchers from hearing the child's frantic cries and him their shouts. The lad would run and run. The heat, even of the night, would dry him up. Likely enough, he would live through the night, but if his rescue were delayed much beyond sunrise it would be too late.

"Women!" he almost shouted to the dogs still wallowing in the troughs. "One woman mooning along thinking of young Tom Mace and no thought in 'er head for that bonny boy; and another woman, high and mighty, looking down 'er long nose at the nigs and 'unting 'em away. They would have tracked the kid down by now. Gawd!"

Taking another long drink of water, he filled a billy-can and hurried out to meet Mayne in the gathering gloom. They did meet half a mile from the hut.

"Have a drink," Todd said, offering the billy, and forcing all expression from his face.

"Thanks! I'm darned dry, Todd. Water ran out about four o'clock."

Not until Mayne had quenched his thirst did Todd tell him of the catastrophe at Atlas, and watch him turn into a man of stone.

Then Mayne burst out: "He's got to be found. To-night! Come on, Todd!"

He ran. Todd laboured behind him. They raced to the hut, Mayne straight to the car; Todd, sensibly, for the water-bucket, from which to fill the radiator. Before Todd was actually in the car, it was off as an arrow from a bow.

There were seven gates between them and the homestead. The first was made of light wood. The car bumpers smashed it to splinters, for Mayne would not stop to open it. The second gate was built of stouter material. The bumpers smashed it, to be sure, ripped and tore it from its hinges, but a flying length of wood smashed the headlights. Fortunately, the engine was magneto-driven, but every light was put out. Leaning now over his side to view the track round the end of the windscreen, Mayne drove as might a madman, but with the cunning of a madman.

Every yard of the twisting track he knew, every bend, every water-gutter. In the darkness he could hardly distinguish it. The scrub trees flashed past them as though they were sticks wielded by an invisible giant flailing the air in the effort to strike them.

The third gate was of stout tubular iron. "Pull up here, or you'll smash us," Todd yelled in Mayne's ear.

The car rocked round the bends, to the passenger invisible. Familiar horizons gave to Todd their position. The car leapt water-gutters as a thing insane for speed. Todd so far forgot himself, when they passed a solitary giant pine tree, as to yell: "Pull up, you fool! Do you want us to walk fifteen miles?"

Mayne jammed on the screaming brakes. The wheels skidded in the deep sand. The car lurched sideways, stopped sideways in front of the iron gate. Then Todd was on the ground, jumping to the gate. Swinging it open, he leapt for the car when it shot through the gateway, and before he had gained his seat it was travelling at thirty miles an hour.

The fourth gate shared the fate of the first two. Between it and the next the car, meeting heavy drift sand, almost turned over, so severe was the sudden skid. Mayne was braking to stop before the fifth gate, but crashed through its heavy timbers. A part of it lay over the wrecked bonnet and across the smashed windscreen whilst they hurtled on. Todd struggled to remove it, and was flung back into his seat with terrific violence when for the second time the car skidded in sand, seemed for a moment to dance on a wire, and stopped with the engine facing the way they had come. A third skid sliced off the off-side running-board, and the tree that did that damage wrecked the hood, which collapsed.

"Go easy over this blasted creek!" roared Todd, knowing that immediately in front lay a steep-banked creek where the road took a hairpin turn in negotiating it. "Go easy, damn you! They want searchers on the Poison Belt, not corpses six miles from the river."

The last gate wrecked the radiator. They then had one mile to travel to reach the homestead. They had covered half the distance when the engine seized. Useless, the machine was as nothing seen outside a car-wrecker's shop. The two men ran the last half-mile. Within the Atlas office was a light. Mayne shouted before he reached the door. A woman came running out.

"Frank! Frank! They can't find Little Frankie," she sobbed.

2

WITH Todd Gray at his heels, Frank Mayne reached the Rest House in the Poison Belt, neither aware that behind them ran Ethel Mayne. A hurricane-lamp was raised to the level of Mayne's face. The flame flickered violently in the raging wind. Red dust swirled and reddened the light.

"Frank! Thank God, you have come!"

"Ann! Haven't they found him?"

"No. We have only just got here," Ann Shelley cried. "The car broke down. It would. But I brought Aunty Joe and Abie and Larry. They've gone in. So has Cameron and several of his men.'"

"How long ago?"

Mayne's voice was quite steady, but Ann Shelley knew that he fought hard to make it so in this crisis. The light revealed his livid face, and the blood where a splinter from the wind-screen had struck him. It was the face of an old man, and almost she cried out.

"Ten minutes," she managed to say, unaware, like those two scarecrows of men, that Ethel hovered behind them.

"We've got to reach the road before the others," Mayne said sharply. "We've got to stop them messing up the boy's tracks if he crossed the road."

He meant the main track from Atlas to Menindee, that track which passed through the Poison Belt over a causeway of logs half a mile back from the river. Its surface was deep with silt, and it would be impossible for the child to cross the road without leaving imprints of his feet for the veriest new-chum to see. If Little Frankie had not crossed the road, the search for the child would be comparatively easy, for it would then be confined to the lantana between road and river, or the clear flats on either side. If the boy had crossed the road and entered the lantana westward of it, covering many square miles, the search would be much more difficult and probably take longer.

With a heart of lead Mayne preceded Todd Gray and the two women through the maze of lantana straight to the road, where they found men and lights. Above the wind they heard guttural shouting. The lights converged to one point. Mayne raced towards it.

"Hallo, Mayne! Look! The lad crossed here," Alldyce Cameron shouted. "Now then, men, spread out, and into the bush after the boy."

Here was the he-man in action, even in such a crisis posing before the women and men used to accepting commands. His magnificent figure was arrayed in immaculate duck. On his head a pith-helmet: on his feet white canvas shoes. Towering above the others, he personally dominated those around him. Every crisis produces a leader, as this crisis produced Alldyce Cameron, the battalion commander, as a leader – until Frank Mayne asserted himself.

"Stop!"

The word seemed to strike on the ears of everyone as a jagged piece of ice. Moving men froze into immobility. Cameron opened his mouth to bark a contradictory order.

"If any man leaves this road," Mayne snarled, his face working, "I'll follow him in and strangle him with my hands. Cameron, you are a fool! Would you have a crowd of men rush in there and trample out the child's tracks? Hi, there! Aunty Joe! Abie! Larry! To me!"

Aunty Joe and the two bucks ran to Mayne.

"Abie, take a lamp. You take a lamp too, Larry. Aunty Joe, if you can't track Little Frankie no one can. You three have got to find him quick. Here, Abie, take this box of matches in case the wind blows out the lamps."

Aunty Joe crouched over the line of distinct little boot impressions, a buck on either side of her, their lamps lowered close to the ground. Looking like grotesque, semi-human animals, the three ran off the road. The first lantana bush wiped out the lighted lamps and those three human bloodhounds from the vision of the small crowd. For a moment adjoining bushes were revealed

267

in the lamplight. The lantana became a high, dense black wall.

How long they were gone Mayne could not judge. He heard a woman quietly sobbing, and another woman's voice consoling her. He saw the shape of a tall woman standing beside Cameron, but did not notice that Cameron held her hand. He knew that Ann Shelley stood on his left, and that Feng was standing on his right. Time had stopped.

Presently he said: "How long have they been gone?"

Feng answered him. "Twenty-five minutes. Take a grip of yourself, Frank, old man!"

At long last! After uncounted years! Someone shouted triumph. From the black wall of lantana, two hundred yards distant, lights winked out. Three forms were revealed coming along the road toward them. The witnesses rushed to meet Aunty Joe and her escort, Mayne foremost.

He saw Aunty Joe's ebony face, saw with amaze the tears sliding down her round fat cheeks. She held Little Frankie in her arms. Ethel Mayne sped past him, outdistanced him and those with him. Aunty Joe held out the boy as though making an offering to her own pagan god.

"Too plurry late, missus," she cried fiercely. "Likkle Frankie, him dead with fear."

Ethel Mayne halted directly before the little body, to stand and look down upon it, motionless, unable to move.

"I'm tinkit, missus, you all the same one big plurry fool," Aunty Joe almost shouted. "You bin driven blackfellow from Atlas, and no stay here to run after Likkle Frankie. Aunty Joe never lose urn Likkle Frankie, my plurry oath! Him run and run and run in the dark, the banshee at his heels, and bimebi Likkle Frankie him see banshee and drop down dead. Good, eh? An' Aunty Joe and blackfellow down on Tin Tin."

Voiceless, tearless, Ethel Mayne accepted her dead. She turned slowly from Aunty Joe, who burst into wailing sobs. She ignored Alldyce Cameron, who would have taken the body from her. And so she came face to face with her husband. For perhaps twenty seconds husband and wife stared stonily at each other. Mayne was unable to speak, unable to move. He was a man of ice. Only his brain was alive.

The light from several lamps fell on them and on the dead

child in Ethel's arms. Strong she must have been during those terrible moments. Feng's hands gripped Mayne's left arm. On his other side came Eva, supported by Mary O'Doyle.

Ethel, seeing Eva, took three steps towards the maid, holding out the body for her to see the more clearly. "You murderess!" she cried softly but distinctly.

And Eva, looking down on the bloodstained, dust-stained little face, looking down at the wide and fixed blue eyes in which remained that last supreme terror, threw back her head and shrieked and shrieked.

3

LITTLE FRANKIE was buried beside Old Man Mayne in the Atlas cemetery, which was situated a quarter of a mile up the creek, beyond the shearing shed. It was impossible to obtain the services of a minister, and the Police Sergeant, who came from Menindee, read the service. Apart from Aunty Joe, who watched from a distance, he was the only person present who cried. Ann Shelley, doubly shocked by Frank's appearance and the tragedy, remained dry-eyed. Ethel moved and looked as a woman of marble.

Mayne stayed three days at Atlas after the funeral. He had done no labour after making the tiny coffin for his son. He came to Feng in the office, a human travesty of what he had been.

"I can't stop here any longer," he said dully. "Ethel does little else but curse Atlas, and Australia, and me for bringing the lad and her out here. She will not permit me to console her, nor does she think *I* need consoling. If only she would weep: if only I could weep! Todd and I are going back to White Well. Should she need me, ring me up."

Feng nodded sympathetic assent.

At the doorway Mayne paused and looked up to say: "After all, Todd Gray was right. The bush is a jealous mistress. I deserted her for three years, and she has avenged herself by ruining Atlas and killing my boy."

And in that mood he had gone back to his sheep, to slave through the red-hot days, cutting scrub with an axe whose blade it was impossible to touch.

Feng saw nothing of Ethel Mayne during the following weeks.

269

Since she had refused Eva entry to Government House, since Eva had no friends in Australia to whom she could go, and since she was verging on a nervous breakdown, Feng willingly consented that Mary O'Doyle should have the girl with her.

It was the ninth day after Little Frankie's death that Mary said to Feng, when she was clearing away the after-dinner coffee-things: "Will ye consent to see Eva, Misther Feng? The maid 'as bin arsting to have worrd with ye all this blessed day."

"Certainly, Mary: bring her here."

Not a little to his surprise, Eva appeared without sign of the hysteria which had so worried Mary, but her big hazel eyes were misty and red-rimmed through constant crying. Smiling cheerfully on her, Feng drew up a chair for her so that they sat almost knee to knee sideways to the table, on which Feng had just placed writing materials.

"Eva," he said softly, when the door had closed on Mary O'Doyle, who for the very first time knelt on the floor and held her ear to the keyhole, "Eva, you must try not to take this thing too much to heart. No one for a moment believes that you were wilfully neglectful. I am sure Mr. Mayne doesn't, and Mrs. Mayne will not either when she has conquered her very natural grief."

In Eva's eyes now burned a strange light. Her tragic face then was beautiful, despite the red-trimmed eyes.

"Thank you for letting me speak to you, Mr. Feng," she said with obvious difficulty. "I wanted to talk to someone. I feel I must talk to someone who might understand, or I shall go mad. You have always been kind to me, and I – I must tell the truth. When you say that no one thinks I was wilfully neglectful, you may be right; but I was wilfully neglectful all the same. If I tell you about it, I – I may not go on having the dreadful dreams."

"Tell me, by all means. Likely enough, I shall be a more impartial judge of you than you are yourself."

Subconsciously Feng drew towards him the blotter and picked up a pencil. Subconsciously, the moment he removed his gaze from her face, he began to draw meaningless figures on the blotter. And when Eva had spoken three sentences he began to make shorthand notes.

"I read in a book once," Eva said, her voice still flat, "that if a woman loves a man she will never betray him, no matter what he does to her. Books are wrong. I am going to prove it, for I hate the man I once loved so much that I would have done anything to please him.

"We were on our way, Mr. Feng, as you know, to lay flowers on Old John's grave. Little Frankie was upset because Beelzebub had gone off hunting. He was still upset when we reached the Rest House, and found there Mr. Cameron sitting on the dead tree.

"We had often met him there. He made love to me. I – I worshipped the ground he trod on. He told me that I was beautiful and – and desirable, and – and he made love to me. How could I think of Tom when Alldyce kissed me? It wasn't because Alldyce is a gentleman, that he has plenty of money and Tom only has little, that I let him kiss me and love me. You see, I couldn't help it. He is so handsome and gentle, and his voice thrilled me, and his touch almost made me faint.

"That afternoon we didn't have much time, for it was late. I told Alldyce so, but he laughed, and said the flowers could wait for another day, and he took Little Frankie from the push-cart because the boy wanted to get out. He kept calling for Beelzebub.

"Let him play around for a bit, dear," Alldyce said, and then he drew me down into his arms. Even as he kissed and kissed me I heard Little Frankie calling for the dog and – and I never thought he would run away to find him.

"But he did. When Mr. Cameron released me, when I – I sort of came round, Little Frankie had vanished. It seemed only a few seconds before that I heard him shouting for Beelzebub. Mr. Cameron said: 'Why, the little brat has gone off home!' I jumped up and ran along the river path as far as the homestead end of the lantana, and couldn't see him. From there I could see over clear ground right to the garden fence.

"I flew back to the Rest House. Mr. Cameron then was down in the river bed crossing to his horse. I screamed at him to come back, and when he did I told him that Little Frankie hadn't gone home.

"'Well, he cannot have gone far, Eva. I'll look for him,' he said crossly. 'You stay here, or you'll get lost too.'

"He was away ever so long. I got so frightened. I didn't know

271

what to do. And presently he came back with a scared look in his face.

"'I can't find him,' he said. 'You run home and tell Mrs. Mayne and everyone that you were sitting here and saw something moving about on the opposite side of the river which interested you, and when you looked round Little Frankie was nowhere to be seen.'

"'Very well,' I agreed, and was going to run to the house when he stopped me, saying: 'Now remember, Eva dear. Don't tell anyone I was here with you. It will look bad. Remember that. Now, off you go as hard as you can run.'"

Eva paused in her confession. Feng's pencil stopped. When he looked at her he noted the hardness that had crept into her eyes. Her voice was stronger when she resumed.

"You see, Mr. Feng, don't you, how it was? While Little Frankie was running about crying for his mummy, while I was rushing to the homestead for help, Alldyce was slinking back to his home. If he had stopped to search he might have found Little Frankie. Don't you think so?"

"It is more than likely, Eva," Feng confirmed in icy tones.

"He said he loved me," the girl went on. "Yet in my trouble he hasn't come forward to share the blame with me. No. He kept back. He's left me to face it all by myself. It is not fair. What is the use of a man being a gentleman if he can't do what – what Tom would have done? That's all, Mr. Feng. Thank you for listening to me. I do hope those awful dreams won't come again. Do you think they will, now I've confessed?"

"No, Eva, I am sure of it," he told her earnestly. "You do not love Cameron any more?"

"I – I hate him. And yet – and yet, if he called me, I mightn't be able to stop going to him."

"He will not call you, Eva. Just wait a moment."

Feng hurriedly transcribed his notes and rang for Mary O'Doyle.

Mary crept along the passage to her kitchen, thence to return with her usual heavy tread.

On her entrance Feng said: "Just sign your name here, Eva." And when she had done so without the slightest protest, though she wondered, Feng got Mary to scratch her signature to accompany his own in witness. "That will be all, Mary," he said quietly, with a significant look.

To Eva he said, when Mary had left: "You loved Tom Mace once, did you not?"

"Yes."

"Deep down in your heart you love him still, don't you?"

"I – don't know."

"But you really do, don't you?"

"Yes. Yes, I suppose so."

"Of course you do. You were merely infatuated with Cameron, that is all. That sort of love has no depth and doesn't last. Now I'll tell you what you're going to do. To-morrow Miss Shelley will call and you will go with her to Tin Tin. Yesterday she rang me up, and among other things she told me that her companion had to leave to go to her sick mother. I suggested to Miss Shelley that you take her place. You will be happy again with Miss Shelley, because she is the most understanding woman on this earth. Wait, please! When Tom Mace comes in again, I'll get him here and tell him about everything you have told me. I know Tom as well, if not better, than you do. I know he will forgive you. If I don't tell him, you will have to some time. You cannot have it on your mind between you. And when the drought breaks you and he shall have a home. Mr. Mayne has promised. Now I give you my promise as well. You will agree?"

"Oh, Mr. Feng, yes!" and Eva at last cried.

Feng himself escorted Eva to Mary O'Doyle's sitting-room. He waited then half an hour before ringing for his housekeeper, foster-mother, and slave. "Close the door, Mary, please."

She did so.

"Mary," he said, leaning back in his chair and looking up into her weather-beaten, likeable face, "Mary, you will do nothing to Mr. Alldyce Cameron. You will leave Mr. Alldyce Cameron to me. Woman, I read your mind as easily as I knew that you were listening at the keyhole. You would like to lay those capable hands on Mr. Alldyce Cameron and cause him acute suffering, wouldn't you? But" – slowly – "you will have to leave him to me. I hope that is understood?"

"Indade it is, Misther Feng. But it was the first time I listened. I had to. I knew the child 'ad somethin' on her poor mind. The blackguard! Mr. Halldyce –"

"You will leave him to me, Mary. Good night!"

Looking down into the black, blazing eyes, Mary O'Doyle received comfort. She was satisfied that she could leave Mr. Alldyce Cameron to Feng Ching-wei.

CHAPTER XXIII

CAMERON'S GREATEST TRIUMPH

1

ALLDYCE CAMERON was able to leave Thuringah Station two days before Christmas. His company had given him a month's notice to leave, or to accept a sixty per cent. cut in his salary of six hundred a year. And he had determined to do one of two things: accept the cut, or get away – with Ethel Mayne.

The newly risen sun already was blazing hot when he drove a new car down-river to Atlas. He, being on the east side, secured no advantage from the long shadows cast westward by the river gums, but as usual he was cool, and exhilarated to the point of intoxication by the imminence of his greatest conquest. Woman, his god, was about to bestow on him her greatest favour. Opposite the homestead of Atlas he swung the car round, facing Menindee, and stopped it.

Then his heart quickened, his lips parted to emit a sigh of utter satisfaction, his eyes shone with desire, when he saw hastening across the dry river-bed Ethel Mayne, carrying but one suitcase. Impulse seized him to shout exultantly when he dashed down the steep bank to meet her. He commanded the strength of a giant when he swept her off her feet into his arms and carried her up the bank to the car. His face flushed a deep red, he set her down in the seat beside the wheel, sprang in himself, slammed shut the door, geared in, and drove recklessly northward.

Neither was conscious of hearing four kookaburras vying with one another in mocking laughter, nor did either of them see Feng Ching-wei standing behind his open bedroom window and smiling that suave smile of his.

"Where was Mayne when you left, sweetheart?" Cameron

murmured, with Ethel leaning against him.

"Oh! He was out at some place with his wretched sheep. Must we discuss him this wonderful morning?"

He laughed gaily. "Just for a moment, dear, and then, well, forget him. You wrote him the note I suggested, and left it in the rack?"

"Ye-es," with just the faintest hint of regret, which vanished in adding: "I explained how impossible it was to go on. I was quite truthful. I said only Little Frankie stopped me from running away with you long ago. I told him we were going to Adelaide, and that we would send him the evidence for a divorce, for which I hoped he would sue so that we both could start afresh. That was right, wasn't it?"

"Quite right, darling,'" he said, squeezing her arm. "We will send him the name of the hotel. You should get your divorce in three months. We can then go to England legally married, and without a shadow to dim our happiness."

"Alldyce!" She uttered the name in a voice that thrilled him as never before had done the voice of a woman. "Alldyce, you will always be happy with me? You will look after me and love me – always – always?"

"I shall love you always, dear," he told her, really meaning it.

"You must, you know" – pleadingly. "You must make me forget Atlas and the horrors I have seen in this dreadful country. You must love me so fiercely that I shall even forget poor Little Frankie. Oh, Alldyce! I loved the baby."

"Perhaps, some day, you will grow to love another," he whispered, and watched her dark eyes open and shine, and her creamy face glow pink.

And so did Ethel Mayne burn her boats, deliberately burn them, for of the two hairs that bound her to her husband and convention by far the stronger of the two had broken with the death of her boy; the weaker, her regard for her father, then having snapped before the onslaught of Alldyce Cameron.

This morning she was not sorry that there was now no possibility of going back. She was experiencing a lightness of spirit, a jocund buoyancy as though for long she had lived in a grey-lit prison and now was free in brilliant sunlight. Already Atlas, with which were associated that sober old-young man, her husband, and that passionless spider-man who sat and schemed in the office or his bungalow, was being pushed rapidly into obscurity by this new life, a life that would so wonderfully realise her happiest dreams.

The first night from Atlas they spent on the train travelling from Broken Hill to Adelaide. They were unaware of the inquiry agent who followed their taxi to the North Australian Hotel, Cameron's car being brought on after them.

Ethel Mayne experienced the joys of the bride that should have been hers when she married Frank Mayne. Now clothes and money were subordinate to love. She would have found joy in living with Cameron in a workman's cottage. His embraces were fresh and supremely delicious to her soul. Yet her passion for this man was restrained; unfathomed and deep in her heart was the knowledge that she would not reach the heights of abandon until she could rid herself of the haunting face of Little Frankie. Memories of the gladsome child were as links of the cable that anchored her to the past.

2

THREE days of bliss had gone. It was the morning of the fourth day, when she sat in the hotel lounge whilst Cameron paid a visit to his bank, that from far-away Atlas Feng Ching-wei struck.

A well-dressed stranger approached her. Looking up, she saw him doff his hat and offer her his card, and whilst she read the superscription he coolly drew a chair close to her and sat down.

"Madam, as my card states, I am a private inquiry agent," he said. "I have been instructed by Mr. Feng Ching-wei, of Atlas Station, to secure evidence for divorce on behalf of Mr. Frank Mayne. I think I may say that I have secured that evidence."

The dark brows lifted just a fraction. Then the pale lids dropped and veiled the woman's eyes. At first she felt a qualm of fear, but this was followed quickly by relief. For would not this man's spying simplify affairs, and hurry them to the conclusion she so ardently desired?

She replied quite coolly: "Mr. Feng Ching-wei need not have troubled. Yesterday I posted to Mr. Mayne particulars to be found in the register of this hotel."

"Your action will corroborate my evidence, madam," calmly

stated the inquiry agent. "However, I have been instructed further. I am to place in your hands these papers and photograph in a sequence dictated by Mr. Feng Ching-wei. First, this short newspaper cutting."

It was a report of a maintenance case taken from *The Barrier Miner*, Broken Hill, in which Olive Clive sued Alldyce Cameron. Judgment had been given in favour of the girl.

Having read this, Ethel Mayne gazed at the tips of her shoes. So Alldyce was not entirely spotless! But what man was? One could hardly expect so splendid a man not to be tempted and fall to the blandishments of a hussy. If Feng thought such a thing as this would destroy her faith in her lover, then he would find out his mistake. "Mr. Ching-wei need not have troubled," she repeated coldly.

The agent offered no comment. He placed in her hand a photographic print. Watching her profile, he felt admiration of her self-control, for Ethel Mayne revealed no outward sign of the shock given her by this photograph of Eva lying in Cameron's arms.

The light in the lounge appeared to grow dull, as though outside a cloud had masked the sun. So, after all, her splendid lover was weak. She had thought him so strong, so true, and here was Feng drawing aside the curtain of deception. Had the agent looked into her eyes he would have seen their hardening, the determination to keep Alldyce from tempting hussies in the future.

"And this certified copy of a statement, signed by Eva Jennings, witnessed by Mary O'Doyle and Feng Ching-wei," murmured the agent, expecting hopefully that now this cold, haughty woman would show dismay.

Slowly Ethel Mayne read through Eva's confession. Yet again, more slowly, she read it through. The heat of her body appeared to die away, leaving her deathly cold. Extraneous sounds became emphasized, beat on her ears, forming a world to which no longer did she belong. Feng's revenge was complete. The subtlety of his Oriental mind had dictated the manner of it. First she was to provide the evidence for divorce proceedings. And then, at the height of her happiness with Cameron – this!

When she rose to her feet the agent rose too. Ignoring him, she passed to the lift and was deposited on the first floor, where was their suite. Locking herself in the bedroom, she almost collapsed on a chesterfield, and again read and re-read one paragraph of Eva's confession:

You see, Mr. Feng, don't you, how it was? While Little Frankie was running about crying for his mummy, while I was rushing to the homestead for help, Alldyce was slinking back to his home. If he had stopped to search he might have found Little Frankie. Don't you think so?

Gently Ethel Mayne's head fell back on the cushion behind her. Her lips began to tremble. Her poor brain was stunned by the roaring clamour of the crashing walls of her castle of joy. The confession was not a forgery. Of that she was convinced. She knew Feng well enough to understand that he was too clever to strike with a faulty weapon.

She shut her eyes to banish those living sentences of Eva's confession. She saw then the tear-stained, dusty little face of the child she so passionately had loved. A child cried in the next suite. It had cried during the night, but its cries in that delirious night she had forgotten. Now the child's cries appeared to be those of Little Frankie frantically screaming for her, with the fearful, shadowy aboriginal conception of the bush spirit racing at his heels. And almost in reach of him the man in whose arms Eva had lain, stealing away that he might not face his responsibilities.

To her it seemed that the little boy was just beyond a black curtain that had only to be pulled aside to admit her to be with him and to comfort him. A strong-willed woman, Ethel Mayne decided to pass through that curtain.

3

ALLDYCE CAMERON was delayed overlong with his bank business. On his hotel-bound way he met a friend who delayed him yet further, and in his heart Cameron cursed his friend for coming between him, if only for a few minutes, and his god. Woman –

Assisted by the liftman, he broke open the door of his suite. They found Ethel lying on her bed. Fastidious to the last, her right arm hung over the edge of the bed, the hand deep in the interior of a water-ewer not now containing water. She had cut the main arteries of her wrist with one of Cameron's safety-razor blades.

Eva's confession, the photograph, and the clipping he found on Ethel's dressing-table. For a little while he was puzzled, for a little while he suspected Feng of having sent them and meditated vengeance. For a little while he grieved at Ethel's death. She was so lovely, and she was beginning to open to his ardour as a bud breaking open into a glorious flower. Finally, he considered himself unjustly treated.

But there! The girl clerk in the hotel office was a stunner. He would –!

CHAPTER XXIV

THE NEW LIFE

1

MR. ROWLAND SMYTHE paid his next visit to Atlas at the end of January, just one month after Alldyce Cameron lost his greatest and most magnificent catch. Smythe came in his big car, driven by his chauffeur, accompanied by his dispatch-cases, which now held the fate of several huge properties. With one of these dispatch-cases between his feet he faced Feng Ching-wei from his chair on the veranda of Feng's bungalow.

"About four miles this side of Tin Tin we met a madman driving a truck," he said in his cheerful non-business tones. "Did he pass through here?"

"No, he started from here, Smythe. It was Tom Mace going to see his sweetheart. After the tragedy of Little Frankie I sent Eva, the nursemaid, to Ann Shelley. Ann rang up yesterday to say that she had at last banished Cameron's influence from her mind, and thought it an opportune time for her former sweetheart to win her back. This morning Mace came in with a load of carcass wool, and it took two hours of my time to get him to see that the girl was more sinned against than he was. When, finally, he did make up his mind to woo his Eva, he lost no time getting away."

"What is he going to do when he gets Sir John's money?"

279

"He hasn't decided," Feng said slowly. "But they are going to be married soon – according to Mace. And they are coming to live at Atlas – according to Frank."

"Hum! Where's Frank?"

"Out with Boynton and Reynolds's sheep."

"Any idea how many left?"

"Frank estimates about fourteen thousand."

"I suppose Frank can't pay anything off that loan? Over fifty thousand, you know. My people are not pleased about it, and I fear that if they get a good offer for Atlas they might accept it."

"What would happen then?"

Smythe sighed and his face expressed anxiety. He said deliberately: "The value of Atlas and all station properties to-day is what they will fetch. My firm, as you know, controls hundreds of thousands of pounds invested in pastoral propositions. This world depression, with the consequent slump in wool, is putting the wind up them. If they got an offer of fifty thousand for Atlas, they'd send Frank packing with a bonus of five hundred pounds."

"They could foreclose on Atlas?"

"They could, and they would," replied Smythe. "They most certainly will if Frank falls down on the payment of interest. How much money has he got?"

"He told me he has now about fifteen hundred pounds. Against my advice he paid a further thousand off Westmacott's selection to Mrs. Westmacott. Your beastly firm can't run him off Westmacott's place."

"I am pleased to hear it, Feng; indeed I am. But how the devil is he going to keep Atlas? The interest will very quickly eat up his fifteen hundred, and he has expenses to pay as well."

"He is going to keep Atlas, Smythe. And you are going to help him."

"Well, I am doing what I can. I should be really saddened to see him lose it."

"I believe you would. You maintain that your firm would accept fifty thousand pounds for the Atlas indebtedness to them. If I paid forty-four thousand of that money, would you yourself find six thousand at five per cent?"

Smythe looked long and steadily at his host. "I did not think you had so much money. But the interest on your forty-four thousand, plus that on my six thousand, wouldn't make the position of Atlas any better. It would be buying out one set of creditors and taking on another set."

"Listen!" Feng urged intensely. "When Old Man Mayne died he left me two thousand pounds he said my father lent him in a drought period. He also left me a further sum of twenty-five thousand, as you well know. That was eleven years ago. I have never touched that principal, which has been earning good interest. To it I have added most of my earnings from Atlas, and twelve months ago I realised all my securities, and placed a few hundreds over forty-four thousand in my bank. All that money has come out of Atlas – a free gift to me. It shall go back into Atlas – a free gift."

From the pale round face and the black, now blazing, eyes Rowland Smythe gazed across the empty Gutter of Australia. His life had been crammed with experience of human foibles, among which was nothing like this. Surely with such a guiding spirit Atlas never could sink into bankruptcy!

"Smythe, now that that woman has gone from Atlas, she will soon fade from Frank's mind," Feng continued. "Dead, I bear her no animosity. There is much I can now forgive her. We did not understand her, nor she us. It is a fact that already Frank's spirit is recovering from that strange indecision produced by the slavish desire to please her. He is becoming his old shrewd, far-seeing self. He is like a man long chained to a stake and now set free. The drought won't last for ever. He'll pull Atlas through it and raise Atlas from the dust."

"It is a pity he never married Ann Shelley."

"He will, presently."

"Oh!"

"I shall will it."

"And you think you will succeed?"

"I am sure."

For a moment Smythe regarded Feng Ching-wei pensively. Then: "Very well," he said. "I'll pay in six thousand pounds to your bank account on the first of February. On that date post your cheque to my principals. You'll want money with which to carry on. I'll find another ten thousand by the fifteenth of next month, making fifteen thousand in all. Atlas can pay me a four per cent.

interest. Hang it! No money could be safer or in safer hands."

"Thanks! In three years after the drought Atlas will have paid back that money. Excuse me for a minute. I must go along to the office and ring up Ann Shelley."

When Feng had gone, Mr. Rowland Smythe sat with narrowed eyelids. If only that fool of a nephew had applied himself to business instead of aping the writings of those damned Russians, he might have become as admirable as this Chinaman.

2

IN the chair before occupied by Mr. Rowland Smythe now sat Ann Shelley. It was the day following the financier's visit, and she drank tea with Feng on the latter's veranda.

"We have been good friends, Ann, haven't we?" he was saying. "I think I prefer the word 'pal' to 'friend' in describing the relationship that has existed between us for so many years. Perhaps the strongest strand of the rope which binds us in palship is our love for Frank. You do love him, don't you – in the way I do?"

"Yes, of course, old boy," she said with conviction.

"Then I will first tell you what I have done for him, and next will point out to you what you can do for him," Feng said. "When he brought home Ethel Dyson I met her in a hostile spirit. I could not help that, because for several years before he went to England I had counted on your future marriage to him. However, when he did marry Ethel Dyson, although I was hostile, I determined to be fair. When able, I counselled Frank on the way to retain her affection, but when I saw that her ideas of financial economy were – well – peculiar; when I saw that she never would regard Atlas as we do; when I saw that her love of social excitement and her ambition of social power far transcended her regard for her husband; I knew that even had this drought not happened Atlas eventually would have been ruined. Ethel Dyson was the kind of woman who ruins everything and everybody she comes across.

"When she eloped with Cameron I foresaw what would have happened had she not died. I believe that Cameron would have tired of her quickly, and that he would not have married her had she secured a divorce. Assuming that she had lived, I think Frank would have divorced her because she asked for it. But when

Cameron refused to marry her, she would have been disinclined to go back to her people, and would have asked Frank to re-marry her. And I believe he would have done so."

"And you sent her the copy of Eva's confession so that she would cast off Cameron and seek re-marriage with Frank the quicker?" Ann asked, with a touch of sarcasm.

"I sent her the confession in the first place to strike at them for what they had done to Frank; and in the second place to make her see the impossibility of coming back to Atlas. I considered that when she knew that the man to whom she had given herself was directly responsible for the death of Little Frankie, she would realise that the barrier she herself had erected would be too strong to allow her to regain her former life here. Evidently, at the last, she recognised that."

He saw her gaze fixed on him and blandly looked into her grey eyes, now perplexed and troubled.

She heard him say: "Ever since that day I saw her in Cameron's arms in the garden-house, I have been governed by one ambition, which was to remove her from Atlas and put you in her place. My ambition has been partly realised, Ann. The remaining part has yet to be fulfilled.

"Smythe came the other day to say that his firm was troubled about their financial advances. We agreed that it was only a matter of time, drought or no drought, when Frank would lose Atlas. Smythe said his people would take fifty thousand pounds for Atlas, which was in their hands. We agreed to buy them out. He is to advance privately six thousand pounds at four per cent., and I am giving back to Atlas forty-four thousand pounds which Atlas has given me. On February the first Atlas will belong to Frank, with but a small mortgage of fifteen thousand on it."

"You will give back all the money Old Man Mayne left you, and more besides?" she exclaimed.

"Yes, dear. I am giving my all, save, perhaps, two or three hundred pounds. Wait! Come with me."

With wonder in her heart Ann Shelley followed him through the French windows to his studio-drawing-room. He led her to the curtained alcove in which she had seen that amazing picture of herself. And there he switched on the alcove lights and then drew aside the curtains.

And Ann Shelley cried out. The picture of herself, with her face flushed, her lips parted, and the lovelight in her eyes, was slashed to ribbons.

"Ann, dear," Feng said softly, "I painted that picture after Frank had given you up to marry Ethel Dyson. When I heard that Frank's wife was dead, and that he was again free to marry, I – did – that. Whilst you were promised to no man I dared to love you, although I saw the impossibility of marriage with you. I sinned against none, against neither you nor Frank. But when he became free again, you became his and he became yours. And, as I have torn and slashed the picture, so I have torn out and slashed my man's love of you from my heart."

Turning to her, he placed his hands gently on her shoulders. The light from the alcove fell on their faces. Her lips were trembling, her eyes were dimmed with unshed tears. He was smiling in that inscrutable way of his. His voice was low but steady when he said: "I have nothing else to give. For Frank's sake I have given all I have. He's my pal. He's your pal. You follow my example, Ann, and give him all you have – yourself when he is ready to ask and to accept."

"You know I shall do that, Feng," she assured him, the tears now falling from her unhidden eyes.

3

"HEY! Wake up, Mr. Mayne, and listen!"

Frank Mayne was shaken into wakefulness in the living-hut at White Well, where he and Todd Gray now lived, directing the battle against the horrific drought. It was one o'clock in the morning. A low, persistent hum reached him. "What is it, Todd? Wind?"

"Come outside and have a look."

Together they passed out into the cool night air. A full moon hung in the clear sky above their heads. Its brilliant light shone directly on the southern edge of the one vast cloud in the north. Its base appeared to rest on the horizon. Upward from the earth a huge black column, and above the column in sprouting mushroom shape tier upon tier of ice and snow, a glittering aerial mass, a celestial arctic field. And from the north came that persistent hum.

"Rain!" Todd said, his unshaven face lit with joy.

"That cloud is dropping water on Westmacott's old place," Mayne declared.

"Tons and tons of water, Mr. Mayne. Gawd! I wish I was over there in it. Do you know where that cloud is going?"

"Not yet."

"It is travelling directly west. It's the pilot-cloud that heralds the breaking of the drought. When was the last time we see a cloud moving from east to west? Years and years ago! That cloud is gonna go half-way across Australia to meet the east-coming rain-clouds. It will come back with 'em and the drought will be over."

"Hope so, Todd. We must take a run over to Westmacott's old place to-morrow, and find out how many points of rain have fallen."

"Of course. And I'm goin' to paddle in the puddle.

They watched the single great cloud pass over the western horizon, when all the sky became brilliantly clear.

Almost as soon as it was light they drove across to the selection, now belonging to Mayne. They had penetrated some three miles when they reached the almost knife-edge of the country on which the rain had fallen. Beyond, as far as they could see, the clay-pans were covered with sheets of water lying on the barren land, gleaming diamond-like in the sunlight. The natural water gutters were still running water. A surface tank that had been bone-dry was now half-filled, and water was still pouring into it along the feed channels in racing brown torrents.

"Two inches fell about here if a point," Mayne said, and laughed for very gladness.

"Ten inches is gonna fall over all Atlas in a day or so," Todd said, laughing too.

"It doesn't look like it by the sky and the wind direction to-day, Todd."

"All right. I'll bet you. I'll bet you a quid it rains before Sunday."

"I'll take you."

And, when they arrived back at White Well: "Here, Mr. Mayne, look here! See these ants carrying their eggs from their ground nest up into this tree."

"You confounded optimist! They've been doing that for

years."

"Have they? They haven't done it for three years. I'll bet you a fiver it rains before Sunday, anyhow."

"I'll take you. That'll be six pounds you will owe me, Todd."

That afternoon Mayne overhauled the windmill at White Well, and Todd Gray worked in the kitchen cooking enough food to last three days, as was their practice now, for the eternal scrub-cutting was kept going. Without the efforts of those two men the Atlas flocks would have dwindled to a few scattered mobs.

Standing on the staging at the top of the mill, Frank Mayne whistled whilst he replaced a broken cog-wheel. Light-heartedly he whistled, despite the scene of barren desolation his elevation revealed. Far away over the sand waste a line of slow-rising dust marked the passage of a flock coming to water, tiny white dots dancing in the mirage.

For lately Mayne had been returning from that world of despair and despondency which had held him for three long years. He was coming back to real life, conducted by the figure of hope which is at the side of every man. He whistled because his heart was lightened of the terrible fear of losing Atlas, the fear that had been banished by Feng's magnificent gift and Smythe's ready assistance. If Todd won his bets, then Atlas would start afresh with about ten thousand sheep. From sixty-six thousand to ten thousand in three years!

The lines of anguish about his tanned face were almost erased by Time. No longer did he regret Ethel Dyson. If he had ceased to love her when she fled with Cameron, he had never been able to hate her. After all, she had come to Atlas in a bad period, had seen it at its worst. The jealous bush, in avenging herself on him, had vented its spite on her. Still, thoughts of Little Frankie saddened him, yet the past was coming to appear to him as a tranquil memory.

The sun of hope blazed warmly in his soul this day in early March. When once the drought broke – and after the terrible rainless period there would be no false breaks – he would show the world how to run a sheep-station. The old prosperous days were bound to return. Rain would quicken this dead land into a surging upward rush of new life. Why, in two weeks' time that, country where the rain had fallen would be covered with a green carpet, and in a month grass would be growing six inches high. Green grass, grass with the wonderful greenness of emeralds. It seemed but a foolish dream, but one that would come true.

Yes, those old days would return, those far-off days of content and happiness, when he and Feng and Ann – Ann! Dear, comradely, lovable Ann! What an ass he had been, what an ass! Perhaps, when he had pulled Atlas out of –

"Hey, Mr. Mayne! I'll bet you another fiver it'll rain before Sunday," shouted Todd Gray from the ground below.

"I'll take you!" returned Mayne, and he deliberately dropped grease on Todd's spotless white trousers worn when cooking. "That will be eleven pounds you owe me, Todd. Must have a lot of money, eh?"

Wonderfully enough, Todd's quick anger was not roused by the black grease-drops. He shouted up at Mayne: "Come down out of that, a-laughing up there like a young gal wantin' to be kissed. Look wot's coming! Look behind you!"

What Frank Mayne did see when, turning, he looked to the north and west, drove him to the ground with the agility of an old-time powder-monkey. From due north to south of west the horizon was blotted out by a rapidly rising wall of dark-brown sand.

Standing at the foot of the mill, they watched the sand-wall rising with incredible speed toward the zenith. Reaching the sun, the sand yellowed it, reddened it, finally dimmed it to greyness and wiped it away.

"It is going to be dusty," Todd observed dryly. "I'm for home and beauty to shut the winders, and bury me 'ead in a blanket, so's I shan't eat about seventeen millions of atoms."

"So'm I," Mayne responded, and together they raced for the shelter of the hut.

Mayne lingered outside the twin huts whilst Todd within slammed shut and fastened securely the trap-door, glassless windows. Earthward from the zenith towered the approaching wall, a vast billowing curtain that threatened to fall on the huts, on all Atlas, and bury their world beneath countless tons of sand. An alternately rising and falling hum, as of some monstrous top, reverberated on Mayne's ear-drums. The face of the sand-wall was ever changing in a short range of colour tints, from the red of those masses pushed outward to catch the light of the eastern clear sky, to the black of vast caverns and orifices made by portions sucked back into the mass. The humming sound grew louder and higher in pitch. Behind the sand-wall lurked the cyclone devil.

Whilst he looked the scrub about a mile distant vanished, eaten up by the racing horror. He saw the dun-coloured specks of sheep half a mile distant overwhelmed, eaten up. Glancing upward, the wall, which now had no summit, seemed to be falling outward and downward upon them. At its base countless little columns of dust rose from the plain to stagger drunkenly into it, as though in ludicrous futile effort to beat it back. Till the last three seconds Mayne stayed, rooted to the spot by the wonder of it. He found Todd Gray seated on his bunk, a blanket beside him.

"She's gonna be a hum-dinger," he said with perverse glee. "She's gonna bring rain."

"Not it! We must have had fifty of these storms since last it rained, Todd," said Mayne chidingly.

"Not this sort. Remember that cloud coming from the east and going to the west. A pilot-cloud that was. Going out across the continent to pilot back the rain. Anyway, if you don't believe me, I'll bet you another –"

The sand-wall struck White Well with a sound of w-wo-woowoof-ff. The dimly seen interior of the hut vanished. Within five seconds it was utterly dark. The air was filled with sand. The roof-iron rattled and strained for a short space, and then followed a silence. The darkness continued, perhaps for ten minutes. The silence became oppressive. Todd spluttered and coughed.

"I told you it's gonna rain. A sand-storm without wind is as abnormal as an astronomer without a telescope. If they could capture and store all the static created by this sand, they'd have enough power to drive all the machinery in the world for a hundred years. Hark! It's gonna rain!"

With a towel now pressed to his mouth and nostrils, Mayne listened. As though he stood on a beach listening to the countless water-bubbles exploding after a wave had spent itself, so now he heard the hiss of sand falling on the iron roof, sand that had been lifted high in the air from somewhere in the heart of Australia, and carried thus far by a mighty wind that now had died, permitting the sand to fall. The light began to return. Vibrations stirred the air – strange vibrations as though caught by imagination rather than by physical nerves. It was as though, at some vast distance, a cosmic bombardment was in progress.

"She's coming," Todd said. "Hark at 'er!"

"But she's going – has gone, almost," Mayne objected, thinking of the sand-storm.

"Oh, that! I'm talking of the break in the drought. Let's go outside. That's thunder, for a million."

"Wind most likely," was Mayne's pessimistic view.

The air quickly was clearing. To the south-west the sand-wall hung from the sky as the train from the dress of Satan's bride. Above them the sun appeared, a grey disk rapidly becoming a dirty brown. Streaks of blue lay over the north-western horizon, and whilst it widened they saw huge blotches of white. The hut roofs, the fowl-house roof, the crossbars of the gate to the fowl-run, the dog-kennel, the branches and the twigs of the pepper tree, everything was covered with sand, loaded as a snowstorm would have loaded every object on which it fell.

The sun became blood-red and set without growing in brightness. From the thinning sand to the north and west masses of white came out as though on a developing photographic plate. The white blotches were clouds. A wind rustled through the pepper tree, and from it fell sand as though from a sieve; from roofs and gate-rails it blew a cloud of sand. The air was filled with strange rumbling noises. The wind freshened, and quickly the thinning sand veil was wafted eastward and they could see the sky clearly. Masses of clouds were growing from nothingness, were forming in the sky before the eyes of the two drought-shrivelled men. Masses of clouds, seemingly miles deep, were rushing together, propelled by high atmospheric whirlwinds. Jove and his army were mobilising with ever louder thunderclaps and ever more brilliant lightning bolts.

"She's coming! I told you so! Look at 'er!" shouted Todd Gray. "You owe me sixteen quid."

Water-drops fell on the fine sand laid smoothly over all the land by the storm. They made dull circular marks as large as florins. The heated earth turned the water splashes into vapour that rose to the nostrils of the entranced men, smelling of newly turned, sweetened earth, of an alchemist's mixture of the scents of every herb and flower and young grass-shoot on all the surface of a luscious earth.

The landscape of barren sand and blackened, dying scrub was fading behind a wall – this time a wall of falling water. Lightning sizzled as water on a red-hot stove, so close was it at times. Thunder beat on their ear-drums with terrific force, and shook the ground on which they stood. And above it – or below – to Mayne and Gray dwarfing the roaring elements, another sound, the gug-guggling of water running away along the sand-choked gutters.

They discarded all restraint. Why do horses gallop, and steers buck, and sheep playfully bunt at the approach of rain? Urged by the same irresistible force, these two who had fought drought to the last ditch tore off their clothes and capered in the puddles with the rain thudding upon them, streaming down their bodies. They laughed and shouted as men made mad, threw back their heads to allow the pelting rain to fall into their open mouths.

"She's come! She's come!" screamed Todd.

"She's over! She's over!" yelled Mayne, and, seizing the fierce-eyed little cook, he whirled him round and round in the nudest and maddest of lunatic dances.

It was over – Drought!

THE END

THE OTHER NON-BONY NOVELS

BY ARTHUR UPFIELD

The House of Cain

When Austilene Thorpe is accused of murder and then disappears from gaol, her fiancé, Martin Sherwood, goes blind with the shock. His adventurer brother, Monty, learns she is in a haven for murderers in Central Australia, and they set out to find her.

The Beach of Atonement

Arnold Dudley jealously murders his wife's lover and flees north from Perth to a lonely beach near Dongara on the Western Australian coast. When almost driven to madness by remorse and solitude, he meets two women who strive to rebuild his life.

A Royal Abduction

American gangsters abduct Princess Natalie of Rolandia from a train on the Nullarbor Plain in Australia, and hide her in caves until the ransom is paid. It was not part of the plan to capture two innocent travellers and imprison them underground as well.

Breakaway House

Harry Tremayne goes to the Murchison region in Western Australia to find out what happened to his brother, a police detective who died there while investigating thefts of gold. Suspicion falls on the extravagant owner of Breakaway House.

The Great Melbourne Cup Mystery

The horse that would have won the Melbourne Cup is killed and Tom Pink, rider of the murdered horse, tries to find out who did it. Born into the underworld, he exposes graft and blackmail reaching the upper echelons of Melbourne society.